Alo

"It was a hot night, and we slept out in the garden. It was nicer out there."

"They slept together," spat Aunt Thelma. "Naked."

Hands trembling, Norman took off his glasses carefully and rubbed his eyes. "Can this be true?"

"They did things to each other," my aunt added, with a supreme sense of satisfaction.

"We didn't, we didn't!" I protested.

"Liar!" screamed my aunt. "Sins build one upon the other. One leads to the next."

Aunt Thelma grabbed my arm and jerked me out of the room. She dragged me into the kitchen and forced me to lay my torso over the table, buttocks up in the air.

"You are a sinful, evil child. You have tempted an innocent boy and ruined him. I shall show you the pain of sin."

The first sharp slap came down on me with intense, searing fire. I fought not to scream.

ATHENA
ALEXIS

Along Came a Spider

A DELL BOOK

Published by
Dell Publishing
a division of
Bantam Doubleday Dell Publishing Group, Inc.
666 Fifth Avenue
New York, New York 10103

ISBN: 0-440-20663-4

Interior design by Jeremiah B. Lighter

Printed in the United States of America

Published simultaneously in Canada

November 1991

10 9 8 7 6 5 4 3 2 1

OPM

To my sister Katina,
who is a novelist in her own right.
Love and kisses.

ACKNOWLEDGMENTS

I would especially like to acknowledge and thank the following people who have helped make this book a reality. I want to thank my sister Katina who writes wonderful books herself. Thanks are also due to Jeanne Cavelos, my editor, who made meticulous and helpful comments throughout the progress of this manuscript. Finally, I thank my friends and family who support me through the good times and the bad.

Along
Came
a Spider

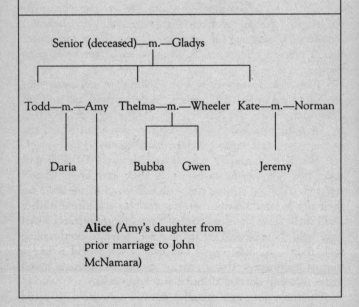

THE BRODERICKS OF CONGREVE

Family Tree

Senior (deceased)—m.—Gladys

Todd—m.—Amy   Thelma—m.—Wheeler   Kate—m.—Norman

Daria   Bubba   Gwen   Jeremy

Alice (Amy's daughter from
prior marriage to John
McNamara)

Prologue

My name is Alice. When the sky turns black and I watch the birds flying frantically to shelter, I remember Congreve, Georgia. It was my home for longer than I care to remember. So short a time, yet so long to endure.

Now that I am grown with children of my own, they often find me in a deeply pensive mood and ask where I am drifting in my mind. I dare tell them only that I am reverting to a bygone time when I grew up too fast and learned the pain of the world all too vividly. No more will I say.

When my youngest reaches eighteen, then I shall give them this manuscript to read that they may know what I suffered. This not so that they will feel pity for me, for I am their mother and do not wish pity from my children. Rather I will show them my story so that they will understand why I have held them close. Perhaps they will learn to do the same with their own little ones. The evil of the world is like a monstrous shadow that is always near, and pain is a red flame that can devour all hope and happiness.

In those long-ago dreadful days in Congreve, I would often look at my little sister's book of nursery rhymes and think of the thinly veiled cruelties that lay beneath those cheerful verses and colorful pictures. This truthful parallel to life is sensed by all children. After each bright day comes a cold journey upstairs to bed in sullen darkness—a trembling child lying beneath the covers while phantoms dance on the walls.

And thus the title for this narration comes easily to me. It is buried in a familiar verse which we have heard so many times. How apt it is to the story which is about to unfold in these pages. Golden little Miss Muffet ate curds and whey.

But *Along Came a Spider* . . .

1

Early Joy

My blood was southern, but all my youth until the time I was thirteen was spent in New York City. My father, John, and mother, Amy, came from Richmond, Virginia, college sweethearts who went off hand in hand to seek their fortune in the wide world. Father was a would-be writer of novels and Mother an aspiring dancer. I never knew my father even in the faintest memories of youth because he left us when I was first born. When I would ask Mother about him, she would affect an English cockney accent and say " 'e was a bad 'un" or " 'e was a rotter," laugh and say no more.

Her easy humor about his disappearance infected me and I neither wished for him nor created elaborate fantasies of him being a prince or plutocrat as so many children do with absent fathers. That was later when I was imprisoned and desperate and could find no solace or hope in anything else.

In addition, it seemed that my stepfather, Todd, had always been there. Todd was a painter and also southern but from a more obscure city, Congreve, Georgia, a port on a river by the sea. He was tall and blond and handsome. He came into my world when I was two, and I remember feeling only the slightest twinge of jealousy at finding him in my mother's bed in the mornings. There was such happiness on their faces, such constant singing and laughter, that I was captivated by their relationship from the start.

Todd was boisterous and full of life and quickly took us

out of a tiny two-room flat into a huge abandoned garment factory loft in SoHo. I remember a world of gigantic canvases, twisted metal sculptures that seemed to reach the sky, and the smell of turpentine and paint. We were happy. Bathed in sifted light from high, wire-reinforced windows, we sang and danced about the broad floors. I loved being up so high. I would stand on the balcony and holler across to a friend in the other building. There was no sense of earth, just space, and if I concentrated very hard I could pretend that I was suspended in midair like a bird.

Dancing jobs were scarce, so my mother mostly was a waitress in a Greek restaurant on 57th Street, and she and Todd and I would spend a lot of time there. The owners were a cantankerous old Greek man and his wife who would sit in the front booth and greet all their customers as they came in. Todd was fascinated. He would go earlier and earlier to pick Mom up from work and Georgios and Evanthia would always invite him to sit down in the booth with them. Todd would place me next to him and Mother would bring us whatever Georgios ordered, usually a huge platter of Greek chicken, shrimp, and souvlakia, a mixture of lamb and beef with yogurt sauce. Then Georgios would make Mother sit down next to me too, and we would all eat and talk together.

"When we are rich," Todd would say, "we will all go to Greece together and visit the islands on our yacht." Many of the pictures Todd painted were of whitewashed stucco buildings, which he told us were what Greece was like. He had been there long ago, when he was a young child, and the fact that Mother worked in a Greek restaurant when he met her was apparently part of the reason he loved her. She reminded him of that wonderful country with its good-hearted people.

"Oh, Todd," Mother would laugh, "you're such a dreamer." Then she would nuzzle up to him and hug his arm, and, sitting between them in the middle, I would feel all warm and cozy inside. They were happy together and so was I, basking in their love for each other.

Soon, Mother became Mrs. Broderick, and Todd officially became my father. Though the wedding photos have long ago disappeared, I remember one of myself barefooted with daisies painted on my cheeks, my hands holding a spray of violets. Around me were bearded artists in overalls brandishing glasses of champagne. Mother—how beautiful she was—wore a chaplet of flowers and looked like an angel come down to earth.

Being only two, I was initially afraid of the vast space of the loft, which seemed fully as big as a basketball court. But Todd and Mother kept me near at night, and as I grew older I came to love the iron and wood cavern and my "room" made of old garment racks hung with canvases. I could shift the room's shape and location and redecorate with all the crazy jumble of materials that Todd salvaged from junkyards and garbage heaps. I had a brass bed and a department store mannequin dressed in a soldier's red uniform—a fragment of a castle from a theater backdrop—a couch on wheels fashioned artfully from the back seat of a Cadillac with the tailfins for armrests. I even learned to ride a bicycle inside! And so my life was always an adventure.

There was never any doubt that Todd was a talented painter. He could do swirling vortex abstractions for the culture-hungry nouveau riches or murals of heaped clouds and rural views for suburban banks. His real talent, however, was in portraiture, and it was there that he exercised so perfectly that magic soul possessed by all artists. His likenesses were exquisite. Subtle mood and character graced each face, and the hands were gentle and smooth with flesh tones of life itself.

Todd painted me from the earliest days, and I rapidly accepted it, like all children, as a verification of my "me-centered" universe. The pictures he did of my mother were of the most beautiful woman in creation, and it seemed utterly natural that she should be exquisitely naked on those canvases just as I was on mine. In my room, I hung many of those pictures of myself and my mother and made up stories about each. One was a nymph who lived beneath the sea—another was a queen with a castle on a mountain high on an island in Greece—yet another, a poor but beautiful girl who lived in a cottage in a deep forest.

When I was eight, Mother announced her pregnancy. And so, I watched her belly swell. I was excited but also sad. The new child would be immediate and obvious competition. Sensing my fears, Mother spent long hours telling me of the joy we would all share, and so I felt confident of her love, yet was old enough to wonder.

I was conscious that Todd was not my father. He had made a baby with my mother and the three of them would be joined by blood in a way I was not. The baby would call him "Daddy" while I would always call him "Todd." In a subtle way, I would be the outsider.

Despite my anxiety, I loved the tiny, squealing little bundle when they brought her home from the hospital. Her name was Daria, after a sister of Todd's who died when she was very young, but I called her "Ria" and everyone thought it so marvelous a name that it stuck and Ria she was.

My little sister soon began to crawl and then toddle around our world of canvas and jumble, and I spent many loving hours following to keep her safe. Because I was eight years older, I was big and yet not big—a person in between her and the adults. I could more easily share her mischief and fun; yet I was also her protector and teacher. At eight and nine and ten, I was anxious for responsibility and so I invested great wells of love and pride in Ria. She was the most perfect little sister in the world.

Her hair was a deep lustrous brown and curled in little knots and ringlets like a drawing of a cherub. Her face was a perfect oval, her mouth a little rosebud. She learned to talk early and by age one could use her stubby fingers to stack astonishing numbers of small blocks in leaning towers of Pisa. She painted on brown wrapping paper in great daubs and used glue to stick colored bits of polished glass on cardboard in wild mosaics.

Life seemed perfect. And any fears I had about our not being a complete family were forever dispelled when I complained that my arms hurt one morning. Thinking that it was from sleeping on my arms, I did not worry, but my parents rushed me off to a solemn gray doctor, who promised me an ice-cream cone if I sat still and did as he said. He took X rays and several days later my parents went back to talk to him about the results.

When they came home, Mother held me close and smoothed my hair. Todd hugged us both and began to cry. They never talked about it to me, but I overheard them telling friends who came to the house. The doctor had diagnosed some horrible disease from which I would soon die.

The days became like a nightmare. My parents took me to the hospital for more tests. Todd slept each night on a cot in my room, and Mother brought Ria to visit frequently. The hospital was such a foreign place, with nurses waking me up at all hours to take my temperature or give me vile-tasting medicine. Always Todd was there, trying to take my mind off of the hospital. He would clown with me, hide my toothbrush, and run his fingers through my hair when I looked sad. Each night when he prayed over me, I reached up and told him I was going to be all right.

Finally the new tests were completed and the doctor pronounced the earlier tests false. My parents were elated. They carried me home, and Todd even took Ria and me to the zoo to celebrate.

Life continued blissfully. Mother, Todd, Ria, and I were a family. We had no one else. My real father was never mentioned. My mother's parents were dead, so we never visited her childhood Virginia home. As for Todd, I realized he had parents and relatives back in Congreve, but he only mocked them in his boisterous way.

"Wouldn't Thelma throw a hissy-fit over this," or "Wouldn't Senior have heart failure to see us now," he would laugh when we were having some childish bit of fun. I sensed that his family did not love him the way we loved each other and that they were very grim and not at all given to joy or laughter. That such people existed in this world was hard to miss in a city like New York. But as a child, I took our joy for granted.

Occasionally, an official-looking letter would come from Congreve which Todd would scan and then burn with much laughter as if he were exorcising a ghost. Once, right after Ria's birth, a thick envelope came from Todd's father, who was called "Senior." It was a letter such as a proud grandfather might send, filled with good wishes and photos of an old man with a white mustache sitting in a wicker chair on the porch of a vast house. He seemed particularly happy at the baby being named Daria and enclosed a check in an amount that I did not appreciate, having no real understanding of money.

Todd kissed the check loudly and boasted of how we'd "spend the old demon's money and still spit on his grave when the time comes." Then he burned the letter with the photos. Briefly, I imagined that a grandfather would come into our lives. But he never did, and Todd and Mother accepted it all as normal enough. The Brodericks, Todd's parents, seemed far away, almost like ogres from a fairy tale that you read about and never really believed existed.

The letter which changed everything came on a hot and humid day. All the newspapers were full of the horrible heat wave. I got the mail myself from the boxes in the foyer downstairs. Mother waited with a curious expression on her face while Todd opened the envelope and scanned the contents.

"My father died two weeks ago," Todd pronounced. "This is a notice from a lawyer about his will. My sister Thelma didn't tell me about the funeral, of course. She wouldn't want me there."

Even as a thirteen-year-old teenager, I thought it strange that Todd wasn't saddened by the death of his father. His voice didn't falter and there was no trace of tears in his eyes.

As well, I remember the sudden burst of excitement when he read further.

"Why, Amy, I do believe we're going to be rich! The old bastard left his money to his grandchildren. We may be able to buy that yacht and cruise the Greek islands yet." He picked me up and whirled me around the kitchen floor wildly. "Money, Alice," he said, "don't let anyone ever tell you that money's not important. Money makes you free and independent. And we are going to have lots of it! Lots of money and lots of freedom!"

Then he frowned grimly and put me down. "We have to go down there," he said to my mother. "The lawyer's letter is quite specific. Senior left the money to Daria, and he stipulated that she had to live in Congreve."

"But Todd," Mother said, suddenly fearful, "you hate it down there, and we're so happy here. Poor, but happy. You used to say no amount of money would make you move back to Congreve. Remember?"

Todd shook his head. "This is different. This is a lot of money. We can even put up with Thelma and her dismal husband Wheeler for this amount of money. We're going back on our own terms. We're going back to money. And we'll get a lawyer to make sure that everything is done right. Otherwise Thelma will steal every penny."

"But how long will we have to stay?" Mother asked.

"You know how Senior always hated it that I escaped that dreadful place. He wants Daria to be educated in Congreve. All of grade school. I guess he figured by then she'd like the place or something. Talk about stupid."

"All those years?" said Mother, horrified.

"We'll find a loophole," Todd said. "It's too crazy for words. I mean he left her the money. She should be able to have it no matter what. As soon as we find a lawyer, we'll get this straightened out."

"But will anybody help us? You've always said that your sister and her husband control the whole town."

"Lawyers jump for money. They're just a pack of jack-als. Don't worry."

"But Todd, will there be enough money for all of us? I mean, I work here and you have odd jobs. How can there possibly be enough money to support a family of four?"

Todd smiled. "Senior was a very rich man, Amy, and he was very tight with a dollar. He probably kept eighty cents of every buck he ever made. He left plenty of loot. The old bastard wanted to control us from the grave. His will provided for the support of all of us as long as we live in Congreve together."

"It is beastly hot right now in New York," said Mother. "It might be nice to get away to the sea if only for a little while."

Todd shrugged. "You don't know what heat is until you've been to Congreve. But big bucks can make anything bearable. You'll see, Amy. Even Thelma and Wheeler will be bearable if we have enough money. And we'll keep our place here in New York—now we have the money to do it. We can come up here to get away when things down there become too insufferable. It'll be our sanctuary."

As foolish as it sounds, I had never thought of being rich before that day. Sure, rich was Fifth Avenue and all the fine shops and apartments on the Upper East Side. But my parents had always scorned money as something that got in the way of fun. The next day, however, Todd gave notice that we were leaving the apartment for a few months and he boasted to some of the neighbors that we had "come into money."

We made plans in a flurry. Todd bought a new suit and train tickets. He called Congreve and told Thelma and Wheeler that we were coming back. He whispered to Mother that they were only giving us the carriage house behind the big mansion. We didn't take many possessions because we didn't have that much and, anyway, the loft in New York was still going to be ours.

I packed Ria's and my things in one big suitcase. I can

almost remember everything we took to this day. My diary that I wrote in every night; my favorite bathrobe and powder; my sketchpad and book of architecture from the Metropolitan Museum; some of the favorite pictures that Todd had given me for birthday and Christmas presents; Ria's fuzzy duck and the Mother Goose book that had once been mine.

We took the train down to Congreve two days later. I daydreamed about where we were going as I watched the train travel down the eastern seaboard. Life seemed so pleasant and the train was such a perfect way to travel. Looking out the window, Ria and I watched as we sped by fields of yellow and green, over trestles high above the water, through big cities and small towns. Periodically, the conductor in his white coat would come by and check our tickets. Mother had packed a lunch of peanut butter sandwiches, apple juice, and grapes. It was as if we were suspended in time. I never wanted the train ride to end!

From time to time, I would read Ria a story. How I loved her. She was five years old, small but determined. Very pretty with her long curly brown hair and green eyes. It was clear that she was going to be even more beautiful as she got older. Beauty may be in the eye of the beholder, but some people are beautiful to all beholders. Ria was like that. No one could look at her without remarking how pretty she was.

"We are going to visit in a huge old house," I told her. "My beautiful little Ria can play on big stairs and in nooks and crannies."

Todd smiled indulgently. "Except now she will be called by her real name. She will be Daria."

"Why?" my little sister asked. "My name is Ria."

"No," Mom said. "Ria is just short for Daria. You must go by your formal name, the name that your grandfather Senior liked so much. Daria is such a pretty name, don't you think? Won't it be fun to have a new name?"

Ria was perfectly content and explained to her fuzzy duck all about her new name. But, myself, I felt a twinge of the old jealous fear of not belonging. Ria was going to a family that was hers and not mine. And she was abandoning the name I had given her.

"I thought Daria was somebody who died," I grumped sullenly. "Why does Ria have to be called that?"

Todd gave me a sharp look, opened his mouth to speak, then closed it again. Mom hugged me. "Dear, don't say that ever again please. It's not something anyone wishes to be reminded of. We are going to Congreve and some things will be different. At least long enough for us to get Senior's Estate settled. But we will still be a family and we will still love each other."

I started to argue. "Well, I don't see why she has to—"

Mom put her fingers gently over my mouth and shushed me. "I'm quite serious, Alice. Think of other people's feelings instead of your own."

I went back to reading Ria her story. She would always be Ria to me and no one could change that. Minutes later, my anger had dissipated. My mother and Todd seemed so excited. The air was expectant.

2

A Strange Land

We arrived in Congreve, Georgia, at nine o'clock at night. "Cun-greve. Cun-greeve!" said the porter going down the aisles of the railway cars.

No one else got off with us into the heat and the loneliness. Heat that seemed like a steamy wet blanket settling over your head—heat worse than sun-blistered asphalt in New York—with a rotting smell like when the garbage men are on strike. And silence like nothing was going on anywhere.

Doors slammed, and seconds later the train glided out of the station past winking red signal lights. We watched until the last car passed from sight around a bend of towering pine trees, heading on farther south toward Florida.

The train station was built of wood with peeling posters Scotch-taped to the walls. Old hand trucks with iron wheels were stacked with mailbags. A shabby man slept in wrinkled clothes on a red plastic sofa. His shoes were off, displaying holes in his socks. A gumball machine looked like generations of kids had licked the glass into foggy filth and never had a penny to buy gum. A lone railroad employee shuffled around behind a counter.

So how proud can you be when you live among dribbled paint and welded sculptures in SoHo? Not very. But that wasn't the point. For days, Todd had talked about our future wealth and I had come to picture Congreve as a cross between Fifth Avenue, Palm Beach, and Disneyland.

"Well, no one seems to be here," said Todd in an un-
naturally loud voice. The railroad worker shuffled some
more, still intent on a comic book he was reading. "And
here I expected Cinderella's coach," Todd continued with
forced cheerfulness. "Or at least a Rolls-Royce."

"Perhaps the most important Broderick among us
should find a cab," Mom kidded.

Todd laughed and went out the door of the station.
Mom went into the rest room. I sat down with Daria on one
of the greasy plastic chairs. I didn't want to go to the rest
room. I was sure that it would be unclean like the rest of the
place.

That was another thing that struck me, I suppose. Todd
had been talking about the importance of the Brodericks in
Congreve. How they owned the town. When they walked
down the street, people moved aside. I knew the grandfather
was dead. But there was a grandmother. And aunts and un-
cles. Where were they with their big smiles and arms full of
presents like in the first-grade readers? I had never experienced that—never gone to see a grandmother on the farm at
Christmas or even to a Long Island suburb. I had been looking forward to it.

In my daydreams, I had even imagined a beautiful
woman in a silk dress holding a big bunch of flowers with
long stems and handing them to Mom as she said, "Welcome
to Congreve, dear." And let's face it, I was kind of thinking
they might have a present for me as well. I wasn't sure quite
what. Daria would be easy to buy a toy for. But my new
grandmother would use her imagination and come up with
something nice for me. She would have called New York
secretly and asked Mom what to get me.

"Look," said Daria, interrupting my thoughts. "I've got
braces." She grinned, showing me her teeth covered with
green chewing gum.

"But your teeth were so straight," I said, playing along.

Daria grimaced to show her white teeth with the gum
removed. "Now they're gone," she said.

"Whups. Guess you have to go back to the dentist."

Daria held out both hands to show they were empty. "I've swallowed my gum. I'm going to choke."

"Don't tell fibs," I chided. "You'll be like the little boy who cried wolf."

"Who's that?"

I told her the story with the moral at the end of no one believing the little boy when he finally told the truth.

"Well one day," she said, "we'll be at the zoo and the alligators will get out and I'll tell you and you'll believe me because I always tell the truth."

"No, you don't. You're telling me a story about having swallowed your gum when you didn't."

Daria sat and thought for a moment. "Well anyhow," she argued stubbornly, "I never tell fibs about animals."

"You're so silly," I said, hugging her close.

Todd came back and got all the suitcases heaped on a rusty-looking metal cart. He was sweating heavily and the new gray suit he had bought especially to travel to Congreve suddenly looked shiny and old. One slow and tired ceiling fan in the middle of the large waiting room hardly helped dispel our perspiration.

"There's a cab waiting outside," he said in a low voice to my mother. "I called the house and talked to Thelma. She and Wheeler aren't any too pleased we're showing up to take Daria's part of the inheritance. I don't think they thought I'd ever come back to Congreve. They said they were going to bed and not to wake them up. Ideal welcome, I'd say. I'm not any too eager to have to lay eyes on my wonderful sweetheart sister and her charming husband."

We went out to a parking lot to find a lone rusty car that was higher on one side than the other, as if the springs were busted. *Quick Cab* was written on the side. It sat in a little puddle of light that swarmed with moths. Except for that light under a round metal shade, the world was dark amid a horizon of warehouses and little patches of trees.

The driver was a skinny man in an undershirt, and his

arms were decorated with faded tattoos. When the luggage was all in, the trunk wouldn't close and he had to tie it with string. I edged into the backseat next to a window with Daria between me and Mom. Todd sat in the front next to the driver, who seemed ready to talk nonstop.

"We're heading across town," Todd said. "It's kind of tricky, but I'll show you the way."

"You're from around here?" the cab driver asked.

"Not exactly," said Todd. "I lived here a long time ago. Now I live in New York."

"You don't say. What brings you here?"

"Business."

"Ain't much business in this town. What there is belongs to the bank."

"How so?"

"Debts. You got to borrow money to get started. So you go to the bank. From there on out, they own you."

"That seems to be true all over the world," said Todd. "Anything new happening in town?"

"Nothing much," said the driver. "Old man Broderick died. He was the biggest banker in town. Owned a piece of everybody."

"Well, do you feel liberated now?" asked Todd.

"Not really. The debts don't disappear. Just have to deal with that bloodsucking Wheeler."

I sensed that Todd was leading the man on. "Who's Wheeler?" he asked.

"Son-in-law of the old man. Just as mean and far craftier. Old Senior—that's what the old man was called—Senior would tell you to your face to do things his way or he'd ruin you. At least you knew where you stood. Do what he wanted or close up shop and get out of Congreve. And he'd be right explicit about what he wanted. A piece of your hide. But he'd leave you just enough to get by. Now Wheeler—there's a horse of a different color."

"How so?"

"He wants everything. He'll string you along for a while

and then cut your line of credit without warning. When you have to sell out, he'll buy the business and suddenly you're working for him."

"He can't own everything in town."

"He's making a right good try at it. Who do you think owns this cab company?"

"Wheeler?"

"Took it from me last year. Five old rusted out cars and a shack with a telephone in it. Barely made enough to live on before that. Now I'm staring at welfare."

My seat was sticky and Daria was leaning on me, her head now heavy with sleep. When I tried to shift my position, she got closer, finally climbing up onto my lap. She clung to me, as if I were the only anchor in her changing universe.

"Who you going to see?" asked the driver.

"Don't choke," said Todd. "Wheeler and Thelma Broderick." Under his breath I heard him mutter, "Broderick—that pig Wheeler not only took the money—he took the name too!"

The driver spit his toothpick out the window and stared at him. "I got a big mouth," he said.

Todd laughed. "Don't worry, I won't tell them what you said. I might as well admit that I'm not in love with them myself. Only reason I'm here is because I have to be here."

"It don't matter I guess. I can't starve to death but once."

"Maybe I can do something to help you out," Todd suggested.

The driver snorted. "Who are you anyway?"

"I'm . . . uh, Todd Broderick. Senior's son."

"Well I'll be a son of a—" The driver caught himself, remembering Mom and me in the back. He stared at Todd hard. "Yeah, you are Senior's boy, ain't you. You've got the same face. How long ago did you leave town?"

"I can't even remember," said Todd. "And I'm not

coming back to stay. Just long enough to get what's mine. At least that's my plan."

"Well good luck on that. I'd say you might have a snowball's chance in you-know-where." The driver checked Mom out in the rearview mirror and then peered at Todd again. He shook his head wonderingly. "You don't look a bit like Thelma though. Not a bit."

"Thank God for small favors," said Todd.

I knew almost nothing about Todd's family, just what I'd overheard. I knew that Todd had two older sisters, Thelma and Kate, each with a husband. Thelma had two kids and Kate one—my cousins in a way, although not by blood. I couldn't remember their names, but one was supposed to be close to my age. I had looked forward to a cousin, but then I had also imagined Congreve as a fairy tale, so I was beginning to have my doubts.

Outside, we passed a trailer camp. Mangy dogs came out and barked at the car as if they wanted to jump in and eat us. Then came an abandoned drive-in movie, the silent screen half pulled down, a used-car lot, an "adult" bookstore, and three fast-foods in a row followed by a motel that advertised hourly rates. It was as grubby as that highway that goes across the New Jersey meadows.

A light drizzle started, but I didn't roll up my window. The raindrops felt good against my skin, though they barely relieved the heat. Steam rose in little feathers from the road. Daria shifted against me, her face leaving a sweat stain on my white blouse. Little beads of perspiration dotted her nose and upper lip.

Then the rain came in a rush, obliterating the windshield and soaking my arm and face. "Close the window," Daria complained sleepily, but I ignored her. Todd and Mother sat getting wet, too, as though they appreciated it like me. So did the driver.

The rain let up finally to show a view of a broad marsh and then the river with a trestle bridge up ahead. I knew

Congreve sat on a river and my interest stirred. Maybe it would be dramatic after all!

The bridge had several spans crossing the blackness down below. Floating lights showed ships at anchor. We reached the far side to find palmetto trees and live oaks lining the streets of more run-down neighborhoods. Stores were closed for the night. We passed dry cleaners, gas stations, and old frame houses with plants growing in tin cans on sagging second-story porches. I watched Mother as she took in everything, wondering if she found it as disappointing as I did.

We splashed through huge puddles in streets flooded by the rain. Black people drifted slowly in the night or sat on their steps drinking from bottles in brown paper bags. The driver raised a couple of fingers in salute to those he knew. Children danced with no music, just writhing to their own rhythms. Someone was selling watermelons out of the back of a truck. Another truck had fish.

"It's all so familiar," said Todd. Without thinking, he explained to the driver how to go the rest of the way.

"Don't nothing never change," said the driver.

"Certainly not my family," said Todd. "It would be too much to hope for."

We crossed a broad street lined with palmettos, bumped over some old trolley tracks, and suddenly the character of the town altered dramatically.

"This is the historic district—the best part of town," Todd told us as we drove down streets where slanting shadows of huge antique houses touched across the road. The lights of the houses were in jumbled patterns showing the lack of uniform design. Here and there, a dark space marked the yard of a house set far back from the street. Thick tropical vegetation poked through the iron fences.

We turned onto a narrow road that ran between two patches of marsh and then a dark, impenetrable mass of trees on the left. We seemed to be on a little spit of wooded land that was running out into marsh.

The car turned again through an open gate of metal sheets topped with spikes, crunched over something white like gravel, and bathed the corner of a huge brick house in headlights.

Suddenly, I had an indescribable feeling of being closed in, engulfed by the darkness around us. It was so quiet, and still, and black. Not a star was in the sky. I held Daria close. She seemed peaceful and untouched by the forebodings which threatened to overwhelm me.

"Do what he wanted or close up shop and get out of Congreve," Todd whispered under his breath to no one in particular. Then more loudly, "Welcome to Congreve. Home of my youth."

3
My Relatives

"End of the line," said Todd in a cheerful whisper as he put one foot out on the grass. "God, it looks as dreadful as I remembered."

"Dreadful?" I questioned.

"He's being funny," Mom whispered, giving Ria and me a hug before helping us out of the car.

"Yeah, that's it. Funny," Todd continued to whisper. "Funny as all get out."

At the time, I didn't wonder why we were whispering. The big house was so solemn and dark and silent that whispering seemed a natural response. It loomed over us, making me dizzy when I leaned my head back to try to see the top. There were no lights on anywhere in the huge mansion except for one at the very top, in what looked like the attic.

In the front yard, a statue of Mercury was poised over a sundial surrounded by thick beds of flowers. Boxwoods higher than my head lined a narrow brick walk. A giant oak like a majestic, sighing inkblot screened the neighboring mansion. Tall palmettos had old fronds still on the trunk giving them a ragged look. Water dripped from all the trees giving them an air of sadness.

"The drive is crushed oyster shells," Mom explained as I scuffed at them with the toe of my tennis shoe. I tried to put Daria down, but she refused to wake up and clung to me relentlessly.

In silence, Todd paid the cabdriver and we stood watching as the car light flared in our faces, backed down the drive, and disappeared into the street. The hot night clung to us without a bit of breeze, and we huddled there among bag and baggage like refugees who had arrived in a city deserted by all but ghosts.

"Is nobody home?" I asked. I forgot to whisper.

"Shhh," said Todd. "Aunt Thelma goes to bed early. She specifically said that she didn't want to be disturbed."

I studied the face of my watch in the dark. The luminous paint had never worked well, but I could see it was barely ten. All the houses we had passed on the street had been lit up. At least early bed wasn't a custom of the city.

"Is Aunt Thelma sick?" I asked in all seriousness.

Todd laughed. "You don't know the half of it," he answered, but he didn't elaborate. "Alice, darling, don't ask too many questions right now. We're all going to be having a hard time adjusting. Things are different down here in Congreve, but we'll all get used to it. Plus we'll be rich. That will help everything."

It took us several trips to ferry the bags around behind the house where a small patch of yard was encroached upon by shaggy plants and bushes. Through gaps, a high brick wall could be seen. A little cottage sat at the very back against the wall. It had a small door with a window on either side and a second floor with three windows. Todd explained that it was a carriage house where in olden days servants had lived who helped the rich people who lived in the big mansion. It was going to be our new home, at least for a while.

"Look, Ria," I whispered. "It's a troll's cottage deep in a magic wood. We're going to live there."

Daria didn't seem impressed. She was half asleep and the darkness was not appealing. "Her name is Daria now, dear," said Mother. "Let's remember that."

The door was ajar. Todd felt around for lights and found them. Downstairs was a tiny kitchen and a living room. The furniture was nice, all covered with chintz and looking like a fancy little hideaway despite a musty smell.

Todd started up a rusty old air conditioner, which clanked and banged a bit before it settled into a steady hum, and I felt the sticky hot air slowly replaced by a cooler draft.

Todd bustled upstairs, leading us like the Pied Piper. He started another air conditioner, which dripped water onto a dark spot on the floor. There were two tiny bedrooms with a bath between. The tub was raised on lion's feet, as though it might walk out onto the small landing.

Two beds in what Mom said was Ria's and my room were made and neatly turned down. There was a child's chair and table. Old prints on the walls had fairies dancing in circles. A stand-up radio from the 1930s filled a corner. It was the kind Mom had once described from her childhood.

Without thinking, I turned on the radio and began flipping the channels. The volume was too loud and when I found a channel, it was deafening.

"ROCKING THE GEORGIA COAST WITH A TRIBUTE TO MISTUH BOHHHH—DIDDLEY! YEA-AAHHHH!!"

I quickly turned it down, but the damage was done. Todd came rushing in, his face red with anger. When he spoke, it was with thinly veiled, unexpected violence. I had never seen him in such a state. It was weird. It was as if he had changed into a different person the minute we came to Congreve.

"Don't you ever do that again!" he ordered, pressing his face up close to mine. "Never never never!"

"I . . . I'm sorry, Todd," I stammered. "It was an accident . . ."

"There won't be any more accidents! You know why? Because you will never again turn on that radio. Ever!"

Foolishly, I argued. "Not even in the daytime?"

He took me by the shoulders as if to shake me. "NEVER!"

He stormed out. His outburst had woken Ria up and she began to cry quietly. She hugged my hand to her cheek. Mother came in and drew us close, talking in whispers. "It's okay, Alice. It's okay," she reassured. "I know you don't understand. It's not just the noise—Aunt Thelma doesn't like noise—it upsets her badly. But more than anything . . . well, it was the channel the radio was tuned in on. You see, some of these people down here are kind of, well, prudish. Your aunt Thelma and uncle Wheeler don't like rock and roll. They . . . well, they don't like a lot of things. We have to try to get along with these people for the sake of the inheritance. But we'll still be a family and we'll still be happy. Things will just be a little different when we're around them, okay, darling? Do you understand?"

"I'm sorry," I said numbly. It all seemed so strange. Suddenly, I wanted to be hugged. I wanted to be little like Daria and go to sleep on Mom's lap and be safe.

"We'll talk about it in the morning. It won't be easy here. But then it won't be hard either. Does that sound crazy?" She smiled. "We'll all be a bit crazy until we get used to each other. But we'll play and have lots of fun together. You'll see."

She saw us both washed and out of the bathroom and kissed us both in bed.

After she was gone, I got up on impulse and hung up one of the pictures I had brought with me. It was a portrait of Daria and me that Todd had done. We were standing in front of a deep blue sea that Todd said was like Greece.

Todd had painted it in watercolor. I was probably ten in the picture and Daria two. We didn't have any clothes on. In retrospect I'm not sure why, but we didn't. Artists paint people like that. There was nothing vulgar about it. We might have been living in the Garden of Eden or something. It was my favorite picture of Todd's, which was why I had brought it. It made the place a little bit of home.

I crawled back in bed.

"This is like the Three Bears' cottage," I said to Daria, trying to be cheerful. I reached out for her hand between the beds, but she didn't take mine. She was already fast asleep. I could not sleep. I was in a strange bed surrounded by strange objects and people whom I had never met. There was an indescribable eeriness about the whole event which threatened to smother me.

I concentrated on a bar of light coming into the room from the hall, making a neat patch on the floor. I could hear Todd and Mom moving around quietly. The light vanished. They whispered awhile in the dark.

Their bed creaked briefly, and I heard Todd say, "No, I can't, Amy. It's weird. When I get around here, all my old inadequacies come back. It's like Senior is still alive—sneering at me. That's why he made it so I would have to come back to Congreve to get Daria's money. He didn't like it that I got away from him in New York. I guess he's had the last laugh."

I was old enough to know what adults did when they were naked together. Old enough that many girls my age had already started to try the joys of the flesh themselves. My parents' obvious physical attraction to each other had seemed to me to be the most natural thing in the world. And many a night I had heard their passion as I lay in bed awake. Sometimes, too, I had smiled to hear one of them protest, "No, the children might hear."

But tonight, the message was different—peculiar. It was like someone else had invaded our world and that someone else was already changing everything.

Nervous and edgy, I got up from my bed and walked across the room. I almost wished that Daria would wake up so that we would have to go see Mom and Todd and turn the quiet house into noise and chatter again. I deliberately tried to make noise, but Daria slept soundly.

From my little window, I could see out in the yard. The moon had come out, dusting the palmettos with silver. Shadows covered the white ground. I thought I could see a small animal—like a bunny or a cat. I wished I could show him to Daria, but she remained fast asleep, her breathing in quiet, regular puffs. Her little hands held her fuzzy duck.

I curled up on my bed, elbows on the windowsill, and

watched the animal. It was a bunny, I could see him clearly as he scampered out of the shadows. He seemed so peaceful and yet I knew he was a hunted beast, always wary, always filled with fears. He had come into the garden to feed among the bushes and flowers on the dew-wet grass. Suddenly I wished that I could shelter a whole world of defenseless animals there. Every night they could come, sensing that they were safe and welcome.

The vast house where my aunt and uncle lived was grim and silent, not a light showing except at the very top. Nothing stirred. The rabbit hopped away. A faint hot wind rustled the leaves of the palmettos. It was a strange swishing sound like an old dress in an attic stiff with age. I followed the rustling leaves up, to the higher reaches of the house where crazy old dormers and chimney stacks jumbled together in black shapes that met a deep blue sky devoid of stars.

A dark form flashed in that one lighted dormer. Something round and white squashed against the glass. It was a face framed by gray hair . . . a woman's face . . . cheeks and nose flattened, lips parted, and . . . they were moving in a private conversation. Fingertips moved up the glass, touching it as if exploring the margins of a prison.

As I watched, a peculiar feeling came over me. She knew how to search the darkness. She had watched us move into our little house. She knew where my bedroom lay. She was looking straight down at me and her eyes could see into my brain! She was whispering something to me. Something so quiet that no one in the big house could hear. But I was expected to hear! I was expected to know her message instinctively. Who was she and what was she trying to tell me?

I thought of olden times and how crazy people were often locked in attics. Suddenly I was scared and lonely. My parents' bedroom seemed very far away, a distance I would never travel again to seek comfort in the dead of night. I walked to the edge of Ria's bed and sat down next to her, held her hand, felt the companionship of another human being, alive and breathing amidst loneliness and fear. Finally, I looked out of the window again. The woman was gone. I told myself that I had imagined the entire episode.

Still, I felt utterly alone in an alien world. I crawled into bed, put my head under the sheet, and closed my eyes very tight. Everything would seem better in the morning. I was in a new place and it was late at night. My imagination was running away with me.

4

Home?

When I awoke the next morning, the sun was shining and all my fears from the night before seemed silly and ill-founded. The figure at the window and the dark shadows were all gone. After all, your imagination can run away with you if you let it. At least, that's what I told myself.

In the light of day, the broad lawn and the promise of the harbor beyond the high wall seemed beautiful and life held much promise. The familiar watercolor Todd had done of Ria and me that I had hung on the wall made me feel that things were normal and right.

Todd and Mom were sleeping peacefully in their room. Across from me, little Daria seemed so sweet as she slumbered, one arm clutching her favored fuzzy duck. I found myself disgusted with my own morbid attitude from the night before. I had to learn to look on the bright side. New York had not been all that joyful. Life was better already and I hadn't even met anyone.

Daria stirred. She was not a morning child and usually awakened in a grumpy mood. It was almost impossible to get her to go to bed at night, but the very idea of morning seemed to tire her.

"I don't wanna get up," she whined as I gave her a big kiss good morning.

"Come on, Ria," I said cheerfully. "You have something new to wear. You're going to meet your new relatives!"

She balled up in her covers. I sat next to her, stroking her back and urging her to get up and be more cheerful.

Suddenly, Todd burst into our room! He was in an unaccustomed hurry, buttoning his shirt as he talked. He stooped at the vanity mirror and began tying his necktie.

"Oh my God, Daria!" he yelled in alarm over his shoulder. "You aren't up yet! Get up this instant! It's late!" He didn't even acknowledge my presence.

I was confused. How could it be late on a Sunday? Sunday was a day of rest. Todd never painted on Sundays, and we would go to the Bronx Zoo or the Brooklyn Museum or the Cloisters. But Todd was acting as if we were missing something terribly important.

"It's Sunday," I protested. "We always sleep late on Sunday." I regretted my words instantly. He looked in a fury.

Mom came in, brushing her teeth and talking with a mouth full of foamy toothpaste. "Get up, Daria," she urged. "Get up right now! Please be a good girl for Mommy." She rushed to the tiny bathroom. I could hear the water running. She came back with a washcloth and began scrubbing at Daria's face.

"I want to do it myself," Ria protested, squirming and trying to pull the washcloth out of Mom's hands. Mom scrubbed my sister's face until it was bright red. Daria pitched a minor tantrum, crying out her protests.

"Ow! Ow! You're hurting me!"

"We're expected for breakfast in the big house right this instant!" said Mom. "And then there's church. Todd says that everyone in Congreve goes to church. Get up, girls! We are expected immediately!"

Perhaps it is not surprising, but in New York we had seldom if ever gone to church. Oh, I suppose we went on Christmas Eve and Easter and to a funeral and a couple of weddings. But that was pretty much it. Church was not a part of our lives. Mom and Todd didn't seem to see any point in organized religion.

But suddenly the rules were changed.

Needless to say, there was considerable confusion between Daria and me, not only over the new routine, but especially over what to wear. Whereas Daria had a pretty blue dress with rabbits embroidered on it and black buckle shoes, I owned nothing appropriate. I needed stockings and a slip and dress shoes. All I could seem to find was a pink and white polka-dot dress and some black and white saddle oxfords.

"I suppose this will have to do," Mom said dubiously to Todd. "We'll have to go shopping tomorrow and buy her some suitable clothes."

"Yes. With our new money," Todd said confidently.

Mom laughed nervously and took Todd by the hand. "We'll have money soon," she said. "When will Daria start drawing her allowance?"

"I suppose Wheeler and Thelma will know something," Todd said. "And I've got an appointment with a lawyer tomorrow to verify whatever they tell me. This is only temporary. Soon the girls will have all the fine clothes they want."

Mother nodded her consent as she brushed Daria's hair vigorously and smoothed it down with a little water. Then she helped me braid mine in a long pigtail down my back. Since that was Todd's favorite way for me to fix my hair, I suddenly felt all right despite my crummy clothes. I was glamorous and my stepfather thought me lovely.

In a little group, we crossed the lawn and walked around to the front of the big house. The hot sun had already dried the dew. Ahead of us, formidable and inviting at the same time, the big house loomed. As we walked in through the screened-in front porch, the smell of heat turned to the smell of age, the odor of a house that has not been properly aired for a long time. No one greeted us at the main front door, but it wasn't locked. We just walked in. Though the house was big enough to need servants, none were around.

Aunt Thelma's house, as Mom and Todd called it, was badly in need of a cleaning. Apparently, Aunt Thelma and Uncle Wheeler had moved in while Senior was still alive. No one ever talked about Senior's wife. I assumed that she was dead. There was dust everywhere covering memorabilia and knickknacks on every flat surface. A Christmas crèche that had never been put away. Porcelain shepherds kissed little girls. Gilt-frame mirrors were spotted where the mercury had worn off the back. Sagging old couches and chairs had broken springs. Lampshades dripped with glass bangles.

We wandered through to the dining room, where two adults waited, as grim as the house itself. There was no welcome. No arms opened to hug us, no smiles to meet our tentative faces. These strange, unknown people stared down at Daria and me. Strange, unknown people who were nonetheless related, at least to Daria and Todd. Alas, they were my family's real alive and living relatives. These were the people whom the cabdriver had so maligned.

Aunt Thelma, my stepfather's oldest sister, was a big, formidable woman, nearly six feet tall and stout, going on obese. She was not beautiful like Amy, my mother. Her body was large and lumpy and her face was ugly. To me, she did not look one bit like Todd, my stepfather. Her eyes were small, furtive, and shiny, like those of a rat. Her legs were like tree trunks and her wrists were creases joining big hands with fat arms. The middle of her body was clearly strapped in by a corset. Her dyed blond hair was puffed up on top of her head and sprayed stiff. I ducked my head, trying not to look at her, feeling that some unspeakable evil would be transferred between us if I did.

Against the wall was a giant box filled with religious picture books. Aunt Thelma's big, sturdy arm reached down into the box. Her eyes locked on mine. They were oddly mesmerizing and I could not look away, much as I tried. Suddenly they lifted and bored in on Daria. Poor Ria reached out for me instinctively, but her hand was snatched away and a religious book was thrust into it instead.

"Do you like Jesus?" Aunt Thelma asked, with eyes only for Ria.

"Thank you," said Daria in a tiny voice. I knew she was just being polite about something she perceived as a present.

Wheeler, Aunt Thelma's husband, seemed kind of handsome with dark hair that had turned silver on the sides and a dimple in his chin. He was a lot bigger than Todd, although he seemed slim and smooth next to his wife.

"I am your aunt Thelma," she gushed at Daria, smothering her with a hug. "And this is your uncle Wheeler. You must be little Daria. Beautiful, of course, just like your pictures." Aunt Thelma did not bother to greet anyone else. Uncle Wheeler simply nodded to Mom and Todd and ignored us kids.

Obviously unused to much activity, Aunt Thelma wheezed to the long mahogany dining room table, which was laid out for breakfast. Eggs, bacon, toast, and grits.

"Breakfast is the most important meal of the day," she lectured. "I never do without my bacon and eggs."

We were each instructed as to what seat to take. Aunt Thelma sat at the head of the table and Uncle Wheeler at the foot. Daria was placed to her right. My aunt took out her compact and carefully powdered her nose while the rest of us sat watching.

At the table, I felt even more self-conscious. I felt I had to be very careful. This was clearly a much more formal environment than I was used to. I didn't want to embarrass my parents. I looked around me to be sure to do what seemed to be appropriate based on what the others were doing. I noticed that I was not alone. Todd and Mother seemed equally hesitant and Ria was still as a mouse. The food was served and we ate in a strained silence.

The walls were covered with framed black-and-white photos of what looked like the same child. A little girl with bobbed hair, sometimes with a big bow, who seemed to be about Daria's age. The photos were faded, so they had to have been taken long ago. She was on a pony. She was holding a big hoop, throwing a ball, playing under a hose, riding a tricycle. I didn't have the nerve to ask who she was or why she merited such prominence.

"I presume Alice has some better clothes," said Aunt Thelma, looking down her freshly powdered nose at me.

My parents exchanged a curious look that I had never seen before. "No," said Mom helplessly. She forced a little laugh. "This is pretty much it. Alice is growing so fast we haven't really bought her too much recently. You know how fast teenagers grow out of their clothes." She stirred her uneaten meal around on her plate.

Aunt Thelma sopped a smidge of toast in egg yolk, put it in her mouth, and chewed it thoughtfully. "I see," she observed coldly. "And what sort of a church do you attend in New York?"

"Well . . ." Mom stumbled . . . "we . . . um . . . we go to the . . ." Her voice trailed off miserably.

Uncle Wheeler made a *tsk*-ing noise of disapproval.

"And the child dresses like this?" Aunt Thelma persisted. "This sort of attire is suitable there?"

"Look, Thelma," said Todd, trying to take up for Mom, "money's been tight. There's no point in pretending otherwise. These clothes are all we can afford. That's why we're here." He cleared his throat. "To . . . uh . . . ease our financial burden."

"If a man can't properly provide for his children," Uncle Wheeler inserted, "he ought to go into a new line of work."

"Well, I was planning on doing that," Todd answered. "Now that Daria owns a share of the bank, maybe I'll take more of an interest in its business."

Wheeler's mouth twitched. Then he smiled broadly, showing a lot of teeth. "I'm not sure that's appropriate," he said. "The Estate is in trust for the grandchildren until they're each twenty-one. Senior placed my bank in control of the assets. After all, I'm the only one who knows anything about business."

"Your bank?" Todd asked.

"Right," Wheeler said. "It could have been yours, but you went off to New York to paint pretty pictures. And Senior needed someone to take over."

"Yes, Todd," Thelma chimed in. "And we have the most number of children. You and Kate only have one each. So it is altogether appropriate that we have the largest say."

"Fine," Todd said smoothly. "It's kind of ironic, isn't it? Now all of us will have to please our children or else we'll be out in the street."

"I don't expect to be out of work," Uncle Wheeler said dryly. "My son Bubba will never . . . take any interest in banking. Our nephew Jeremy will become a minister like his father and have no concern for material possessions. As for my daughter Gwen and little Daria here . . . well, they're girls." He cleared his throat. "And you're an artist."

"Well, I certainly plan to learn more about banking," Todd insisted, still in his forced good humor. "I've got to look after the interest of my little chick. And who knows? There might be some more to join the brood. May as well increase my family's share of the bank."

"I won't have vulgarity in my house," Thelma snapped at Todd, as if he were a nasty child.

Todd looked surprised. "Vulgarity? What did I say?"

"Don't try your little-brother cuteness on me," Thelma sneered. "Senior is no longer here to be taken in by your guileless act. I run the house now. And I won't have talk of sex at my table."

"Thelma, give me a break, will you?" Todd replied incredulously. "All Senior ever talked about was our having kids. Surely you remember. He was always bugging us to get married and have kids. That's why he set up the will the way he did. To encourage us to get into a competition to create the most grandkids."

For a moment, I thought that Todd's words had silenced the woman. But I was mistaken. "Did I not make myself clear?" Thelma demanded. Her lips had become a thin line and her teeth were clinched in hate. "I do not intend to repeat myself again. I will not tolerate this sort of talk. If you persist, then you can find a change of address. Perhaps someplace more in line with your income and religious practices."

Todd held his tongue, but I could tell that he was steaming underneath.

A wintry smile on her lips, Aunt Thelma wiped her mouth and stood up with difficulty. She flung down her napkin. "By dragging in for breakfast you have made us late to church. I am thoroughly disgusted."

With some alarm, I felt my aunt staring at me hard for the third time that morning. "Alice, you will stay here," she said harshly. "The others will come with me."

I looked to my mother in consternation, feeling tears welling up at the corners of my eyes.

"Why on earth, Thelma? What's wrong?" Mom asked.

"I have already spoken on the subject of her clothes," asserted Aunt Thelma.

"For goodness' sakes, Thelma, aren't you being a little silly? It's just for today, after all. We'll get Alice some new clothes when the stores open on Monday."

My aunt held her ground. "Then just for today she can stay home. It's an insult to God's house for the child to appear there looking like a ragamuffin."

Todd stood up from the table. "Let's not argue, Amy. Alice would probably rather stay home."

Mother stood up as well and put her arms around me. "Well, Alice dear," she said. "What luck."

"I suppose *she* would rather stay home," said Aunt Thelma. Her emphasis on the *she* was not lost on me, as if I was some lower animal, devoid, even, of a name. "My Gwendolyn sings in the choir," Thelma said, pointing up the contrast. "She's in church now. We do not permit her to be a slugabed. Or a heathen."

She turned to Daria. "Come, child. You are such a pretty little thing with such a pretty dress. You will sit next to me. I want to get to know you."

Timidly, Daria looked up at the huge, ugly woman.

"Go on," urged Todd. "Take your auntie Thelma's hand."

Instead, Daria turned and hugged me. Wheeler made his *tsk*-ing noise of disapproval. Aunt Thelma stared at her sternly, but she didn't seem to notice. For myself, I loved Ria as she kissed me.

With my barely touched plate of food in front of me, I watched them go out the door. Still, Daria refused to hold the woman's hand. I felt like cheering her on.

Alone, I tried to comfort myself. Todd was right. I didn't want to go to church. The thought of sitting next to Aunt Thelma in a pew was yuck. But what disturbed me was the way my parents seemed to accept Thelma and Wheeler's being in charge. And, I suppose here in Congreve they were, in some strange way, because of what the cabdriver had said —they owned most of the town.

And, also, for the first time, I realized how much more important Daria might be in the scheme of things than I was. After all, it was money we had come to Congreve for, and the money was tied to Ria.

As I sat alone the house seemed even more dark and sinister. Uneasily, I got up from the table and looked around. It was an old house that had perhaps once been elegant, with servants to keep the moldings free of dust and the silver shiny and polished. Now everything was worn and unkempt. The paint was peeling on the twelve-foot-high ceilings. A huge carved door had come off the rusty hinges and stood in a corner of the room.

I went out into the hall where the broad stairs rose up toward the darkness. The worn carpet was held in place by dingy brass runners. I started up the stairs, the boards creaking beneath my feet.

At the first landing there was a big stained-glass window with a coat of arms. Rose shield with a big Gothic *B* crowned by a knight's helmet. *B* for *Broderick*, I guessed. It looked like one of those phony designs you can buy in shops. In the rest

of the window were various heraldic angel designs like you'd
see in a church window, except toward the bottom was a
little girl's head. She had dark hair cut like Buster Brown. It
was the little girl from the pictures in the dining room. Then
an awful realization struck me. Except for the haircut, she
looked like my little sister.

I thought of the old woman I had seen on the third
floor the night before. Uneasily, I looked up the staircase.
Suddenly the house seemed to have eyes. Spooked by my
thoughts, I ran back through the dining room, through the
kitchen and out the back door, the screen slamming behind
me!

Outside in the sunshine, my fears suddenly seemed silly.
There were grass and trees around. In New York, even the
parks had been dirty. This was a novelty to me.

On impulse I decided to explore the grounds around
the house, which were as immense and as unkempt as the
inside of the house. Still, it was wonderful to be able to
wander on so much ground. With my limited knowledge of
such things, I reckoned that the Broderick estate inside the
walls alone covered many acres.

I went to the gate and looked right and left. A curved
road faced out to broad marsh, yellow-brown in the summer
sun. Red-winged blackbirds perched on tree limbs and white
egrets waded long-legged among the tall grasses. Beyond was
a strip of blue that became the harbor with a distant skyline
of the city. Other than a vine-tangled frame house next door,
we were alone on a peninsula islanded by marsh and water.
We might have been on a ship.

Suddenly, it fitted into place. This was the Broderick
estate that Todd had described. Senior's father—Todd's
grandfather—had built the house on a wooded spit of high
land eighty years ago. And he had built a house for his son
as well. That son, who came to be called "Senior" with the
death of his father, had moved to the big house. Senior's old
house, the one next door to us, now belonged to Todd's
sister Kate Woolcott.

The neighboring house was a serious mess. I had noticed it earlier because I could see it from the bedroom window in the carriage house. It was two stories high and maybe half the size of Aunt Thelma's, but still huge to a kid used to being cooped up in a New York apartment. A gabled house of peeling white paint and jutting angles, it had thick coils of grapevine and wisteria climbing all over the porch and walls. The backyard was a jungle. Birds had dropped seeds and every variety of tree was sprouting above the tangle. No one seemed to live there. A cupola on top had broken-out windows.

At the back wall, behind Aunt Thelma's house, was a ramshackle old garage stacked high with newspapers and magazines and old rusty tools. Beside that was a flower garden that badly needed weeding and a falling-down grape arbor. I sat in the shade and imagined our family with great wealth.

It would be the way Todd had described. We would live in Italy in perfect sunshine and he would paint and we would spend our days in a villa on a cliff. Mom would dance to the music of flutes and Daria and I would learn Italian and explore old cities and Roman ruins. We would take boats down the Rhine and the Danube and live in whatever castle struck our fancy. I added in a bit about me meeting a wonderfully handsome boy who would fall in love with me.

For a long time, I sat lost in my daydreams. So it took me a while to realize that someone else was in the yard with me.

A hulking teenage boy was crouched in the corner made where one of the chimneys joined the house. He had freckles and bright red hair that hung down over his shoulders. He was stooped over, sucking his thumb. His furtive eyes were fixed on me, making me certain he had been watching me for some time. Some queer part of myself forced me to stare back when my legs wanted to run away.

He was huge, nearly as big as Aunt Thelma. And in some odd way he looked like her. It was the eyes. The same feral, shiny points. He wore black gloves without fingers, a T-shirt with a skull on it, and big work boots with steel toes. He did not stop sucking his thumb.

If there's one thing New York has, it's an abundance of creeps. You learn early not to be timid. I crossed the garden and approached him. "I'm Alice," I said brashly.

The boy said nothing, just stared at me mean and hard, his thumb still in his mouth. His eyes darted right and left, checking to see who was around.

"Who are you?" I asked him. "What's your name?"

For a minute I thought he was going to come at me; he seemed so angry at my questions. He took his thumb out of his mouth. "You get outta here!" he hissed. "This is my place. It's the one place where they lets me alone! Bubba don't want nobody in his place! You hear?" He jammed his thumb back in and began sucking it again.

"I didn't mean to invade your privacy," I said. Was this Thelma and Wheeler's son? Was this one of the "grandkids" who, with Daria, was supposed to inherit Senior Broderick's money?

"You get outta town too," Bubba growled, gaining confidence when I did not talk back to him. "You all just pack up your bags and get your asses straight out of town. You don't belong here. Daddy says he's gone run your asses outta here!"

I swallowed hard. "I don't think we're staying long." We certainly weren't going to if I had anything to say about it!

"Y'all want all the money, don't you?" Bubba accused. "That's what Mumma says. She says you're nothin' but a pack of thieves, you New York Brodericks come to take all the money Senior made for us. And she'll fix you for it, my Mumma will. I oughta know. I done seen her do some terrible things."

I held my head up with false pride. "That's not true!" I choked. "We don't care a thing for the money!"

Bubba did not like my attitude. In a flash, he grabbed me by the shoulders and squeezed tight.

"Liar!" he yelled. "Shit-ass liar!"

Squealing with pain, I tore away and backed up several steps away from him.

Bubba glowered at me, but he didn't pursue. His gloves had brass studs along the knuckles and he rubbed those against his face. "I can hurt you!" he threatened. "I can hurt you real bad! I can hurt you so bad you'll wish you'd never met me! That's what I do to folks what I don't like!"

He began to laugh in a wild, unhinged way. Then backed away from me, disappearing around a corner of the dark house.

I retreated to the carriage house, the only place where I felt a faint solace. There, in that house, were our few possessions. My shabby clothes. Daria's fuzzy duck. The pictures Todd had painted. There, I had a link with our life before we had come to this horrible place seeking money.

The word rang in my ears. *Money.* Bubba was exactly right. Money was why we had come.

I needed to talk to my parents. I needed to tell them that we had to leave. We didn't need money. We were happy before.

5

Aunt Thelma

Church made my parents strangely talk-ative. Since Todd had seen all the familiar people he had known as a youth—people he had gone to New York to escape—it had clearly been a deathly ritual of propriety that he despised. At home with Mom, Ria, and me, he imitated their mannerisms in a grim burlesque: the restaurant owners, the insurance agents, the lawyers all bowing and scraping to the Brodericks.

The minister had delivered a sermon on giving, and Uncle Wheeler had pledged a large amount of money out of Senior Broderick's estate. Outside the church, Aunt Thelma had taken Wheeler to task for his extravagance, railing about the ingratitude and envy of the world. Among us, Todd called her a "biblical pestilence."

Still, Mom showed a quiet strength. Daria had been a huge success in church, and everyone had fussed over her cute curls and mature speech.

Lunch of fried chicken and potato salad was brought to us in the carriage house on three stacked-up trays by a poor elderly woman with blue-rinse hair and one leg shorter than the other. Alberta Pratt was Aunt Thelma's only servant.

Overworked she was, beaten down and stepped on. When we tried to talk to her, she wouldn't meet our gazes. "Mr. Wheeler and Miz Thelma are dining at the Country Club," she mumbled before limping away across the yard. "You aren't to go in the house when they aren't there."

At lunch, I confronted my parents boldly about moving back to New York and gave an account of Bubba and his threats. I said I didn't see why we needed Ria's money, not if we had to stay in Congreve to get it.

Todd laughed nervously and remarked children didn't understand real life. He said that Bubba was "brain-damaged" at birth and I should not be afraid of him. Bubba was weird but harmless. We were here for a purpose, and we should all stick it out together. This was an opportunity for us to gain so much money that we would never be poor again. We were a family and we would all be tough. If we stuck together, we would be unbeatable.

Listening to him, it all made a certain amount of sense. I wanted to believe in his dream. I wanted to believe we were a loving, loyal unit.

Still, I didn't understand why we had to stay in that awful carriage house or why we couldn't at least cook for ourselves sometimes. Todd tried to explain. He said that we were obliged to stay in the carriage house until Daria's inheritance was secure. It all had to do with Senior's will and how he had wanted the whole family to live together as a unit. Plus, Todd explained that the carriage house did not have facilities for a working kitchen. It would be very expensive to renovate and dangerous as well because of electrical wires buried underground in the marsh that was Congreve.

For the rest of that day, Daria and I were true friends and companions. We took a walk on the rim of the marsh and down to the edge of a wall around an old graveyard. We played Old Maid. We hid from each other in the yard around the small carriage house. Life was almost bearable for that short moment.

But Monday morning dawned bright and clear, and again Todd and Mother rushed us off to another detestable breakfast in the dark house with Aunt Thelma. Alberta toiled in the kitchen frying the bacon and eggs that would become so familiar. Uncle Wheeler had already gone to the bank. Thelma mentioned this pointedly as an example of work ethic rectitude in an otherwise slothful world. The whereabouts of the perfect churchgoing Gwendolyn and the thumb-sucking Bubba were unclear.

Again we were surrounded by the grime of age, the salt-crusted windows, and the walls full of pictures of the mysterious little girl. On second viewing, they seemed sinister. Familiarity took away the initial edge of naiveté in the eyes of the child, leaving them with a touch of sadness like those of a forlorn ghost with a secret to tell.

After breakfast, my mother took me aside. "You must go shopping this morning, Alice. Just you and Aunt Thelma. She was so bent out of shape about your clothes yesterday, that she's offered to buy you something more . . . well, suitable."

In the kitchen, my aunt was loudly scolding Alberta for a variety of faults. The bacon was not high quality and had been fried too crisp. The eggs were too watery.

"Suitable?" I queried. "I don't want suitable clothes. Why can't you come too? Anyway, I thought we were going to be rich. Why do we care about her?"

Mom took a deep breath. "It's not quite that simple, darling. I know it's hard to understand, but it has to do with lawyers and estates and wills. Uncle Wheeler and Aunt Thelma control the bank. The bank has control of Daria's money. Thelma is a very opinionated woman. She feels it's more appropriate for you to go alone with her. This is a small thing for you to do. Please, Alice darling, cooperate. And try to show some gratitude even if you don't feel it."

I acquiesced and dressed up as best I could—in my same Sunday clothes that had gotten me banned from church—and rode with my aunt in her large black Cadillac to downtown Congreve. In the daylight, I could clearly see the geography of where I now lived.

The Broderick mansion was truly isolated out on a spit of wooded land that jutted into a broad marsh at one end of the harbor. A one-lane paved road followed the edge of the short peninsula past an old graveyard and ruined church—

the high land narrowing at the neck of the peninsula with deep marsh on either side—to the broader road that rimmed the harbor. There on the deeper water, big houses of a similar age to the Broderick's stood amidst shady trees and orderly streets a few blocks to the downtown.

Sun sparkled on the water. Gulls wheeled. Under other circumstances the harbor and the quaintly antique mansions might have been a rapturous view. But I was in the clutches of the opinionated Aunt Thelma.

At least she didn't speak to me until she had parked the car on the main street in a no-parking zone. No one would give her a ticket, she explained. The police knew her car. We were situated right in the middle of Beau Street, the main shopping street in town. It was a bright, hot morning, and the sidewalk was thronged with people. Once more I thought of the poor cabdriver and his tale of Uncle Wheeler's stealing his business. Aunt Thelma did behave as though she owned the town. She and Uncle Wheeler were clearly very powerful.

Aunt Thelma powdered her nose from a small compact, touched up her hair in the rearview mirror, then began a rocking motion that heaved her bulk out of the car. I got out and waited for her to come around. Then she turned those beady eyes on me.

"How old are you, child?" she asked.

"I was thirteen in May," I answered shortly. I would not make undue conversation with the woman. I would answer her questions and keep all my other thoughts to myself.

"I suppose you're menstruating," Thelma said sternly.

My brain registered shock. "Yes," I said, blushing brightly.

"I suspected as much," she said. I couldn't believe she had said that. I followed her up the street, quickly forgetting my vow of reticence. "Why do you ask me about that?" I said, my heart beating faster.

"I need to know what I'm dealing with," she replied

darkly. "At this stage you'll present problems. You're at the age for problems."

My face grew hot with shame. "What do you mean problems?" I asked. "I don't cause my parents any trouble."

"A girl who is becoming a woman is always a problem!" Aunt Thelma pronounced. "You let biology rule your brain. And, unsupervised, with the wrong sort of boy, you're certain to succumb to the ultimate evil." Her tongue darted over her lips, making me think of a poisonous snake.

Of course, I knew what she was talking about. I knew where babies came from and about love and sex and all that. We were very open about things in our family. Todd thought nothing of painting Mother or me with no clothes on. For certain, I knew that Aunt Thelma would not approve of that. But I wasn't some roaring furnace of lust. "I'm not going to do anything wrong."

"Don't play innocent with me, child," my aunt continued. "I am raising two children of my own and have dealt with many a servant. I know the child's brain intimately. And I am never deceived. I am not like your parents."

I stared at her in amazed blankness.

"I was raised to work," Aunt Thelma lectured. "Although there was plenty of money for servants, I was made to do servants' chores. It was good discipline. Mother objected, but she was a weak and foolish person. Senior knew best. I have raised my two children according to his precepts."

"Housework is nothing to me," I said quietly. "I do it all the time. No big deal."

"Gwendolyn does very rigorous housework. And in the summer months when she's out of school, the work doubles. It saves us money on servants. Senior always said that if you watch the pennies, the dollars take care of themselves. And it keeps children out of trouble."

I wanted to add "particularly menstruating girls," but I wisely kept my mouth shut.

"My Gwendolyn is a year older than you. Her morning

is devoted to chores, her afternoon to improving activities. Piano. Guided reading. Choir. Devotional studies."

"Is she allowed to play?" I couldn't help asking.

"She finds her joy in improving herself," Aunt Thelma sniffed.

"Doesn't she have friends?"

"Gwendolyn is shy and does not make friends easily. As such, I have thought it advisable to improve her morally and intellectually until she can be a leader in society rather than some flibbertigibbet who marries the wrong sort of boy and ends up in the gutter."

"So she doesn't date," I continued, surprised at my own brashness.

Aunt Thelma looked at me sharply. "Certainly not. All boys are the same. They use those encounters with young girls to try to take what they consider their due. I will not condone it."

At that moment she took me firmly by my left arm and shepherded me through some revolving doors into a large department store. There was a vast room with departments selling perfumes, glasses, household wares, men's clothes. Just like the dark Broderick house, it had once been grand, but now seemed seedy. There were no escalators, only elevators with tired old black men on stools who closed accordion gates and asked you which floor you wanted. I didn't know such things existed.

"You are going to meet Miss Dawling," Aunt Thelma said as we rode up. "She is the only clerk I permit to wait upon me. A woman of good family but distressed circumstances. I see to it that she makes her monthly sales quota so she can keep her job. It's the least I can do, having known her family intimately. She is grateful."

The door opened, accordion gate swishing back. "Watch your step please," mumbled the old man for probably the eight hundred millionth time in his life.

Certainly, I didn't want to ruin Miss Dawling's commission, but still I was surprised at the clothes in her department. They were dowdy and designed for older women. Nothing bright, only black and tan and gray. "Are these really clothes for kids?" I asked.

Aunt Thelma licked her lips in that now familiar snake-like manner. "This is the only proper store in Congreve for respectable young women. Especially a respectable young lady who will soon be attending the Ashcroft School for Girls."

"School?" I asked, puzzled. I guess I had refused to think beyond the summer, but it was true. I would have to stay in Congreve—until Daria was out of grade school. Todd had explained it to Mother and me and there was no doubt he meant it.

Thelma pulled out a plain-looking tan shirtwaist dress with a high collar, viewed it dubiously. "Apparently, you're not aware of the way things are done down here in Congreve. New York is a different kind of place from down here."

"But . . . what do you mean? I haven't talked about this with Mom and Todd." Panic filled me. What on earth was the Ashcroft School for Girls?

"I don't approve of your referring to your stepfather as 'Todd,' " Thelma said. "I think 'Stepfather' or 'Stepfather Broderick' is much more appropriate. See that you make that change in your vocabulary." She added a navy blue skirt and plain white blouse to the clothes she had laid over her arm.

"Sure. Seems like a mouthful. But okay." There were moments when I couldn't quite take my aunt seriously. "But I've always gone to public schools in New York. My parents would have told me if it was going to be different down here. I know they would."

My aunt flashed a strange, smug smile. "I neither consult the opinions of my children nor share with them my plans. That was Senior's way, and that is my way. I am glad to learn that my brother has at least retained some of what he was taught."

"But that's not their way," I protested. "They're . . . different."

"I wouldn't disagree with that. Todd has shown that amply over time. Much to the shame of this family. *Your parents*, as you call them, must conform to propriety by sending their eldest daughter to the Ashcroft School. I shall see to that if no one else does."

A timid woman with thick glasses approached us, dutifully lifting the clothes from Aunt Thelma's arm and hanging them in a dressing room. Thelma and I followed her. The mirror in the dressing room was cracked and the chair was wobbly.

"This is Alice McNamara," my aunt introduced. "And, Alice, this is Miss Dawling. Alice is my brother Todd's stepdaughter by marriage. Todd who has now come back to us since Senior passed away. Of course he had to. Senior left his daughter Daria a lot of money, but Todd was obliged to return to Congreve to live before he could have the use of it. How fate does play strange tricks on us."

Aunt Thelma sat regally on the lone chair. "You would not believe the clothes that this girl brought with her from New York. Disgusting, Miss Dawling, disgusting. When I saw her, I knew I would have to interrupt all other obligations to bring her here for something proper."

Miss Dawling nodded, withdrawn into her world of subservience and loneliness, of servility and humility and mumbled agreement. She pulled the tan shirtwaist dress off the hanger and held it up to me tentatively. "She'll be going to Ashcroft, of course. This type of dress will be quite appropriate there."

"Naturally," Aunt Thelma continued. "Although I have my doubts about her preparation. She may have to stay back a grade. I have no confidence in New York schools. How many years of Latin have you had, child?"

"None," I admitted. "We get to choose a language next year. I figured on Spanish. So many people in New York speak it. I thought it might be useful."

"Just as I feared."

"Feared?"

"Senior always called Latin the foundation for properly learning the English language and a superb lesson in self-discipline. When schools abandon Latin, they abandon all self-discipline."

"Todd . . . Stepfather . . . says that Latin's a dead language and it's of no use to anyone," I said matter-of-factly. I felt strangely comfortable taking a parent's word as the absolute authority.

"Yes. He would, of course. He'd pay no mind to preparing you with a proper education. This is going to present a difficulty for me. Ashcroft has Latin required from the third grade. I may not even be able to get you admitted as a student."

"Oh, I'm sure you can, Mrs. Broderick," Miss Dawling insisted. "They wouldn't refuse you anything."

Aunt Thelma stared hard at the sales clerk, irritated that anyone might contradict her. Miss Dawling turned sheepish. "Well, perhaps you're right. They are very strict about academic performance at Ashcroft."

Personally, I felt overjoyed at the idea of being disqualified from the Ashcroft School, which I was sure would be horrible. I pictured it filled with Aunt Thelmas in ascending sizes from first to twelfth grade.

"My niece Daria, however, should have no difficulty being admitted to the preschool," Thelma told Miss Dawling smugly. "You will meet her soon. She's Todd's daughter. His real daughter. This one"—she waved in my direction—"this one is the child of the woman he is currently married to . . . and some other man." She grimaced. "McNamara," she added once more to distinguish me clearly from the Brodericks.

Again, I had a premonition of my aunt Thelma pulling our family apart. In her mind, I clearly did not belong. I was an interloper. The Broderick blood did not grace my veins. From her chair, Aunt Thelma barked instructions.

"Now, child," she said to me, "let's get on with this. I don't have all day to cater to you!"

I was somewhat taken aback. Both of these women were going to stay in the dressing room while I tried on my clothes. Stripping down in front of strangers—I felt humiliated. I had been raised to be casual about my body, yet these people made me feel dirty.

"Go ahead, child," Thelma said, reading my mind. "I have two children of my own. I've seen naked bodies before. Yours is nothing special to me. And you're not God's gift to mankind like you think you are."

I steeled myself and began to take off my clothes.

"She's going to have quite a figure soon," said Miss Dawling in a weak attempt at flattery.

Thelma's shiny eyes never left my body. "Yes, I fear so," she said. "Which will be one more problem for the Brodericks."

I scrambled to get into the dress, and hide myself from those evil encroaching eyes!

"Well," said Aunt Thelma critically. "It doesn't look like much on her, but nothing really would. Take her hair down from that ridiculous pigtail, Dawling, and fix it up on her head somehow."

Obediently, Miss Dawling acquiesced, putting my auburn hair in a tight knot with bobby pins she took from the pocket of her dress. I stared at myself in the mirror. My face looked sallow and drawn. I was no longer pretty.

The rest of the clothes were a blur. I followed directions and tried them on, each in turn, keeping my modesty as best I could. They prodded and poked at me and turned me this way and that. My hair kept falling out of the bun. Aunt Thelma said it ought to be cut.

Together, my aunt and Miss Dawling piled up a large purchase of drab clothes for me. "Now how about a bathing suit?" asked Miss Dawling slavishly. "There's still some summer left, and Ashcroft has that very nice heated pool during the winter."

The thought of the water seemed the only bright spot in this depressing day. Even if Gwen was only allowed to go to choir and scrub floors, perhaps if I had a bathing suit, my aunt would have to let me have some fun. Anyway, Mom and Todd would not allow her to run my life. They had promised Daria and me days of fun on the beach. Broad white beaches, as Todd described them, with exotic seashells and tropical vegetation and brown pelicans that flew in low lines over the water.

"Oh, yes, please, may I have one?" I asked eagerly.

"Well . . . if there's something suitable," said Aunt Thelma to Miss Dawling. "You know my opinions on this matter."

"Yes," said Miss Dawling. For a moment, I felt a small twinge of solidarity with the poor woman. Like maybe she recognized me as a fellow prisoner of Aunt Thelma's tyranny.

She was gone for a few minutes while I concentrated on going through my clothes so as not to catch my aunt's gaze. Finally, Miss Dawling came into the tiny space with several bathing suits. I picked the red one. It was one-piece and cut low in the back. I kept on my underwear to try it on.

I daydreamed as I put on the suit. I dreamed of meeting a handsome boy and having him overcome with my beauty. It didn't seem such a bad thing to want boys to be attracted to you. In two years, I'd be in high school. Everyone had a boyfriend then. Even Ria wanted the boys to like her.

"Stop that," Thelma snapped. "I won't have you fondling yourself. Do you hear? Take off that suit immediately."

"Fondling . . . ?" I fixed on the forbidden word.

"I've warned you to not play the fool with me, child. Did you hear me? I said take that suit off. Dawling, I can't believe you tried to talk me into this."

At that moment, the poor saleswoman's face began to come apart. The cause was apparent. Depending upon Aunt Thelma to keep her lowly job. A sense of her waning, purposeless life. At that moment it was more than she could bear. Her face turned up in that awful smile people get when they cry, and the tears started to flow.

My aunt turned on her indignantly. "Take hold of yourself, Dawling," she commanded. "I can't have you sniveling like this over nothing."

Miss Dawling fled from the dressing room. Clucking her tongue, Aunt Thelma laboriously got out of her chair and picked up the stack of clothes. I got dressed and followed her out. Miss Dawling was nowhere to be seen.

A skinny man in a suit came out of the back of the store, his hands fluttering in concern. A little plastic badge identified him as the manager. "What's wrong, Mrs. Broderick?" he asked anxiously.

"Nothing at all," my aunt said smoothly, but her voice belied her words. "I simply don't know what came over that foolish woman! She always was weak. I suppose that's why she . . . well, no mind. No harm is done. I trust this won't mar Miss Dawling's record."

"Oh, no, of course not," the manager gushed.

"Senior knew her father well," my aunt continued. "A fine man. Were he alive, it would destroy him to know that his only daughter . . . was in . . . such a . . . state!"

The manager put all of our purchases in two large boxes and even carried them to Aunt Thelma's car, all the way assuring her that he would deal with Miss Dawling himself. "I do hope we'll see you again soon," he repeated.

I did not talk to my aunt on the way home. I just listened while she made nasty remarks about the "witless Dawling woman" who had made some tragic error in the past that had marked her forever.

On the way home, Aunt Thelma drove me by the Broderick bank, the fountainhead of all the family wealth. What a dismal place it was. It was a drab brick building, six stories high with two lions crouching out front kind of like the New York Public Library. A big clock on the outside wall struck the hour with a loud tinny sound that could be heard for blocks.

Aunt Thelma seemed particularly pleased with the clock. Apparently, Senior had always kept the time accurate, but now it was off and my aunt saw this as symbolic of her husband's inadequacy. It was the first hint I had that she had not been pleased with him. She especially resented his having to take her name when they got married.

On our way home, we drove past the harbor. The iron railing on one side was decorated with lines of preening seagulls. With their fading, worn-out opulence, the big brooding houses were across, on the other side, facing the water. Then we turned onto the narrow road that skirted the graveyard and went out onto the isolated peninsula where the Broderick and Woolcott houses sat at the end.

When my aunt stopped at last in the drive, I forced a smile and thanked her. I reached for the box of new clothes, but Aunt Thelma put a possessive hand on it. "I'll keep the clothes for now," she explained. "I will present them to your parents myself. Now away with you, girl. You have put me through too much exertion as it is."

I knew what she was up to. She wanted to rub it in that I was to be dressed properly only out of her charity. Her brother Todd was obviously inadequate to the task of supporting us.

So I found myself again in my new fenced-in, marsh-isolated, oppressive world. The huge mansion cast its early afternoon shadow across the lawn, creeping slowly longer with the passage of the sun, reaching to within inches of the carriage house.

I stood in that patch of sunlight thinking that I had somehow missed a day of living. What I had experienced had not been real life.

6

The Big House

That shopping day was among the longest in my life. When we returned, it was barely lunchtime. Aunt Thelma lectured us all on the misfortunes of Miss Dawling. My clothes were unmentioned. Afterward, we went back to our little carriage house and talked together like a real family.

Todd had been to see a lawyer. He feigned high spirits, but the news was clearly bad.

"You know," he said, "I'm not sure we should have come back here after all. Thelma and Wheeler are such pirates. And Senior died the same son of a bitch that he always was. He wanted to rub my face in it. And he sure set the Estate up to do just that."

"What do you mean, darling?" Mother asked. "Is it really all that bad? Can't anything be done to change the will?"

Todd shook his head. "Well, there aren't any loopholes, that's for sure, plus these lawyers are all basically in Wheeler's back pocket. I mean, money talks and Wheeler has the money just like that poor old cabdriver told us the first night. About the only thing I can demand, it seems, is some sort of access to the bank records."

"Well, isn't that hopeful?"

"Yes and no," Todd said. "They have all the cards and they'll show me only what's convenient to show me."

"Well, when will we be able to move out of here—to somewhere else in Congreve?" Mother asked.

Todd gave a hollow laugh. "I wouldn't count on it,

Amy. Senior wrote in his will that he wanted us all to live together. I mean, he didn't miss a trick. We'll have to stay put here in the carriage house, either that, or we'll have to move back to New York."

Mother hugged Todd briefly and gave us her widest smile. "Well, we'll just have to bear up, won't we? After all, it will all be over soon and we will be very, very wealthy with not a care in the world."

When Mother asked me about the shopping trip with Aunt Thelma, I suppose I was ugly to her. I said probably Aunt Thelma was planning a ceremony where she dressed me in clothes like a novice nun or something. It truly seemed like being in Congreve was bringing out the worst in all of us. Mom pulled me to her and smiled. "Try to put up with her and laugh inside, Alice," she said.

After a while, I went to my room to play with Ria. Mother appeared at the door almost immediately. Her face looked drawn and tired. "Alice, Thelma has summoned you back to the big house," she said.

"Aw, come on, Mom . . ." I protested.

"Please don't kick up a fuss, darling," she said. "I think Thelma wants you to get to know Gwen. She is your new cousin—at least by marriage."

"Jeez, Mom, I hate these people. I can't believe they are related to Todd."

Mother looked away. "I know," she said. "But we have to try to get along with them. Please, Alice. Go on over there. Oh, and use the back door."

No one seemed to be in the big house. An unsigned note said *Alice to scour oven—Gwendolyn scrub floor.* There was a sponge and scrubbing powder on the drainboard in the kitchen. This was no joke. My alleged cousin was nowhere in sight. I looked at my watch. Oh, well, I thought to myself, I might as well do the work. I couldn't go back to Mother and Todd and pitch a fit. I had to be mature. I set to work. I had done that kind of housework before and hated it. The oven was especially dirty, crusted over with layers of filth.

No doubt Alberta was so pressed with making meals that she had little time to clean, and besides, with one leg shorter than the other, she moved slowly. Apparently, Alberta was the only person my aunt could lure into domestic service. I thought of myself as helping her rather than my aunt. But after half an hour, my resolve began to flag. I had made little headway, and my arms ached.

I was so absorbed in my own thoughts that I didn't immediately notice the girl who came into the kitchen after some time. She was a few years older than I, dressed in very baggy jeans and an old shirt, her pale blond hair tied up in a rag. She was badly overweight. There is really no other way to put it.

She didn't say hello or introduce herself or anything. She just began to haul cleaning materials out of the adjoining bathroom. Dumping several detergents into a metal mop bucket with wheels and a place to squeeze the string mop on the far side, she began mopping the kitchen floor with soapy water. Watching her, I realized suddenly that this must be Gwendolyn—Aunt Thelma's daughter who spent her time improving herself.

"Do you do a lot of this kind of work?" I asked, trying to strike up a conversation.

Gwen looked around before she answered. She seemed afraid of being overheard, as if talking while she worked was frivolous. "This is good training," she told me. Her voice was peculiarly high and hollow. "It will help me to grow strong and morally decent." Hair had fallen down into the middle of her forehead, and she wiped at it with the back of her arm.

"It will?" I said unbelieving. Frankly, I failed to see much moral gain in cleaning a dirty oven.

Gwen ignored my comment. "I must learn not to be proud of my social position," she lectured me. "I must know what it is to work for a living like less fortunate people. It will teach me not to put on airs."

I stared at her. Did she live in the real world? "There's

never been any danger of me putting on airs," I said. "I've never had anything to be snobby about."

I could see my aunt in the look that Gwen gave me then. "That's because you live in squalor in New York."

Strangely, what she said did not make me mad. "In squalor?" I asked, almost laughingly. "How in the world do you know how we live in New York?"

Gwen looked surprised at my question. "Why . . ." She groped for words. "Why . . . Momma said so. She knows all about you."

"Well, that's interesting since your mother has never seen where I live." I paused. "Actually, it's nice in New York."

"Yes, but you have a stepfather."

"Yeah?" I said. "What does that have to do with New York being nice?"

Gwen put a wisp of hair in her mouth and began to suck on it. Her voice became low, as if she was going to tell me a great secret. "Momma says it's important that you aren't Uncle Todd's real child. She says it means that Bubba and I will get . . . more money."

"Right," I said. "Maybe when you come into your wealth you can hire an oven scrubber."

Gwen gaped at me, then ducked her head and scrubbed furiously at the floor with the mop. It was then that I realized that Aunt Thelma was standing in the doorway.

"The first lesson for you, Alice McNamara, is humility," my aunt stated. "Money does not bring leisure. It brings responsibility. Senior taught me that lesson well."

I said nothing, simply took up my sponge and oven cleaner once again and went back to work. I felt like laughing in these people's faces. They were so weird and unreal.

Aunt Thelma examined the floor with disdain. She was permanently angry with everyone and everything, even her own daughter. "Gwen, use some elbow grease," she chided. "It's no wonder you can't lose any weight. You don't have discipline or will power. I can't believe that Broderick blood is in your veins."

"I'm sorry," whined Gwen, the tears welling in her eyes. "I must try harder. I must do what you want." Again she spoke with that same hollow voice, as if she was reciting memorized lines.

My aunt smiled with pleasure. "I've long ago given up any hope of change," she said. "I know it's my fault. I indulged you as a child. I let you eat whatever you wanted. It's a mistake to love too much. And what do I get for loving? An obese child." She said *obese* as if it were a disease. She put her face in Gwen's. "An obese child," she repeated, "who does not have the will to make herself presentable before God and the world. You could be slim like Alice if you'd just make the effort."

I was appalled. It was no wonder that Gwen was crying. And it was apparent that Aunt Thelma had laid heavy guilt and even concentrated cruelty on her daughter for many years. Suddenly I was overcome with love for my parents and how they had treated Ria and me.

"I'm sorry I'm so fat," Gwen wept. "I'll try to do better. I promise I'll try! I'll make you proud of me!" She reached out for her mother, wanting comfort.

"Stop that!" Aunt Thelma snapped. "Your hands are filthy. Look at you. Blubbering over nothing. I won't hug a dirty, crying child. You're just a big baby. Still wetting the bed. Sneaking food. Maybe you can get Alice to show you how to lose some weight. Lord knows I've tried everything. I wash my hands of you."

After her mother left, Gwen sat down cross-legged in a puddle of water and cried behind her hands. Silently, I went over and held her heaving shoulders.

"I'm sorry," I said. "I don't know why she has to be so mean to you."

"I deserve it," Gwen sobbed. "It's all my fault. I know it's all my fault. If I wasn't so dumb in school . . . if I wasn't so fat . . . things would be happy. I've brought unhappiness on the whole family. On all the Brodericks. Myself. I did it all myself."

She said it with such conviction that I realized she truly believed what she was saying. And I was stunned. How much emotional pounding had it taken to convince her of this?

"You're wrong," I argued. "It's not your fault."

"No, *you're* wrong!" Gwen countered vehemently. "What do you know? It *is* my fault! It is—it is! Admitting to it is the first step toward self-improvement! Senior always said that!"

I stood back, dizzy with her defiance. "Okay, okay. Jeez, if that's the way you feel. I mean . . . I'm sorry . . . I mean is there anything I can do?"

Gwen shrugged her shoulders and went back to scrubbing. "Yeah, go back to New York so she won't compare us."

I tried to laugh, but it came out false and hollow and I felt stupid.

In silence, we worked on and on. The bars of sunlight shifted as the hours passed. At last we were finished.

"Does she have to come back and inspect it?" I asked finally.

"No," Gwen said, getting up with difficulty. "She's gone out. She always goes out after she gets mad at me." Gwen dragged the heavy bucket of filthy water across the floor on its wheels and clumsily dumped it into the toilet bowl off the kitchen.

"Hey . . ." Gwen said tentatively.

"Yes?" I answered. I was through and I wanted to get out of this place as fast as I could.

"I suppose there is something you could do for me," she blurted out.

"Sure," I said. "What is it?"

"My room is up on the second floor," she whispered. "Turn left at the top of the stairs and it's the first door. There's a Psalm taped up. I'm going up there."

"Yeah?" I asked.

Her eyes had an expectant glow. "There's some cake in

that covered dish over there. Chocolate cake. If you'd bring some up to my room, we could share it. And then Momma would never know . . ."

"Gwen, I don't think . . ." I hesitated. The thought of discovery by my aunt filled me with dread. If Gwen wanted to sneak food, let her do it herself.

Gwen's eyes filled with tears again. "Please," she begged. "I thought you wanted to be my friend! I won't let you come to my room if you don't bring cake!"

"Well, I dunno," I said, trying to think of a halfway reasonable excuse. "It's late and I should be finding my parents and . . ." And who wants to come to your dumb room with the Psalm taped up anyhow, I wanted to say. You can't all drag me down to your level.

"You're just like all the rest," Gwen went on. "You hate me! You hate me because I'm fat!" She fled the room and ran pounding up the stairs. I heard a door slam.

Silence engulfed me and with it a nervous feeling that someone was lurking. I opened the kitchen door gingerly and looked around. Not a soul.

The chocolate cake sat under its glass lid. The icing was fudge. It looked rich and moist. With only a moment's hesitation, I got a knife out from the drawer and a plate from the cupboard. How much could I take without someone noticing? I cut a big wedge. Gwen could have it all. I wouldn't eat any.

I went up the creaking stairs. Rosy light filtered through the stained-glass window with the shield and angels and the little girl's head. The door was just as Gwen had described. Psalm 6 was Scotch-taped there.

O, Lord, rebuke me not in thine anger, neither chasten me in thy hot displeasure.
Have mercy upon me, O Lord; for I am weak: O Lord, heal me; for my bones are vexed.

I tapped lightly.

"Go away," said a small voice from inside.

"I've got it for you," I whispered.

The door opened quickly. My cousin had eyes only for the cake as she hustled me inside and shut the door. I noticed that the lock had been removed and the room had little furniture and few personal objects, as if no one lived there. There was only a picture of Christ kneeling at Gethsemane, a Sunday school perfect attendance certificate, a cross over the bed, and a withered flower arrangement on the chest of drawers. It wasn't at all like my room in New York or even the room I had begun to decorate in the carriage house. It was as if Gwen had been allowed no personal possessions.

Gwen had already begun packing the cake into her face. She didn't offer me any. I wandered around the room. Tucked away in a far corner was a framed photo on the wall of the same little girl featured in the dining room. She was sitting in a bucket of water having a big time on a hot day. A hose lay on the lawn.

As though accepting that I wasn't going to ask for any cake, Gwen slowed down. Or maybe she did not want it to disappear too quickly. She ate the remainder slowly, saving the icing for last.

"That's Daria," she said. "Momma's little sister who died. Momma used to say I looked like her until I got fat."

"I'm sorry."

"She used to love me more when I looked like Daria. When I lose weight, she'll start loving me again."

I shrugged. "Yeah. I guess."

"You are my friend, aren't you?" she said finally.

"Well, I suppose I'd like to be," I whispered. "We can imagine we're really cousins, even if I don't have any Broderick blood. I don't have a real cousin."

"Yes," Gwen agreed. "I guess that would be okay." She paused briefly to take another bite of cake. "I'll tell you something . . . if you promise not to tell."

"Okay," I said. It was an easy promise since I had no one I could confide in.

"Have you met my brother?"

"Yeah," I said. "Sort of. I mean, I think I did. He was outside the house . . . next to the chimney."

"Was he sucking his thumb?"

"Yeah."

Gwen tried her first mouthful of icing. She held it in her mouth a long time, letting it melt, savoring it. "He's not quite right in the head. Momma denies it, but it's true. I mean, he is right in the head, but he is really . . . I mean, there's something wrong with his head."

"How old is he?" I asked.

"He's sixteen. We're twins. I came out first and there was some problem with him. You have to be careful of him."

"Why?"

"He's not right. He's mean. He'll do . . . ugly things to you."

"Like what?"

At that awful instant, the door to her room was flung open and Aunt Thelma appeared. With one fell swoop, she knocked the dish from Gwen's hands and sent it spinning across the floor. The dish didn't break, but icing smeared all over the rug.

"Clean that up," she growled at Gwen. "Immediately."

Scurrying to do her mother's bidding, Gwen wept. "I'm sorry. I'm sorry. I won't do it again," she repeated.

For the first time, I realized that my aunt was holding a leather-bound whip. It was truly bizarre. I had never seen such a thing except in the movies. It was limber and Aunt Thelma bent it between her two hands. Her sinister gaze was entirely on me. An air of unreality surrounded the whole scene.

"Who sneaked you that cake, Gwen?" she asked, looking straight at me.

"I didn't do it, Momma!" wailed Gwen. "I didn't do it! I promise you, I didn't!"

"Then tell me who did," my aunt said triumphantly. She knew that she had caught me.

"She did." Gwen pointed firmly in my direction. "It was her! She did it, Momma!"

The whip swished in the air.

"Wait a minute," I said. "This is ridiculous. Don't get me caught in some stupid contest you're having between yourselves. Gwen asked me to get the cake for her and I did. Maybe I shouldn't have, but I did." I could hear my voice as I spoke. It sounded scared. I was scared.

My aunt was clearly pleased at my reaction. "I do believe you're arguing with me, Alice McNamara. Splitting moral hairs, aren't you? Gwendolyn is helpless around food. It's made her an ungainly mess. It's destroyed her looks and her future in society. No boy will ever want to marry her. And you've given her cake. You've given her exactly what she can't control herself around. That's like giving liquor to an alcoholic."

"I'm sorry," I said, sincerely. "She had worked so hard . . . she wanted it so much . . . She asked me if I wanted to be her friend . . . I felt so bad about how—"

With a stinging *thwack*, the whip stung my arm. I yelled as I backed up, but Aunt Thelma grabbed me by the wrist and held me with a grip of steel. She was incredibly strong. There was clearly no reasoning with her. It seemed unbelievable that getting a piece of cake had put me in such a position. My aunt was crazy.

I twisted and yelled as the blows landed on my thighs. On my buttocks. On my back. I didn't want to yell. I wanted to have the grit to be silent. But it hurt.

"You wretched, wretched, evil girl!" Aunt Thelma screamed.

I squirmed and struggled.

"This is nuts," I yelled at my aunt. "All I did was give her a lousy piece of cake! Leave me alone. Leave me alone or I'll tell my parents and they'll . . ." I was speechless trying to explain what my parents would do. This was too unreal for words. No one sane would believe it.

My aunt paused for a minute and a smile crossed her lips. "Yes," she said. "By all means tell your parents. But they won't do anything. They don't want to get in a fight with me. After all, Wheeler is my husband and he controls all of the money. Every single bit of it. They have to get along with me. That's what Senior wanted. That's why he made Todd move back to Congreve."

She lifted the whip and more blows came. I sobbed uncontrollably. I struck back at her. "Leave me alone!" I screamed. "Leave me alone!" I tried to run, but my aunt held me.

"Don't you talk back to me, Alice McNamara," she spit out. "Stand still and take your punishment. Didn't your wonderful parents teach you even that much?"

Still, the blows came. I willed myself to stand firm, but I knew that I could not. I was crying.

"Please stop! Please stop hitting me!" I pleaded.

"You are an evil girl, Alice McNamara!" Aunt Thelma raged.

The blows and the pain became a blur. I fought with my aunt as best I could. Finally, she began to tire and she stopped.

"There," she said. She was breathing hard and her eyes were red with hate. "And you clean up that rug," she ordered Gwen.

Gwen was crying, but she worked quickly. I could barely see for my tears. I hurt everywhere.

Aunt Thelma held tightly to the banister as she walked downstairs; she was red from exertion and muttering to herself.

She's crazy, I told myself. Stark, raving crazy.

Aching all over, I stumbled out into the hall.

"Go away! Don't ever come back to my room!" Gwen yelled after me. "You're not fit to be in this house! You're not a Broderick!"

It was dark outside. I would collect myself. I was surrounded by madness, but I would be all right. My parents wouldn't believe this. They would leave Congreve when they heard about it. The money wouldn't matter anymore.

7

The Truce

When I got back to the carriage house, my mother and father were playing a game of Old Maid with Ria. They looked so happy and it was such a contrast to what had happened in my aunt's house with Gwen.

But they knew instantly that something was wrong. Mother got very pale and Todd put down his hand of cards. "What on earth happened to you?" Mother gasped. She pulled me to her and searched my tear-stained face.

I could feel my heartbeat quicken. "Aunt Thelma," I said. "She's . . . she's . . . crazy . . ."

"Alice . . ." my mother insisted, "what happened?"

"It's too gross for words," I said, sitting down at the table. "She hit me. . . . She has this whip . . . it's . . . unbelievable. Really . . . I mean I don't even believe it myself."

Daria's eyes were big with fear and she was tuning up to cry. She came over and hugged me.

"Alice," Todd said, taking charge. "Tell me exactly what happened. Step by step." He took a handkerchief out of his back pocket and handed it to me, touching my hand gently.

I told the whole story right up to Aunt Thelma's finding us with the cake. "She said that I was helping Gwen to be big and fat. She took out this awful whip and she hit me with it again and again."

Todd pulled the back of my shirt up. The marks were

clearly visible. He was furious. "This is outrageous," he said through clenched teeth. "She's gone too damn far."

He stood up. "Todd," Mother cautioned, "wait and catch your temper. You have to think about this before you storm over there."

"Are you suggesting that I should sit back and allow this to be done to my child?" he demanded.

"Please," I said. "Don't do anything. I tell you the woman is crazy. Let's just get away from here. Let's go home."

"Let her drive us out?" Todd said. "I'm not going to give up Daria's fortune because my crazy sister goes berserk. Senior always hated her and said she was crazy. This is living proof. We've got her where we want her now."

He stormed out of the house, but Mother ran behind him, trying to subdue him. Daria clung to me for dear life. "Alice," she said, "are we going to go home?"

"Yes," I said. "I know we will. Now why don't you get in bed and I'll read you and the fuzzy duck a story."

It was hours later before Todd returned home. Mother and I had both fallen asleep together on my bed after we had read Ria a story, overcome by the need to be close to each other in the face of what had happened. Mother had sponged off my wounds and put some salve on them, shaking her head in disbelief the whole time. Then she had helped me get dressed in my pajamas and tucked me into bed. I was barely aware of it when Todd came in to call Mother to come to bed with him. I was exhausted. Both of them kissed my cheek.

"What happened?" my mother whispered in the dark.

Todd shrugged. "She doesn't deny doing it," he said. "And she says she's sorry. She just lost control, apparently. She is so frustrated by Gwen. God knows her two children are messes, both of them."

"You sound almost sorry for her, Todd."

"Not a chance. Thelma is a bitch. And I think Alice hit

the nail on the head. She is crazy. But she apologized to me. And so did that bastard Wheeler. They don't want this to get around town. They're very concerned about what everyone thinks of them."

"And?" Mother said. "Is she going to apologize to poor Alice, Todd? I cleaned off those wounds and they are positively horrible. It's unbelievable that a grown woman would do that to a poor child. Unbelievable."

"Yes, Amy, I totally agree with you, but we have to move slowly. Thelma says she'll be more civil to Alice, though she insists that Alice keep her distance from Gwen."

"No doubt Alice has that intention."

"Anyway, they agreed to let me come in to the bank starting immediately—tomorrow—to work there and to learn more about the management of the Broderick Estate and Daria's money. Wheeler even agreed to give me a salary. I can see my way clear. The money situation will ease up almost immediately."

"Oh, Todd, it's too good to be true!" Mother exclaimed. "Can it really be so? Frankly, darling, looking at poor Alice tonight I was inclined to agree with moving back to New York right away. We can't let them treat us like dirt."

"I understand totally, Amy. Except that this is almost an ideal situation. Between Daria's inheritance and the salary that Wheeler has promised to pay me, we'll make three times as much as we made in New York. And you won't have to work. You can stay home with the girls and give them your full attention. I mean, Wheeler even agreed not to charge us any rent for this carriage house."

"But why, Todd? Why on earth? It doesn't make sense. I thought they wanted us out of here."

Todd shrugged again. "Thelma lost it tonight, and she's always been borderline crazy. Senior knew that. Wheeler only married her for her position and money. Wheeler is no dummy. He's a shrewd man. He knows I'll play hardball if I need to."

In the doorway, Mother hugged Todd. "Oh, darling, can it be? Can our lives have really turned around?"

I drifted off to sleep in the euphoria of my parents' happiness. Maybe life in Congreve wasn't going to be so bad after all. The beating had been horrible, but maybe in some perverse way it had been worth it.

8
The Bank

All was not as perfect as we had imagined.

The next day, Todd went off to the bank in his new suit. He kissed Mom dramatically at the door and announced he would come home a banker. He looked so handsome and bright.

At seven o'clock that evening, he came home. He was not as happy as he had been when he left. He and Mom shut themselves up in the tiny kitchen and talked in low voices. I could hear only snatches. Apparently he had gone to see the lawyer about the Estate. He had a copy of the will and he read aloud to Mom from it.

" '. . . income from the corpus of the trust to be distributed for education, support, and maintenance so long as Daria Broderick shall reside in the Broderick household and be educated in the city of Congreve. Sufficient funds shall also be distributed for the support of her parents should they reside with her.' It's right there, just like he told us—in black and white."

"But that's just crazy," Mom protested. "I mean, how can they make her live in some particular house? If he gave her money, can't she just go where her parents want? The money's hers regardless."

"That's not what the lawyer says," Todd answered. "It's so like Senior. He hated me for leaving Congreve, and he always swore he'd disinherit me. But then Daria came along, and he had to figure out some way to give her something.

Though he had never seen her, he adored her. . . . She reminded him of . . ."

"Your sister . . . Daria," Mother whispered.

"Yes . . . Daria," Todd said. "He adored her memory to his dying day."

"So," Mother continued, "how was the bank? How did things go?"

"Not much to report," Todd replied. "Boring, squalid, hideous, but tolerable. It was fine. I'm in a training program like a kid just out of college. I have to start as a teller and learn all the chores from the bottom up. But I got my first paycheck. Wheeler advanced me a month's pay to tide us over plus a month's advance on Daria's income from the Estate. A nice piece of change."

That night was the first time I saw the liquor bottle appear. Todd had brought it home in his briefcase. I had never thought much about liquor before. Among the artists in New York who visited our house, someone was always drinking something. Many were blind drunk a lot of the time, and there was the constant possibility of drugs. But Mom and Todd had always been sparing in their use of liquor, finding joy in life and not in a bottle.

I recognized the signs of whiskey in Todd at dinner in the big house that night—the slurred speech, the clumsy movements. Aunt Thelma and Uncle Wheeler exchanged malign glances. Wheeler loudly suggested Todd was tired from "unaccustomed labor" and ought to retire early. Todd ignored him.

"Some people go to college and study business," said my uncle. "They come to us able to be of use. We don't need any paintings for the bank except from established artists."

With a massive effort at control, Todd laid down his napkin and rose from the table. He turned bright red. "I think that I can learn more than just painting, as you have agreed," he said softly. "Anyway, I'd better go on back to the carriage house. No need to open up old wounds."

When he was halfway across the floor, Aunt Thelma

stopped him with an icy word. "Todd?" she said, her voice rising.

Todd stopped, but said nothing.

"Senior never drank to excess. Yes, he liked his toddy in the evening. Sometimes two. But never to excess. I follow his precepts."

Todd walked out of the room. He lurched against the door frame, caught himself, and went on. The rest of the meal we finished in a total silence. Gwen was given only a carrot and a piece of celery while the rest of us had pork chops and applesauce jazzed up with brown sugar and cinnamon. When she whined about being hungry, my aunt told her to shut up.

Later that night, as I lay in bed, I could hear Todd and Mom talking loudly. Todd was really upset about what had happened at supper.

"The nerve of him saying that I'm not an established artist," he said. "The greedy rat. Those people at the bank hate his guts. He's got some kind of lie detector down there that he hooks them up to when there's the slightest suspicion of dishonesty. Plus everyone knows he married Thelma for her money. I mean, Amy, it's obvious since he even agreed to change his own last name to Broderick. The price of Wheeler's wealth was for Thelma always to be a Broderick and any heirs they produced to be Brodericks."

It was true, I thought. Aunt Thelma had kept the Broderick name. I had no idea what Uncle Wheeler's family name was.

Upset, chasing ghosts no one could see but himself, Todd reminisced about his youth in Congreve and why he had fled for his sanity. The dark house had been built by Senior's father in 1900. Senior was a penny-pinching miser who never spent a dime. That was why the place was so rundown. Thelma was just as bad. She had moved into the big house when Senior was still alive. And once Senior had died, Thelma determined to keep everything exactly as it was when he was alive. She was too cheap even to have the vines cut off her sister's house next door, so it looked like it was being slowly pulled apart.

I was upset to hear Todd in this state. I got up from the bed, went across the tiny hall, and stood in the doorway. Todd noticed me and came over. "What's wrong, Alice?" he asked, hugging me gently. "Can't sleep?"

I nodded my head and kissed him on the cheek. "Please, Todd," I said. "Don't worry so much about all of this. It doesn't matter. We all love you."

Mom hugged me as well. Finally, they both walked me back to bed, kissing me and the sleeping Ria on their way out of the room.

They returned to their bedroom, closing the door behind them. I could hear nothing else, and so was left alone with all of my own morbid thoughts.

Though I finally fell asleep, I was unsettled. No matter how he tried to hide it, Todd was obviously unhappy. Everything that had tormented him in his past was now alive in his present existence.

9

Futile Pursuit

The days crept slowly by, defined increasingly by the bank and what Todd did there. He was frustrated by what he was and was not allowed to do. Still, the paychecks came, and on paydays everything seemed all right. One evening Todd came home proudly announcing he had arranged to review the books and quarterly reports of the Estate. Wheeler wasn't thrilled, but he hadn't been able to object.

As had become a pattern, the liquor bottle was brought out, but this time there was happiness and laughter behind the little kitchen door. We all ate together in the big house and Wheeler wasn't there since he was "working late." In his absence, Todd was the man of the table. He made conversation that Aunt Thelma icily ignored.

The following day, Todd went off to work singing. He and Mom were feeling more in control of their lives.

When he didn't return at the normal time, Mom became alarmed. She tried to hide it, but I could sense her anxiety. The dinner hour came, and we were obliged to go to the big house. Gwen had a dab of cottage cheese while we ate two-inch-thick pork chops and heavy gravy with sweet potatoes and biscuits and succotash and apple cobbler for dessert. Uncle Wheeler and Aunt Thelma stared at us fixedly but said little. Mom lacked the courage to ask them where Todd was. Afterward, we scurried back to our little home.

Time for bed came and went. Mom looked at her watch

frequently. She gave Daria her bath and made us both go to bed. Daria was exhausted and fell asleep immediately. I lay there in the dark worrying. Finally, Todd came through the front door.

I slipped downstairs and lurked outside the kitchen door. They had closed it, and I could barely make out the conversation.

"I was worried about you, Todd. Why didn't you call? What happened?"

Through the crack in the swinging door, I could see Todd. He had loosened his necktie and was searching the pantry for the liquor bottle. "You don't want to know," he said, "and I don't want to talk about it."

He got ice from the refrigerator and put it in a large glass. He poured the glass full of liquor. Then he sat down at the kitchen table. Mother bustled around him, setting him a place with food. She had slipped back to the big house and filled him a plate from the dinner.

Todd didn't touch his food. He drank and refilled his glass. The story came out. They had inundated him with books and papers that he hadn't understood. He didn't know accounting, didn't know how to read balance sheets or evaluate loans. Wheeler had smirked in triumph and the other executives had followed his lead. Defeated, Todd had gone back to his menial job as a teller.

Then things had turned even worse. His accounts had not balanced at the end of the day and Wheeler had been openly contemptuous. Like a naughty child, Todd had been made to stay until he got them right.

"Did you fix it?" Mother asked.

Todd shrugged and made himself another drink. "I had to. And it wasn't my damn fault at all. It was the head teller. She had taken money out of my drawer while I was in the lunchroom. She's not supposed to do that. It's against the rules. Finally she gives me this little smarmy 'Oh, I'm so sorry I forgot I had done that.' I mean, I'd checked the transactions like a million times with her sitting there watching!"

"Oh, Todd, you poor darling," Mother comforted. "Did she do it on purpose?"

"Are you kidding? Of course she did. They were all gloating. Wheeler huffing out the door at closing time but leaving the head teller in charge to make sure that I couldn't get away without correcting the mistake. He doesn't like me messing in the books of the Estate one bit. He doesn't want anything the bank's done to be questioned. That's why they cooked up that little stunt."

"So, sweetheart, why don't you leave the whole thing alone? Just work in the bank and look after Daria's money. Is it worth your sanity to push these people? The Estate has to be profitable enough to pay off Bubba and Gwen too."

My mother had never been a combative person. She was a peacemaker, always compromising. She won people over through gentleness and affection.

Todd grunted. "I suppose you're right. It's just that I don't trust Wheeler."

"Do you want to go back to New York?" my mother asked.

"We can't, Amy. They'll steal everything. I can't let them take Daria's money."

"Daria gets her share free and clear when she's twenty-one."

"They'll strip the assets out of the Estate—sell things off at a loss in phony deals—and leave her with nothing. Wheeler will be sitting there fat, greasy, and stinking rich laughing at us. They took everything from me when I was a kid. My happiness. My joy. My sanity. I'm not going to let them take from my child as well."

My parents talked into the night. Their conversation moved between Congreve and New York and how their finances were finally getting straightened out. I had heard them talk about money often in New York, and I knew that they had borrowed money at times. They were excited that they could pay off their debts.

Later, Todd came in and kissed me good night. I pretended to be asleep.

After he left, I lay in bed listening to Daria's gentle breathing. In my mind I pictured the twin lions out in front of the bank. Todd had taken Ria and me there one day the week before, proudly showing us off to the staff. There had been big gold lettering and marble columns. A large clock on the outside wall could be heard all over Congreve when it struck the hour. It was stiff and formal and filled with tension. It seemed like a place that Todd would not like. There was no artistry there, no joy, no laughter.

I stared up at the shadow-darkened picture Todd had painted of Daria and me when I was ten and she was two. Not once in the weeks we had been in Congreve had he drawn a picture or painted. Everything that meant anything to him had been sacrificed to this strange pursuit of an inheritance. It didn't seem right.

10

Family Madness

     In the morning, Todd was distant and sullen. He called into the bank sick and stayed in bed most of the day. He did not play with Ria and me as he usually did, just lay in bed, either staring up at the ceiling or sleeping. In the evening, we were invited over to the big house for dinner. Though Mother, Ria, and I went over, Todd stayed at home.

     When Mom tried to take him a plate of food, my aunt refused, saying, "In my house people come to the table or they don't eat."

     Mom stood there paralyzed. I held my breath. "Don't be ridiculous," she said breezily. "He's sick, and it's not going to help to starve him."

     Aunt Thelma's nostrils flared, but she didn't raise any further objections.

     When we went back to the carriage house, Todd was up and in the kitchen. The liquor bottle was out on the kitchen table, and he was drinking heavily.

     "Todd," I said. "What's wrong with you? Don't you love us anymore?" Ria ran up to him, pulling on his arm and reaching up to hug his neck.

     Mother came up behind us and hugged all three. "Come on, children," she said. "Of course your father loves you. Let's read a story to Daria."

     Gently, she led us upstairs and we all sat on Ria's bed. Todd's eyes were red and he smelled of liquor, but he announced firmly that he was going to do the reading. I will never forget the story. It was *The Little Engine That Could.* Todd's voice was unsteady, but Ria sat on his lap and I sat at one elbow, Mother at the other. We were once again a happy family.

Until it became clear that we were not alone. Midway through the book, Aunt Thelma was standing in the doorway. I hadn't heard the door open or the stairs creak. She had made it all the way upstairs without a sound.

"Todd, you're drunk," she pronounced. "Disgustingly drunk."

Unsteadily, Todd got to his feet. The book fell to the floor.

"This is our house," he said. "We're entitled to some privacy."

"That's what everyone would like to imagine," my aunt sneered. "Privacy to display your depravity before a small child."

"Depravity? What are you talking about?"

Mom stood there, shocked. She reached tentatively for Todd, but he pushed her hand away.

"Drunk in front of a child," said Aunt Thelma. "Letting her see you in this drunken stupor. I won't have it. I won't have you corrupt an innocent child."

Reaching down, she snatched up Daria. Ria started to cry, pushed against that powerful body with her little hands. "Lemme go!" she cried. "I don't wanna go with you! I want to hear the story!"

"P-put her down," said Todd. He was trying to be forceful, but he only seemed weak and fragile.

"I think she should come and live in the big house with me," pronounced my aunt, "until you learn to control your degraded instincts. That's what Senior wanted, after all. That's why his will requires Daria to live in Congreve. He wanted to make sure I was in her life to guide her moral development."

Daria began crying. "I don't wanna go with you! I want my Mommy and Daddy! I want Alice!"

"Oh, you'd love it in the big house," said my aunt in a gooey voice. "We'll have a lot of fun. And such good things to eat. There's all kinds of candy and cake. You can have as much of it as you want." She picked Ria up in her arms and turned toward the door.

"Thelma, have you lost your mind?" Todd suddenly demanded. "Put that child down!"

My aunt looked shocked. Her mouth twitched at the corners. For a brief moment, her eyes held a touch of terror. "Lost my mind?" she whispered. "Of course not. I'm as sane as the rest of you." Slowly, she put Daria down. Ria ran to me.

Then my aunt saw the portrait on the wall that Todd had painted of Daria and me in New York. Her whole facial expression changed and she seemed to gain new strength.

"They're naked!" she gasped, pointing at the picture.

"So what?" asked Todd.

Her face contorted. "Nakedness! *Children displayed naked!*"

She snatched the picture off the wall and tore it into shreds that sifted to the floor.

"You are despicable, Todd Broderick. You're not a man. You're not fit to carry Senior's shoes. You were always a sickly, sneaky child, sniveling and currying favor with Mother. You never had the backbone to be Senior's son. You wanted your little colored pictures and paint pots. You couldn't go to college and learn the business. You had to run off to the big city and live in your dream world. Borrowing money from Senior. You were too good for the Broderick way of life, but not too good to live off Broderick money."

Todd's hands twitched. He pulled away from my mother and stumbled across the tiny upstairs hall. The door to their bedroom opened, then slammed. The bed creaked as he fell on it.

Mom remained standing in the open doorway. Daria

clung to me for dear life. My aunt stared at us briefly, then stalked down the stairs. I heard the screen door bang. From our upstairs window, I watched her cross the lawn to the big house. No lights came on as she entered. I thought with horror of my aunt threatening to take Ria away from us into that dark, gruesome house and my heart ached. My little Ria who was scared of the dark. I held her close and kissed her hair.

"Mom, what's wrong?" I demanded frantically. "Why is Aunt Thelma so mean to all of us? What's her problem?"

She sat down heavily on my bed. Her eyes were dry. I sat beside her, and hugged her. I was scared and wanted comfort.

"Please, Momma, please tell me what's wrong," I begged. "Why is Todd so upset?"

Mom's eyes became glazed and distant, seeing a vista I could not share. "Alice, my darling Alice, sometimes we are the victims of the past. Todd—your stepfather—has never gotten along with his sister. It's like old jealousies coming to haunt them. I'm not sure any of us can really understand. We just have to try to help him."

"But Mom," I said, "we have more money now, can't we move somewhere else?"

"Daria's money is in trust, Alice. That means the bank will look after it until she's an adult. In the meantime, Daria's money is not hers free and clear until she turns twenty-one."

"But what about lawyers and things? What about them?"

"Todd is looking for a lawyer to represent us. They're all afraid of Wheeler. It's such a small town . . . and he's so powerful." She put on a brave smile. "But he'll find someone to help us. I know he will. Someday soon we'll be able to leave."

Mom stroked my hair and hugged me. Ria clutched at my hands. Suddenly, I felt horribly ashamed. I was thinking more about myself than I was about Todd. I was sorry that he and his sister hated each other. I wished there was something I could do to help.

Finally, Mother stood up and went toward the bedroom. Taking Ria's hand, I followed her.

Todd was sprawled out across the bed, still fully clothed, asleep. With all the tenderness I had in my heart, I leaned down and kissed him, just as he had kissed me every night since I could remember. Ria did the same. Then we went back into our own bedroom.

Ria ran to the pieces of the picture that Todd had drawn, which were in a neat pile in the middle of the floor of our room. Tears brimmed in her small eyes. "It was a pretty picture," she said. "We can glue it back together, can't we, Alice?"

"Later," I said. "Later we'll try to put it back together." I pushed the tears from my eyes as I picked the shreds up off the floor and tucked them away in my top dresser drawer. It could not be repaired, but maybe Ria would be comforted believing we would put it back together.

I picked up *The Little Engine That Could* and read it to her. Eventually, my sister slept. Her grip on my hand relaxed and she turned over in her bed.

My parents seemed to be asleep, too, but I could not sleep. I did not even want to get ready for bed. Quietly, I cut off the upstairs lights and crept downstairs. For a while I sat in the open front doorway watching the dark house.

A flash of anger surged inside me, making me restless. Walking silently across the lawn, I prowled in the dark outside around the big house. Listening. Peering.

A slash of light came out of the one lighted window downstairs and fell in a rectangle on the ground. I stepped around it and crouched under the window. Peeped over the sill. My aunt was pacing up and down the parlor, wearing a steady path in the carpet.

"I have not lost my mind. There's no insanity in our family," she was saying. But she was talking to no one. Not a single soul was in the room with her.

"Never been one bit of craziness in this family. This whole town is filled with nuts and folks being shipped off to the crazyhouse every day. But no Brodericks are crazy. Not a one. Not since the first one stepped off the boat two centuries ago. We're good, solid, hardworking people. Folks who give their all and receive the Lord's blessings in return. Oh, sure, everybody's jealous of us Brodericks. Jealous and spiteful. Saying mean things about Mother just out of spite. She's up in the attic now. I didn't put her there. Senior did. Anyway, Mother's going to be well. She's just a little tired. That's all. Just a little tired."

It was uncanny. My aunt kept pacing up and down the room. Pacing and talking.

"Give value for your money. A good day's work for a good day's wage. That's what Senior would say. He was a respected man. He had the respect of the whole world. He ran this town. Folks stood up when he entered the room. They came up to him on the sidewalk wanting to shake his hand and thank him for all the good things he did for folks.

"He'd come out of the bank at six-thirty each evening and check his watch against the bank clock. Both were always right on the dot. Don't you know he saw to that. I was so proud to be his little girl. He wanted a son but he got Todd instead. Todd wasn't a man. He wanted to mess with little colored pictures and paints like some kind of sissy. So Senior put all his hopes and dreams on me. And I was so proud. All decked out in my Sunday dress and patent leather shoes riding with him in the front seat of the big car, walking into the church holding his hand with everybody bowing and scraping."

My aunt leaned up against the window, pressed her face against the glass, and stared out into the dark. I crouched down lower, holding my breath. Eventually, she turned and went back to pacing. She was pointing and gesturing menacingly now, facing down an imaginary audience of enemies.

"There's no madness in this family, I can tell you that. Nothing that can't be cured. Mother's going to be well one day soon. Senior was wrong to lock her up in the attic. Now, Todd, he's shiftless and irresponsible. But there's no madness there. There's nothing wrong with Broderick blood. Mother's going to be cured. She'll be up and around same as always. We just couldn't use a hospital and all those doctors because we couldn't have folks talking and spitting out their evil bile. Using it as an excuse to slander the Brodericks and say we are no good. She'll be up and around. You wait and see."

I crept away like one more frightened night creature.

What on earth was she talking about? Madness in the Broderick family. Her mother locked in the attic. A chill crept over me, and I ran back inside and locked all the doors.

11

My New Friend

The days passed as Ria and I had come to expect. We had no friends our age. We simply stayed near the carriage house, playing together, sometimes walking down the small peninsula to watch birds in the marsh. There were always chores for me to do in the big house. Cleaning, dusting, scrubbing. I did not mind. It was something to pass the time.

But, one day, there was bustle and activity in the vine-covered frame house next door. Though it was in bad shape and needed repairs, it began to take on a life of its own. There were people moving in.

Windows were thrown open. Someone swept a broom out the back door. A small moving van drove up and men unloaded boxes. Pots and pans clattered and banged in the kitchen. A boy's voice shouted and feet could be heard on the stairs.

Ria and I watched, fascinated, from our bedroom window. There was new life on our isolated peninsula. The movers came and went and engaged in normal activities. I even heard laughter.

Gladly, one morning we went with Mother and Todd across the lawn for the familiar bacon-and-egg breakfast. Something exciting was about to happen.

At the big house, I learned that the rest of the Broderick clan had arrived. The Woolcotts. Norman and Kate. Kate was the sister of Todd and Thelma. They had a boy,

Jeremy, fifteen. Two years older than I was. Like us, they had returned to Congreve because of Senior's will.

But my new relatives were not at breakfast as I had expected. Todd and Mom said nothing. Since the horrible night, they had fallen into a pattern of silent acceptance of everything that happened—small humiliations, slights, open insults. Gwen brought things to the table and stared wistfully at the biscuits and grits running with butter. A thin, solitary slice of melon lay on her plate.

"The vultures have come home to roost," said Uncle Wheeler from behind his newspaper.

"I don't think that's an appropriate attitude in front of the children," said my aunt. Of course, she approved of his attitude. She just didn't want it voiced in front of Alice who wasn't of Broderick blood. And Gwen who was bound for heaven.

Uncle Wheeler snorted with disdain. "Your foolish sister marrying some damn moron minister who can't hold a job. Dragging her from one cannibal land to another. And now they come swarming around Congreve because of the will."

"He was discharged from his post some months ago," my aunt corrected. "You know he can't hold a job."

I sat silently eating the bacon and eggs. Gwen gnawed her melon down into the rind like someone biting their fingernails. I tried to imagine what Jeremy Woolcott would look like. Maybe he was handsome and fun. A dismal thought struck me—he came from Broderick genes. Even if they were named Woolcott, they were still Brodericks and, so, had the famous blood. Jeremy would probably be as big a creep as Bubba.

The day dragged by filled with my usual chores. Gwen mostly hung in corners staring into space. Her lips moved slowly in inaudible conversations with herself. One time, when she thought no one was looking, she sneaked a big mouthful of grits and wiped her lips repeatedly to remove all traces of her sin.

In the evening after dinner, I waited impatiently for the mosquitoes to settle and around nine o'clock went out in the garden. Insects made a million night noises in the marsh. From far across the harbor, at the docks, there came a wail of a ship's horn. The air held that ever-present odor of alluvial silt from the endlessly flowing river that washed through Congreve and out to sea.

It was inevitable that I was drawn to the narrow wooden gate—to look into the neighboring yard. There were people over there and I hadn't seen them yet.

On tiptoes, I could just see over the top. A boy was there, shrouded by the darkness. I could see him. He made no effort to hide himself. He could see me. Our eyes made contact by a sort of electricity.

"Hi," he said boldly. He came forward until he was easily visible to me and took hold of the top of the gate. Since he was tall, he looked down on me easily.

"Hello," I said shyly, stepping back a bit. He was very good-looking with kind of wavy hair that looked like it would be brown in daylight.

"You must be Alice. You certainly aren't grotesque enough to be Gwen. Even though I haven't seen her in five years, she couldn't have altered so radically."

I smiled. It was the first pleasant conspiracy of hatred I had enjoyed. Maybe he was all right, even though he was a Broderick. He gave me a fighting spirit. "Yes, I'm Alice."

Jeremy laughed. "You are the dreaded foundling who has crashed the family without sharing the Broderick ancestry. Dark things are whispered of you."

He sounded melodramatic and yet so serious at the same time that I was shocked. "What sort of things?"

He looked around cautiously, then spoke in a whisper. "Mater and Pater"—he called them that, Latin for mother and father—"are all tucked up in bed. They can't stay awake past eight o'clock. But you'd best come over into our yard to avoid the gimlet eye of Thelma the Disciplinarian."

The lock on the gate was rusted shut, but I had no trouble climbing over. Jeremy took my arm when I got to the top and guided me as I jumped. His touch gave me a thrill. I fell to my knees and found myself looking up into his face. His eyes glowed in the dark like fireflies.

"There's a secret hideaway here on these haunted premises," he said. "It's good you learn it. I only survived my early childhood by being able to secret myself there safe from the fire-breathing Auntie Thelma."

"Do you always talk like this?" I asked.

"Shhh," he cautioned. "Whisper. No, I don't always talk in orotund phrases. I read Shakespeare all the way on the plane. It took three days. Engines falling off. Delays in Cairo. Pater dithering and losing our tickets. Mater being carried off and ravished by Egyptian police in red tarbooshes."

I giggled. "You're lying to me."

"Here and there. But you have to make the story a good one. Otherwise you get mired down in reality and that is such a bore."

He led me among the growing honeysuckle and blackberry, down to a winding path overhung by locust trees. Faint bits of weathered white paint showed among a jungle growth of vines where there was an old gazebo down at the very foot of the garden! With a little umbrella-like roof over a masonry slab with latticed sides shaggy with twined leaves, it was deliciously ghostly. Yet it didn't seem like much of a hiding place when a determined adult was intent on finding you.

"Allow me to point out the salient features," said Jeremy. "You will note that you are completely concealed from the houses by foliage. If you are quiet, no one will ever know you are here. I used to lie concealed for days living off Cheerios and rainwater caught in flowerpots."

"Why couldn't someone have simply come down here and found you?"

"You wouldn't believe quite how inept Mater and Pater are. They have trouble finding their shoes in the morning. It takes them the entire morning to get through breakfast. And as for the loathsome Auntie, look here." He took my hand and guided it in the dark to the edge of a brick wall. There were broken-out chunks here and there.

"Handholds," he pronounced. "Over the top of the wall and you're in the old St. Michael's graveyard. The church burned twenty years ago. The graveyard was filled up back before the Civil War. So no one goes in there. Could you picture Auntie dear trying to scale that in pursuit?"

I laughed at the image.

"I escaped many a sound beating in early life by going over that wall."

"Did she beat you a lot?"

"Savagely. She's a big believer in spare-the-rod, spoil-the-child. Except Bubba and Gwen don't seem to have turned out as model youth. Bubba is a serious cretin and Gwen belongs in a madhouse. Has my aunt flogged you yet?"

"Yes," I said, amazed that he would know.

"Did she use the barbed wire?"

I almost laughed, but the memory of the beating was too vivid. "Don't make jokes. It hurt horribly. She used some whip bound in leather."

"Ah, the dog whip. Did she beat you about the eyes?"

"Don't poke fun," I said resentfully. "It hurt like hell."

"You know how to curse. Marvelous! Just the sort of cousin I've always longed for. Let's sit down and curse together. Shit. Damn. And then there's the dreaded f-word."

He led me into the gazebo and flopped down on one end of an old black iron garden bench. Tucked his knees up under his chin. In spite of the sophisticated language he was using, he seemed very boyish.

"You'll get used to the beatings. Either that or go mad from the pain."

"I hope we'll be able to leave here soon."

"Take the money and run? I'll bet Uncle Wheeler is having conniptions over the idea of giving away part of his bank. He was over here today blistering Pater about how he was not going to allow an institution he had worked so hard to make solvent be torn to shreds by thieving relatives too lazy to work."

"Todd works," I insisted. "He's an artist. He supported us, no matter what anyone says."

Jeremy laughed. "Pater works, too, after his fashion. He just can't seem to hold a post. He's always being bounced from one desolate wasteland to the next. The Africans all think him deranged and give him the sort of guarded respect they accord the insane."

"What do you mean?"

"They think the insane are in touch with the spirit world and so are not about to harm them for fear of angering spirits. It's probably the only way we've survived. There was a big massacre in Uganda while we were there and dozens of foreigners were killed. While we were in Zaire, the army mutinied and wiped out our entire village. Except for us, of course. We were in direct communication with evil spirits."

"Is your father really that strange?"

"You'll see for yourself soon enough, providing Mater and Pater manage to get through breakfast one day in time to receive visitors."

"You mean you're allowed to eat meals on your own? We have to spend every one with Aunt Thelma and Uncle Wheeler."

"That's part of how they dominate the family. We're exempt because Mater and Pater never seem to make it to meals on time and that drives Thelma into a frenzy."

"Where have you come from?"

"From Kenya. A lost little village near Meru. They were having their puberty rites when we left."

"Their . . . ?" I clapped my hand over my mouth, realizing what he was saying.

"The missionaries have tried to get them to stop for a hundred years, but of course they won't. Pater solves the problem by pretending it doesn't happen. He's asleep by eight o'clock anyway, which meant I could come and go as I pleased in the evening. I was invited to watch."

"To watch?"

"It was marvelous. Naked girls dancing in lines. And then the screaming and the blood."

"What are you talking about?"

"They circumcise the boys . . . and the girls."

"The girls? How do they . . . ? No, don't tell me. I don't want to hear it."

"But it's so fascinating. You see they—"

"Shush," I interrupted. I stood up abruptly. "I have to go back. They'll be looking for me."

He led me back to the gate and helped me back over the top. I stood there in the dark with the gate between us.

"I don't want you to think I'm a prude," I said. "It's just that . . . well, things here are so awful. There's no one to talk to and Mom and Todd are acting so strange. They are getting quieter and quieter, almost like they're retreating into themselves. Meeting you seems, well, refreshing. I'm just having trouble getting used to it."

"I understand," he said. "You have to learn to live in a world of imagination. It's the only way to survive."

"I'm . . . glad you're here. I need a friend. Desperately."

"We'll slit our wrists and mingle our blood. I'll infect you with the Broderick curse."

"Stop being so silly," I giggled.

"I know. You can wear this." He slid a white lump threaded on a string from around his neck and handed it to me. The lump felt smooth, like enamel.

"What is it?" I asked.

"It's a witch's tooth—from a witch who was flayed alive in Zaire. An amulet. It will protect you from the Broderick evil. Don't let grisly Auntie see it, though, because it'll drive her into a frenzy."

Without another word he slid away catlike into the darkness. Leaving me standing there lost in wonder and excitement.

12

A Talk with My Mother

Another day passed slowly. Because Gwen had committed some unnamed sin, she was kept in her room and I had to do all the laundry including ironing sheets, which is a clumsy chore and, of course, my efforts didn't satisfy my aunt at all. I did notice that the laundry smelled of urine and realized what Gwen had done. At age sixteen, she had apparently wet her bed.

I also had to iron Bubba's underwear, if anyone could imagine anything so gross. He wasn't around very much because he seemed to live somewhere else, but last night he had spent the night in the house for his annual bath and shearing. The sound of his bellowing could be heard through the house as his mother forced him to practice some minimal hygiene.

Working alongside Alberta in the kitchen, I tried to engage in conversation. She whispered to me that Aunt Thelma didn't like people to talk when they were working because it would distract them from doing the best possible job. It was truly bizarre. Whenever I'd say something, Alberta would just look around furtively. So at last I got the hint and quit trying.

Alberta was a terrific cook, and it is ironic that I never had a bad meal in that awful house. I tried to praise her, but she would become very nervous. She reminded me of a stray dog who has been kicked and beaten by everyone it meets and can't believe that anywhere in the world is a decent person.

In late afternoon, Mom and Aunt Thelma finally returned from town in the Cadillac. Ria had gone with them. They had gotten her hair cut, which Ria didn't like one bit. Oh, Mom fussed over her and said it looked pretty, but Ria clearly didn't agree.

"Ugh," Ria said to me. "I don't like it. Do you, Alice?"

"Of course Alice likes it, Daria," Mother interrupted before I had a chance to say anything. "Now it won't be any trouble to fix your hair. Remember how you hated combing it when it was long and had all those big tangles?"

"I don't like it," she insisted. "I want hair like Alice's."

"Daria," Aunt Thelma said sternly. "Now you look more like your heritage. You look more like a real Broderick."

It was then that I realized why Aunt Thelma had wanted the haircut. She wanted my sister to look like the little girl in the dining room pictures. The resemblance was uncanny now. Aunt Thelma wanted Ria to look like that little girl, just like she wanted her called Daria and not Ria.

That night, after supper, I went out into the garden and stood by the narrow gate for a long time wondering if Jeremy was around. I hadn't seen him or his family all day. I wanted to talk to him about the strange dead girl. I wanted to know why she had died.

There were lights on in the house. I scaled over the gate and walked in the neighboring garden, sat in the gazebo hidden from all eyes, half imagining that Jeremy was watching and would jump out and say "boo." I took the witch tooth out of my shirt and rubbed it, wondering if I could bring out its magic, and draw him to me with its power.

I imagined him in Africa wearing sandals and shorts with the air all clean and the stars bright and perfect in their constellations. A lion would roar in the distance and I would shiver and press up against Jeremy. He would hold me in his arms gently. It was a nice daydream, and banished some of my morbid fears, but it did not make him come.

The lights began going off in the house. Giving up hope of Jeremy's coming, I went back over the gate. Mom was waiting for me right on the other side. Standing there in the dark, she gave me quite a start. "Alice, what on earth are you doing?" she said in a harsh whisper.

"Mom, I've met the neatest guy," I said excitedly.

"Oh please no!" she said in alarm. "Not him!"

"Not him? What's wrong with you?" We were talking in intense whispers.

"Don't you know who that is next door?"

"Sure, they're my relatives. Or sort of. Isn't he sort of my cousin? And, Mom, he's really neat. I mean, he's been all over the world and talks in the funniest ways. He's the only bright spot in the past month."

I was startled by what happened next. My mother grabbed me by the shoulders and shook me. "You sneaked over there in the dark to meet him? I can't believe it."

"No, I didn't," I argued. "I mean, he wasn't there. But I would have liked to meet him. And what's wrong with that?"

"You mustn't go near him. Aunt Thelma wouldn't approve. She has very strict ideas of morality. You know that. And how does it look? A teenage girl sneaking around in the dark to meet with her own cousin."

"Hey, Mom," I said. "It's me—Alice—your daughter. You've known me for a long time. Are you trying to suggest I'd do something with a cousin I barely know? Have I got it right? Are you talking about sex, Mom?"

That really rattled her. Something had changed about her. I mean, in New York, Todd had regularly painted naked women. Even my mom and me. And sex had never seemed dirty. My parents hadn't been prudish. But here under the glare of the mighty Aunt Thelma, it all became dirty. Aunt Thelma had destroyed one of Todd's pictures. And now in the garden my mother was speaking with the morality of

Aunt Thelma, assuming that my relationship with Jeremy would be dirty.

"You know I trust you, Alice. But think of how it looks from her perspective. Cousins meeting in the dark. She'd imagine the worst. You know what incest is, don't you?"

"How could I not, Mom? I mean I'm thirteen. I'm from New York City. There are girls in my school class who are pregnant. I'm not Gwen Broderick or someone who probably takes a bath in her underwear."

Then the enormity of what she had said struck me. "Incest? What are you talking about?"

Her voice sounded on the edge of breaking. She sniffed back tears. "Alice, I trust you. You know I do. I know it's been hard on you here. It's been hard on all of us. Poor Todd . . . he's . . . Alice, you're a beautiful girl. You're a healthy young animal. And I've heard stories about that boy. Something could happen between you two. He's very . . . well, he's very precocious."

"Mom, aren't you being ridiculous? I'm not going to do anything with him. I just met him and talked to him for twenty minutes or something last night. That's all."

"Don't argue with me! Don't argue, I say!" She struck me across the face, a stinging blow. My head snapped back. My hand went to my mouth. I was more startled than hurt. Mom hadn't hit me in years. I could barely recall her doing it even when I was a kid. Instantly, she began to cry.

"I'm sorry. I'm really sorry," she moaned, hugging me to her. "I'm so upset. Trying to look out for you and Daria and trying to hold Todd together. I'm sorry, Alice. I'm taking all of my frustrations out on you. Forgive me."

"Has something happened, Mother?" I asked. "You seem—well different—on edge. And Todd . . . he's always drinking these days. And around Aunt Thelma and Uncle Wheeler, I mean, you're both horribly silent. It's weird. What's going on?"

"Oh, Alice." My mother hugged me. "It's terrible what they're doing to Todd. Truly terrible." There was a long pause. "And there's no one to talk to. Todd has been back and forth to lawyers, but your uncle Wheeler is so powerful in this town that there's nothing Todd can do." My mother clung to me as if she was drawing strength from me.

I hugged her back, wanting her love, wanting to feel like a little girl again, safe and warm in her arms. I cried. "Please, Mom, please. Can't we go home? Can't we forget about the money? Or make them send it to us?"

She shook her head. "Wheeler has canceled the lease on the loft in New York. He found out about it and got his lawyers to just . . . to just write the landlord and cancel the lease." She waved her hands in a futile gesture. "I don't understand it. We were just somehow put out. We have nowhere to go back to. And, Alice, everything is gone from there—all of our possessions were gathered up and dumped. It was so cruel and unfeeling. Todd is devastated. All of his paintings—his life's work—gone."

"What do you mean?" I asked. "How could they do that? It's not fair."

"Oh, Alice, life's not fair," my mother sobbed. "Wheeler and Thelma did it out of spite. It's like the worst thing we could have done coming back here. We've put ourselves under their thumb. Now we're dependent on them for everything. The bank paycheck. Daria's allowance. It's driving Todd crazy."

She put her head on my shoulder and cried. I found myself stroking her hair, comforting her. "We'll make it, Mom. We'll hang tough."

We sat there a long time, hugging each other and trying to collect ourselves. Finally, we felt composed enough to go back to the carriage house.

As we were walking back, we both gasped simultaneously. There was an awful white face in the highest window of the big house. The woman's hands scratched at the glass. Stroked it. Tried to wave at us. It put a chill right through my whole body. Mom choked back a scream.

"Who is that?" I asked. "She lives up at the top of the house. I saw her the first night."

Mom became vague. "It . . . it must be Todd's mother, Gladys. I don't know why I haven't thought . . . but Todd never mentions her ever . . . so naturally I didn't . . . I'll tell Todd we've seen her. Yes, he'd like to know that. Come. We must go in. And you must promise me to never go over that gate again."

"Sure, Mom. Sure. Anything."

I held her close as we went in. She was trembling. Moths were bouncing off the outside porch light, which was shaped like a little lantern.

When we came in, Todd was drinking at the kitchen table. He tossed back a small glass of bourbon as we came in and poured another. His speech was slurred. "You can scratch three more lawyers off the list," he said. "I've certainly gone the rounds. None of them want to represent us. They all say there's no problem with the Estate and that we have no need of an attorney. They're calling Wheeler to report on me before I even get out the door."

"You . . . you don't know that, dear," said Mom, sitting down at the table.

I stood in the doorway. Todd kept a tight grip on the bottle to prevent Mom from getting it away from him. It had come to be a little ritual they had worked out. Her trying to slide the liquor away, trying to be subtle and not hurt him, trying to get him to stop and go to bed. And him drinking all the more heavily.

"Of course I know it," Todd said, suddenly belligerent. "I see their faces. I'm the one who's there, not you. You don't see how they're laughing at us. Laughing because they know Wheeler is going to pick us clean."

Mom cringed. Violence seemed right under the surface. I found myself wondering if he would hit her. It was something I had never dreamed of between them before.

"It's okay, Todd," I said. "No matter what, we'll be a

family." I meant it as a plea, but it came out as me playing parent. And adults don't care for that one bit.

"Go to bed," he snapped at me. "Thelma has a lot for you to do tomorrow."

"Please can't she have a day off?" Mom asked. "She's worked so hard. Couldn't we go downtown together as a family? Have lunch with you or something?"

"And have everyone laughing at you on the street? I won't have that. Not while I'm alive. And Alice needs to pull her weight. She's thirteen. A little manual labor is good for her. I have to sweat. By God she can too!" He slugged down another drink.

"Sure, Todd," I said. "Sure. I'm okay. Don't worry about me."

"I've had eleven years of raising your kid, Amy," he said in an ugly voice. "I'm sick of it. What good is she? Another mouth for me to feed."

"I work, Todd," Mom argued, flushed with anger. "I work just as hard as you!"

"Not since coming here, you haven't. You haven't lifted your hand. Look at this place! It's a freaking mess! What do you do all day?"

I slinked out of sight. There was no point in me butting into an argument like that. But it made me feel sick right down in my guts. Sick, thinking of the life we had once had not so very long ago—without a cross word among us. Mom had always worked. Todd knew that. He was just angry and saying whatever he could think of to hurt us all. He was taking out his own frustrations on his family.

"I saw your mother this evening, Todd," I heard Mom say.

Silence filled the kitchen.

"Don't make fun of my mother," he said.

"I . . . I wasn't. She was at a window . . . outside just now . . . I saw her, that was all."

"I said don't make fun of my mother."

"I wasn't, Todd. I swear I wasn't."

"They all laugh at her. They always have. They say she's insane. She's not insane. There is no insanity in my family. It's not true that I left this town because I was scared of insanity. I don't care what you're hearing. It's not true!"

Upstairs, I found Daria in bed with a light on looking at picture books. Mercifully oblivious to the horrible scene downstairs, she was telling her fuzzy duck a story as she turned the pages. I got on my pajamas and climbed in bed with her.

"I don't like my hair cut," she said. "I want it long like yours."

"Don't worry," I tried to reassure her. "If there's one thing I know about hair, it always grows back."

She thought for a while.

"Daddy is my daddy and Mommy is my mommy," she said.

"That's right."

"And Mommy is your mommy. But you have a different daddy."

I was surprised she was picking up on all these distinctions, but it was no wonder these days since all the adults were constantly discussing them. She couldn't really miss it. "True. Your daddy is my stepfather."

"And you're my big sister."

"Half . . . yeah, right. We're sisters. Forever and always."

"I don't ever want to go away from you."

"We won't, little Ria. We won't ever be separated."

"Promise?"

"I promise you with all my heart," I said. And with every drop of my McNamara blood, I thought.

13

Bubba

In a dilapidated frame garage that stood separate from what I had come to call the Woolcott house was an old Ford Galaxy from the 1960s. It shook and quivered as Norman tried to turn the engine over. From my window in the carriage house, I watched.

Norman emerged from the garage to join his wife, who stood pigeon-toed, twisting the wedding band on her finger, face soaked in stupefaction. "I think perhaps if we raised our voices to the Lord," he said in all sincerity.

"You're always right about these things," said Kate. Her voice held a faint ecstasy, as though she were about to get a glimpse of some hidden excitement.

I gaped as they lifted their hands, fingers spread like supplicants, and Norman began a rambling prayer that touched on God's mercy and justice, spring rain and growing crops, and unfortunates of the world born without the advantages of Woolcotts. He didn't mention the car directly. The two of them looked incredibly thin and fragile, like dandelion puffs that could be blown away by a whisper of a breeze. Their clothes draped across them, hanging in flaps.

From downstairs, I heard my mother's voice calling me. There I found Aunt Thelma, Bubba, and Gwen.

"It is time to meet the other members of the family," my aunt announced. She led us three kids across the yard, pulling a key from her pocket to unlock the garden gate.

The introductions were formal. Jeremy and I pretended we had not met. Bubba and Gwen fidgeted.

Norman and Kate were both pale, as if they never went out in the sun without big hats. They had thin wrists, paper-white skin, and eyes drained of color like invalids after a prolonged bout with fever. They seemed distracted, as though confused by a swarm of visions—as if they could see life in the dust motes in the air. I recognized this manner from Jeremy's description.

"What a ole junk heap," sneered Bubba, kicking the bumper of the car.

"Norman, what do you imagine you're doing with that old car?" demanded my aunt sharply.

Norman explained they were trying to start it up. He made vague gestures. His eyes were pale and remote, like those of someone who lived in a world of thin dreams.

"It needs new points and plugs," said Bubba authoritatively, changing suddenly from the cringing weirdo to the gas station master-of-mysterious-machinery. "I'll fire that mother up."

With a confident swagger, he went over and slid in under the wheel. He pumped the gas pedal several times. The engine finally started with a deep roar.

"Bubba is something of a mechanical genius," said Aunt Thelma. "We figure on sending him to study engineering in college once he gets straight with his high school work."

Kate blinked as if she had a facial tic and touched her fingers to her waxen cheeks. "I thought he had dropped out of high school," she said. There was nothing malicious in her tone. It was just the voice of a person who was confused by what little information she had retained on the subject.

Aunt Thelma glowered at her. "What would you know about that, Kate? Stuck off in Africa somewhere, what would you know about anything?"

"You . . . you wrote us, I believe." Kate looked helplessly to Norman for support. "A long letter. I'm almost certain."

Norman folded his hands across his stomach as though protecting himself from surprise blows. He realized they had sullied the sanctity of Thelma's firstborn, yet he hadn't the slightest idea how to correct the error. All he could do was plow foolishly on. "I'm convinced you're right, Mrs. Woolcott. It was very long. Perhaps seven or eight pages. I've kept it somewhere." He looked around as though the letter might be lying in the yard.

"Bubba has decided to take a year off to master automotive mechanics," my aunt interrupted. "It's a way of finding himself and getting some direction in life. Given that he is working and earning his own way in the world, it strikes me as more healthy than the activity of most young folk today." She looked pointedly at Jeremy. "Bubba will be returning to school. In the meantime, I intend to arrange a private tutor. If he applies himself, he might be able to actually skip a grade once he returns."

Bubba gunned the engine loudly. Abruptly, he stopped and let it idle. Climbing out of the car, he swaggered back to our group with his shambling gait. "Yeah, it needs a tune-up," he said.

"Well, I think you should take it to your garage," said Aunt Thelma. "Do whatever needs to be done. I'm sure Norman will be more than happy to pay your bill. After all, the work needs to be done."

Kate fluttered a bit. "It seems to be running now, Reverend Woolcott, wouldn't you say?" she asked.

"Well, yes, it does," said Norman. "And you see, we're a bit short on funds. We haven't received a regular income for some time now and—"

"Then I'll handle the bill for you," said my aunt. "As I always have in the past."

"Once we start drawing the money from the Estate . . ." began Norman, then he stopped and gazed off into eternity.

"A man who can't support his own family . . ." said Aunt Thelma, but she checked herself in midsentence and became all sugary. "Well, no mind. It will all come out in the wash. Why don't all you children ride along with Bubba? It will give you an opportunity to get to know one another. You will also profit from his example of responsible behavior in this world of toil. By being responsible, Bubba has earned the privilege of a driver's license."

"Do . . . you think this is wise?" questioned Norman. "They're all so young."

"Certainly," replied my aunt, never in doubt about anything.

And so, we were all bundled off in the car, Gwen sprawled in the back by herself, me in the middle of the front seat, Jeremy to my right. Aunt Thelma gave us final warnings about good behavior and stressed that Bubba was in charge.

Bubba ran over some shrubs in the yard before he cut out into the street, burning rubber as he made the turn. He laughed loudly.

"Dumb shits," he said. "What a pair of dingdongs you got for parents, Jer. Don't even know how to look after a car."

"You shouldn't say bad words," said Gwen piously.

"Shut up, lard-butt," Bubba hurled.

Jeremy stared out the window at the passing graveyard and marsh dotted with red-winged blackbirds. He had apparently had long practice ignoring his parents and the remarks made about them. There was a calm about him that was . . . well, it was kind of beautiful. A method of acceptance that never surrendered its dream of a better place. His faint impish smile told me that he would never be dominated by these hateful people. It was inspirational.

We drove along the harbor and then through a run-down area of wharves, old warehouses, and machine shops. Spirit high, Bubba talked loudly about "pulling the engine" on the Ford and putting in a "409 Chevy," whatever that meant. He seemed to think we should be impressed. He kept putting his hand on my leg and looking at me to see what I'd do. I decided to ignore him, like Jeremy. He babbled on about "four-barrels" and "glass packs" and other automotive wonders. He sang "Plastic Jesus" loudly to get Gwen's goat.

> *"I don't care if it rains or freezes*
> *Long as I got my plastic Jesus*
> *Sittin' on the dashboard of my car!"*

"I'm gonna tell Momma," Gwen whined.

We came to an abandoned patch of railway switching yard that backed on one of the fingers of marsh that threaded the city. Banged over the unused, rusty rails choked with weeds. Old boxcars read *Southern Serves the South* in faded white paint. A roundhouse with the roof pulled off had its windows boarded. There was a tangle of lightwires overhead. What a dead, gray, lonely, desolate place.

"See that?" Bubba demanded, pointing to a patch of snaky-looking woods that lined the marsh.

He was pointing to a tar paper shack back in there barely visible for the trees smothered in kudzu. Oil drums surrounded it like a fort.

"That there's my place," he said proudly. "Bet you'd like to come out there and stay with me, huh, Alice?"

"Not really," I said.

I turned in the seat to gaze back at the dismal spot. With all her propriety, could Aunt Thelma really permit her son to live in such a spot?

"Nice, ain't it?" Bubba crowed. "I can do anything I want out there. Smoke, drink, look at dirty magazines." He laughed and put his hand back on my leg, rubbing me, feeling me up. I tried to move it off, but he gripped me like iron. Finally, Bubba put both hands on the wheel to swerve and run over a dead dog that lay among the tracks. The carcass exploded with a squish.

"Got the sum-bitch!" he howled with pleasure.

A sharp nausea engulfed me and I put my face in my hands.

On and on Bubba talked: about how he was on his own and nobody told him what to do, how "old lard-butt Gwen" still wet the bed and got whipped for it and had to do chores and had to stay in her room when she was "on the rag." Whenever he'd say something dirty, he'd look over at me to see how I was taking it and leer back at Gwen to see if he was making her cry. Predictably, he got to her.

"You shut up, Bubba!" she wailed. "I don't wet the bed! You know I don't! I'm gonna tell on you for talking dirty!"

It was hard to believe they were both sixteen years old.

The garage where Bubba worked was on the outskirts of town, a frame building with three bays and antique gas pumps out front, all shaded by a lordly oak. Red Coca-Cola shields flanked the words DWAYNE'S SERV. The ground around the gas pumps was covered with bottle caps. Behind a fringe of trees was a landscape of fallow fields and an abandoned farmhouse.

The car fishtailed slightly when Bubba screeched to a halt. Ramming open the door, he emerged. "Hey, Dwayne!" he yelled, slamming the flat of his hand down on the roof. "Get yore sorry butt out here while I pop the hood on this bad boy!"

A big man came out, wiping grease off his hands and onto a rag, peering in the sudden glare of sunlight. He had a slicked-back tidal wave of hair and a chew of tobacco like a lump in his cheek. Unshaven jowls. A faded tattoo on his hairy forearm. He didn't look like the sort who would take lip off a teenager.

"You can charge whatever you want," Bubba continued. "Mumma's gone pay." He pounded on the roof of the car, making a clangor. "Big bucks. Charge her out the wazoo."

Dwayne looked Bubba over tentatively. Did a slow spit of brown tobacco juice that splashed in the dust and then puddled there. Took a deep breath and got his courage up.

"Bubba, I done told you I can't have you around here no more. Not after what you done."

Bubba glowered at him. Showed his Broderick brutality with a sneer of yellow teeth. "You can't get rid of me. I'll tell my daddy. He'll call your loan at the bank."

The threat struck home. The prevalent fear of being devoured by Wheeler's bank. Still, Dwayne persisted. "No. Not on this one you won't. It's one thing cracking an engine block or tearing up some injectors. I can eat the loss on them if I have to. But what you done to that cabdriver . . . well, you don't want your daddy to know about that. Now you just get on out of here."

"You ice-hole," Bubba drawled fiercely.

Dwayne looked down at him. "Somebody's gone smack the shit out of you one day, Bubba. One day you're gone get smart-mouth with somebody who ain't a-scared of your daddy and it gone be 'that's all she wrote.'"

Bubba climbed back in the car, clashed the gears, and scratched off, sending bottle caps flying. "Ice-hole!" he yelled back over the noise. He was looking backward at the garage and nearly ran into a ditch, jerking the wheel back to get onto the road. We went flying along at fifty miles an hour.

Pine forest passed. Old black people tended little stands selling boiled peanuts and woven baskets to the few tourists who passed by. Small houses had yards littered with junk cars.

"What did you do to get fired?" Jeremy couldn't resist asking.

Bubba seemed to rise to the idea of male camaraderie. "Stupid old cabdriver come in needing brake fluid. He's an old fart. Daddy keeps him in business. I drained all the brake fluid out so he'd crack up. Sure enough he did. But not down the road like I figured. Hit a gas pump on the way out. Dwayne like to shit a brick. Came boiling out all mad at him swearing he couldn't drive and might have blowed himself up with flaming gasoline. Tells him he's blind as a damn bat. Then Dwayne gets in, backs the car up and hits the wall of the garage. Did you see where he tore up the corner of the building? Boy was he pissed!" Bubba laughed, feeding hungrily on the memory of his escapade.

Poor guy, I thought, remembering the driver who delivered us to the Broderick house the first night and wondering if it was him.

"You shouldn't do stuff like that, Bubba," said Gwen primly from the backseat. "It's not nice to people."

"I ain't no Holy Roller like you," Bubba retorted. "Folks get in my way, I stomp their ass good just like Daddy does."

I looked at Jeremy. He rolled his eyes and shook his head at me. Behind him, the trees were whizzing by. The speed had increased to seventy.

"Bubba, slow down," commanded Gwen. "You're going too fast."

"I got to blow the carbon out of the pipes," he said. "Got to get it up to top speed." His eyes were alight and wide like a fanatic's. His hands held the wheel tight. The gas pedal went steadily to the floor and was kept there.

We passed a vast plain of marsh grass with its underlying rich mud. Ribbons of brackish water coursed through it. White birds fished among the brown, watery beauty.

Gwen gripped the back of the seat, leaned forward to yell in Bubba's ear. "Bubba, you slow down! I mean it!"

"Eat shit and bark at the moon," he said, his mouth spread in an exultant grin.

"I'm gonna tell, Bubba! I'm gonna tell Mumma about what you did to that man's cab!" She grabbed Bubba around the neck and began to shake him.

"Lemme go, you sorry bitch!" he yelled.

The road rose as we approached a small bridge. I closed my eyes. The bridge blipped past with blinding speed and a sparkle of light on water. Gwen kept shaking her brother. He turned to fight her off.

Suddenly, we sheared through a metal barrier and were flying down a slope of broomsage. Everything went into slow motion. Gwen's screams seemed long and drawn out. My mind clearly was speculating on whether to try to throw open the door and jump free. Jeremy was in the way. I rejected the idea and braced myself. Bubba emitted a long howl of laughter.

The car rolled over and over then came to a stop upside-down just short of a patch of trees. We had bounced around inside like beans in a jar. Gwen was lying on top of me in the front seat. Inside my ribs, I could feel my heart pounding.

Briefly she was quiet. Then, when she realized she wasn't badly hurt, she began to wail. "I'm dying! I'm dying!"

Jeremy got the door open and crawled out. There was a heavy odor of gas in the air. He pulled me out behind him and I stood there looking at the car and aching all over my body. The engine was still running.

Bubba staggered out, blood running down from his nose where he had hit the steering wheel. "It's gonna blow!" he yelled. "Just like on TV! Get back! It's gonna blow!"

Inside, Gwen was still wailing. Before I could think, Jeremy had gone back and was pulling hopelessly at her. Dragging at her fat ankles. A shoe came off. "Lemme alone!" she protested. "I'm hurt! I need an ambulance! I need a doctor! You can't move a hurt person!"

"You're going to burn alive!" I yelled.

Galvanized into action, Gwen fought her way clear, mashing Jeremy in the process. He came out behind her, and we stood twenty yards back from the car. Bubba danced around, sniffing back the trickles of blood from his nose, his movements excited, erratic.

"Come on and blow, you sum-bitch!" he encouraged. "Blow up!"

"I'm gonna tell," Gwen wailed. "I'm gonna tell Mumma what you did!"

"You keep your yap shut or I'll fix you good!" Bubba threatened.

Cars had stopped up on the road and people were looking over the edge of the hill where we had gone through the metal fence. Bubba saw them and took off into the trees, running clumsily, crashing through the brush. The three of us were left standing there.

After a time, there was the wail of an ambulance, first thin, then harsh and near. When the EMS men came down the slope, Gwen sat down on the ground and started to cry about how she was hurt. As she attracted attention, her complaints grew in their energy. "I'm all torn up inside," she said. "Something's busted loose!"

When the EMS men tried to examine her, she kicked them away. They shrugged and stood back. They were gangling and straw-haired, barely out of their teens. Not about to lay undesired hands on a Broderick.

Then Aunt Thelma's bulk appeared at the top of the hill. "Gwendolyn, you get yourself right up here, young lady." In her triumph at our disaster, she seemed stronger than ever.

Gwen jumped like she had been shot with a gun. She struggled up the slope clutching at handfuls of broomsage, one shoe missing, her big shoulders up around her ears. Jeremy and I followed along behind her. We were puffing when we reached the top. Gwen was heaving, as if she might throw up.

Norman and Kate were standing near Thelma's big Cadillac. They gazed down at their wrecked car in silent acceptance of the destruction. Like everything in their world, it seemed slightly unreal.

"Jeremy did it," Gwen sniffed, rubbing at her eyes. "Jeremy drove too fast. I told him to slow down and how he didn't even have a driver's license and didn't know how to drive and he was going too fast and he just laughed at me and kept on and now look at what he's done! I'm all tore up inside! I need a doctor!" Her tirade ended, she began to heave and puff again like she might vomit.

"But he didn't . . ." I began vainly.

Jeremy took hold of my arm to silence me. Without a

word, he went over and got into the Cadillac. His face was neutral—without the slightest trace of bitterness at his cousin's treachery.

"Jeremy, was this a wise thing to do?" asked Kate, making a hopeless gesture with her arms.

Aunt Thelma maintained a pretense of decorum since a crowd of witnesses were present. "I'm very disappointed in you children," she said.

Gwen continued to make whining noises, half asking for medical help, half entreating mercy. She looked eagerly to her mother for any trace of pity or tenderness. Of course, it never came.

14

The Secret Place

All through dinner the evening of the wreck, we heard from Aunt Thelma about how worthless Jeremy was. The very idea of that boy inheriting part of the bank was truly outrageous. Norman couldn't hold a job. Couldn't work. Wouldn't work. The greed of Norman and Kate wanting things that other people had worked all their lives for. My parents didn't say a word. It was clear the lecture was intended as an oblique slap at them.

And yet, by the following morning, the car wreck had ceased to be of importance. I had expected to hear it harped on forever, but just as suddenly as it had happened, it was over.

It was replaced by what began as a nothing event.

I mark the beginning of my serious resistance to the Brodericks from that moment. For it was the breakfast where poor Daria dared to sing at the table. It was a nothing event. Daria sang at the table. She was five years old and she sang a little song while she was sitting there eating her cereal. Frankly, it was amazing she had never done it before. Daria was always singing, as I remember her. But apparently she hadn't done it before in the company of my aunt, judging from the reaction she got that morning.

"*Three blind mice,*" Ria sang, banging with her spoon on the edge of the dish. She was not raucous; she was just having a good time. But she was singing. "*Three blind mice.*"

Gwen's head snapped up from her lone piece of dry

toast and glass of prune juice. Her face went pale. "Sing before you eat, die before you sleep," she said under her breath.

The morbid ditty grabbed at me. Daria didn't hear. She laughed, happy to be holding the center of attention and sang on.

> "See how they run,
> See how they run!"

There was horror in my aunt Thelma's face. "No one sings at the Broderick table!" she roared.

Daria looked around, frightened of the bellowing voice. Ria was not big on being yelled at. She would tune up and cry at the smallest remark if she thought you really meant it. "I'm just singing," she said in a small voice. Her mouth closed up. She put her spoon in the milk and stirred it slightly.

Aunt Thelma's eyes showed white over the top edges. An image flashed in my mind of her when she whipped me. It was the sign of her wrath. "Are you talking back to me, child?" she demanded.

Ria's head sunk lower. Tears began in her eyes. "Don't be mean to me," she said.

I looked to Uncle Wheeler and caught his eye. He snapped the newspaper in front of his face and began turning the pages, as if he was looking for something. He made his tsk-ing noise.

Mom sat stiff, staring at the big oil portrait of Senior over the sideboard. Todd was pinching the bridge of his nose. They seemed to be ignoring the whole thing.

Aunt Thelma's big hand reached out to seize Ria's arm. She jerked the little body around and shoved her face within inches of my sister's. Her big lower lip poked out, eyes staring madly. "You do not sing at the table. No one sings at the table. Senior never allowed it. Good little girls do what Senior wanted. You must be good. You must be a good little girl. You must never do what's bad and evil and sinful and wrong."

Ria retreated more within herself. Even sitting all the way across the table, I was scared. My aunt had a bad temper and I knew that she was capable of being totally irrational. Her eyes were wide with hate and anger. Her mouth curled in a horrible sneer.

Aunt Thelma did not let go of Ria. She shook my sister until Ria's teeth rattled. "It's sinful to sing at the table! Who has taught you to be sinful, child? Is it your mother? Your father?"

Ria began to wail, tried to pull away, but she was trapped tightly.

"Stop that screaming!" Aunt Thelma yelled. "Stop it, I say!" She drew back the flat of her hand—her hand was as big as Ria's head. Was she going to smack my sister in the face?

"Stop it!" I yelled. "Don't hurt my sister, you big cow!"

In an instant, I had knocked my chair over backward and raced around the table. With my fist balled, I hit my aunt as hard as I could. The blow landed beside her eye, rocking her, but not really making much of an impact. She did let go of Ria. I tried to gather my sister in my arms. She was crying violently.

Aunt Thelma was out of her chair in a second. She grabbed for my hair. I could have dodged her, but I was too busy shielding Daria with my body. The big hand wrapped itself in my hair, snapped my head backward.

Everything went into slow motion. Todd's mouth was wide-open. He was speechless. Uncle Wheeler threw down his newspaper.

And in those slow-moving moments, I was twisting around, trying to hit Aunt Thelma again. Instead, I got a hard flat-hand blow straight to my jaw. I saw stars before I felt the jolt. Then came pain.

"Thelma!" Todd thundered. "Stop that!"

"You mustn't sing at the table," said Gwen in a lost voice. "It's bad manners."

My head jerked in a tight pattern because my aunt still had me by the hair. Weakly, I tried to kick her, but it only came out as a tap. The floor was tilting. Nausea rose from the pit of my stomach.

"You wretched child, Alice McNamara!" my aunt shrieked. "You evil, sinful child! How dare you strike me! How dare you!"

My knees sagged. The room continued to spin. Daria was holding tight to my leg. "Don't hurt my sister Alice!" she yelled.

I fell to my knees, feeling like I might throw up. I was still dizzy.

"Stop it, Thelma!" Todd yelled again. He was holding me now.

Mother was up now, crouching over me, holding on to me. "Stop it! Stop it!" she yelled.

"It's not right to sing in the dining room," parroted Gwen. "Senior never allowed it."

It all became confused in my mind. A dozen things going on at once. Gwen talking in that dead monotone. Todd and Wheeler arguing about who had started the fight. Mom spilling out ideas in a jumble.

"Why are we doing this to each other?" she said plaintively. "What's wrong with us? What are we doing?"

In an instant, my aunt regained her poise. Just like that, she turned all sugary. She purred at Daria. "I've got a surprise for you."

Daria stared at her suspiciously.

"I'm going to take you way up in the house," said Thelma. "To a special, secret place that no one knows about. There are toys there."

"I don't need toys," Ria sulked.

"But they're very special toys, Daria darling. The toys of a good little girl who died young. A little girl who knew right from wrong. Good from bad. But God took her up to heaven anyway because he needed perfect little angels. He took her up there by making her die very, very young. And now she's a little bitty angel."

"Thelma!" exclaimed Todd in a shocked voice. He had suddenly turned from Wheeler. "Thelma, what in God's name are you saying?"

My aunt actually looked flustered. She had mentioned something dreadful. Without another word, she hurried from the room.

15

My Mother of the Seagreen Eyes

The following night, I lay in bed miserable listening to my parents fight in their bedroom. Their light was out. They were cooped up together in the hot darkness amid a growing hatred and inhumanity.

The reek of fog smothered the yard and crept in through the cracks of the house. In bloodthirsty hordes, mosquitoes whined against the screens. Far off in Congreve, the clock on the Broderick bank struck ten. At night, it carried across the water. Fifteen minutes off, as my aunt pointed out frequently. Senior had made it run on time, but Wheeler couldn't seem to manage this feat of clock maintenance.

It was as if everything had changed with that scene the day before. Mother and Todd had argued bitterly. Nothing either had done had pleased the other. They were miserable with themselves and so they took it out on the world around them. And especially on Ria and me. In some strange way I suppose they held us responsible.

Mother had even let my aunt take Ria away the next afternoon. It was like she didn't believe that Aunt Thelma would hurt Ria. But I knew differently. I had felt the whip weeks before and her anger yesterday. I wasn't around. I was doing chores in the big house—vacuuming floors and beating out rugs.

I had never before really thought of my mother as being so vulnerable and weak. My mother of the seagreen eyes. I hadn't coined that expression. Todd had when I was in first grade and had to write a description of my family. And ever since I had thought of my mother's eyes as something magical. I would look for them specially every time I saw her.

In school, whenever careers were discussed, I always wanted to be a dancer like her. I wanted to go to work wearing leotards, a big coat, and tennis shoes, carrying a shoulder bag with a change of clothes. I vowed to walk with her springy walk and live with my head full of music just like she did. It was strange to be thirteen and still worship your mother. Most of my friends in New York hated their parents and were going through awful teenage rebellions.

But things had changed. My parents were fighting horribly. Lying in my bed, late at night, I could hear every word.

"Take off that nightgown," Todd growled. "I feel like I'm sleeping with Old Mother Hubbard."

"You're drunk, Todd," Mom said wearily. "You're always drunk now. I can't stand to be touched by you when you're drunk."

"So what am I supposed to do all evening? Sit around here and listen to you dither and whine? I'm going nuts and you don't care. You're too self-centered to do what we have to do to make money."

"I won't have any more children. I won't, I say. We can't support the two we have now."

There it was. The dreaded subject of sex. It seemed to obsess adults, yet terrify them at the same time.

Sex. More children to be Broderick heirs.

"Okay," he brooded. "If that's the way you're going to be, then I want to adopt Alice."

"What on earth for?"

"You know why. The more kids we have, the bigger the slice of the pie we get. The will doesn't say anything about adoption. I can play loopholes as well as Wheeler. Then maybe I can leave that hateful bank and stay home and paint. Money for Alice would make that possible."

"I don't . . . know. I guess we can ask Alice if she'd like to be adopted."

"What difference does it make what she wants? She has no memory of her real father. I'm all she's ever known. He doesn't pay child support. He never writes or sends a present. Just tell her I'm adopting her and that's all there is to it. She'll be a Broderick."

Mom's voice turned sarcastic. "I'm sure she'll be overjoyed at that. The Brodericks are so important in Congreve. Why, folks will just get off the sidewalk for her once she has that name."

I heard the sharp blow and Mom quietly crying. The tension had reached a state of disease. Todd had taken to hitting her frequently. I didn't know how hard. I didn't know if he said he was sorry later and hugged and kissed her and begged forgiveness. I was closed out of their world.

"If you don't get your hands off me, I'm going to tell . . . Wheeler!" my mom screamed.

"You don't say," Todd sneered. "You ready to play footsy with the enemy?"

Ria padded across the floor on little bare feet and crawled in bed beside me.

"Duck wants to sleep with us," she said.

I didn't know what to say to her. I knew she had heard. Ria missed nothing. She was just learning to kept her mouth shut.

I held my sister close and felt her heart beating peacefully.

I dreaded what I knew I had to ask. I had to probe the horror that stared at us so steadfastly.

"What did you do with Auntie Thelma, Ria? You know, this afternoon. When you went over there to play?"

"We went upstairs."

"But what did you do upstairs?"

"It was very dark. There is an old woman who lives up there. She sits there. She doesn't do anything."

"What is she called? What's her name?"

Ria screwed up her face in thought. "I don't know. She wasn't called anything."

"What did you play?"

"There were lots of toys."

"What toys?"

"Well, there were dolls. And a little horse with wheels on him. And a bear."

"Who did they belong to?"

"It was very sad. They were a good little girl's who died. She burned up."

"How?"

"Her Christmas tree caught on fire, and she got burned up in it."

Ria had begun to cry. I hugged her and smoothed her hair. She spoke to me between sobs. "She's gone up to heaven to be an angel. There are dogs and kitties up in heaven too. Everything that dies goes there."

"That's right, Ria. And little mice and squirrels and rabbits and ducks."

"When I die, I'll go to heaven."

"You're not going to die, Ria. Not for years and years and years."

She thought for a moment. "One day I'll have babies and you'll be a grandmother."

"I'm your sister. I'll be their aunt."

"Like Auntie Thelma."

"No. Not like her. I'll be a nice aunt."

She started to cry again.

"Don't cry, little sweetheart. What's bothering you now?"

"I don't like to think of the little girl burning up. It makes me sad. She had a favorite song. Auntie Thelma taught me to sing it."

"Let me hear it."

In an odd plaintive monotone, little Ria began to sing. It was a very familiar nursery rhyme.

"Little Miss Muffet
Sat on a tuffet,
Eating some curds and whey.
Along came a spider
And sat down beside her,
And frightened Miss Muffet away."

"I don't like that," I said. "I don't like to think about spiders."

"They gave me a dolly," said Ria. "I put her in bed because she's sick."

"What's wrong with her?"

"She's burned too."

"Show me."

Ria went back over to her bed and returned with an old-fashioned doll with a cloth body and china face and hands. The cloth was scorched black. Half the face was also black with carbon.

"The dolly told her to be careful of fire, but she didn't listen. She wanted to get the pretty things off the tree before they burned up. And . . . and she caught fire."

While I hugged and sang lullabies to her, Ria cried herself to sleep. Surrounded by thoughts of dying and decay. Like the marsh smell on hot nights in this awful town.

The whole place was dying around us. Mom and Todd were dying too.

16
First Love

My fears for Ria were dampened somewhat the following weekend. Because then we finally got to take the trip to the beach that Ria and I had been anticipating so eagerly.

It all started at breakfast. Aunt Thelma was steaming like a kettle ready to boil. Gwen had been banished from the table, as though something unclean were about to happen. Picking up on the ugly vibrations, everyone ate silently.

"I always like a good breakfast," said Aunt Thelma, packing away the bacon and eggs as usual. "Breakfast is the most important meal of the day." Then she added for the eight-hundredth time. "Good old bacon and eggs. Can't beat 'em."

Today my aunt's tone was really grim. It was more a recitation designed to get everyone's attention. Even Uncle Wheeler looked tense.

Aunt Thelma dabbed her prim lips and put the cloth napkin carefully next to her plate. She fixed Mom and Todd with hostile eyes. "Kate and Norman . . . who I have serious doubts about . . . have taken it upon themselves . . . and I find it most ill-advised . . . but they have done it all the same . . . they have taken it upon themselves to invite the two girls to accompany them to the beach. They have been quite insistent."

"The beach?" said Daria brightly. "Swimming?"

Thelma continued. "What worries me is that they have

always had a measure of difficulty understanding basic proprieties. As a consequence, Norman has bounced from one
muddle to the next in his missionary work."

"Well, he can always become a banker like me," said
Todd, trying to inject a light note into the conversation.

I was suddenly angry at Todd for saying anything. Here
we were actually invited to the beach. It was the first pros-
pect of fun since we had arrived.

Uncle Wheeler made his now famous *tsk*-ing noise and
folded his newspaper. He poured more coffee for himself.

"As it is a Saturday," my aunt said forcibly, "I find
some difficulty in blocking their request. Mind you, Gwendolyn will not be going. Her skin is far too fair to take direct
sun. We learned that to our consternation when she was
quite young. She will engage in improving activities here at
the house while the other children . . . cavort about foolishly."

I refused to pay much attention to my aunt. I was too
excited. We were actually going to escape the confines of the
horrible Broderick house.

Aunt Thelma stared firmly at Mom and Todd. "I feel
certain you will not want to be involved in this foolishness,"
she said harshly.

"Of course we will," said Todd, and I could have kissed
him in gratitude for his sudden spark of life. "I haven't been
out to the old sandbar since I was a teenager."

"No," said Aunt Thelma. "You spend your time in bars
of a different sort."

Todd let the jibe pass. He grabbed Daria up out of her
chair, and swung her around. "We're going to the beach!" he
exclaimed. "Hot diggety dog!"

"Yay!" went Ria, waving her fists above her head.

"Alice will clear the table," said Aunt Thelma, determined to inject as much gloom into the situation as possible.

Still, the chore flew past. Gwen was already in the
kitchen. With her arms in soapsuds up to the elbows, she

pouted. She had sneaked half a pot of grits and a stick of butter.

"I didn't eat those," she said fiercely. "They were no good. I only took a taste and threw them out. Grits aren't good for you. They just make you fat."

"Right," I said, shoving the last of the dishes onto the drainboard. I tried to sidle out the kitchen door, but Aunt Thelma's big hand seized my bicep.

"I'd like a word with you, young lady."

"Uh, okay. Sure."

"I know what's on your sullied little mind," she said.

That was her word. *Sullied.* Gwen was smirking at me, drinking in every word.

"Jeremy is an ignorant young boy who bears the Broderick name on his mother's side. You think you can flaunt yourself in front of him and trap him."

"Trap him? Into what?"

"Don't play the sweet innocent with me. Your aunt Kate and uncle Norman are fools to allow their son to be exposed to such as you. I have no doubt they'll live to regret it."

"I won't do anything," I answered smoothly. I was determined that she was not going to spoil my fun.

"There will be no provocative behavior at the beach; do you understand me?"

"No. Nothing. I'll be good. I swear it."

"Don't swear. It's sacrilegious."

Behind Aunt Thelma's back, Gwen stuck out her tongue and made a face at me. I didn't care. I was free while she remained in bondage. Happily, I scurried away across the lawn.

Back in the carriage house, Mom was packing a lunch. Todd was mixing up vodka and orange juice in a thermos. Mom didn't object. She was as excited as we kids were.

There was the problem of a bathing suit for me. Mom produced one that Aunt Kate had lent her. It was way too big and we had to safety-pin it in a bunch of places. I looked like a fool in it. Still, I didn't care. Jeremy wasn't the type to care about that kind of thing. He would think it was funny.

Kate and Norman wore enormous matching straw hats and sunglasses with big smears of sun block across their faces. They had that same entranced air about them, vague, slightly lost and confused, as if they were afraid they had left the stove on or forgotten some vital article.

Todd seemed shy with his sister. "Hello, Sis," he said. "It's strange to all be back together once again." He walked up to her and hugged her gently. It struck me that they sort of looked alike. Aunt Kate had blondish hair like Todd and blue eyes, plus they both had the same full mouth. Not at all like my aunt Thelma with her rat eyes and thin, mean mouth.

"I'm sure it's part of God's plan," Kate said. "In which case it's not strange at all, but preordained."

"Well," said Todd, trying to make a joke, "you've survived cannibal shores only to return to a far more savage environment."

"Cannibals?" blinked Norman, taking him literally. "Oh, no. There are no cannibals. That's a myth. They're quite good people. Good Christians."

Aunt Kate seemed scandalized. "Todd, we can't have talk of cannibals! It's not proper for the children to believe such . . . such . . . Reverend Woolcott does not approve of such talk." It was her habit to call him by his title like that. Jeremy looked at me and rolled his eyes. I bit my lip to stifle laughter.

In the already blistering heat, we packed into the car. The old Ford had been hauled back from where Bubba wrecked it and repaired in a crude way. It rattled and banged a lot and the brakes seemed sluggish, but that didn't really matter since Norman drove so slowly. Naturally, this infuriated everyone else on the road who was trying to get to the beach, and they honked their horns and yelled at him. He didn't care. At every stop light, he would take the car out of gear and go into a daze. When the light turned green, Jeremy would have to tell him. Then Norman would struggle to get the car in gear and lurch off. Horns behind us became deafening. Todd and my mom scowled and squirmed.

Still, it didn't matter. We were going to the beach. Aunt Thelma was far away.

Jeremy was funny and charming in a way that soon had my parents actually hanging on his conversation with something like gratitude. We went across the long stretch of marsh on the causeway over to the barrier island where centuries-old houses nestled amidst greenery. Jeremy talked to us of the history of the old wooden houses, told tales of yellow fever in plantation days, buried treasure and Civil War blockade runners. Since he'd grown up in Congreve, Todd knew the stories, but hearing them afresh from a fifteen-year-old boy seemed to revive his sense of fun.

We drove way down the island past the bait-and-tackle shops and cottages on stilts. At the very end was a stretch of palmetto jungle tangled with vines and spiky plants. Norman parked the car and spent a long time speculating as to whether it was placed properly. Wearing her look of trouble and concern, Kate agreed. Perhaps they should pull it a little more off the road? Had the parking regulations changed? It had been years since they had been home. It wouldn't do to disobey the local laws, Reverend Woolcott being a man of the church and having such a prominent position.

The rest of us got out and made for the dunes, climbing around them to find a broad white beach with breakers rolling in. A line of brown pelicans flew by. It was enchantment. The spark of life was rekindled in my heart to burst into passionate flame.

Ria absolutely exploded with excitement. It was all so novel and exciting to her. The tidal pools of water. Driftwood. Tiny limpets bubbling in the wet sand. Her joy was infectious. I was equally thrilled. I felt renewed and free and clean. There was a world outside the dismal Broderick confines, and it was beautiful.

Aunt Kate herded Jeremy and me aside. Norman stood

hesitantly on the edge of her lecture. She wrung her hands and twisted her simple wedding band as she spoke.

"Children, I know you're pleased to be here. And the water looks most refreshing. I trust you can swim, Alice?"

"Sure. Of course I can."

"Well, I . . . I'm not quite sure how to express this . . . but . . ."

"We're okay, Ma," said an exasperated Jeremy. "Okay?"

"Well, yes, certainly you are. I mean, I know you're both fine children. Jeremy, I raised you. Or rather Reverend Woolcott and I raised you together. Not without our differences here and there, of course. But, basically, we have been of one mind and under the guidance of the Lord. We believe in outward forms and conventions and know there's some real message for living in society's restraints."

"We're okay, Ma."

Norman took a tentative step forward. He couldn't seem to look at us. His eyes were fixed on the farthest line of waves. The creases in his face deepened and slacked as he made grimaces. "What your mother is trying to say is . . . um . . . in the confusion of the surf . . . well, you must be careful to not . . . to not bump up against one another." He swallowed hard. Still, he couldn't look at us.

"We won't get hurt," I said stupidly.

Norman stared at me wide-eyed for a moment and then went back to studying the surf. "Oh no, it's the . . . um . . . it's the . . ."

"It's the suggestive possibilities," said Jeremy in a disgusted tone.

"The what?" I said.

Norman let his hands go slack at the wrists and sort of flapped them at us. "Well, run along now. You've been warned. A word to the wise et cetera."

I thought Jeremy's body looked very strong even if it was incredibly lean as he raced heartily into the surf. He slowed, but still plunged on up to his knees, his thighs, then dived in. I followed, gasping at the shock of the cool water.

Dived in and stroked violently against the strong pull of the current.

Together, we treaded water, our hair plastered down, spitting out the salty wet.

"I ought to make fun of my parents," said Jeremy. "Or apologize or something, but I won't. I'm just happy they managed to get through breakfast and get us here."

I laughed. "Don't you dare apologize. My parents are screwed up too. This place seems to do that to people."

"Yes," Jeremy said dramatically, "the ancestral castle blights everyone."

Kate came down to the edge of the shore, shouting and waving frantically. "Jeremy! Alice! You're too far out!"

We rode the easy swells, rising and falling together.

"She can't swim," said Jeremy. "Just sort of turn away casually and look out to sea. She doesn't know if we can hear her or not."

My leg brushed against his.

"Whups," he said. "Carnal contact."

"I'm sorry," I said instinctively.

"Don't be foolish. I think we should touch each other a lot just to show them." He reached for me and I shoved his hands away giggling, splashed water in his eyes.

"No!" I protested. "Don't! She'll have a hissy-fit. And maybe tell the awful Aunt Thelma."

"Perish the thought!" Jeremy proclaimed with mock emphasis. "Tattle that we've been naughty, smutty children. Aunt Thelma will cut off our genitals and grind them up for mystery-meat dinner."

"How can you talk like that?" I yelped.

"It's easy. Plus it's also a nice revenge on them. They can't know that we're talking about the deadly *s-e-x*."

"I don't know anything to say about *s-e-x*. Even if it is revenge."

"Sure you do. It's what you start to feel at our age. You feel it all through your body. It surges in you like the promise of spring. It's always there. Desire. Longing. A lust for touching, love, deep passion."

I knew I was blushing. "You're doing this deliberately just to shock me."

"No, to thwart them. Just to show them they have no ultimate power over us. Even if they can't quite know it, they must guess I'm talking about *s-e-x.*"

"Jeeeremy!" called his mother. "Jeeeremy, can't you hear me?"

He was two years older than I. An older boy. I found myself wondering about women who married older men and knew now why they did it. I was captivated by him. I wanted to make some passionate pledge to him. I wanted to touch him, hold him, kiss him.

I knew even then it was only a teenage crush, but I felt the pangs of it just as surely as if I had believed it something deeper. And looking at his handsome face and bright eyes, I was convinced that this was a perfect boy for first-time love.

17

A Social Call

The store clerk Miss Dawling was dead. We heard it whispered behind closed doors. Miss Dawling had killed herself. Aunt Thelma was scandalized, but she insisted that we were obliged to make a social call on the woman's aged mother.

Of course, we drove there in the Cadillac, with the air-conditioning going full blast. The sun was so hot that the hazy air felt more like smoke. The ground was parched and dusty.

"This woman is absolutely crippled up with rheumatoid arthritis," Aunt Thelma lectured. "So don't stare at her infirmity."

"No, ma'am," said Gwen dutifully.

"There are foul rumors of Miss Dawling having taken her own life. People are saying that she ate rat poison and died screaming in agony in the hospital. The truth of the matter is that her appendix burst and she got to the hospital too late."

"She didn't kill herself like everyone is saying?" asked Gwen eagerly.

"You heard me say she did not. So not another word on the subject. Your father is making certain there will be no coroner's jury probing into the matter. The doctor's death certificate will suffice."

"It won't seem the same without her working in the Junior Miss department," said Gwen. She seemed proud of her contribution to the conversation, like she was a grown-up society matron and an equal with her mother.

Men were digging up the pipes in the street where Miss Dawling's mother lived, piling dirt in a rampart.

"I don't understand why grief is no longer respected in this town," said Aunt Thelma, her mouth prim and bitter. "When Senior ran things, the proprieties were respected. A mourning family would have their street blocked off to traffic. Now we've just got chaos. I don't know what's happening to the world these days."

Pulling into a drive lined with thick azalea bushes, my aunt parked the car. She opened her compact and carefully powdered her nose. Then rocked back and forth on the seat to build the necessary momentum to launch herself out of the car.

Down the street, a screen door banged. One of the men in the ditch was loudly telling an off-color joke. Aunt Thelma glared at him. Gwen lagged behind as if she wanted to hear the punchline.

The old woman, Miss Dawling's mother, was unable to come to the door. She just sat in a wheelchair, frail and defeated, with the door open. Her body seemed frozen, locked up, as though her bones would crack into splinters if you tried to pull them apart. Her head remained permanently down in deep sorrow. She wore an old flannel bathrobe that looked tired and worn-out. A ladder of bone went up her chest to a neck composed of loose folds of skin.

A mustiness clung to the room. Aunt Thelma seated herself regally in an armchair with a little green tea towel pinned to the headrest and pronounced the room in need of a good airing. Gwen wrestled briefly with her girdle and sat down as well.

I slid into a straight chair and looked at a cabinet filled with little rose-colored glass animals: horses, lions, giraffes, tigers. I tried to picture Miss Dawling as a little girl taking the animals out of the case and playing with them carefully so they wouldn't break. Making up fantasies about them.

A broken clock sat on the mantel, its hands marking midnight. Light trickled through the old lace curtains in a kind of smear. Water dripped in the kitchen sink.

The old woman's lower lip hung loose and it was really gross. Saliva would fill it up to the brim and then go over the edge in a long drool. It embarrassed her a lot, and she would scuff at it with her clawed hands.

My aunt expressed her condolences. "It's a tragedy that you've outlived your daughter. It seems unnatural. Gwendolyn, stop fidgeting."

A small fan on the floor made slow rotations to the right and left, bathing our ankles in brief coolness and then passing on again. Gwen smiled at the fan, as if she were losing herself in the blur of its blades.

"The welfare sends a girl around with my meals," said the old woman. "She'll stay and feed me and do some housework. Helps me take a bath."

"It's good there are charitable organizations able and willing to help," replied Aunt Thelma. "So much is wasted on the undeserving poor. People who could pull themselves up by their own bootstraps if they had the gumption or the moral will."

"It's not very much, but it helps."

"I gotta go to the bathroom," said Gwen.

Thelma scowled at her. "One thing for sure," she told the old woman, "is that you can't go on living here by yourself. It's too dangerous with the crime rate what it is. There are men in this world of such animal character that they would victimize a person such as yourself."

The woman shivered as if with cold. "I'm not sure what I'll do."

"The welfare agency will make a determination."

"But how will I know what's going to happen?"

"You will be told."

"It just don't seem right I should end up like this."

"Don't take it personally. God gives us the burdens he knows we are capable of bearing."

"It just don't seem right."

"There is a divine plan. I have faith and I believe it with all my heart. I have known the healing spirit. When my little sister died, a part of me died with her. My poor mother was simply devastated with grief. Senior never quite got over it himself although he was outwardly such a strong man you would not have known he was grieving inside. Grieving every hour of every day. I grieved too, of course. But I knew the healing spirit of the Lord. He healed me and made me a better person for my loss. He gave me the mission of serving Congreve, and I carry out His will to the best of my ability."

"You do so many good things," the old woman murmured. "You never used to forget us at Christmas."

"Christmas is a special time for the Brodericks. It was the time of our tragedy. We always mark the date by particular kindness to the unfortunate."

"Momma, I really gotta go," whined Gwen. She crossed her legs and squeezed them together.

"It's just down the hall," said the old woman.

"I told her to go before we left home," Aunt Thelma contradicted. "She must learn restraint."

"I'm sorry, Momma," said Gwen. She crossed her legs the other way.

I looked at the glass animals, trying to make up names for each of them. There was a dried rose on the bottom shelf of the cabinet lying on top of what looked like a theater playbill. Someone had kept it as a treasured memento.

"There are nasty rumors flitting about the town," said Aunt Thelma, "that your daughter took her own life. I have put a stop to them."

The old woman's lips trembled. "Thank you," she squeaked.

"There is nothing more shameful than suicide. So there could be no more vicious rumor in creation. It was only proper that I should act as I did. It is a Broderick tradition. I sometimes find myself wishing that one of those spiteful people would dare contradict me. I'd give them what for."

"It is a lie," insisted the old woman. She flailed a bit with one of her stiff arms. "There's not a word of truth in it."

"If it were true, we'd know. The town would know. The truth always follows a person."

The old woman rubbed her teary eyes with a twisted wrist. "She was such a pretty little girl. I remember giving her baths in the kitchen sink. She'd play in the water and splash it all over the kitchen floor so I'd have to mop up afterward. Her father was alive then. He loved her so."

"Men always dote on little girls," said my aunt. "Senior was particularly fond of our Daria. And of me."

"We had some money then," the woman went on. She wasn't even quite listening to my aunt. "Her father had a good job at the waterworks. We had a car and one of the first color TVs on the block. We had encyclopedias. We took subscriptions to five or six magazines. *Ladies' Home Journal. The Saturday Evening Post. Life. Reader's Digest.* We had lots of things then. We had big hopes for our daughter. We figured she'd go to college and maybe become a schoolteacher or a nurse. Meet a good man and marry. She'd have the kind of job where she could follow him around if his job moved him. Be like a second income. Then my husband died and everything just fell apart. I took sick. So she had to go to work in the store. It was just going to be for a little while until I got well again. But I never did.

"She was always such a model daughter," the old woman continued in a monotone. "She was always dutiful and good. She was only bad the one time. You know, marrying that sailor who already had another wife. One of them orientals he had met in the Philippines and never really properly divorced. She wasn't really bad. It was just a mistake. There's no way she could have known the truth. He didn't hardly realize the truth himself. She left him as soon as she found out. It's not right that folks should talk about her and hold it against her for so many years."

"Stop staring, Gwendolyn," Aunt Thelma commanded.

"It's not polite to gape at other people's misery. I've told you that often enough." My aunt rocked back and forth in the chair to stand up. One of the wooden ends of the chair arms cracked.

"Rotten old thing," Thelma pronounced.

The old woman stayed frozen in her wheelchair, her pinched face staring after us. "You're so kind to always remember us at Christmas," she said to our backs.

We went outside and got into the streamlined Cadillac. Aunt Thelma lectured Gwen on making a spectacle of herself by demanding to go to the bathroom. Gwen sat, covering up the air-conditioning vent with both hands, taking her hands away and sucking at the gush of cold air.

"There's men who will rape old women, aren't there, Momma?" she said.

"Don't talk about such disgusting things," Aunt Thelma corrected. "You know it's true. It's enough to know the truth without talking about it."

"There was a seventy-five-year-old woman who got raped last month in Atlanta. Our teacher in school said the man who did it had some hatred of his mother and she was like a mother figure. Isn't that just about the sickest thing you ever heard? Can you imagine someone being so hung up on their parents that they'd take it out on an innocent old woman like that?"

"I don't have to imagine it," said Aunt Thelma. "I have better things to occupy my mind."

Gwen sagged back into the seat. "Going to see old cripples," she muttered.

"What?" said Thelma.

"Nothing."

"What did you say?"

Gwen tucked her two chins down onto her chest. "I said nothing."

"You better not have."

When we reached the house, Bubba came across the lawn at a dead run. He jerked open his mother's door. "Is it true? Is it true what they're saying that Miss Dawling killed herself with rat poison?"

Aunt Thelma viewed her son with constraint, squinting at him.

Still, Bubba went on, inflamed with excitement. "They're saying she just couldn't take looking after that sick old woman anymore and ate rat poison. You know, just gobbled it up like powdered sugar and died with the screaming heebie-jeebies in the emergency room of the hospital. They said it took two men to hold her down, her body was jerking so from all the puke. I mean, green puke, just exploding out of her like a geyser!"

"Momma, don't let him talk like that," whined Gwen. "It's not nice to talk about people like that."

"Boys like to think about gory things," chided Aunt Thelma. "It's in their nature." Heading for the house, she left us standing there, so Bubba turned his attention to me.

"I wish I could of seen her croak. Old lady Dawling was such an old toad. I'd like to have watched her scream with the pain and throw up the green puke all over herself."

"You're disgusting," I said. "You should die yourself."

"It'd be slicker'n eel shit to watch somebody die like that from rat poison. Like sticking a pin through a worm and watching it squirm all around except there'd be blood and screaming and kicking and stuff."

"I always hated her," Gwen joined in maliciously. "Having to go down there to that horrible old store and buy clothes with her and Momma standing in the dressing room with me and poking and pulling at me."

"You just hate it because you're a lard-butt and they tell you so!" jeered Bubba.

"I'm not fat! I'm losing weight! Everybody says so!"

"You're fat and you wet the bed! Bed wetter! Bed wetter!"

"I hate you! I hate you!" Gwen wailed.

Bubba went off with a jaunty stride. Gwen stood there

crying and hugging her shoulders. Her legs were pressed together tightly, as if she was trying not to wet her pants.

Miss Dawling had killed herself. She had reached a point where she couldn't take life anymore. It made me sick to my stomach.

18

The Nursery

After our one trip to the beach, Aunt Thelma seemed to feel the need to compete with the allure of Kate and Norman. Or maybe she just wanted to get close to Ria.

At any rate, my aunt opened up a dusty old nursery on the second floor where Daria was allowed to play. I was even permitted to accompany her. The insides of the door panels were painted with a faded lion and a unicorn. The windows were thick with cobwebs.

There wasn't much to play with in that mournful room. A chalkboard with no chalk. A rocking horse, wooden animals on strings to be pulled about, and a broken electric train. The one thing Daria did like a lot was a playhouse of heavy wood with two front windows with windowboxes and a door and a chimney. I could get through the door on hands and knees and sit squinched up inside with her.

On the wall were mildewed prints of little children in footie pajamas saying their prayers and some old photos of Todd, Thelma, and Kate as little kids. It was weird how you could recognize them. Todd looked distant and dreamy, Kate totally spaced out, and Thelma pompous and nasty. There was one with four of them, the last apparently being Daria who died. That was a creepy picture. Kate looked spacey and Todd disinterested. But Thelma was holding the little girl on fat knees and smiling at her with malign eyes. You could actually see hatred in her eyes.

We only played in the nursery twice. The second time we went there, something horrible happened. Daria had gone out to the bathroom. I was sitting in the playhouse waiting for her return when the yucky Bubba appeared.

His face leered at me from the small doorway. There was awful fuzz on his upper lip, a mustache that he wouldn't shave. "Playing dolls, are you?" he drawled.

"I'm playing with my little sister," I snapped. I don't know why I felt embarrassed. He was nothing to me. It was just an instinctive reaction.

But when he came shoving into the playhouse with his head and shoulders, I was suddenly afraid. He was squarely blocking the only door. The roof didn't lift off. I was caged in. He made a guttural chuckle, an empty-headed laugh.

"What are you doing here?" I demanded. "I thought you didn't live here anymore."

"I don't. But I likes to come back and visit. Mumma likes to see me. She don't care for that fat pig sister of mine at all. She likes me."

"That's a real honor."

He came in up to his waist. His shirttail was pulled out so his flabby belly showed. There was a tuft of hair around his navel. "We ain't really cousins, you know that?"

"Thank God for small favors," I said sarcastically. But a knot was shaping in my stomach. I didn't feel the courage I was trying to project. In the far corner, I tried to make myself small.

"That means we can be in love."

"Don't make me puke!" I snarled. "Get out of here."

"Mumma done beat the hide right off your little butt, didn't she?" leered Bubba.

"What of it?"

He crawled farther in, his face right up in mine. "I like to think about that little fanny of yours being all red and hot with her laying the strap to it. She used to do that to me before I got too big."

"I'm warning you, Bubba . . ." I said, but his hands had reached out to grab my breasts.

"You want to love up to me? Huh? You'd like some lovin', wouldn't you?"

I tangled one hand in his greasy hair, grabbed an ear with the other, and yanked hard.

"Yiii!" he yelped.

"I'll pull that ear right off, Bubba! It's real easy! Want to find out how easy!" I yanked again.

"Ow! God damn you, you bitch, I'll fuckin' kill your ass!" he wailed, hatred and fear filling his shallow eyes.

I yanked again. He struggled and backed out of the little house. "I'll tell my Mumma you hurt me! She'll beat you raw!"

I didn't want to follow him outside the little house. He'd have the advantage of height and weight there. As his head went out the door, I let go of my grip.

He got to his feet and gave the wooden house a terrific kick, which shook it violently. "You fuggin' bitch! Don't no girl treats Bubba like that! I'll fix your ass! I swear I will!"

"You and what army?" I sassed back.

He kicked the house again and stalked off.

When Ria came out of the bathroom, I talked her into doing something else outside.

Later that day, I decided to tell my mother about what had happened with Bubba. I mean, if some boy had made a pass at me in New York, I would never have mentioned it. But here in Congreve the small, entrapping nature of our world compelled me to share the incident with her. Bubba's glittering snake eyes. The strange games with Ria in the attic. I had to make her understand.

My mother was sitting in the kitchen with an ironing board and a pile of ironing she was not quite doing. Even in New York, she had never been big on domestic chores. I mean, we all pitched in, and things got kind of halfway done somehow. Now, in Congreve, she felt this need to act all domestic and virtuous, but her heart just wasn't in it. Like all of us, she was used to living carelessly. I sat down beside her on a kitchen chair.

"Mom, something really yuck happened today."

A momentary concern passed over her face. The sea-green eyes flickered lightly. "It's not something with Jeremy, is it?"

The obsession about propriety with Jeremy—it should have been a warning. "No, it was that disgusting Bubba."

"When did you see him? He lives on his own, doesn't he?"

Having actually to describe what had happened made me so depressed that I couldn't put the sentences together right. "I . . . I was playing with Daria in that dumb big wooden playhouse up in the old nursery . . . she went to the bathroom. And he came pushing into the house and started putting his hands all over me."

"Oh, Alice," she said, "you know we don't need this right now. Really. Todd just can't deal with it, plus I'm sure you're exaggerating."

Her tone sent me off the handle. I became almost hysterical. "He did! He did! He grabbed my . . . my breasts . . . and started talking about loving up to him in that awful hick accent. I grabbed his ear and tried to pull it off. He sucks his thumb and he's always lurking around staring at us. I'm afraid he'll do something to Daria."

My mother didn't reach out for me. She didn't touch my hair or hug me—nothing like that. She just got up and started messing with the ironing. Sprinkled a bit of water on a shirt, giving it a hit-and-miss with the iron. Her voice was like . . . in a trance. "I think you've got an overactive imagination, Alice."

I held my elbows and rocked back and forth on the chair. My mother didn't want to hear what I had to tell her. It wasn't that she wasn't interested so much as that she couldn't deal with it. Her plate was already full.

Mother looked at me tenderly and there were tears in her eyes. "Alice, darling, you must be strong. Don't tell

Todd this story about Bubba, you must promise me. He has so many things to worry about, and this would really upset him. You know you're exaggerating. I mean, Alice, you're from New York. You know how to deal with this kind of thing."

I was flabbergasted. They didn't want to have to worry about me. It made me feel sick to my stomach and awfully alone.

"Alice?" my mother said finally.

"Yeah?"

"Since we're having this little talk, maybe I should mention something to you."

"What's that?"

"You know Todd loves you very much."

I sniffed and wiped my nose on my sleeve. "I know."

"And he's really been the only father you've ever known."

I sniffed again. "That's true."

"Well, he and I have been talking. We'd like for him to adopt you. I'm a Broderick. You could be one too. We'd be so much closer as a family. You'd be completely one of us. No different last name from your sister and us."

"I don't know, Mom," I said evenly. "I just don't know. I mean, now just doesn't seem like the time."

"Why not, Alice? Todd is so counting on this. I don't want you to hurt his feelings."

"Well, Mom, I just kind of like my name. McNamara. I've always had it. I feel comfortable with it."

I was shocked at the anger that suddenly came out of her. "You are an ungrateful child, Alice. Todd has supported you all these years and now you want to reject him." She shook a finger at me. "I am very disappointed in you. You expect to share in the money, but you won't do anything to help. You've made up lies. You're being horribly ugly to us. Do you hear me?"

I went away to my room and sat alone in the dark telling myself about life's injustices. Of course I loved Mother and

Todd, and I was very grateful. But I didn't want to change my name to Broderick. Not for any amount of money.

I was a pearl inside an oyster's blackness. And one day the shell would be opened and all my brilliance would shine forth. I would be valued at my true worth.

19
Mission of Justice

One night after dark a man came to our carriage house door. He wore red pants and a lime-green sport jacket with a fat tie striped with both colors. I knew him from church, where Todd, Mother, Ria, and I had gone regularly since we moved to Congreve. Tom Duncan owned the Chevrolet dealership. He was often in church, where he'd be backslapping people as we all came out, saying "No problem" and "Can do" in a loud voice. He was always smiling, and he could make the little foyer of the church ring with laughter.

The first time Tom Duncan spotted Todd, he made a beeline for him and started pumping his hand, telling him how glad he was that Todd was back in town and how he had always wanted to buy one of Todd's paintings to put in his office. On and on he talked, about could Todd draw cars, and, of course, he could because he could draw anything and paint just something wonderful.

Uncle Wheeler and Aunt Thelma hadn't been happy with how nice Duncan was to Todd, introducing him to people and saying how much Todd looked like Senior and wasn't it just great he had come back to Congreve permanent like.

That night, Tom Duncan's mournful face and bleary eyes appeared at our door after dark. Like an escaped felon, he slipped inside, and Ria and I were banished upstairs. Still, I listened as best I could. The bank clock had just banged eight. It sounded worse than usual, like maybe the works were coming apart inside.

"Yeah, boy, I'd love a drink. I'm just about falling apart. Sick with worry. My wife Mabel is filing for divorce, and you know what that means in Congreve even in this day and age."

Todd's voice was calm and untroubled. He seemed utterly in control. "And you're about to lose your business?"

"It's Detroit. I call them Detroit. I mean General Motors. They say if I don't move out of the old downtown lot to the edge of town and put up a big new high-volume-low-margin place, they'll exercise their buy-out rights and take back everything I've sweated and bled for for twenty-two years. You know I started out in this business twenty-two years ago selling old used-car clunkers out on the harbor road to sailors. It took me ten years to get the franchise money to buy a new-car dealership and really get going. I used to go out at night to repo cars wearing black clothes and tennis shoes. I've come up the hard way, I tell you. I've paid my dues. I've walked the stairs when other folks took the escalator."

Todd interrupted the torrent of passion. "Why won't Wheeler lend you the money? You're the only Chevy dealership in town. There's no way you could lose."

"Well, the excuse that's being given is . . . well, you've heard it surely."

"No," said Todd. "I haven't."

He winced. "Well it's about me and Rhonda, my secretary."

"I haven't heard a word."

"You mean Wheeler ain't bad-mouthed me to you?"

"Wheeler doesn't like to talk business with me. He considers me a threat since my child owns part of the bank."

"We . . . well, Rhonda and me been having a little bit of an off-and-on affair for some time now. One of them damn cops told Wheeler—they tell him everything that goes on in this town—one of them spotted us coming out of a motel—

and Wheeler told Thelma, and naturally she didn't approve."

Todd laughed. "That's putting it mildly."

"That Thelma, she's what you'd call a well-nourished gal." Duncan laughed briefly and then stopped abruptly. "Not meaning to be rude or nothing about your kin."

"Thelma is no friend of mine even though she is my sister."

Duncan warmed to his subject. "Well, I just don't get it. I mean, I know she's a Broderick and all, and you're a big proud family—you got every right to be—but her making Wheeler change his name instead of her—well, it just seems strange. Women's lib kind of stuff, except it was all years ago, before we'd ever even heard of women's lib."

The bottle clinked against glasses.

"Good stuff," said Duncan, admiring his drink. "I mean, don't get me wrong. I ain't got nothing in particular against women working. It's just all this demanding stuff they ain't earned, and all this marching with signs and bringing crazy lawsuits."

"Sure," said Todd. "Of course. But what's the real reason for Wheeler denying you a loan?"

"Well, I mean, can't you see? He wants my business. I've got one of the biggest cash cows in town that he don't have his finger in. He's offered to buy fifty-one percent of the thing more times than I can count. He knew he had me when I came crawling in this time. He just sat there smirking, talking about Thelma's overdeveloped sense of morality, and how with her taking a particular interest in the matter, his hands were tied.

" 'So how can I ever get the money?' I asked him, and he gives that smile like his mustache is tickling his mouth at the edges. 'If you didn't fully have control of the dealership, she might be mollified,' he says. 'Figure you were suitably humbled for your wayward ways.' That's what he said. 'Wayward ways.' Does that sound like Thelma or what? Could have been her very words."

"That's Thelma all right."

Duncan's voice sparked with anger. "They're going to end up owning the whole town! Even your father was never that greedy. Sure he liked his money just like anybody, but he was satisfied to see his loans repaid with interest. He didn't expect you to just hand him what you had worked and sweated for. It ain't right for a bank to operate like that in this day and age."

"No," said Todd. "It's not. And I'm trying my best to put a stop to it."

"Do you really mean that? Damn that's wonderful! I knew you were Senior's son. You've got the Broderick blood all right. You've got the steel."

"Don't thank me. I'm doing it for my daughter Daria. The bank is a fourth hers."

"Daria. That's a pretty name. Pretty little girl, too. Wasn't that your sister's name? The one that got burned up?"

"Yes, it was."

"I remember when it happened. It was way back when I was just fresh in town and starting out. Senior was all tore up about it. And your poor mother . . . she was never . . ."

"Let's not talk about it," said Todd. His voice was like a December wind. "My family problems are my own. What we have to address is your holding on to what you worked for."

"Lemme just slip out quietly," said Duncan with a fear-tinged voice. "If Thelma or Wheeler thought I was here to see you . . . sometimes I think that big old house has got eyes in it."

Todd talked to Mom way into the night with nervous excitement. He was going to confront Wheeler and straighten him out about poor Tom Duncan.

The lines were drawn. There was to be no backing out. His voice held a reverence for his mission of justice.

20
The Spider's Web

It was night and I had come awake to lie for a time staring at the other bed, unsure of the time or how long I had been asleep. I listened vaguely for the gentle breathing that was always there.

Distantly, the bank clock clanked one time. Was it the half hour? Or one in the morning? Something was wrong. I tried to clear my head.

I could see the chair with something white lying on it: underwear and socks. Mom always made us lay our clothes out the night before.

A flash of horror went through me. Ria was gone.

I jumped up and went quickly down the stairs. The front door was open. A feeble light from far off in the street did nothing to illuminate the hot, blank night. The yard wore its shapes of bushes and trees.

I heard a whimpering noise and saw her little white nightgown halfway across the lawn. She looked tiny, like a little sparrow that had fallen out of the nest.

Then I realized my sister was sleepwalking.

Even as I watched, she woke up and stood there, hands clapped to her mouth, calling out for help, for friends, for love.

"Mommy! Mommy! Alice!"

I rushed out onto the lawn sodden with dew and took her hands in my own.

Ria's face screwed up. Tears poured out of her eyes. She began to bawl with fear like a small hunted animal.

I hugged her with all the compassion I could show, whispered to her to be quiet and watch for the bunny rabbit that came out on the lawn. I tried to shield her from that looming house of sickness, the abiding place of evil.

I looked fearfully up toward the attic window where I had seen the cadaverous old woman stand—her hair matted down, face drawn and white as flour, eyes ever watchful.

"It's all right, Ria," I whispered. "Everything's okay. Alice is here."

"I'm scared," Ria went on dolefully.

"You're fine. I'm here," I soothed.

"I had a bad dream. There was a fire. I was walking into it. Bad things were happening. And I was in the attic."

"Ria, Ria, why do you think such bad things? What did you do with Aunt Thelma in the attic?"

"There's an old woman. I'm supposed to help make her well."

"What do you mean?"

"Auntie Thelma says I will make her well if we play a game."

"What kind of a game?"

"We played a game. It was Christmas and Santa had come and there were presents and toys and oranges. And I was Daria. That's what they called me. But I was another Daria. I was the little girl who burned up in the fire. And I was supposed to pretend I was on fire and scream for help. At first it was funny, but then it made me very sad and I cried and cried. And Auntie Thelma hugged me and it was all right then. But I think of it all the time."

As she talked, Ria gave fearful looks toward the big house. Finally, she could utter no more words.

Dreading to do so, I turned and looked at the high window. It was a blank blackness.

As softly as possible, I gathered Ria in my arms and

carried her back into the house, up the narrow stairs. Her quiet sobs cut into my heart.

Mother was waiting at the head of the stairs. A rush of gratitude poured over me. She took Ria in her arms, lay down with her, and they both fell asleep.

I sat in my bed patiently waiting for Mom to rouse herself and go out again. But they both slept peacefully.

Yielding to my own insecurities and fears, I woke Mom and pulled her outside the room and downstairs. Todd was snoring heavily, and I was afraid of waking him. Mother yawned and rubbed her eyes, saying that she was incredibly tired and that she was always tired these days.

We held our conversation in the kitchen in a deep whisper. As I talked, I trembled with anxiety. I described the Christmas tree fire and the old woman in the attic and the hideous game they had played with Ria.

"The woman in the attic is Todd's mother, Gladys," Mom said, as though giving me some reassurance.

"Is she crazy? Have they locked her up there because she's crazy?"

Mom frowned. "I'm sure she's perfectly all right. She's just old. Todd loves her. She was the nicest person in his life when he was growing up."

"You mean the only nice person," I said bitterly.

Moisture was shining on my mother's cheeks. "You are making me perfectly miserable," she said.

I stared at my mother, wondering what had become of her. I used never to see her without feeling a touch of pride. When I was a first-grader and she would pick me up at school, I would run to her laughing and shrieking with joy. Now her beautiful color, which had never faded even in city winters, was receding even under the intense sun of Congreve. Here, in this dismal place, she was hopelessly lost in the wilderness. Everything I remembered of her seemed obliterated.

With a sad, sick heart, I went back to my room. The awful burned doll was sitting on the chair. Ria never played with it, but it was there—an unceasing reminder of the attic and the girl who had died in the fire. Without a moment's hesitation, I carried it out into the night and heaved it over the fence into the old graveyard to be lost among rank weeds.

My feet were wet in the dew-soaked grass. A spiderweb decorated a bush. The sight of it constricted my throat and made me think of the web Aunt Thelma had spun around us.

Along came a spider.

21

The Demon Rite

"There's a dark secret in the family, that's for sure," said Jeremy.

We were down in the dank cavity of the Broderick cellar, where ooze and slime came out of the foundations from the high water table. Fungus was growing on the cement walls. Light trickled through the dirty panes of the tiny windows set high up in wells. Far away, there was a faint cry of birds in the marshes.

Jeremy seized a lizard and let me hold it carefully, feeling its little heart beating against my hand, its neck puffing in and out, its color changing from green to tan. When I put it back on the wall, it didn't run away, just sat there staring at us with its big yellow eyes. We were two strange creatures who had invaded its world yet done it no harm, so it could not truly assimilate our existence.

"Mater talks about the dark secret a lot," Jeremy continued. "She's vague about it like so many things. But there was the death of the little sister, Daria, years ago, of course. Mater was little. So were Aunt Thelma and Uncle Todd. They were all little kids. Daria was the youngest, barely five. After she died, nothing was ever the same."

We probed deeper into the cellar, pushing aside the cobwebs, picking a path among wooden crates and empty bottles and sodden old mildewed furniture.

"I truly hate this place," I said. "I expect to find big clusters of bats hanging from the ceiling."

"Yes, but we're in search of truth. Here, in this darkness, we will find the evil that lurks in the human soul."

"Do you always talk like this?"

"It's a bad habit, I know. I get it from missionary parents, the mixed-up mess of the King James Bible, classic books, and ministerial homilies. It's a handicap. I may never be able to consort with real people."

In a dark corner, we found an old musty box. It was full of boy's things: worn-out tennis shoes, a deflated basketball, a baseball glove, a faded blue Cub Scout uniform, a clip-on bow tie. A small Bible was inscribed *May your path be straight as you grow strong and true—to Wheeler Junior on his 10th birthday. With love, His Parents.*

It was hard to think of Bubba as a small boy. Wheeler Junior. His parents must have had big hopes for him.

"It's like the refuse of the boy they wanted Bubba to be," said Jeremy. "Then he shed this carapace and revealed himself for the nasty insect he is."

"Did you know him when you were younger?" I asked.

Jeremy nodded. "Once or twice we would visit here and he was so awful he got kicked out of everything. Sunday school. Scouts. Sports teams. Birthday parties. You name it. Even as scared as everyone was of Senior and Uncle Wheeler, Bubba was so awful they couldn't tolerate him. He used to make himself vomit in school right in the middle of the classroom so they'd send him home."

"What? He'd just stick his finger down his throat and barf?"

"I guess. And he'd deliberately pee in his pants in church. Just sit there and do it on the floor. He'd get animals out of the marsh—lizards and snakes and little birds and things—pull them out of his pockets and squish them in front of people. Eventually they gave up and let him roam around as he pleased. I figure it's a fitting punishment for them."

"Punishment?"

"Sure. Have you never thought of how adults are punished by their children? Here Aunt Thelma longs to have an heir to the great Broderick banking tradition and gets Bubba instead."

"Banking tradition? These people don't know real banks. Great big ones like in New York with billions of dollars and huge eighty-story buildings and thousands of people who work there. Chase Manhattan. Citibank. Those are banks."

"Yeah, but it doesn't diminish their pain. They think they're important. They're obsessed with being big deals in this hick burg, and their seed is bad."

"Their seed—" I stopped myself. A sexual allusion. Why couldn't I stop thinking how good-looking Jeremy was? Stop trying to picture him naked?

"Breeding mistakes compounded over time," he went on. "Their lineage has turned to decay and madness. Uncle Wheeler will be the last and then they lose it all."

"You could be the heir."

"Me? They wouldn't let me. Anyhow, could you imagine me with a briefcase going down to that awful bank every day?"

"Not really. But then what are you going to do?"

"I don't know. Perhaps I'll learn to fly an airplane and carry stewmeat to cannibals all over Africa. What about you?"

"I'm going to be a dancer like my mother."

"A dancer?"

His surprise seemed genuine, not deliberately rude. Still, I was put out. "Sure. Why not?"

"I dunno. You just somehow seem kind of fierce. Combative."

"Combative?"

"Yeah. Like you're always ready to fight back. I mean against injustice and evil and things."

It was a weird insight that somehow rang true. Still, I couldn't accept it. "Well, I'm sure dancers are combative. It's all part of being creative."

"If you say so. I just don't see you as being particularly like your mother. I don't mean to be rude. I don't think I'm like my parents. At least I hope I'm not."

"And I'm glad you're not," I said. "You'd still be eating breakfast now."

We both laughed and felt warm like pals together.

There was a constant drip of water into a big metal barrel. Getting closer, I saw it was floating with mosquito larvae. Next to it was an old bucket with the bottom half out of it. Some rusted tools in a rusted metal box. A sawhorse. A huge old furnace with a coal heap and shovel beside it.

Jeremy stopped to examine a collection of license plates and hubcaps nailed to a beam. "The handiwork of Neanderthal man," he said. "I detect a trace of the esteemed Bubba."

"What?"

"Don't you see? His first small attempts at crime hung up here in his moment of triumph. Stolen hubcaps brought back as trophies like scalp locks from the enemy camp. I bet at one time he had some kind of lair or den down here. Probably gnawed on bones and conducted weird religious rites. Sacrificed dogs and cats."

"God, it's so nasty and yuck!"

"That's Bubba. My fine young cousin whose blood runs in my veins. What could be more attractive to him?"

"I don't know. Surely he could find some other place in the house. Some room. The attic." I caught myself even as I said it.

"She lives there," said Jeremy.

"The old woman?"

"My grandmother."

"Has she always been there?"

Jeremy didn't smile anymore. "I think since the little girl died. I think that's the secret in the family. She went mad, and they put her away up there."

A curtain was suspended from the ceiling at the back, a hanging army blanket held up by string through torn holes. Pronouncing it "the demon's lair," Jeremy pushed it aside.

An old sleeping bag wet with damp and slime was wadded next to a stack of mildewed Batman comics. A crucifix hung on the wall. Jesus with bleeding hands and feet and uplifted eyes. It was carved from wood about eight inches long. Roofing tacks had been shoved into it and filled the body like a pincushion.

"The demon rites of the simpleton's brain," said Jeremy. "I knew we would find Bubba's spoor here."

"Spoor?"

"His track. Evidence of his coming and going."

Jeremy might have been filled with his usual cynical mirth, but I felt chilled to the bone. "Do you think he still comes in here?"

"No. The trail is cold. The Bubba creature lives in the shack that he showed us the day he tried to obliterate our car. This belongs to the immature Bubba—before he had grown to full prowling manhood. The days when he wore Buster Brown shoes, had a bowl-on-the-head haircut, wore short pants and a little bow tie as he was dragged to church to sit peeing onto the floor while Gwen yowled with the infants' choir."

Jeremy opened an old cake tin with a sleigh painted on it with holly leaf trim and the words *fruit cake* in old English script. Inside was a teddy bear blackened by fire, one side of the plastic face bubbled up, the hair scorched off. A note was stuck to it, held on by three plastic swords like you'd find piercing olives in a martini. Three swords and three colors— blue, red, green.

The note was a childish scrawl: *They dunt lov nobudy but ole ded girl. I want to kil her ded ded ded.*

22

Poison Tongues

Daria never asked about the burned doll I had thrown away. Perhaps she was relieved to be rid of it. I didn't know. Her inner life had become too intensely private. She no longer chattered to me about whatever popped into her mind the way she once had. She would sit through meals at the big house without saying a word, something I never would have believed her capable of in New York.

But every meal was the same—a barrage of insults from Aunt Thelma and Uncle Wheeler—a crippling emotional blur notable only when it reached a virulent fever pitch. And the night they began really shoving Todd out of the bank was one of those.

The food was piled high and steaming. Poor old Alberta could certainly cook. Thick slabs of clove-spiced ham glistening with juices and brown sugar seasoning. Corn on the cob was stacked like cordwood on a platter and running with butter and sprinkled with ground black pepper. Ripe red tomatoes were heaped with mayonnaise.

Gwen had wet her pants at choir practice and come home howling with shame. Now she was being punished by having a small dish of lettuce and celery. She was in agony, longing to ransack the succulent dishes that she was forbidden.

All of us sat in the usual deathly silence except for the clink of forks on the plates, the scrape of a chair here and there. Occasionally, Aunt Thelma would make some offensive remark, feasting more upon her hatreds than upon the heaped food.

"This is not very high quality ham. You can't get decent meat at the supermarket these days."

No one commented.

"When Senior was alive, they always had the best meats for us at the butcher counter," she continued. "They wouldn't have dared to do otherwise. Mother would drive up and they'd come out and open the car door for her. There was always a special treat for me."

I tried to imagine my aunt being given a "special treat" at a meat counter. Did she pack her face with raw chops and liver while men in white aprons stood around her beaming?

Ria and I had learned to clean our plates—you did not waste food at Aunt Thelma's table—so we ate and tried to ignore her.

Todd was not present. I knew he was over in the carriage house. I knew he was drinking. Mother was so incredibly tense, she nearly went through the ceiling when he entered the dining room through the kitchen door. He stumbled at the edge of the carpet but steadied himself.

Staring straight ahead, Aunt Thelma refused to see him. However, Uncle Wheeler cut sly eyes in his direction.

Todd turned a chair around and sat down, legs straddling it, arms across the back. "We've gotta get a few s'ings straight," he announced, looking at my uncle. Mom gave a little gasp. Todd's speech was badly slurred.

Aunt Thelma's deadly gaze went from Todd's posture in the chair to his slack face with growing contempt. "When Senior was alive, we did not sit at the table in that fashion."

Todd pointed a finger at her. His chin lay on his other arm. "You stay out of this."

Aunt Thelma reared back like a snake ready to strike.

"Todd, please . . ." said Mom plaintively.

"Shut up, Amy!" he snapped at her. "I'm talking business."

"You are disgusting," said Aunt Thelma. "Get out of our presence and sober up."

Silent tears had begun to run down Ria's face. She had become so withdrawn lately, unable to let things out the way she once had.

Elaborately, Uncle Wheeler wiped his mouth and mustache. Made the familiar *tsk*-ing noise. Folded his napkin carefully on the table. "Now, Thelma," he said in a cautious voice. "We know he's . . . laboring under a difficulty. Perhaps it would be best if we at least tried to talk."

"Not with the children present. And Amy."

"The children don't understand, but perhaps they should be excused from the table. And as for Amy, well, it's best she see what I have to deal with at the bank."

Todd snorted. "*You* have to deal with. Hah!"

"Children," said my aunt loudly. "Go and find a game in the parlor."

The three of us got up from the table. Ria stopped and looked up at the pictures of the little girl playing. They must have seemed incongruous even to her. She slipped her hand into mine and we went out. Gwen tugged her girdle down, made a whining noise, and followed us.

I hated the parlor. It was grim and smelled of mildew. The books were all Bibles or religious tracts. The only game was Parcheesi, which Ria couldn't understand and is a boring game anyhow. Gwen sat there with us being sanctimonious. The loud voices of the adults carried perfectly to our ears.

"I am going to be given responsibility at the bank," Todd asserted. "I will have loan authority of some amount. I realize I'm only in a learning stage, but I've got to be given some authority or I'll never get anywhere."

"The Duncan loan was simply not bankable," said Uncle Wheeler sternly. "I have been over it repeatedly with you."

"You're just shutting the man out because you want his

car dealership. You expect him to hand you everything he's spent a lifetime working for."

"That's absurd," said my uncle.

"The man's an adulterer," said Aunt Thelma. "He's thrown away his life's work on some honky-tonk hussy."

Todd's fist hit the table. "I know for a fact you made him an offer for his business, and when he refused, you cut off his line of credit!"

"And your source is Tom Duncan, of course," said Uncle Wheeler silkily. "Who would never tell a lie. Who would never see you as some poor sap he could hoodwink with ugly stories."

"Yeah, that's me. A sap. But you're a goddamn crook."

Uncle Wheeler's tone remained level. "A poor sap who drinks during the day."

"That's a lie!"

"During business hours—out of the bottom of his desk drawer."

Ria crawled into my lap. I hugged her close. Gwen simpered with virtuous delight. I wouldn't meet her eyes.

"You've got them all spying on me!" raged Todd. "Watching me and making up lies. They're all in your pocket. They'll say anything for you and you'll spread it around town with your poison tongue."

Mom cried while Aunt Thelma muttered, "Lowest of the low. I never saw such shocking degeneracy in Senior's time. It wasn't permitted."

Todd was losing all control. "Do you want to hook me up to your lie detector and see if I'm telling the truth? Is that what you want? Has it come down to that?"

"I'm afraid under the circumstances," announced Uncle Wheeler, "I'm going to have to take steps."

"What are you driving at?" asked Todd. His voice was low and ugly.

"I'm going to have to forbid you to enter the bank until you've . . . resolved your problem."

"You can't do that."

"I have our reputation to think of. We can't maintain the confidence of our customers and depositors if we keep someone around in your state."

"That's a joke. Everyone crawls to you for money. And you eat away at them like a cancer. You're taking an equity position in their little struggling businesses and getting them deeper and deeper into debt while you learn their weaknesses. Then you spring the trap and take them over completely."

"You're a sick man, Todd. I'm sorry to have to say that. You don't seem to have the slightest notion how the capitalist system works. You see evil behind the most basic facets of free market enterprise. I truly feel sorry for you. Perhaps if you stuck to your painting, you'd—"

"You're not driving me out of the bank!"

"How do you propose to stop me?"

"It belongs to the grandchildren. It belongs to Daria!"

"And Gwen and Bubba!" said Aunt Thelma loudly.

There it was. I had no family membership. Not that I cared about their money, but I wanted to be on Ria's side. I wanted to be with Mom and Todd. I wanted us to be a family—a phalanx—a fighting unit.

"It's held in trust for all of them," said Uncle Wheeler. "You know that. And as president of the bank, I happen to be the duly appointed trustee."

"It's not fair," Todd said. I could hear tears in his voice.

"I can't help the law," said Uncle Wheeler. He knew he had won, and it was giving him great pleasure.

"I think you should check into the hospital for a while," said my aunt. "Dry out."

"There's nothing wrong with me!" Todd shouted. "Nothing except for this stinking rotten town!"

In the parlor, there sat a huge Chinese pot with scenes of dragons and warriors on horseback with long bows and arrows all in lurid reds and greens. An arrangement of dried sea oats had been put there probably thirty years ago and allowed to become brittle and broken and ragged. Gwen got up and began fluffing the arrangement, as if she were some perfect Congreve matron making her house beautiful for a visit from a ladies' magazine photographer.

"It's not right to drink alcohol," she said.

Todd went out the door and then I heard the words that sent a horrible chill through me: "Daria is dead!"

23
The Kiss

Despite Wheeler's threats, Todd was still allowed in the bank the next day. But he came home more upset than ever. He said he needed a drink, just one, and he'd limit himself. Of course, he didn't.

All day, Norman, Kate, and Jeremy had pecked at the tangled mess of the back garden with digging tools. There was no danger to our secret gazebo hideaway. Jeremy deliberately goofed off and Norman and Kate didn't press him. A lot of breaks were taken. Lemonade was drunk. Inspired by his close contact with nature, Norman lectured on God's divine plan.

At the end of the day in the fall of darkness, I sat before the upstairs window. I was dazed by the heat. The hot, heavy night was weighted down by growing storm clouds, a mix of nameless smells, and the sharp whine of mosquitoes. I daydreamed of winter in New York. The freezing sleet and wind that whipped down the canyons of the buildings. Of my ratty old overcoat and wool hat that Mom had gotten in a thrift shop. Of shivering with a red nose and blowing on my hands against the cold.

From my vantage point, I could see one light on in the Broderick house. The Woolcott house was lit throughout the downstairs with silhouette figures of Norman and Kate seated still reading. Norman read by tracing the sentences with a finger. The time passed and the mosquitoes settled.

A liquid birdcall floated. I peered into the black-leafed

tree limbs and crisscrossed shadows seeing no one. It had to be Jeremy. I slipped down the stairs.

Ria was asleep and Mom and Todd were at their usual posts in the kitchen fighting.

"Just what do you want me to do, Amy?" Todd was saying angrily. "I want to know! Just what is it you want me to do?"

Mom was talking low and quiet, trying to slide him out of his mood, trying to do I don't know what.

"Tell me what you want me to do, dammit!"

I slid out the door, closing it carefully. Crossing the patch of grass and bushes stealthily, I scaled the gate and dropped into the wild black tangle of our secret place. Shrouded by the dark, Jeremy was waiting.

Very breathless, I stood beside him, gazed into his shining eyes, which were all full of mischief and fun.

"I saw you in the window," he whispered, knowing normal-toned voices would carry in the still night. "Rapunzel locked in her tower."

"You're a real nut, you know," I said. I felt very self-conscious, nervous and excited all at the same time. I had a huge crush on him and I desperately wanted him to like me. No, more than that. I wanted him to adore me and to love me in rich waves of hot passion.

Jeremy whirled around, as if he were spinning out the world for me. "But it's so true. The grotesque ogre in the big house. I think we should call her that. Our own name for her. Ogre."

I giggled. "And Ig and Og for the two kids."

"Our fabulous cousins."

"Not mine. I'm not a Broderick. Daily, I'm reminded of that."

"You're flat-out lucky, is what you are. And me too."

"Why?"

"Because we can be in love."

"What?"

He suddenly took my shoulders in his hands and kissed

me on the cheek. I was stunned. He drew back just a bit, as if he expected me to hit him. When I didn't, he leaned in again and kissed me where my neck joined the collarbone. A strange thrill tingled all the way to my toes.

"Ooooo." I shivered. "Where did you learn that?"

"In the wilds of Africa. Dusky maidens taught me all the arts of love by moonlight. Come on. I'll teach them to you."

He took my hand and led me through the hanging vines, honeysuckle, blackberry thorns, and mimosa. The gazebo was dark and spooky. A growing hot breeze bore the smell of the sea and swished in among the dead palmetto leaves. Huge clouds were piling up, blotting the moon and stars and putting us in utter blackness.

"Are your parents likely to miss you?" I asked.

"They're exhausted from toil. Pater is jotting notes for sermons on Man's Oneness with Nature. Mater is gripped with an air of preoccupation. I think she's sleeping with her eyes open like a fish. Meanwhile, the Broderick manse is silent except for the occasional belching of Gwen as she forages for cheese in mousetraps."

I giggled. "I think Gwen has been on a diet for years. She just keeps herself blown up with helium or something."

Feeling flirtatious, I put my head on his shoulder but pulled it back instantly. He ran his hand through my hair and caressed my cheek. Brought my head back to rest there. My arms fit naturally around his waist. He felt very big next to me.

There was a sudden zigzag flash of light and detonation of thunder. I pressed into him and felt him squeeze me tightly, both of us startled.

"That was close," I said.

His lips kissed my cheek. His teeth lightly took my ear lobe and squeezed it. Like the kiss on the neck, the thrill went through me and I shivered.

Yet I found it hard to take him seriously. "You really know your way around making out, don't you?"

"The dark passion of Africa. Drums throbbing at night. Everyone has sex over there all the time. Poor Mater and Pater simply look through it. It's as though it's not there for them. I'm not sure they really know where babies come from."

"Have . . . have you done things with a girl before? I mean serious things?

"Constantly. Since I was in the cradle."

Suddenly his lips were on mine. I felt a fire and a joy I had never known before. My heart was pounding.

There was a huge lump in his pants. I knew what was there. I knew what boys liked to have done to them. Some of the girls in my class at school had done that—at least those who were going steady. I had never had a boyfriend, and despite vivid word pictures from those who did, I felt innocent, shy, and even a little frightened.

I put my hand on him there and held it gently. He sighed and closed his eyes.

"You show great promise, Miss Alice," he said. "I'll take you away with me to Senegal. We'll live in a grass hut and keep a pet crocodile which we'll name Thelma. When it gets unruly, we'll roast and eat it. You can have a necklace of its teeth for warding off all demons."

He made me feel very sad. I began to cry. I couldn't stop myself. "I'm sorry," I said. "I'm being silly."

"Feeling sad for Thelma the croc?"

"No. I'm wishing we could go away to that crazy world you describe—just you and me and my sister Daria. I couldn't leave her behind to them."

"To them? You mean your parents?"

"Yes. They're not real anymore. They're not themselves. They don't care about us. I'm nothing to them and Daria is just a key to the bank vault."

He traced my eyebrows with his fingertips and dabbed at the tears. "Don't take your hand away from me," he said. "I want us to be part of each other."

"Please kiss me again. Let me lose myself in you."

Before he could respond, big drops of rain splatted and rattled on the roof, raising a smell of dust. The drops came quickly and turned to a torrential downpour that seemed as though it would sweep the garden and the gazebo away. Suddenly, the ground was a dark, churning lake.

Thunder cracked and blasted and we clung to each other as electricity with a pale blue zipping flame skittered over the ground water. Safe on the platform above the water, we stood holding each other until the flashing thunderbolts had passed to leave only a steady gush of rain in their wake.

Water streamed off the roof of the summerhouse on all sides, surrounding us like a curtain. With a seemingly careless movement, Jeremy stepped out into the pelting rain, spread his arms and soaked himself. He turned his face up at the sky and opened his mouth to the falling water, drinking in the cool.

Gusts of windblown rain thrashed the tree leaves. He's crazy, I thought. He's wonderful—he's crazy—he's wonderful!

I went out into the rain as well. Stood up to my ankles in water. Felt my body turn cool and wet, my hair plaster against my head.

We held hands, both wanting to whoop with joy and laughter and celebration, yet knowing we couldn't. Even in the rush of rain, we had to be quiet.

He touched my breasts, which were standing out so against my wet and clinging T-shirt. I didn't resist as he peeled up the shirt and held them, one in each hand. Bent his head and kissed them each in turn. The witch tooth lay whitely between them.

He seemed overjoyed that I had let him touch me there, let him kiss me in such an intimate way. I wanted him to touch me more, to touch every part of my body, to kiss every part of me. But he was hiding his shyness in bravado.

"Let's go and spy upon the City of the Ghouls!" he proposed.

I was amazed that he was afraid to go any farther with me—to touch my other parts. "What? The Brodericks?"

"The freak house! The Mansion of Desolation! The Mausoleum of the Living Dead."

As ever, I laughed at his crazy wit, urging him to banish the Brodericks with mockery.

"Peep through the windows to watch Gwen looting the fridge," he said. "Wheeler cackling as he counts his gold. Find Thelma snoozing in her coffin and drive a stake through her heart."

"Yes, yes!" I said. "We'll watch the ogre and she won't know we're there!"

The rain never stopped, falling so heavily, you could barely see three feet. Holding hands, we made our way by memory through the garden and over the gate. Ahead, the big house was like an apparition in the pelting water. The one light in the parlor seemed dim. We crept up beneath the sill and crouched there. The sash was open several inches and murmuring voices leaked out. Slowly we peeked in.

My aunt sat in the parlor with Bubba. An eerie half-smile was on her lips. They were talking . . . about Miss Dawling!

"Yes, Son, if you must know, she died of poison."

"Did it hurt? Did she just kinda go to sleep or did it kill her real slow and painful?" Lusting after the gory details, Bubba was on the edge of his chair.

My aunt spoke calmly. "It was very painful. The worst kind of pain."

"Did she scream and yell? Did she spit up green puke?"

My aunt did not bat an eyelash at her son's coarse language. "I understand that she did. Poison is not pleasant."

"What kinda poison was it?"

"Something very simple and ordinary. Rat poison. Strychnine. Like you can buy in any store."

"I wanna get some. Can we buy some at the store?"

She made the eerie smile again. "Do you have some rats you want to kill?"

He paused and thought. "Yeah. Yeah. Sure."

"I'll give you the money to go to the store on your own," she said. "Don't say anything to anybody though."

That was it. Jeremy and I exchanged silent looks, frozen beneath that window as the rain poured, soaking into our skins.

24

The Woman in the Attic

August dragged to a close and the blasting heat became almost mellow. In the marshy creeks and estuaries of the town, shrimp harvests began. One day, Alberta bought a huge box of shrimp from a black man who walked the length of the peninsula to our gate with his catch balanced on his head. They were big shrimp, like you'd see only in the most ritzy restaurants in New York. They lay there in their bed of dripping ice, pinkish and plump and curled, smelling of richly brackish water. Though it took me three hours to peel them all, I was still excited.

Dinner was mounds of shrimp boiled with sausage and potatoes. Corn bread. Fresh green beans in olive oil. Avocado with a creamy dressing. Pineapple upside-down cake. Gwen was permitted green beans with no oil or butter. Her lips were absolutely tremulous as she gazed yearningly at the food she was denied.

Todd looked horrible. His eyes glassy and unfocused, he knocked over his glass of iced tea and sat helpless and slumped as everyone stared at the spreading brown stain.

He hadn't been to the bank that day. Instead, he had been in the carriage house drinking. It had begun as just one drink to steady his nerves and spread to a series throughout the day.

"We missed you at the bank today," said my uncle maliciously.

Thelma spoke of Todd as though he weren't in the

room. "Perhaps if he'd go ahead and check into the hospital he'd be able to go back soon. Senior always said that an alcoholic can't be helped unless he wants to help himself."

"He's not an alcoholic!" argued Mom fiercely. "He is a sensitive, good man. He's just spent a lifetime in this dismal hole, and it's getting to him."

My heart leapt! Mom still loved Todd. She was going to defend him against these ogres. I wanted to cheer.

Aunt Thelma and Uncle Wheeler exchanged evil looks. "He's free to leave this 'dismal hole,'" said my aunt, "whenever he wants. But—if he stays—his family had best mind their manners or else they can move elsewhere. If they can afford it."

Unsteadily, Todd got to his feet. He swayed back and forth like a tree in a breeze. He was looking at the pictures on the wall of the little girl playing.

"She was very beautiful," he said slowly. "Innocent. Sweet. Filled with joy. She didn't deserve such a—"

"Sit down, Todd," snapped my aunt.

He rocked back and forth indecisively, then straightened. He seemed infused with a sudden determination. "I think it's high time I paid Mother a visit."

He pushed his chair back from the table and it fell over behind him. He lurched, stepped over it, and walked around the table, out the dining room toward the stairs.

Uncle Wheeler and Aunt Thelma gaped at each other. There was fear on their faces. I had never seen my aunt move so quickly. In an instant, she sprang up and raced after Todd.

My heart was pounding. Todd was doing something that was a threat to them. Going to see his mother? The old woman in the attic. The woman who had stared down at me when we had first arrived. I didn't understand it all, but instinctively I was on Todd's side.

"Todd, you come back here right away!" Aunt Thelma shouted from the hallway.

Todd's laughter floated downward as he climbed to the second floor. Two sets of feet began pounding up the stairs.

I stood up abruptly.

"Sit down, young lady!" my uncle ordered.

"*No!*" I shouted.

I went after them. Uncle Wheeler pursued me. He was moving fast. But I sprinted up the stairs two at a time. I raced on light kid's feet while my uncle huffed and puffed behind me.

"You get away from her!" my aunt bellowed. "She's a sick old woman! You'll upset her and then I'll have to deal with it! I'll have to clean up your mess after you just like when we were children! Just like I have to now!"

I passed the first landing with the stained-glass window with the dead Daria's head forever memorialized beneath the fake Broderick coat of arms. I ran on—up and up.

Ahead of me, my aunt was puffing. "Years I've spent nursing her while you played in New York. I've given my life to her."

"Get away from me, Thelma!" Todd yelled. "Lemme alone! I just want to see Mother!"

I was beyond the second landing and onto that narrow, dark stretch of stairs that led to the attic. My aunt and Todd were struggling at the top. Uncle Wheeler was yelling at me from down below. I stopped.

Todd was jerking on the doorknob shouting, "Mother! Mother! It's me, Todd!"

Aunt Thelma reached him and pulled at him. "Leave her alone! Leave her alone!"

I grabbed at my aunt. "Get away from him, you big cow!" I shouted.

She gave me a backhand blow that sent me sprawling. Stars flashed in front of my eyes. I found myself on the floor, half against the wall. My head was spinning. Squeezing my arms in a grip of iron, Uncle Wheeler had his hands on me now. Kicking with all my might, I fought him.

"You can't keep me from my mother!" Todd shouted.

"You put her there!" yelled Aunt Thelma. "You drove her mad! You killed Daria! You put her in the fire!"

As I watched, Todd slowly collapsed, oozing down the wall into a heap on the floor. Like claws, his hands scraped down the wood of the door. He was weeping inconsolably. "I didn't! I didn't!" he sobbed. "It's all a lie! It's not true! I was only nine years old!"

Aunt Thelma was red and heaving. She had played her trump card and won. "You know the truth. You know the truth about everything. You ran to New York to hide from the truth and blacken your soul in low, tawdry living."

"I didn't do it," Todd wept. "I wouldn't have. I couldn't have. She was too pretty and sweet. I loved her."

"So did I," said Aunt Thelma. "So did we all. Mother loved her so much she became sick with grief. That's why she's in there. But she'll be well soon. She loves to be visited by the new Daria. It's so good for her."

"You will not lock my daughter in there again!" said Todd fiercely. "I will not permit it!"

"I will do what I please in my own house," spit my aunt. "I will do what needs to be done to help our mother recover."

"No!" said Todd. "No, you won't!" He was yelling up at her from the floor. Using his last reserves of emotional strength, he pulled himself to his feet. He jabbed his forefinger in her face, making her flinch back.

"Not with my daughter, you won't. You touch my Daria and I'll raise a stink that the precious Broderick name can't overcome in a year of Sundays!"

"You wouldn't dare," yelled Aunt Thelma, but it was clear she knew he would.

"What would Senior think of that, hey?" stormed Todd, his eyes wild and gleaming with the ecstasy of power. "Senior —with his watch chain across his vest and his pomposity and his greed! Senior—who blighted everything he touched! Senior—who locked his wife in an attic because he couldn't admit to the community that she was insane! Would he like a scandal? Would he like it, Thelma?"

My aunt stuttered. Her jowls shook and her face flamed red. She gripped the stair railing dizzily. For a moment, it seemed as though she might pitch over the edge and fall tumbling into the void at the bottom.

Todd's eyes were misty and he wiped them furiously with the back of his sleeve as he stumbled down the stairs.

There was bravery in his soul. There was poetry and art in the man who had named my mother's eyes seagreen.

25

The Chinese Pot

On a sultry afternoon with a land breeze that brought a plague of bugs, I was set to scrubbing out old Alberta's bathroom. She had nearly passed out from the heat while making lunch and had had to go home despite a tongue-clucking harangue from my aunt about how nobody wanted to work these days.

Alberta's bathroom was connected to the kitchen and was a general junk hole where my aunt shoved the cleaning stuff and anything else that needed to be dumped out of sight. It took me forever to haul everything out just so I could get at the floor and scrub.

Gwen was supposedly playing with Daria in the parlor. There were moments with my little sister when Gwen would actually come out of herself and be halfway human, like maybe Daria's innocence brought out a forgotten true goodness in the frustrated, miserable mess that was Gwendolyn Broderick.

As usual, I made the time go past by daydreaming. I pretended I was scrubbing dishes in the trendy restaurant where all the young dancers worked when they were not in a show. And Jeremy was an airline pilot who had flown into Kennedy Airport from Cairo or Cape Town. He'd come in with his buddies. They'd be short on waitresses that day, and I'd have to go out and handle his table. Or—maybe the pilots would be all rowdy and nobody could handle them but me.

I'd be looking really good and Jeremy would recognize me—the big recognition scene like in the movies. He'd make some cryptic remark about Congreve that no one would understand but me. And after work, he'd be out on the street waiting for me.

I was up to my elbows in the commode when I heard a noise in the pantry. Gwen was in there, stuffing big lumps of sugar into her mouth and sucking on them.

Surprise and confusion gave way to fear. Her face turned florid. "I'm not doing anything bad," she said.

"Where's Daria?" I asked.

Tears began to stream as she replied with bitter reproach. "Don't you be mean. Don't you dare tell on me. I haven't done anything!"

"Fine. I'm not about to tell. I just wondered where you had left my sister."

Gwen sniffed back her tears. "She's okay. Bubba's with her."

"Bubba?"

There was no point in railing at her. I banged open the swinging door to the dining room, listened to the silent house.

Something ominous hovered in the air.

"I don't want this," said a small frightened voice. "I don't like it! It hurts!"

I knew the voice. It was Daria's.

For one deathless moment, I became frozen.

"Please stop! Please stop!"

Daria's voice was louder now. It had become a wail. What was going on?

She was crying violently. I ran toward the parlor.

All I could see was Bubba's bulging, rounded back. Then I realized that he had his hand down in Daria's pants.

I didn't stop to think. Ria saw me. Her appeal flashed like electricity.

The big Chinese pot with the sea oat dried arrangement was there on the sideboard. I snatched it up. It didn't seem to weigh anything at all. With two hands, I lifted it over my head and smashed it down on him.

There was no noise, just a big *thunk*. The pot shattered into a million pieces. Sea oats went everywhere. Bubba rolled to the floor.

Daria was in my arms. I was petting her, crying over her. "Ria, Ria darling. Please tell me you're okay!"

She was crying, holding between her legs.

I gathered her up in my arms and started out of the room with her. I stopped and looked back. Bubba lay sprawled and still. His head was running with blood. It was gathering in a pool under his face.

I didn't care if I had killed him. I didn't care if he drowned in his own blood.

I trudged out of the parlor carrying my sweet burden. Ria had her face in my neck crying.

Gwen came into the hall. Her cheeks were pushed out with sugar lumps like a chipmunk's. "What's wrong?" she slurped around her mouthful.

I laughed wildly. I was triumphant. I was as deranged as the rest of them.

26

The Broderick Name

I found Mother as she always seemed to be now—surrounded by a pile of unfinished ironing, a magazine open on her lap, gazing dreamily into space with her sea-green eyes. Daria crawled into her arms and wept. Whispering, I told Mom what had happened. She held my little sister close, but only stared at the wall when I described the dreadful event with Bubba.

Mom simply wouldn't talk. She didn't ask how I got Daria away from this monster. She didn't ask whether I had killed him, which I was growing convinced of.

"Todd's asleep," was all she said. "He's not feeling well. We mustn't wake him."

"Mom, didn't you hear what I said?"

"If only Todd would do what Wheeler says and settle down in banking. Learn the business and give up this silly dream of being a painter. If I could just make him listen to Wheeler more, maybe he'd get the hang of it."

Then the ambulance rolled up, its siren going at full pitch.

Mom wasn't interested. She took Daria into the bedroom where Todd was sleeping while I went out into the yard.

Uncle Wheeler came flying up in his Cadillac right behind the ambulance. He was red-faced and angry, irritated at having his day interrupted.

"Here I am in the middle of a real estate closing and this has to happen," he growled.

As Bubba was wheeled out on the gurney, my uncle started shouting at the EMS men. He told them he owned most of the hospital and half the doctors in it and could have them fired whenever he wanted. In the heat, he jerked off his jacket and hurled it to the ground. He yanked at his necktie, loosening it at his throat. His forehead was glistening with sweat and his armpits were big brown stains. He kept yelling for no particular reason.

With the siren blaring and lights flashing, the ambulance finally took off. Uncle Wheeler jumped into his car and gunned the engine, following them out.

Drawn by the commotion, Jeremy came over from the Woolcott house. He was reserved since he knew he shouldn't act like we were pals in front of the bad guys.

Todd stumbled out of our little house. At first, I thought he was groggy from sleep, then I realized he was drunk, absolutely reeling drunk.

Aunt Thelma boiled out of her house, dragging Gwen. She actually had Gwen by the ear. Gwen whined and whimpered.

"You did this!" my aunt shrieked, pointing a finger inches from Todd's nose. "You tried to kill my son! I'll get you for this if it's the last thing I do!"

Todd blinked at her incoherently.

"Get in the car, Gwen!" Aunt Thelma yelled. She struggled to get under the wheel of her Cadillac and backed over shrubs getting it turned around. Gwen bounced around inside as Thelma spun the wheel and jarred over the brick margin of the drive. The car went out the gate.

Todd stood staring after them a long time. Finally, Jeremy took Todd by the hand and led him over to the Woolcott house. He seemed very gentle and kind with Todd, as if he was actually concerned for his well-being. I followed along, too, hugging Todd and kissing him myself. I loved

him. He was my father, and Aunt Thelma and Uncle
Wheeler were horrible people.

Later, I went back into our house. Mom had come out
of the bedroom.

"Alice?" she said vaguely.

I cringed. It would all come out now. The enormity of
the thing had finally sunk in. "Yes?"

Her voice sounded like that of someone coming out of a
coma and not tuned into reality exactly. "Has something
happened to Bubba?"

"Yes," I said. "I hit him with a Chinese pot. I may have
killed him."

"Hit him?"

"Yeah. I hit him as hard as I could."

Still, she wasn't listening. She was just gazing out the
window into space dreamily. "What on earth for?"

I was dumbfounded. My words came flowing out in
high-pitched passion. "What for? Because of what he was
doing to Ria. He had his fingers up in her, Mom. Didn't you
listen to a word I said? He was doing vile, horrible, awful stuff
to her and she was crying and begging for him to stop."

"Did you hurt him?"

"Yes I hurt him. I wanted to kill him. I hope he dies."

Her voice was disapproving. Spacey. Weird. "You
shouldn't say such mean things, Alice. That's not very well
brought up. Aunt Thelma wouldn't approve of such talk."

"Mom, can't I get through to you? He was molesting
Daria."

My mother turned peevish. "Don't raise your voice to
me, Alice. You have too vivid an imagination . . . or else
you're telling some awful story. I refuse to believe such a
thing."

"Great. Now I'll go to prison."

Mom didn't seem to hear. She walked away, upstairs
into the bedroom, and closed the door. I ran a bath and put
Daria into it. Mom came out of the bedroom, got a magazine, and went back in again.

For a long time, Daria played in the bath with rubber animals. She seemed to be developing the ability to block things out of her mind. I wasn't sure if that was good or not. Mom and Todd were such a mess and that was what they did.

I didn't know what to do. I wasn't a mother or a psychologist or a schoolteacher. What do you do after your sister has been molested and you've possibly killed the creep who did it? Should I talk to Ria about it? Or make up some fairy tale and pretend that it all happened in our imagination?

Long after dark, Aunt Thelma and Uncle Wheeler drove up together. As they got out of their cars I could hear my aunt berating Gwen, who was sobbing. Her angry voice floated up and into my window.

"You children have been nothing but trouble from the day you were born."

Gwen continued to weep.

"You stop that crying or I'll give you something to cry about."

"I'm sorry, Momma," Gwen gulped, trying to contain her misery.

"Now you go tell those sorry relatives of ours to get over to our house P.D.Q. We're going to get to the bottom of this."

As she approached our door Gwen's step quickened. I came down in response to her banging.

"Boy, is Uncle Todd going to get it," Gwen said maliciously. "He is in dee-eep trouble."

Mom came down looking as out of it as before. "You were all gone off . . ." she said to Gwen vaguely. "I didn't know if I should do anything about supper. None of us have eaten."

"My brother may die," Gwen said melodramatically. There was an odd edge to her voice, a glint in her eye, as though she looked forward to that possibility.

I found myself taking charge. "You stay here, Mom," I

said. "Daria's not going near those people, and someone's
got to be with her."

"My mother said you were to all come," said Gwen.
Smug. Filled with the importance of her mission, the authority of Her Eminence the Great Spider Thelma.

I pushed Gwen back and closed the door behind me.
"Mom's staying here," I said through clenched teeth. Taking
Gwen's arm, I led her back across the yard. Glancing back, I
saw Mom staring blankly after me through the screen.

"My mother is not going to like this one bit," Gwen
predicted saucily.

Uncle Wheeler was sitting at the head of the dining
room table drinking a cup of coffee. Aunt Thelma ranged
against the mantel. Behind her, the pictures of the dead
Daria were frozen in play.

Todd was sitting with his head in his hands, rocking
slightly back and forth. I couldn't figure how he had known
to come.

"I don't know," Todd was saying. "I don't know anything about it."

"You're going to jail for this for a long time, brother
dear," my aunt crooned. "The motive is clear. Reduce the
number of heirs and your precious Daria gets a bigger cut."

"Thelma, I don't know if we should lay our cards on the
table like this," began my uncle. But she cut him off.

"That's your son lying in intensive care," she bellowed.
"You've never loved him. I'm all that protects him from
those who are jealous of the Broderick position in this
town."

Uncle Wheeler spoke through clenched teeth. "Thelma,
I'm warning you. Don't talk like that in front of . . ." He
jerked his chin in my direction.

"You stand against that wall, young lady, and don't say
a word," Aunt Thelma snapped at me. "And where is that
wretched mother of yours? I distinctly recall saying you
should all be here, even little precious."

"They're not coming," I said with brave defiance.

"I said to not open your—what do you mean they're not coming?"

Todd had his face on his arms on the table, crying in utter confusion. "I don't know anything. I swear I don't."

"Just as I said," I replied to her. "And I'm the one who hit Bubba."

"*You what?*" my aunt shrieked. She grabbed me by the shoulders and shook me until my teeth rattled. "*You did what?*"

Uncle Wheeler sprang up, grabbed her wrists, and made her release me. "Stop it, Thelma. Let the child tell her story." Then he turned to me, all silky and smooth. Stepped back a pace. Folded his arms. "Tell us about it, Alice. What happened?"

"He was molesting my little sister so I hit him. I'll do it again if he messes with her."

"That's an absurd lie," yelled my aunt. Even at the time I remarked how she didn't even blink. She just spit out her denial as if she had expected the accusation. Or else had some advance knowledge of Bubba's little ways.

"Quiet, Thelma," said Wheeler. "Now, Alice, tell us, what do you mean by molesting? That's quite a word for someone your age. Was he playing too rough with her?"

"He had his hands in her pants and . . . and up her thing. That's what I mean by molesting. How would you define it?"

My aunt drew her big hand back to strike me. "You impertinent little . . . !"

Uncle Wheeler pushed her aside again. I had never seen him so bold with her. "That's a very serious accusation, young lady," he said in his still smooth voice. "And you've admitted to a very serious action yourself. I hope for your sake you know what happens to girls who tell lies, particularly girls who might have killed someone."

"I'm not lying," I said stubbornly.

"Well, I'm glad to hear that, because I'm going to take you down to the bank for a lie detector test. And if you don't pass, I'm going to turn you over to the police for prosecution."

My aunt suddenly gasped. "You'll do no such thing. The scandal."

"Yeah," I said. "Besides, I'm telling the truth, and you know it. You don't want everyone to know the truth, do you, Aunt Thelma?"

"Shut up, Alice," Uncle Wheeler said. He turned to my aunt. "Of course, you know she's lying, Thelma. We'll prove it easily. The polygraph machine is wonderful. We're going to prove she's lying. She might even be lying to protect her stepfather. And then we'll have them where we want them."

"I won't have the Broderick name smeared by scandal. Can you imagine what people will do to us if they get the least bit of dirt on this family?"

"The cops know how to keep their mouths shut. They've hushed up plenty of things before."

"I won't take that risk. Just one person . . . This has got to stop here. And go no further."

"You want to stop?" said Uncle Wheeler incredulously. "When we're so close to . . . when we could possibly . . ."

"Yes," she said firmly. "It must end here. If there is one thing Senior always made clear, it's that no breath of scandal should ever touch the family."

She turned savagely to me. "Do you understand what's happened here? You may think you're getting away with something, young lady, but you're not. I must find a way to deal with you on my own. I know you're lying, Alice. My son would never do such a terrible thing. You've made this up and I'll deal with you for it. I'm not sure how just yet, but I will. And you'll live to regret the day you injured him. Now get out of my sight."

Gwen drifted along behind me to the kitchen door.

"She's gonna get you good," she taunted. "You're going to be sorr-ry for what you did."

"Fatso," I sneered.

Gwen looked as if she had been slapped. Then she tuned up to cry.

27

A Place of Appeasement

I took my Aunt Thelma's threats seriously. I had no doubt that she'd lie in wait for as long as it took to get me. So I watched my step: did my chores meekly and was very, very careful about meeting Jeremy in the garden at night.

Bubba survived. Unfortunately. Although I was glad enough at the time. He lived at home while the bandages were on his head. At least my aunt didn't make me take him his meals. Gwen had to do that, and she'd come out of his room crying each time from something he had said or some pinch or slap or blow he had given her. The injury I had inflicted hadn't noticeably reduced his intelligence. Now he just had a better excuse to lie in bed looking at horror comics and sucking his thumb. After a week, he went back to his tar paper shack.

September came, still blanketed with the oppressive southern heat. Despite dire predictions of disaster, I took the placement test at Ashcroft School and ended up in my proper grade. The lack of Latin didn't seem to bother the school nearly as much as it did Aunt Thelma. I put on my drab department store clothes and mixed in as best I could.

Jeremy was enrolled at a private boys' school where he was kept occupied in the afternoons with required sports and other activities. His family didn't take their meals in the big house, so I seldom saw him.

Since Ria was in preschool at Ashcroft, we walked together each day down the long peninsula into the streets of big houses, live oaks, and gray Spanish moss on sidewalks cracked and broken by countless tree roots. Yards were filled with banana palms and palmettos. Ria talked about her new friends, their dolls and pets and of things they made together with cut paper and glue. Though Ria made friends easily, no one was ever permitted to come over to our house, and so no one invited her to theirs. We had the plague—the Broderick plague.

By the time we had the school in view, Aunt Thelma's Cadillac would flash by and stop at the front gate. Ria and I would hang back as Gwen dragged herself out of the car, dropping her books at least once, complaining about the food in the cafeteria. The car would roll off as Gwen went into the school, smirking at everyone.

There had never been any talk about my aunt giving us a ride to school or of Gwen introducing us to her social set. Not that Gwen really had a set. In fact, she was totally friendless. Her friends were only those girls whose parents were afraid to be mean to the Brodericks. Those unfortunates would always make a special point of saying something nice about Gwen's clothes or asking her about a class first thing in the morning and then ignoring her for the rest of the day. It was like their parents quizzed them each night on their contact with Gwen and they had to have something to report.

The school was surrounded by a high brick wall, cracked in places and hanging with honeysuckle vines. In the center of a vast tree-shaded green lawn, sat a huge old mansion with white columns and little iron balconies on the upper windows. In an outlying L-shape were modern classrooms, a gym, an indoor swimming pool, and some tennis courts. A fountain had a sculpture of nymphs and fish spouting water. The nymphs had their breasts bare. I sometimes wondered if my aunt wanted to take a sledgehammer to them —or make them wear brassieres.

The headmistress, Miss Carson, resembled a stork. I

always expected her to stand on one leg. One day a week, each class was admitted to her large sitting room to have tea and cakes and learn social graces.

The girls found me strange, but it wasn't because I was a Yankee from New York. It was because, brought up in the confines of this seacoast southern town, they had seldom thought of the outside world. They were expected to be debs at a thing called the Catherine Society Ball, go to a junior college, and marry fraternity boys from the state university— preferably fraternity boys from Congreve. Afterward, they would carry on just like their mothers: have babies, car-pool the kids, play golf or tennis at the Country Club. Perhaps bridge. Have an occasional love affair with someone entirely appropriate.

Thoughts of being an adult seemed far away to me, but to them, it was as real and preordained as church on Sunday. So they behaved like their mothers and actually talked about curtains, carpets, new station wagons or vans, and kitchenware brand names along with the usual teenage girl stuff. It was weird, to say the least.

At first, they weren't particularly mean to me. After all, I was a Broderick—of sorts. Daria was pretty and cute and popular with the teachers and older girls as well as the pre-school gang. She was a small talisman for me. If Daria was my sister, I had to be basically okay.

They asked me about New York but weren't particularly interested in my response. Their mothers went to New York in groups to stay in hotels on Park Avenue, go to plays and shop, or have their hair done at the famous beauty salons. They would return a bit dazzled, but grateful for the security of their own world. Their daughters accepted this as right and proper.

My world of SoHo was a total unknown to them— someplace dirty where subhuman people lived, a place the mothers avoided by taking cabs wherever they went, having their change ready, and sprinting from the cab into the building. Unless they were up near the Plaza at the bottom corner of Central Park where everyone was rich and perfect. In that case, they would stand on the streets or browse in shops without looking for danger.

The schoolwork wasn't hard because the girls had little interest in excelling. Since they were only destined for junior college, they had no real need for higher math or foreign languages. The Latin teacher was ancient and nearly blind and everyone cheated freely on the tests. I found I could make A's without cracking a book. No one seemed particularly interested in my achievement. Aunt Thelma hated me, and Todd and my mother were lost in their combined misery.

Although she was three years older, Gwen was in my class. Even with the lack of rigorous academic standards, Gwen did abysmally. She was only passed due to pressure on the school from my aunt. She couldn't seem to read at much more than a fourth-grade level, and the teachers simply ignored her in class. She would sit staring out the window, her head filled with goodness knows what poor daydreams.

The other girls hated her for the usual reasons that bring out viciousness in teenagers. Gwen was dumb and fat and slow at games. At kickball, she was always put out before reaching first base. Sometimes she'd fall down and just sit on the ground. She was terrified of the water and refused to learn to swim. She took church far too seriously and tattled to the teachers every chance she got. Still, Gwen was treated with remarkable tolerance because of the girls whose parents depended upon Wheeler's bank.

I didn't like the school particularly. I wanted to be back home in New York in the world I knew. Still, the school was preferable to life with the Brodericks. Daria and I would dawdle on the way home and find places to hide away. The best was the old St. Michael's Church graveyard that ran from the neck of the peninsula to directly behind the Broderick mansion.

Like fugitives, we went there. Hiding from my aunt and Gwen and from all the unhappiness of our parents. So close to the somber Broderick mansion, yet hidden by wall and foliage. Safe in that hushed and quiet place with cooing pigeons and the whisper of slow decay, a place of slow, creeping neglect, a place of all variety of green shades, a place of appeasement.

No one ever came to the graveyard. Flowers never appeared on the graves. There were no mourners or philosophers to sit pondering life among the weathered stones. The dead were long dead, centuries-old dead. The tombstones dated from history books. 1703. 1816. 1834. There were graves of little children who were carried off in the age of yellow fever, malaria, and a thousand other vanished mortal ills.

There was a statue of an angel and a mausoleum with a caved-in roof, the interior choked with briars, sumac, and honeysuckle. To the far side of the crumbling wall was the Woolcott back garden, the secret spot where Jeremy and I met after dark on the rare occasions when he could slip out of the house. The graveyard was my sanctuary with Daria, the more tangled and hidden Woolcott garden my spot for Jeremy. I kept them compartmentalized like the two forms of my love.

To the north, beyond the shaggy treetops, were the steeples of the newer churches and the stubby silhouette of the city against a bleached-out sky. The top three stories of the six-story bank building where the two lions sat crouched. The Broderick bank with the clock set on the outside wall that rang the hours with a sound of mechanical clanking over the drifting noise of traffic in a town so frozen in time, it seemed as though it ought to have horses and carriages.

St. Michael's Church itself was long burned and the fire-seared ruins overgrown with weeds. Jeremy said he only remembered going there once as a child. The charred wood had been removed, leaving the vaulted masonry of the church skeleton. Brick and stone like dinosaur bones. Flesh rotted away and the skeleton remaining until time took its toll of that too. A worn plaque that commemorated a new steeple put on after Yankee cannonballs had demolished the old one during the Civil War.

Under the cool shade of the arching oaks, I would do what little homework I had, and Daria would play among the tumbled stones, smelling the rich stink of the delta mud. A distant throbbing of ship engines and the occasional sharp hoot of the steam horn.

Sometimes, I felt sluggish and lazy. I would drowse and dream and remember SoHo. Daria played mother with little babies and made tea parties and arranged imaginary houses behind a big gravestone with a winged skull and the inscription *Time is Ever Fleeting Josephus McGee 1705–1760*. Little lizards skittered on the stones or sat pulsing and watching me curiously. Sometimes we found dead birds, which Daria buried and erected little crosses over and finished with a feeling of completeness.

We were untouched by the dead except for a sense of security. We could lie on the grassy hummocks of the graves or the cool flat stones and find sanctuary among these lost ghosts. Watch clouds plodding across the sky and gulls drifting in gentle cartwheels on high-altitude winds. We would idle there until the sun would flare at the edge of the horizon and dusk came in like pale blue smoke. Then we would thread our way through the stones to the rusted iron gate that led into the Broderick domain, always pausing and gazing back as if waving farewell.

One day, Daria and I walked around opposite sides of the graveyard. Watching each other, we waved at figures so distant, they appeared inches high. A simple game. Following the vine-covered wall and watching each other and waving and ultimately arriving at the same point.

A squirrel scurried in a tree. There was a smell of diesel fuel from off the harbor. A persimmon tree was ripening its fruit for the approaching autumn. Then I saw the small stone, a stone not as old as the others. It was smooth marble with delicate veins of blue and pink and rose coloring shot through it. Heraldic angels blew on trumpets. The cherub's face smiled wanly. It was the same face as on the stained-glass window. A tender pea vine coiled around it. The writing was clear.

I stood still, arrested by the sight.

> Daria Broderick
> Forever an Angel
> Beloved by All
> Untouched by any Taint
> Of Sin or Shame

A pale summer lightning flickered far in the distance somewhere out over the harbor. I stood trembling before the carved marble, thinking of the tiny body that had long ago decayed in the earth with the worms. Her small bones turned to dust. The little mahogany coffin.

I wiped off a sudden bit of sweat that appeared on my forehead and moved warily away.

I didn't show it to Daria. I knew she could recognize the name and would know instantly that buried there was the good little girl who had played with fire despite the warnings of her dolly.

Haunted by some unexplainable need, I returned after supper and put wild daisies on the grave. Strewed them gently and watched their white beauty, knowing that in the morning they would be wilted and brown.

The nighthawks were swooping.

28

Pearly Tears

Life was almost calm in those hot September days. Todd took to calling in sick to the bank a lot and going out in a leaking old skiff that was tied up under a warehouse at the docks, visiting places in the marshes and sandy beaches where he had found solace as a youth. The sea was familiar to him, he knew its secrets, could handle it with skill. He still didn't paint, but he would bring back fish with strange names and dull, glinting scales and white underbellies. He held them aloft proudly, finger hooked under the gills while Daria danced and clapped her hands. He was sunburned and bug-bitten. He smelled of fish and salt water and mud and he hugged us and seemed almost happy.

Todd drank while he fished, but he seemed to handle it better. His eyes were bright with liquor, but also with a vision of something lost and beautiful. He would talk to me about being a teenager, and promise to show me the haunts of his youth. I liked that closeness even though he always broke his word and never once took me. On the weekends, Daria and I would walk him down to the boat and hang around wistfully while he pushed off, loudly promising that next weekend we'd go out together. Always, there was an excuse. We had to get a life jacket for Daria. The weather promised to turn rough. He was going too far and we'd get bored.

I wasn't really hurt. I wished him well and actually believed he was growing stronger, making some kind of a recov-

ery. Daria and I would go back to meet his return by starlight
and watch the fish flopping in the water-filled bucket, squat
patiently while he gutted and scaled them, listen while he
talked about tide and birds and boats he had seen. Gulls
decorated the pilings, waiting for the scraps. Daria pretended
she could distinguish them and gave them names. Timmy
and Josh and Randy. Names of boys from her preschool.

It was Mom who worried me the most. She had become
withdrawn, and I couldn't figure out quite what she did all
day. She didn't do much of anything really. She just seemed
to talk out loud to herself about things that didn't make any
sense. When she did work at chores, she would drift for
hours—letting the water boil over on the stove, or not noticing when the cookies were burning.

Sometimes, when her talking made sense, she reminisced about her hometown of Richmond, Virginia, and
growing up there. Stuff I had never heard before. She said
her father had been an executive for a power company,
which didn't seem very exciting to me, but she acted like it
was something really important and gave them a big place in
society. It didn't sound at all like her. I mean, I couldn't
picture my mother in society, not even as a child. Once,
when I found her crying, she became angry and told me to go
away and leave her alone.

The worst thing was that Mom nagged Todd a lot. What
had begun as a mistaken notion on his part—that he could
fit in at the bank and learn the business—became something
of an obsession for her. It wasn't harsh or strident nagging
like Aunt Thelma handed out, but still, it was always there
between them, her whining little digs spiced with oblique
remarks about how much money Uncle Wheeler made.
Eventually, they avoided each other altogether.

Of course, Todd's frequent absences from the bank
were commented upon by the Brodericks. Naturally, my aunt
denounced him loudly. She couldn't believe that Senior's
blood was in "such a weakling." If Senior could see Todd
now, he would surely turn over in his grave. Incredibly, even

Norman and Kate ganged up on Todd and asked him why he couldn't do better. Todd responded by dragging his boat out of the water, scraping and caulking it, and going back out on one of his solitary cruises.

Once the Coast Guard—some polite young men in white uniforms and crew cuts—even had to bring him in to the big house. They said they had found him asleep and drifting out beyond the harbor mouth. An empty liquor bottle was mentioned.

Unctuously, Aunt Thelma thanked them as she shoved them out the door, promising letters of commendation to their commanding officers. Once they had disappeared, she lit into Todd about being passed out drunk and how it would be good riddance to all if he'd float out to sea and die. Her jowls shaking, she even told him it would have been a blessing if he'd died during childhood instead of their sister Daria. Todd smiled dreamily and walked out of the house. Went down to the docks to patch the sail on his boat. He was humming "Whistle While You Work." Ria and I went with him. We loved him and wanted to let him know.

One morning on the way to school, Daria was withdrawn and distant. I tried to talk to her, but she said nothing. Little pearly tears formed at the edges of her eyes. I stopped and tried to get her to talk, but it was getting late and we were due at school. I gave her a hug outside her classroom. But she pushed me away.

In the middle of geography class, I saw a strange car pull through the gates and stop in front of the school. A woman got out and went inside. This was meaningless in itself. Except that five minutes later, my aunt Thelma's Cadillac roared up and screeched to a halt behind the other car amid a spew of gravel. Clearly in a wrath, Aunt Thelma rocked herself out from behind the wheel and stalked inside.

Shortly afterward, my teacher was called out of the classroom. We had been answering questions on the crops of Brazil. I couldn't concentrate. Something awful was going on. I thought of Daria and her strange mood on the walk to school earlier that day.

Finally, the teacher returned long enough to summon me out into the hall. Twenty heads turned to stare at me. As I passed through the door, a whispering broke out behind me. My heart was pounding.

The teacher was a nice lady whose husband was always out to sea with the navy. She was lonely, and so she spent a lot of time with the students.

"Daria is very upset," she said quietly. She paused, choosing her words carefully. "She began crying in class and told her teacher something which . . . well . . . necessitated Headmistress Carson calling the Welfare Department."

Somehow I knew what it was. "Oh no!" I gasped. "Not Bubba! Not again!"

My teacher hung her head. "I'm not allowed to say anything more. The school . . . well, the school is very touchy about its reputation. The less that's said, the better."

I started to cry. She gave me a squeeze and told me to go along to the headmistress's office. "Chin up," she said bravely. "Things will work out. You'll see."

I felt like a condemned prisoner walking to the electric chair as I went, knowing that everyone in geography class was watching my back.

The door to Headmistress Carson's office was closed, but voices carried through it. I could hear Aunt Thelma speaking her mind.

"She's a five-year-old child. This is some fantasy she's cooked up."

"I'm sorry, Mrs. Broderick," the woman said. "I can't tell you how sorry I am about this. But state law requires that incidents of child abuse be investigated."

"You call this off—or I'll have your job," my aunt threatened.

The woman held her ground. "I didn't make the decision, Mrs. Broderick. My department head did. I'm just carrying out her orders. The child has got to be examined by a physician and a welfare caseworker. Your position in the community will certainly be given all due consideration. No one will breathe a word about this."

"It will leak out. I know it will. I won't have the Broderick name dragged through the dirt!"

"We will do everything possible to . . ."

"You can bet you will. I'll have lawyers coming behind you every step of the way. You don't play fast and loose with Senior Broderick's family without lawyers getting involved."

In an instant, the door was flung open and Aunt Thelma stalked out. She saw me sitting there and raged at me vehemently. "You're behind this somehow, Alice McNamara. I know you are. You and Daria cooked this up together."

I stared at her. Words choked in my throat.

She clenched her hands as if she wanted to strangle me and then stormed away.

In Headmistress Carson's office, I summoned my courage and told the welfare lady the entire story as I knew it. The playhouse. Hitting Bubba on the head. Miss Carson and the welfare worker sat together, listening gravely.

Apparently Bubba had gotten hold of poor Ria again yesterday. Miss Carson was very delicate about exactly what had happened.

I had to protect Ria. I didn't care what Aunt Thelma did. If she drove us out of the house, maybe we could go back home—to New York—and put all this horror behind us.

At last the welfare lady closed up her file and left. I remained behind with Miss Carson. She made a tent of her hands and stared at me for some time. At last she spoke.

"I have had a long experience with young girls," she said. "I have seen them come and go in all their vagaries. Seen them do many foolish things they later regretted. Things that had ramifications which their immature minds could not conceive of when they committed rash actions on a moment's impulse."

I sat silent.

"At your age, laws and the working of the law are a mysterious thing of adults. It's sad you have to get mixed up in something so harsh and unforgiving."

"I can take it," I said defiantly.

Headmistress Carson paused again and looked directly into my eyes. "If you aren't telling the truth, Alice McNamara, I hate to think what might happen to you."

Though her words rang in my ears, I was not afraid. Ria and I had taken the right path. I was certain.

29
Staff Psychologist

"I don't want a shot," protested Daria.

"It's not a shot," I said. "They're just going to talk to you."

Daria was going in the car to see a psychologist. The Welfare Department wanted an assessment done of her. She sat, discouraged, in the front seat between Uncle Wheeler and myself. Whenever she would say something, my uncle would stare grimly at her. Eventually she fell silent.

Mother and Todd were not there. Probably because they hadn't been told what was going on. Ria and I were alone. We had to do this by ourselves.

We drove out a shabby street of secondhand furniture stores to the edge of town. Behind us, clouds of dust rose in the air. A mess of shacks was being bulldozed, big yellow machines pushing tar paper and sticks and boards to one side, leaving the earth scraped down to red clay. A billboard boasted: CONGREVE HOSPITAL EXPANSION—A BRODERICK BANK PROJECT.

A heavy silence hung over the hospital as we entered a parking lot with no trees, its asphalt blistering with heat. In the halls and waiting room were old people slouched on couches or being transported in wheelchairs.

Uncle Wheeler might have been attending a funeral. When she recognized him, a hard-eyed nurse became instantly subservient and directed us to the top floor. Emerging from the elevator, we found an office with the door marked:

PRISCILLA DAVIS, PH.D.
STAFF PSYCHOLOGIST

Dr. Davis was thin-faced and hollow-cheeked with eyes set close together behind half glasses. She wore a white lab coat with pens in the pocket. Her hair was cut very short. Her movements were brisk and forceful. The office was decorated with splashy fingerpaint pictures drawn by little kids.

"Do come in," she said with a professional smile. Then she turned to Ria. "You must be Daria Broderick."

Confronted by this woman, Ria panicked. Her little fingers groped for me. "No, Alice, don't leave me alone. Please come with me."

"Your sister cannot be with you, Daria," Uncle Wheeler said with obvious satisfaction. "It's not allowed."

"I won't! I won't!" Daria insisted.

"Stop this nonsense!" Uncle Wheeler snapped. His temper had flared. "And Alice, you quit encouraging this behavior. I've had it up to here with you two children."

Daria continued to cling to me crying. I shrugged my shoulders at my uncle and played helpless. I didn't blame Ria for not wanting to face this alone.

"It's all right, Mr. Broderick," said the psychologist. "I can handle this. Both of you girls come in."

Uncle Wheeler pursed his lips but consented.

Dr. Davis led us in and seated us on straight chairs in front of her desk. Closed the door. Sat back down. Barred light through the venetian blinds fell on her long desk covered with neat stacks of papers. Her white coat was starched so it crackled. She looked at me over the top rims of her half-moon glasses.

"And you are Alice," she said in a manner she meant to be pleasant but was clearly officious. She was irritated that I was in the way. She consulted her file. "You're Daria's half sister."

"Yeah," I said sarcastically. "I'm not a Broderick and they never let me forget it."

"Who is 'they'?"

"Uncle Wheeler and Aunt Thelma."

"How about your parents? Do they remind you of it as well?"

"Some," I said sulkily.

"Do you feel left out of the family circle?"

"Yeah. Sometimes."

"And you sometimes resent them for not loving you as they should."

I looked at her suspiciously. "No. Not really."

"What do you mean 'not really'? You do resent them, don't you?"

"Sure. I'm a problem teenager. Problem teenagers always resent their parents."

"Who has described you as a problem teenager? Have you been receiving counseling?"

"No. Of course not."

"Have you been a problem at school?"

"No."

"Do you feel you're a problem at school?"

"No. I try to fit in."

Her face had turned cold and unfeeling. "But you don't feel you're quite the social class of the other girls at Ashcroft School?"

"No. I'm not a Broderick. But it doesn't bother me at all."

"You're very brave. But I'm sure there are times when you feel the resentment of the other girls. Of the teachers. Of your aunt Thelma."

"Look," I said with an angry edge to my voice. "We're here because a retarded creep Broderick called Bubba won't keep his hands off my sister. That's it."

"And you hit him on the head once, I believe—with a very heavy and dangerous object?"

"You're durn right I did. And given half the chance I'd do it again. I'd kill him to keep him away from my sister."

She had begun to write notes on a pad. "You'd kill him, you say."

"I feel that strongly about my sister. I mean, she's an innocent little kid. She doesn't understand what he's doing. She's not able to make him stop."

"But you do understand what he's doing?"

"Of course I do."

"Have boys done that sort of thing to you?"

I blushed hotly. "No. No, they haven't."

"Has anyone?"

"No."

"An adult perhaps?"

"No."

"Tell me about your stepfather."

"Todd? What's there to tell? He's an artist."

She was watching me closely. "Is that the most important thing to you about him?"

"I don't know. He's nice and loving usually."

"Has he been different lately?"

"Yes. The Brodericks are driving him crazy."

The slightest touch of rose came to the pallor of her cheeks. "I don't think you should be rude about Mr. and Mrs. Broderick. It will not get you very far. And besides, I've heard quite enough."

She ordered me out of the room. I went grudgingly, wondering if Daria would start crying again. She didn't.

I sat out in the waiting room by myself. Uncle Wheeler had disappeared somewhere.

All the magazines were ragged and they made me feel vaguely unclean. We were in the psychiatric ward. In a nearby room, someone was moaning. Attendants wheeled a gurney past with a man strapped on it. He stared with glassy eyes at the ceiling as the attendants pushed him through swinging doors where they all disappeared.

What seemed like hours later, Daria finally came out. She wasn't happy, but she wasn't sad either. Dr. Davis seemed distant, but satisfied. Concerned that Uncle Wheeler wasn't there, she went to look for him, almost like she was afraid Daria and I would get up to no good on our own. I noticed uneasily that she and Daria didn't say good-bye to each other.

"What did you do in there?" I whispered.

Ria looked down at her feet. She seemed ashamed. "We played with dolls."

I heard my uncle's laughter traveling down the hall. He sounded very pleased with himself. He rounded the corner with Dr. Davis. She was smiling too.

30

Black Evil

"**Y**ou've been doing something nasty, Todd," accused Aunt Thelma.

"Wha . . . whaddaya mean?" he asked. He sounded drunk as usual.

"You know exactly what I mean."

"No. No, I don't."

"Tell me what you've been doing that you're ashamed of, Todd. Tell your big sister."

After dinner that same night, Aunt Thelma had marched Todd into the parlor and sat him down for a serious talk. Mom had taken Ria away. I tried to get her to stay by saying we were a family and should stay together, but Mom insisted that Todd needed to talk with his sister alone about something private. Still, I stayed behind. I hung outside the parlor listening.

The night was pungent with the rot that floated in the thin rivulets of the surrounding marsh. The compost odor had crept in stealthily, filling the house.

"Tell your big sister," Aunt Thelma urged some more, leaning forward, elbows on her knees, offering a false forgiveness of sins.

Tears started to run down Todd's face. "I shouldn't drink so much, I know that, but I can't seem to stop. It just smooths everything out."

"Tell me about Daria, Todd. Tell your big sister. You

can open up to me. I'm supposed to look after you now that Senior's not here. Tell me about Daria."

"Daria? I dunno. What about her?"

"You've done nasty things to her. Unspeakable things. Things you will burn in hell for."

Todd stared at his sister openmouthed.

"I should have seen it coming. Your . . . fascination with young girls. That picture you painted of Alice and Daria naked. It was a sign. Evidence of your evil."

Tendons strained in Todd's throat. "I haven't done anything," he repeated dumbly.

"Sure you have, Todd. Admit it to your sister. You started out so young. Our sister Daria and the terrible fire. You may as well have killed Mother too. And now you're an evil pervert with your own daughter."

Todd stared at his sister with a sort of wide-eyed, shocked innocence. His voice sounded almost retarded. "I haven't done anything. I haven't done anything wrong. I've been good."

"You killed your sister. And now you are doing these unspeakable things to your own little daughter."

"I didn't kill my sister. I didn't."

"The doctor thinks it's a sickness. That's putting it too politely for me. Black evil is what I call it."

"What doctor?"

With a flourish, Aunt Thelma produced a typewritten piece of paper. She read aloud. " 'Using anatomically correct dolls, subject correctly demonstrated sexual penetration with both penis and digits. Evasive answers regarding her father clearly show a mental blockage of repeated traumatic events. Abnormal affection for father and sexual acting-out with doll representing father figure indicate the father as the perpetrator of sexual molestation.' " With a sly, filthy grin, Aunt Thelma put down the paper.

I gagged. That dirty doctor. That soulless dirty woman laughing with Uncle Wheeler. She had tricked Ria. She had tricked Ria into saying that.

Todd looked uncomprehending. "Subject? What do you mean 'subject demonstrated'?"

"Daria Broderick."

"Daria? Daria's dead."

"Your daughter, Todd. Are you unable to tell the difference between the two? Or is it some way of pretending your vile actions never really took place? In your evil brain, you did things to someone long dead?"

"I haven't done anything wrong," Todd insisted desperately.

"You ought to be put to death for what you've done. As it is, you'll go to jail for a long time. Wheeler and I will see to that. We'll protect that innocent child from you at all costs."

I couldn't stand it any longer. I burst out of hiding and confronted her. I put my arms around Todd and hugged him.

"You can't blame it on him!" I shouted. "You evil, vicious witch! I know the truth. Daria will tell the truth. That woman tricked her. It's your animal of a son who did it. I was a witness. I saw it with my own two eyes."

Aunt Thelma pursed her lips. Her big, sturdy hands reached out and grabbed me by the hair. She kept her grip with one hand as she whacked me fiercely across the face with the other.

"No one talks to me like that!" she yelled. "No one in Congreve talks to me like that! Not to Thelma Broderick!"

Todd stood there watching as if the action were something on TV.

I sank to my knees, but my aunt held me tight by the hair. Blood pulsed in my brain. The carpet smelled of bug spray. My gaze fell numbly on a stocking sagging about one of my aunt's thick ankles.

She hit me again. My lower jaw snapped up into the upper one, catching my tongue in my teeth. Stars flashed before my eyes and I tasted blood.

"I know what you're up to," she snarled. "You think you can lie and save your wretched stepfather. But why?

What do you care? He's not your blood. You're not a Broderick." She hit me again with her fist.

Something galvanized Todd into action. Drunkenly, he reached for Aunt Thelma. His hands collided with her and bounced off, but he managed to give her a huge shove. He lost his balance and nearly fell. She went over backward and struck the floor with a thud.

Todd stood there shocked at what he had done. Thelma stared back at him. Her mouth worked, sucking at air that wouldn't enter her lungs. The fall had taken the wind out of her.

"Wuh-wuh-wuh," she gasped, her mouth working like a blowfish's.

We stood back, both of us horrified at what had happened. Violent thoughts raced through my head. Maybe she would die. For that brief moment, I wanted very badly for her to die.

At last her breath came. Red anger surged through her face. "You-you-you!" she stammered incoherently. She gulped air in fits and starts.

Todd gave her a strange smirk.

"You can't . . . no one . . . I'm a Broderick!" she finally burst out.

We left her there trying to get herself upright, pulling at the arm of a couch to regain her feet.

Todd and I walked outside. He did not talk to me. He spoke only to himself. "She's crazy," he whispered. "But I won't let her destroy us."

31

Bright Promises

The next morning Todd staggered off to the bank without bothering to shave. His shirttail stuck out from under his suit jacket. Mom didn't even straighten him up. They had been up talking all night, and she was tired. Plus she didn't like confrontation. Like an ice cube left on the kitchen floor, her resistance had simply melted away.

I didn't want to go to school. Letting the morning sunlight soak into me, I sat in the living room. Daria played on the stoop outside, waiting for me to come.

My mother was wearing perfume. It was subtle but the smell was there all the same.

"Mom, what are we going to do?" I asked.

She moved around the room with easy grace, even doing a few dance steps. "I was the top dancer in the class, Momma," she said. "Remember how people used to come from miles around just to see me dance?"

It was truly awful. My mother had changed, and it was like she was in some other part of her life. She wasn't there with me then. It was as if she had reverted to her childhood and was talking to her own mother.

Images went through my mind of when I was a little girl and Todd was new to us both. His taking me somewhere way in uptown Manhattan where we went up in a creaking freight elevator. It had been all dark and black and I had been afraid of this strange man who had come into my mother's life.

And then we had emerged from the elevator to find a big open hall with beautiful women in black leotards all in a line while someone played on a piano. I recognized my mom and tried to run to her, but Todd had held me back. He wasn't stern or corrective. He just whispered that they were in a perfect magical spell and I would break the spell if I made noise. He urged me to stand and watch and be in love with the beauty.

And so I had stood and watched the dancers move in magical unison. My mother had been as fine as a fairy princess with golden hair pinned up in a bun at the back and her legs and arms so graceful. I had wept a little child's tears at how beautiful it was. Every elegant grace in the world was imprisoned in that room like a treasure box of majesty.

"Momma, you warned me this would happen," my mother said in a resigned voice. She put her arms straight out on the mantel and stretched her body, as if she were at an exercise barre.

"What do you mean?" I whispered.

"Todd's a drinker. Just like Daddy. I know the signs. The bright, brittle gaiety. The laughter that comes only when that bottle is opened. The glittering eyes once those first drinks hit the system. It takes hold of you and one day you just can't stop."

It was true. She was really talking to her mother. Had she flipped out?

"Mom," I pleaded. "Do you understand that Aunt Thelma is trying to send Todd to jail? I mean this is a really filthy thing she's doing."

She kept her posture at the mantel. "Momma, you told me that men would always disappoint me."

"What?"

"Daddy disappointed you. He never provided for you the way you were entitled. And you predicted the same thing would happen to me. Well, you were right." My mother looked up to the ceiling. "John McNamara disappointed me. He never could do anything right. Then came Todd. Todd

Broderick. He was from a crazy family. Oh, he told me I was perfect and beautiful and brilliant. But they all say that. They want to be allowed to love you and to make everything perfect for you. They promise you that, and you're supposed to mold yourself around them. Merge with their dreams. Be a cheering section and a mother and a damsel in distress they can rescue. If you ever get tired of those roles, they'll leave you. John McNamara left me because I wanted him to grow up and provide for me and make me a home like men are supposed to."

"Mom . . ." I said. "Please, Mom." Hot tears ran down my face and onto my lips. "Please . . ."

She didn't hear me. "Daddy became a drunk and lost his job and threw away all our money. So when you got sick, Momma, there was nothing I could do but put you in the nursing home. I won't end up old and decrepit in a county home like you, Momma. Do you hear me? I won't."

She began a new set of ballet steps and pirouetted around the room. "Todd was going to be a big important artist and make all kinds of money, and we were going to live in Connecticut in a country house with ponies and dogs. We were going to cruise the Greek isles in a yacht. He never made any money. His paintings wouldn't sell. I tried to suggest another line of work, but he wouldn't listen. He was heir to a big fortune. The huge Broderick fortune that was going to set us up royally. We'd travel abroad and take a villa in Italy for a year. The girls would learn to speak Italian and study painting."

She laughed after that. In little gulps. She was laughing so hard, it kept her from dancing. "It was all fables and lies and moonglow. And now it's come to this, Momma. My wonderful rich husband, Todd Broderick. He's molested his little daughter. Did you hear that, Momma? He molested her."

She broke down then. The laughter turned to hysterical tears. I reached for her.

"Mom," I whispered, "Todd didn't do anything to Ria.

I know. Ask her. She's a little kid. She wouldn't lie. It was Bubba."

"Don't ever believe men," my mother kept saying, really to no one in particular. In fact, I am not sure that she knew I was there. "Momma, you were right. I should have never believed those bright promises. Once you give them sex, they've got all they want. There's nothing more. Just lust and lies. Hear that, Momma? Sounds like the title to a movie, doesn't it. Lust and lies."

"Mom," I pleaded. "Stop this. You've got to stop this." I was sobbing. I knelt down in front of my mother and hugged her shoulders. "Please, Mom, tell me you're going to be all right."

She pressed her face to my knees. I felt her fine blond hair so like spun gold.

"Alice," Daria interrupted us, from out on the front porch, "isn't it time to go to school?"

"Yes," Mother said. "We must go to school. I have to pack up my ballet clothes, and then we'll go."

From outside on the stoop, her face pressed against the screen door, Ria looked puzzled.

"Let's go," I told her. "Come on or we'll be late."

I didn't want Ria to know. Our mother had gone crazy.

32

Gossip

At school, I saw Gwen talking to little knots of girls. They all turned and stared at me when I came down the hall. Some giggled behind their hands.

The hideous Jennifer Rowland was sitting behind me in French class. I couldn't stand her. She was such a priss-pot. The teacher had gone out of the room, and we were conjugating irregular verbs on a work sheet.

"Psst," she whispered.

"What?" I said rather loudly. Heads turned. Jennifer went silent.

Finally, when I had forgotten she was there, she poked me in the back with the sharp end of her pencil. "Hey, Alice," she hissed.

"What?" I said again, just as loudly.

"What's it like?"

I seized up. I knew what was coming. "What's what like?"

"What's it like to *do it* with your own father?"

The room was dead silent.

Then wild laughter burst forth. Gwen was hooting along with them.

I couldn't believe it. Things were bad enough without this. Gwen must have told everyone. I knew it had to be Gwen. Aunt Thelma would never tolerate a breath of scandal about a Broderick. I dug my nails into my hands and cursed to myself soundlessly. Gwen was truly a twisted, horrible bitch.

At lunch, I found myself alone at a table in the cafeteria. No one would sit with me. Giggling and laughing, Gwen was strutting around like she was some social queen bee.

I picked at my food. When Gwen flounced over, I groaned inwardly. Was she going to be all virtuous and try to lift the sinner up from the gutter?

She settled herself heavily in a chair.

"Why are you by yourself?" she asked.

"You know why," I answered. I felt like dumping my plate on her head.

"Some folks like to think Ashcroft girls are snobby and stuck-up," she said, "but that's just because they're jealous of us. And they're afraid of us because they know we have high standards of both academic achievement and deportment. We know that our position in society brings with it the responsibility to maintain a strong moral order. This is something that you are simply going to have to learn if you intend to remain among us."

"Who helped you memorize that mouthful?" I asked.

Gwen looked startled. The wheels turned slowly in her head. "Todd murdered his own sister!" she spat out. "He hated her because she was pretty and Senior loved her the most—so he set the Christmas tree on fire and put her into it."

I was hard. Hard as nails. Nothing she could have said would have startled me at that point. I was cool. Cool as ice. I wanted to savage her in return. "Does your mother know you're spreading that around town?" I retorted. "If she knew you were letting out scandal about the Brodericks, she'd whip you bloody."

Gwen's face turned a deathly pale.

"Bed wetter," I added viciously.

Gwen's composure disintegrated. She knocked over the chair and stood in the middle of the floor bawling. Her fat knees rubbed against each other and a trail of urine ran down her legs to puddle on the floor. Every eye in the cafeteria was on us.

My cousin's crying got worse and worse and finally reached uncontrolled hysteria. Though she was taken to the school nurse, she still wouldn't calm down. My aunt had to come and pick her up. But Gwen screamed and yelled and wouldn't get into the car.

"I didn't do anything," she wailed. "I didn't do anything wrong!"

While every girl in the school watched from the windows, Aunt Thelma gave her daughter a good cuff to the head.

Naturally, I was sent to Headmistress Carson. She scowled at me as she instructed me to stand in front of her desk.

"Just what did you do to your cousin?" she asked sternly.

"I'm not sure."

"*You're not sure,*" she said, emphasizing each word.

"I mean it could have been my calling her a bed wetter, but more likely it was my telling her Aunt Thelma would whip her for spreading lies about the Brodericks."

Headmistress Carson didn't react to my smart-aleck response. She was moving cautiously. "I see," she said. "You know, Alice McNamara, when you were last here, I expressed fears that something unpleasant might grow out of the . . . the incident with your sister."

"Yes," I said simply. "You did."

"It's not easy for outsiders to understand what we are all about here at Ashcroft. There are those who, through jealousy, feel that Ashcroft girls are snobby . . . or stuck-up. In fact, they're afraid of our girls and of their achievement, which is gained through the highest academic standards as well as deportment."

"I know," I said. "Position in society brings with it the responsibility of maintaining a strong moral order. That's something I'm simply going to have to learn if I expect to remain among you."

Headmistress Carson bridled. An imperious eyebrow shot up.

"Gwen taught me that," I said. "She likes a strong moral order."

At that moment, I wanted to be expelled. I didn't want ever to have to spend another day at Ashcroft School.

But Headmistress Carson proudly held her temper. She was dealing with Brodericks, after all. Even if I was a fake one. "In my opinion, you would be much happier in the public schools. Your aunt Thelma, however, insists that you remain here."

I was dismissed without further ado.

When school let out, I trudged out of the classroom building with girls staring at me and talking behind their hands. Out on the lawns, Daria was being chased by a group of small boys from the preschool. I couldn't tell what they were saying, but she was crying. I ran them off. Afterward, we sat on the edge of the fountain and I held her in my arms.

We sat for a long time, holding each other. From our spot we could see the cars roll up to get the girls. Mercedeses, Cadillacs, Jeep Wagoneers, vans, station wagons. Endless car pools of girls being carted around by mothers in perky, sensible haircuts and practical clothes.

At last they were all gone and silence fell upon the grounds. An old janitor pushed a cart along the walk and disappeared into one of the classroom buildings.

Daria sat perfectly still in my arms. Her lethargy was unnatural. Yet I knew the cause. Our world had become a nightmare. We were lost in a dreamscape and couldn't find our way out. All we had was each other.

At last, I stirred and lifted her up. "Come on, Ria. Let's head for home."

Then I noticed someone standing across the street. I could barely see him since he was leaning up against a tree behind a parked car. He was very still and watchful, as if he had noted every face that emerged from the school and not found ours.

It was Bubba. He was wearing his brass-studded gloves with the fingers cut out. He was sucking his thumb.

33

Distant Sadness

The next day, Todd and Mom were waiting outside school at three o'clock. I briefly felt solid and good. Maybe Mom was all right again and we would be a family, unaffected by the ugly things the kids said about us.

Mom led Daria toward home and Todd told me we were going downtown together. Silently I accompanied him through blocks of big houses until we got to the shabby small ones and then the streets of downtown. Finally I asked him what was going on.

Todd walked tilted slightly forward, like he might fall over if he wasn't careful. "We're gonna see a lawyer," he mumbled in a slurred voice. "I'm gonna adopt you and make you my daughter the way you're supposed to be. It's the only way to get at them."

I didn't say anything. I didn't care exactly. He wanted me to be his daughter for the money. Fine. If that was what he wanted, I'd do it. What did I care what my last name was? I would be loyal to Todd and Mom.

"Sure, Todd," I said finally. "Will that make it all better? I mean, you and Mom seem so upset all the time."

Todd put his arm around me and pulled me to him. "Maybe," he said. "Maybe it will make it all better."

Down rows of dingy brick facades we walked, past neon, faded green awnings, and aluminum siding. We passed the Paramount Theater, which was devoted exclusively to kung fu movies now. Passed the Delight Luncheonette, where a policeman was the only one at the counter, his cruiser parked outside in front of a fire hydrant. Jake's Shoe Repair. Woolworth's.

Todd was talking not really to me—more to himself. "Best durn lawyer in town. If anybody can win a hopeless case, it's Byron Mizell. Senior used to swear by him. Not for the corporate work, mind you, just when the bank got sued."

I followed along, reached out to hold his hand.

Eventually we stopped outside a run-down frame building. Inside, the stairs had carpet with big holes in each step. At the top of the staircase was a paper bag and Coke bottle where someone had sat and eaten their lunch and left the trash. Also, there was a door that said:

BYRON MIZELL
ATTORNEY-AT-LAW

An old secretary with bifocals and a chintz-pattern dress crooned into the intercom to announce Todd and me. A big watermelon and a basket of squishy-looking tomatoes sat beside her desk. "Come on in!" boomed a deep voice. Obediently, we went into a room of old oak furniture with cigarette burns on the edges like the tick-marks on a ruler.

The first thing I noticed was a Norman Rockwell calendar with boys swimming in a fishing hole hanging on the wall. Bird dogs on a point in a broomsage field were under dusty glass. Plus a framed diploma from the state law school with a date forty years ago.

Byron Mizell had dark sweat stains under his armpits and red suspenders that slouched to either side of his big stomach. His white shirt spread between the buttons. He had snow-white hair and a fat tie with a sunrise handpainted on it.

He was filled with loud good humor. "This your daughter? Mighty pretty girl. Mighty pretty. How old are you, sweetheart?"

"Thirteen," I answered.

"Lord, you're about the age of one of my granddaughters." He rubbed the back of his neck, hit his gut with his fist, and slapped the desktop to emphasize his pleasure in meeting someone so perfect as myself.

From under the desk, his feet were visible. He was wearing leather bedroom slippers with crushed-down backs.

"Todd, it's good to see you. Been a long time. Too long. We've missed you down here. Hope you're here to stay. I been knowing you since you was scampering around behind Senior. You were quite the boy. Always did have a mind of your own. Standing up to your daddy right from the beginning. Talking back to him before you was even in school. Old Senior he was proud of that. Uh-huh, you bet he was. Used to show you off. 'That boy's got a mind of his own,' he'd say. 'That boy will measure up. Yessir, he will measure up.' "

His chin down in his chest, Todd mumbled a reply. "Yeah, right."

"So tell me all about New York," Mizell continued. "You making a living painting and all that? What do you think of that picture of bird dogs there on that wall? Think it's worth any money? Hell, I ought to hire you to paint me something. What kinda pictures do you sell up there in New York?"

I looked at the door. Half of it was pebbled glass. You could read *Attorney-at-Law* backward through it. I looked back at Byron Mizell. He was talking to fill a void. Almost like he didn't want Todd to have a chance to say anything.

"Look, Byron," Todd interrupted finally, "I need some help. I want to adopt Alice."

Byron looked surprised. "What? Adopt? I thought she was your daughter."

"I already explained it all to you over the phone. The whole sordid thing. You knew Senior. You know how the Brodericks operate. I need help. Are you going to help me or not?"

Byron leaned back in his chair and folded his hands. "Well, now, I'll be glad to help you, m'boy. But . . ." He lowered his voice. "Excuse my French but you've shit pretty bad in your own bed. I don't want to have to talk harsh to you. I know you artist types are kinda wild—drinking and running around and liking to shock ordinary folks. Being a Broderick, you maybe grew up thinking you could get by with anything. But some messes nobody can clean up."

Todd twisted the buttons on his shirt. "Hey, wait a minute. What are you talking about?"

"To adopt a kid, you got to be adjudged a fit parent by the Welfare Department."

"Fit? Of course I'm a fit parent. I've raised my daughter Daria. And I've raised Alice since she was a toddler. Come on, man. Pull out the legal forms and let's get this thing going."

Byron opened his desk drawer and slammed it shut again. "Todd, I don't think you want Welfare looking at you too close right now. I mean I wouldn't push the whole thing."

"What whole thing?"

"Word is pretty much out that you . . . uh . . . well, word round the courthouse is there might be an investigation by Welfare and maybe your real daughter gets taken from you."

Todd put his head in his hands. I couldn't tell if he was crying or not. But when he looked up, his eyes were clear. "Wheeler and Thelma are behind this. All that crazy crap about what happened to Daria. It's all lies. I have witnesses."

"Who?" Byron asked. "A five-year-old who hardly knows what's going on. Alice here? Look, Todd, they'll twist that around. They'll say the only reason she's on your side is for money."

Todd stood up and propped himself on the back of his chair. He seemed very unsteady. "So what do you suggest I do? Crawl over in a corner and die? Let these bastards get the best of me?"

Byron looked out the window for a long time. It, too, was painted with BYRON MIZELL ATTORNEY-AT-LAW, as if he was afraid someone might not know who he was. Pigeons roosted on the air-conditioning unit, drinking the water from it, throwing their heads back to swallow. The silence was deafening.

"You don't know the half of it," said Byron. "I'm an old man. I've seen near about everything. But this here is particularly vicious. Look, Todd, I'm willing to help you in every way that I can. I like you. Even more, I believe you. But you know as well as I do that Wheeler and Thelma are very powerful in this town. They talked that psychologist into their corner. They will threaten and terrorize and do whatever is necessary. I've seen them in action. Everybody in this town has at one time or another."

"So what is it, Byron? Spit it out. You're beholden to Wheeler in some way or other, aren't you? You've got to ask his permission, haven't you?" Todd's voice had risen with every word until he was virtually yelling. "You've got to call Wheeler and get his permission to do this. Well, I don't want you, then. I spent my whole life bowing and scraping to Senior and now I'm supposed to do the same to my sorry, thieving brother-in-law. Well, I'm not doing it."

"I'm sorry," Byron Mizell said. "I'm really sorry. It's just that . . . well, my daughter-in-law works for Wheeler and my son just took out a big loan for a restaurant he wants to start. I know it's a bitch."

Todd gave out something like a groan. "Who else will help me if it's not you?"

"Hey," Byron said, "why don't you let me give you some advice? Get out of here with your family. Forget about the money. Go somewhere and start all over again. You're young enough. Who knows, maybe someday Wheeler and Thelma will croak and you can break the will. Otherwise it's only a matter of time before they strip you of everything."

We walked home past trees with leaves withered by heat. Todd tried to talk and even make some jokes, but his voice was husky as he choked back tears.

I wanted to make him laugh. "Todd, remember how we

used to go into Chinese delicatessens in New York and eat eggrolls and have those awful bean curd milkshakes that tasted terrible? And when Daria was little, she'd take a sip of one and say 'nassy nassy' and we'd try to explain to her that it was supposed to be 'nasty' and we'd all laugh?"

Todd's eyes took on a deep and distant sadness.

"Todd, let's go away together just like Mr. Mizell said. We'll start all over again. I'm even old enough to help out and get a job. I can lie about my age and pick up some money. We'll be all right. And then you can adopt me. I'd love to be your daughter. If we go back to New York, it's too far away for them to care about us. One day we'll come back and beat them."

Todd wasn't listening. He wasn't even beside me. I looked back. He was just standing there staring off into space. I walked back and took his hand. He looked down at his shoes and pulled them slowly from the pavement. Long strands of pink bubble gum had fastened to them as if to hold him to the hot cement.

He seemed puzzled, disoriented. "It's only a matter of time before they'll strip you of everything," he said, repeating Byron's words.

34

Mater and Pater

The sun went down, making the clouds orange rags. Todd had been dazed and lost all the way home, dragging the foot with the gum stuck to the bottom, muttering inaudibly. Once he had even called me "Thelma" and looked at me as if he wasn't really sure who I was.

I barely got him home and into the carriage house before Jeremy was at the door telling me I was summoned to see his parents.

"What on earth have you been up to?" he whispered outside. "All hell seems to have broken loose over at Ogre Mansion from the sounds of the shouting. Mater and Pater were ordered over there, which provoked even more extensive shouting and yelling."

I shrugged, knowing the truth.

At the Woolcott house, Jeremy and I sat in the sunroom waiting for Norman and Kate to appear. We could hear whispering and movement in the other room, signs of their usual vague consternation now made more intense.

Finally, Aunt Kate came in wringing her hands. "We . . . we want you to stay for supper," she said. "It's acceptable to your mother. And your aunt Thelma."

Jeremy and I exchanged glances. "Okay, sure," I said. "Thanks." It was moments like that when I felt I needed to study a nineteenth-century etiquette book.

Kate went to banging around in the kitchen. Norman joined her. Cabinets opened and closed.

"What on earth is going on?" I asked.

"It's just them," Jeremy said. "They barely get through breakfast. The idea of another meal is defeating them. I usually feed myself."

After more time, Norman came in looking tentative. "Your aunt Kate neglected to put any meat out to thaw. She's going to drive to the store."

"You don't need to go to that kind of trouble," I protested. Actually, I felt a great urge to get out of there.

But Norman had all the time in the world. He pulled up a chair, set a book on his lap. "No. No. It will give us an opportunity to talk. We don't really know each other."

"Oh. Hey. Great," I said without enthusiasm. Jeremy rolled his eyes in disgust.

"Alice . . . um Alice, what is your last name?" said Norman. "I find my memory has taken a sudden lapse."

"It's McNamara," I said.

"Oh yes. McNamara. A very attractive name. Even a noble name."

"Yeah. I guess. I don't think about it much. It's just my name."

He clutched the book to his thin chest with bony hands. It was deep blue. I couldn't see the title. For the first time, I became aware of how old Jeremy's father must be! He was more like a grandfather! Except he couldn't be that old. His hair wasn't entirely gray and there weren't all that many wrinkles on his face. He just acted old—as if every bone in his body ached.

"Do you love your father?"

"I've never met my father."

That seemed to throw him. "Oh. Well, you can love him anyway."

"It's a little tough," I said ruefully. "I mean I can't picture how he looks. And I don't know anything about him."

A light bulb seemed to go on in Norman's head. "Well —well, yes. You can love him like you love God the Father."

I reacted like any teenager confronted with adult idiocy. Monosyllables. "Sure. Okay."

This encouraged him. "Well, we've established that you still love your father. Good. Now, you wouldn't want to hurt him in any way, would you?"

The light turned on in my head. I was disgusted. "Don't worry. I'm not getting adopted by Todd. No lawyer in town will touch it. Unless we go somewhere else to do it. New York or someplace."

Blood drained out of Norman's already pale face. "Oh, you wouldn't do that."

"No," I said sourly. "We're never going back there."

"I mean you must agree it simply wouldn't be right to be adopted. There's not just your father's memory to think of. There's all the feelings of others. Daria, for instance. I mean it's like you'd be taking something from her. Kind of crowding into her parentage where you didn't really belong. Confusing things for her. And for Jeremy."

"Pater, what are you talking about?" Jeremy interrupted. "What's going on around here?"

This threw Norman into even more of a fluster. "This . . . this whole business with the money is so complicated as it is, I just get confused. Trying to read all those unfamiliar documents with all that legal language. I'm trained in the church, which has a different sort of language altogether. And now, Alice McNamara, if you create even more complications . . . why . . . why it would just get all snarled and twisted around . . . and . . . and there'd be lawsuits and goodness knows what all."

"Pater, you're making no sense whatsoever," said Jeremy.

Norman sprang to his feet as if he had sat on a tack or was on a spring or something. "I have to check on Mrs. Woolcott," he exclaimed. "She should be back by now. There's dinner to think of. We have a guest."

"She hasn't left yet," said Jeremy.

But Norman didn't hear. He scuttled out into the

kitchen. "Mrs. Woolcott," I heard him say distantly. "You're back. My that was quick."

"Back?" she said in her nasal voice.

"From the store."

"Oh." There was a silence. "I thought I'd best water the plants before I went. Guess I got preoccupied. You know how I am."

"Oh dear," said Norman. "Well, perhaps we'd best forget the whole thing. We can find something in the cupboards. Never mind."

They banged around some more in that kitchen that was festering with mildew, peeling paint, wood rot, and cockroaches.

"Perhaps a nice lentil soup?" suggested Kate.

"Yes. Yes, that would be fine."

"I'm not sure we have any lentils. And they properly should be soaked for several hours beforehand."

Jeremy apologized for his parents. This was worse than normal and hard even for him to bear. He had never quite seen them so bad. Uncle Wheeler and Aunt Thelma had been bellowing at them and had put them into utter confusion.

Norman returned, still holding his book. He sat down again. "Since things are a little delayed, I thought we could talk some more. We're getting along so well and making headway on major issues. Settling our differences, so to speak."

"Pater, don't read that awful thing to Alice," objected Jeremy.

He didn't seem to hear. "You and Jeremy are becoming such fast friends. I know you wouldn't want to do anything to injure him. Diminish his . . . his status with the Broderick family. And . . . and given your age . . . both your ages . . . best that you understand a few basic matters."

"Pater, please. This is embarrassing. Ridiculously embarrassing."

Undeterred, Norman held up the book. "This is a volume of the *General Statutes.* I'm going to read to you from the criminal code."

Scowling and drumming his fingers together, Jeremy thrashed around in his chair and threw his legs up over an arm.

"Now I'm not accusing you of anything, Alice McNamara. Far from it. I just want to avoid problems in the future. I . . . my sister-in-law—your aunt Thelma and I feel it best if you understand how . . . how serious certain actions can be."

He opened the book to a marked page and began to read aloud concisely, emphasizing each word with a dry precision.

"Criminal sexual conduct: definitions.

a. 'Intimate parts' includes the primary genital area, anus, groin, inner thighs, or buttocks of a male or female human being and the breasts of a female human being.

b. 'Sexual battery' means sexual intercourse, cunnilingus, fellatio, anal intercourse, or any intrusion, however slight, of any part of a person's body or of any object into the genital or anal openings of another person's body, except when such intrusion is accomplished for medically recognized treatment or diagnostic purposes."

I stared at Jeremy, but he wouldn't meet my eyes.

Next, Norman began reading selected parts that applied to my age. As he began to roll the words off his tongue, he produced something like oratory.

"Criminal sexual conduct with minors.

A person is guilty of criminal sexual conduct in the second degree if the actor engages in sexual battery with a victim who is fourteen years of age or less but who is at least eleven years of age."

I was stunned beyond belief. The man was a lunatic.
No, that was wrong. He was just a nitwit. It was Aunt
Thelma and her ridiculous obsession with the evils of sex.
She had put him up to this. He was frightened half to death
just reading it.

Aunt Thelma. Thelma the spider. Thelma who didn't
want me in the family stripping Bubba and Gwen of their
share of the money. Thelma who didn't want me around at
all. The scarlet New York City tart leads Jeremy to sin and
destruction and the Broderick bank along with him. The
bank collapses and all Brodericks end up in the gutter because of Alice McNamara's uncontrolled harlot lust.

It was laughable on one hand. But on the other, it was
too horrible to bear.

35

The Dreadful Image

As had come to be customary, Daria and I walked through the St. Michael's graveyard on our way home from school. On our approach, a flock of birds scattered and took to the treetops. I kept Ria away from the tombstone of the first Daria. Daria the First. Princess of the Darkness to Come.

Everyone snubbed us at school now—like they had been told by their parents we were unclean and even picking on us would spread our infection.

The earth among the graves seemed cool and rich. Oak tree shaded in the heat of midafternoon. I dropped my books and held my arms up to the clouds, asking them to take me up to a dreamland of cloud-cushioned ease and peace. Throwing my head back to see only sky made me dizzy. Daria asked what I was doing and I stopped, collected my books and walked on. She said I was a "silly Billy." We went through the rusted gate into the space behind the carriage house.

When we got home, we ate peanut butter crackers. I took my shoes off. Daria went upstairs followed by warnings from Mom not to make a mess with crumbs.

Across the broad lawn, Uncle Wheeler drove up in the Cadillac. Todd was beside him in the front seat. I went barefooted out into the yard to greet Todd. Mom was right behind me.

Uncle Wheeler climbed out of the car. I ran a few steps

toward the car, then stopped. My uncle flashed a smile of false warmth. "Your stepfather will be feeling better soon," he said to me. "He needs to lie down."

Staring across the yard, Todd sat in the car. He didn't seem to see any of us.

"Todd . . ." Mom began.

"Go back in the house, Amy," he whispered. He wasn't looking at us. It was like he could hear, but not see. "I don't need your pity."

"Todd had a little problem at the bank today," explained my uncle. "Word seems to be getting around about his . . . perversion. The employees find his presence . . . well, shall I say less than wholesome."

"You told them all," Todd said softly. "You've disgraced my name. You had a special meeting just to humiliate me."

"You're a sick man, Todd, I'm sorry to say. I don't know which is worse—your imaginary fears of everyone you meet or the demented way you work out your frustrations. I'm not as religious as my wife. I'm more practical and more inclined to believe man finds his own salvation right here on earth through good works. Maybe because I'm practical I'm inclined to believe in solutions for most things. Thelma's the fatalist. I think there's always hope for even the worst among men."

"I knew when they all came out of your office that you had told them," Todd whispered. "I could see it in their eyes."

Todd had never been in such a state. But I knew what was happening. They had broken his will. In that one instant I understood the Broderick madness. The vacuous mindlessness of Norman and Kate, the craziness of Gladys in the attic, the perversity of Bubba and Gwen—it was the only true escape.

Uncle Wheeler stood leaning on the open car door looking in at Todd. "I want to send you someplace where you can get professional help. Not here in Congreve, of course, because there's too much risk of word getting out."

"Bullshit," muttered Todd. "You've told everyone. Word is already out. Todd Broderick is a pervert and no child in Congreve is safe. You've told everyone and now the bank is at risk and depositors will run on the bank and the panic will spread. The whole banking system of the state of Georgia will come tumbling down like a house of cards despite the best efforts of the Federal Reserve System, the U.S. Treasury, and the White House." Todd gave a cackling laugh, cynical, mirthless, mad. He even slapped on the dashboard and stamped both feet several times.

"I'm really sorry for you, Todd," Uncle Wheeler continued. "But accepting the reality of your sickness is the first step toward a cure. That's one thing I learned from Senior himself."

Todd turned burning eyes on him. "You're not locking me off in some nuthouse!" he said fiercely.

"It's a sickness, Todd. It's in the family. Craziness runs in the family and can strike anywhere. Look at your mother." He gestured toward the upstairs windows.

Todd suddenly boiled out of the car in a violent wrath. "I'll kill you for saying that, you son of a bitch! I'll kill you."

Uncle Wheeler backed up. He seemed truly frightened, but was unable to run or lift his hands in defense. "Don't you—don't you—don't—" he stammered.

"I'll kill you, do you hear me!" raged Todd. He was out of the car now, his fists balled, his face flaming crimson. He was filled with the furor of an outraged beast.

Silently, I egged him on. I wanted him to hammer Uncle Wheeler into the dirt. Beat him down into broken bones and jelly and grind the muck into gobs.

"*Todd!*" bellowed the familiar voice. There, in the doorway of the big house, stood Aunt Thelma, hands on her hips, head thrust forward.

Todd froze. His fists fell to his sides. His shoulders slumped. In that short span of time, Uncle Wheeler regained his courage. "Perhaps you'd enjoy a taste of jail," he said sternly. "Assault upon prominent citizens is frowned on in

Congreve even in these lax times. A good thirty days for threatening me might give you some idea of what it would be like if the whole sordid incident regarding your daughter was brought to a court of law."

Todd wasn't listening. I don't think he really heard a word of what was said. His face was a window on an abandoned house. Slowly, he trudged toward the carriage house. Halfway, he peeled out of his suit jacket and let it drop on the grass. Uncle Wheeler followed behind him with threats and commands.

"You will stay in this house until you agree to professional help. I'm calling some hospitals tonight and making arrangements. If you balk, I'll keep you here until you submit. If you try to go out, I'll have the police arrest you and hold you for sex crimes."

Todd staggered through the door and out of sight.

Filled with relief and bravado, Uncle Wheeler shouted after him: "No one threatens Wheeler Broderick without regretting it, I can tell you that! Your life has been a bed of roses up to now. You're nothing but a spoiled, immature brat. But it's all over! I'll show you! I'll fix you!"

36

Solitary Sleep

Her head bent with fatigue, Alberta
trudged down the street toward her home off the peninsula.
The sounds of twilight had come out of hiding. A hot wind
came in off the sea and crooned among the trees around the
dark house. A loose windowpane rattled. The rusted rooster
weather vane on top of the turret creaked.

The house was filled with shadows like gathering ghosts.
It was a dusty crypt where no joy ever entered.

I stood in the dining room looking at the photos of the
lost Daria and trembled to think of her fiery death. Her
happy face had such a haunted look.

I thought of the crazed old woman at the top of the
house with her dirty gray hair hanging like tangled Spanish
moss in the trees outside. Her brain banished by tragedy.
Solitary in her madness, yet ever watchful through that upper window like a baleful eye. Dwelling in the dreadful dark
attic where the sun never seemed to enter.

Ria had told me the woman just sat there staring. Once
the woman had touched her curls. Said nothing, just
touched poor little Ria's curls.

I wondered if the woman would talk to me if I spoke to
her through the door. Maybe she'd like a kid's voice? She
might say something that could help us. It was worth a try.
What was one more whipping?

I went up the stairs as if I were undertaking a long, dusty
journey. Tentatively, I passed the weird stained-glass window

with the fake Broderick coat of arms and the little girl's head
set with wings in multicolors. The higher I went, the more
doubts assailed me. Fears crept in. Would Bubba be waiting
to grab me in an embrace of twisted passion? Would he bur-
row into me with his dirty fingers and ravenous eyes?

Would the old hag come rushing out with a carving
knife or a blazing Christmas tree to hunt me down in some
corner where my screams could not be heard?

A long, dark shadow swung past my eyes. Slowly.
Slowly. Then returned. I looked up. I saw the feet just
slightly above my head. The toes of old tennis shoes were
pointed downward.

Someone was hanging. Twisting slowly at the end of a
rope.

My brain seemed abstracted. "Who is it?" I said aloud
to myself. Stupidly.

I received no answer.

A note was pinned to the trouser cuff by a safety pin. I
went up two more steps. Touched it with trembling hands.
The legs still swung just a bit. I grasped the trousers and held
them still. Read the farewell message.

I have done no wrong. All I ever did was try to love.

                                                        Todd.

His face was purple and twisted. His tongue protruded
and his eyes bugged outward. It wasn't Todd; of course it
wasn't Todd. It was some hideous copy of him. I forced myself to look. Grasped the rail so as not to fall backward.
Stifled a cry.

The choking expression. The purpled gagging. It was
Todd. Truly Todd. Hanged. Strangled to death. Perished
with all his sorrows and wrongs and troubles.

Yet, somehow, he was sleeping. Sleeping like a child.
Lost in solitary sleep.

As I watched I imagined his head gave a little jerk, but
knew it was only an illusion. He was gone to some never-land

where dreams and hopes and things that could never be all went.

I wanted to say something to him, to remind him of something funny that had happened when we had all been happy. The time he had bought a car we didn't need, for eight hundred dollars: an old Chevy Malibu with the back window busted out and one side a mess of rust primer. New York has opposite-side-of-the-street parking. At night you can park on one side; in the day, the other. Which means to avoid paying for a garage, you have to shift your car with the time changes. And everybody is fighting for the limited spaces. So, to be ready for the big traffic shift, Todd would go out into the car an hour in advance and read a book. We thought it was a scream. But he got bored with that and the car didn't work very well anyhow, so he sold it to somebody for four hundred dollars. That was how we had lived. Not sweating the small stuff. And Todd with his free-spirited attitude had been the center of it all.

The rope creaked. In the heavy gloom it was impossible to see from where it was suspended. I didn't even want to think about how he had strung it up.

Without noise or clamor, I turned and walked back down the stairs. I might have been sleepwalking out of that dream world where Todd had gone and from which he could never return.

My mind was filled with such a jumble of recollections that I could not sort them out. I could not even focus long enough to feel grief or passion.

I remembered walking over the Brooklyn Bridge and down to the giant iron chickens and ducks in the park. Ria was a little baby and Todd would push her in the stroller and I'd roller-skate. How many people have you known who've roller-skated over the Brooklyn Bridge? Not many, I'll bet. But I thought nothing of it at the time—except we were way up in the air over the river and we were happy and free. I didn't really know what freedom was then. I just felt freedom, just sensed that something special and rare was happening.

In the Congreve sky, the ibis were flying in squadrons to their nests on the islands in the river. The trees were black and sullen.

I walked into the carriage house, my mind in a daze. My mother was there. Her cheeks were flushed with the red of alcohol. Her eyes were glittering and bright.

"How's my pretty girl?" she asked.

"Todd's dead," I murmured.

She looked at me in the most calm and quiet manner imaginable. "Dead?"

"He . . . he's hanged himself in the stairwell."

"He's actually . . . dead?"

"Yes."

"Did a doctor come?"

"I don't know. When I left, he was still . . . hanging there."

My mother was so placid and unmoved. "Well. I suppose he won't be able to adopt you now. You won't ever be a Broderick. You won't be able to increase our share of the money."

I couldn't help it. I broke down. I began to scream uncontrollably.

37

Final Darkness

They wouldn't let Jeremy near me at the funeral. I could see Kate holding tightly to him and pulling him back whenever he tried to slide in my direction. The regular minister, with Norman to help, said things I've completely forgotten. Not a word of it registered even at the time.

Nameless men carried Todd's coffin out. Daria watched with a kind of dumb misery. I wasn't really sure she realized what had happened. We all filed out slowly and packed into long black limousines with tepid air-conditioning. There was a police car in front and a line of cars behind us with their headlights on. The limousine driver talked in callous platitudes about how the town was changing so much, he hardly knew it. The Broderick bank was really backing good growth.

The graveyard was new and treeless, baking in the heat. Old women held umbrellas over their heads against the sun. Aunt Thelma and Gwen got hold of Daria and pulled her away. Mom raised no objections. She was humming a snatch of a tune which I couldn't identify. For a moment I almost thought she was going to dance.

I remembered cold winters in New York where the soot seemed pasted to the buildings, the pipes froze and hung with icicles, and our breath made puffs in the air. Todd would take me to a restaurant in Little Italy for a steaming cup of cappuccino with thick cream and chocolate flakes and little rolled lemony cookies.

An awning shaded the open grave. The coffin was a mahogany box with brass handles sitting on a pile of dried-out earth. Garish floral wreaths on little tripods adorned the tomb. Uncle Wheeler kept looking at my mother and fingering his thin mustache.

I remembered Todd reeking of turpentine, in his paint-soaked overalls like he had rolled in vermilion and crimson and Prussian blue and cerulean blue and aquamarine. He would have wanted his coffin painted like a Gypsy wagon, covered with bright designs and magic symbols!

I looked at my mother's profile. The lines of her face were so perfect and beautiful, slim and fine-boned. Her eyes were as green as a warm tropical sea. No man could help but be attracted to her. Todd had loved her.

I remembered how Todd took us out to Southampton one summer to stay in a tiny rented room and play in the surf among the gilded rich. And how he and my mother laughed in the sun, sand, and surf and said we were rich in spirit. We were artists and better than anyone with money because we were free.

Beneath the awning, one hand lifted limply, Norman stood in his ministerial white over black.

"So beloved of all, this man who sought beauty in the midst of pain and who fought valiantly against the perils of life."

Norman was like an apparition, a wavering candle flame. The words didn't seem to be coming out of his mouth. They were disconnected, like his own vague grip on reality. I felt dizzy. Then, as if acting out my dizziness, Norman tottered on the edge of the open hole and simply fell in.

A gasp went up from the crowd of mourners. My throat felt clogged.

Norman emerged from the dry, dusty hole, struggling, climbing out with the assistance of many hands, brushing red dirt from his cassock.

"Lost my grip," he mumbled helplessly. "Don't quite understand it. The heat. Overwhelmed." Then he simply sat down on the pile of earth. A slumped-over, pale man, talking gently to himself and plucking at his cuffs.

"It's sunstroke," said Kate. "He was nearly killed by it in Uganda. He should never go out without a hat."

I remembered the galleries in SoHo where Todd would take his work. Each of us would carry a huge canvas, parading like circus performers to meet the owners and applaud as the pictures were hung on the gallery walls.

Throughout the endless ceremony, my mother seemed calm and composed. Her mind was a million miles away and she did not shed a single tear.

The coffin was lowered into final darkness.

As the crowd dispersed we walked apart from the others and wandered as if by design out among the stark new tombstones littered with rain-ruined paper flowers.

"Mom, let's cut and run."

She looked surprised. "What do you mean?" she asked.

I tried my best to sound practical, sane, and organized, and to act like I had a viable plan. "I mean, let's get out of Congreve. Let's get out before we end up in a box too. Or something even worse happens to Daria. Now look, I know we don't have any money so don't raise that as an objection. We'll hitchhike back to New York. It shouldn't take more than two days. We'll pack enough food from the kitchen to last. We'll stay with your friends in the city until you find a job. I'll work after school. We'll make it somehow."

"I am going to have to rely on you, Alice."

"Sure. But I'm tough. A concentration camp would seem fun after Congreve."

"You'll have to look after Daria a lot more. You're going to have to grow up and get rid of your childish fantasies."

"Fantasies?"

"Yes. About Bubba and . . . and things you imagine he's done to your sister."

I might as well have been talking Chinese. My mother hadn't heard a word I'd said.

"With Todd gone, everything falls to me. I feel like a huge weight has been placed on my shoulders." She gave a little laugh. "You're going to have to put these problems you've had at school behind you, Alice, and make a fresh start. I think you should begin by making friends with Gwen. She's terribly popular with all the girls at Ashcroft, and she could be your entrée into Congreve society. Gwen's very insulted by the rude way you've treated her. I really think an apology is in order. And one to your aunt Thelma as well."

"To Aunt Thelma?"

"She's had a lot of her time taken up by your bizarre tales to the social workers. It's been a great strain. But that's all behind us now. If we approach it right, we're going to have a bright and happy future."

I couldn't believe my ears. "Doing what?"

"Why, taking our place in society. There are so many things that go on in Congreve. With fall setting in, there'll be oyster roasts on the beach. And there's always something at the church. You'll meet young men your age instead of that silly, immature Jeremy. And Wheeler thinks you should move into the big house. That way, you can get to know Gwen better and you can become close friends."

Suddenly, I realized I was with an alien presence. My mother had gone mad. I had witnessed its beginning that morning many days ago before I went to school with Ria. There was no way I could reach her. I could never pierce her mask of insanity.

Then I saw Daria, her hand vanished in the big ham fist of Aunt Thelma. I had to take her and run away. We'd go off on our own. But where would we go? Roam the country like the runaways one sees on TV movies? Fall into the hands of Welfare Departments that would shove us into foster-care homes? No, we were trapped. There was no way out.

That night, the moon was like a rind of cheese eaten by rats. I dreamed of drug addicts and winos and babbling derelicts in the worst areas of New York. They had me surrounded. I ran and ran, fell over garbage cans, and saw Todd's body lying still and silent on the pavement. Jennifer Rowland, the hateful girl from school, stood at my elbow and hooted because Todd died and he was a child molester. Aunt Thelma lurked in the background slowly clapping her hands.

38
The Attic

I ran home from school as fast as I could, sprinting until the stitch in my side became unbearable. After school, Ria had been picked up by Aunt Thelma in the Cadillac. I had come out to meet her only to see them drive off together. They didn't want me with them. My aunt was up to something evil.

Birds scattered as I ran through the graveyard and crossed the big lawn to bound into our little carriage house. I called Ria's name. No one answered. Dropping my books in the middle of the floor, I sprinted across the lawn to the big house. Alberta was in the kitchen making applesauce. She looked at me out of the corner of an eye, refusing to catch my gaze. I rushed past her.

The attic. I knew it. My aunt had taken Ria there. Todd was barely buried in the ground and Aunt Thelma had control of my sister again.

Up the stairs I went. Then I heard Daria crying. I pressed my ear against the sealed entrance.

Daria was crying with soft, low sobs of misery.

"Come play with the nice toys under the tree," my aunt Thelma was saying. "Here, look here at this one."

I hammered on the door with both fists and kicked it with both feet. "You let Ria out of there!" I shouted. "You let my sister go!"

My aunt appeared at the door. She was snarling incoherently. Her bulk filled the space of the narrow door.

She shoved Ria out into my open arms.

"I'll deal with you later!" she threatened.

Her violent hostility followed us down the stairs. I heard the attic door close and a key turn in the lock.

Silently, I took Daria out of the big house and across the big lawn. Over into the St. Michael's graveyard to smell the rich earth and leaves, hear the song of birds, and be hidden from the brooding dark house with the upstairs windows.

I talked to her about anything that came to mind, desperately trying to fill the air with cheer. "We'll be going home soon. Mom will get a dancing part in a musical show and we'll move back home to New York. It's probably getting cold up there already. We'll have to have new overcoats."

Daria hadn't heard a word. Her face could have been shaped by wax. Everything was pent up inside her. Fear, hatred, loathing, pain. Nothing came out. She had retreated into internal safety. She was taking the same way out that Todd had taken.

With Todd's death, our family had been broken apart. And all of the pieces of the jigsaw puzzle were lost. Our world of the past had become a fairy tale, something lost deep inside a mountain, and we had forgotten the magic words to take us back.

I lavished tears on my sister and covered her with kisses. "Please, please talk to me, Ria," I begged.

"I shouldn't play with fire," she said at last. "The dolly told me not to."

"N-no," I gagged.

Her head lolled on her shoulders and her voice was low and intense. "If I play with fire the tree will catch fire and I'll burn up. And it will be my fault, not anybody else's."

I hugged her until her bones might have broken. "You're not that girl," I protested wildly. "She lived a long time ago. She's not here anymore."

"I'll be a bad girl if I play with fire," Ria repeated like a little wooden doll.

And then the dreadful silence fell over her once more.

I carried her through the weeds and bushes to the far end of the graveyard under the shadow of the crumbling wall. The world was bending and tilting at funny angles. I held her in front of the accursed gravestone—the gravestone of the older Daria Broderick. I used her fingers to trace the cherub's face and the wings.

"Here is where that other girl is, Ria. They put her here so she could go up to heaven. You are not this girl. You are alive. You are my little sister."

She listened. Finally, she clawed at her face and began to weep. She fixed me with a plaintive gaze. "I don't understand. I'm scared of that old woman in the attic."

I was speechless.

"Auntie Thelma wants me to tell that old woman that I'm dead and Todd did it. She says Todd burned me up." She clutched at my hand. "But I'm not dead. I'm Ria and Todd is my daddy."

I wept and hugged her close. My sister was back from the dead. She was mine again.

39

Castles in Spain

By day, the sky was a blazing oven. At night only the least breeze would come, carrying with it the sounds of frogs, insects, and other throbbing creatures of the darkness. I spent a lot of time with Ria, playing child's games, talking to her, soothing her, helping her to stay in touch with reality.

Bubba was poisoning small animals. Each day after school, I found their little furry and feathered corpses around the yard. I thought of poor squirrel souls and bird ghosts floating over the dew-wet grass by night chittering in the language of animals. He had been infatuated with Miss Dawling's death by rat poison, and Aunt Thelma was letting him play with it. Just one more twisted, sick indulgence from a woman who, I was now certain, had burned up her own little sister. Why else would she be so intent on getting Daria to play out the whole scene again?

One evening, Norman and Kate invited me over to dinner. I suppose they felt sorry for me.

The peas were gray mush and the potatoes tasted like paste, but somehow Kate had managed to pull a meal together. The ice in the tea had melted while waiting for the roast to bake in the oven into coarse strings.

Steamed from the kitchen, Kate smelled of sweat layered over with toilet water. A red rust stain from the plumbing on the floor above had leaked through the dining room wall and bubbled the wallpaper.

Long moments of silence went by as none of us could
think of anything to say. I listened to the ticking sounds of
the Woolcott house at night. At last, Norman cleared his
throat several times and revved up with some of his ministerial talk. As the meaningless words poured forth, his voice
grew stronger, instilled with the faint authority of the
church. On he went, monotonously serving up platitudes
that defined his role in a world full of sin.

"We must accept death. Life is coin of base metal. Death
levels all, the proud and humble alike. Imperial pomp is ultimately brought low. Beggars and emperors both end as dust.
Corruption, opulence, extravagance, loafing, idleness, and
sloth are all sins brought low." He folded his hands and I
wondered briefly if he intended this as a prayer. He looked
upward for his vision of the afterlife.

Jeremy gave me sympathetic looks. Though we were separated by the table, I was drawing closer and closer to him.

I wondered if this was what marriage was like? To sit
with in-laws and try to be polite to people who seemed to
have descended from the moon? To feel closer to someone
because all the rest of humanity was so macabre?

The dinner plodded along. We sat glumly with long peri-
ods of silence.

At last Norman turned to me with a sheepish confes-
sion. "There is an unfortunate affliction in the family," he
said. "Contained, yes, but only barely."

A look of shocked horror passed over Kate's face.
"Don't talk about madness, Reverend Woolcott," she whispered. "It's not appropriate in front of children."

Norman blinked at her. Clearly he had no intention of
talking about madness. "No . . . I meant that the family
values perhaps overmuch . . . although there is much good
done with it . . . still . . ."

I stared at him without the least curiosity.

"It's money, you see. There is quite a good deal of it.
There was a will leaving it to the grandchildren."

"Reverend Woolcott," Kate chided, "we shouldn't talk

to Jeremy and Alice of business matters." She seemed truly alarmed.

"Mrs. Woolcott, I know whereof I speak. This girl should realize why the Woolcotts are idle, for it is not in our nature. We toil in the vineyards of the Lord. There is no rest for us under ordinary circumstances. But we're here for . . . well, for the money."

I fought back a sudden surge of tears. "Why does everyone care about money?" I asked. "Why don't you just leave if you're unhappy?"

"Well, you see," Norman explained earnestly, "it's ours. Or that is to say, Jeremy's. And . . . well, much good could come of it if it were devoted to God's work."

Kate exited abruptly, announcing that she needed to water the plants. When she finally served dessert—rice pudding—it had subsided into sludge. Wordlessly, we spooned it into our mouths. Afterward, Norman insisted on having a Bible reading and a long-winded prayer.

Finally, Jeremy announced he would walk me home. Kate and Norman exchanged flurried glances. "Is that quite . . . wise?" asked Kate.

"Well, I don't know . . . I guess it's acceptable," said Norman. He pursed his lips. "I don't enjoy these kinds of problems especially after a heavy meal." There was a touch of reproach in his voice, as if I were responsible for his discomfort. "She really shouldn't go home unescorted. Her mother would not approve of that. Doubtless, she would think us very poor hosts if we let a young girl out on her own to return home."

"You will hurry right back?" Kate called fretfully after her son.

In a world populated by multitudes of teenagers who have had sex, Jeremy's parents were nervous about their son walking me twenty yards to the carriage house. Still, they acquiesced and didn't follow us to the door or watch us the whole way. They probably were afraid of getting lost and not being able to make it back to the dining room. Or maybe Kate had to water the plants again.

Jeremy closed the front door behind us and put an arm around my shoulders.

"The night is filled with mystery," he said dramatically.

I laid my hand flat against his chest and placed my face there too. A fierce excitement was growing within my body. "Oh, Jeremy, what would I do without you?"

"That was a revolting dinner, wasn't it? And Mater and Pater with their piety. They're just as bad as the others. I've heard them in bed at night talking about what they'll do with the money." He laughed. "My money. Your sister's money. Maybe once we get our hands on it, we three kids can all move to Spain and live in a castle."

"Castles in Spain," I murmured.

"And we can raise horses and little baby bulls and wear suits of armor and tilt at windmills like Don Quixote."

And hold each other close at night, I thought.

Jeremy took me down into the tangled garden and showed me a tired old cur dog tied to a tree by a length of clothesline. The poor thing licked Jeremy's hand and seemed very glad he had come for a visit.

"It's a starving old stray dog," Jeremy announced proudly.

"I can see that," I said. "But what's the point?"

"It seems so appropriate. He's a vagabond like us. You know, like royalty in exile or nobility brought low by fate. We will keep him hidden and feed him and doctor him and bring him back to something resembling life. As he grows stronger, we will too. He'll be a symbol of our healing. I call him 'Black Dog' because that was a pirate character in *Treasure Island*, and also the dog is black. But if you have some preferred name—Mozart or Bizet or Beethoven or whatever —feel free to change his title."

I touched the curl of Jeremy's hair at the nape of his neck and gave it a playful tug. It was my teenage girl's signal that I was unbearably attracted to him.

"Nothing matters but you and me," he said huskily. "The rest of the world fades to ether and mist when we choose to ignore it. It only exists because we permit it to. And all its nastiness we allow as a test of our love."

I took out the witch's tooth that hung down in my blouse and pressed it to my lips, kissed it and rubbed the kiss along his cheek.

He leaned down to seek my mouth. A flicker of electric fire ran along his lips and touched mine with a spark. I opened my mouth and let his tongue go deep inside.

I felt drenched in the love he was pouring forth. I was on fire with his growing passion.

I could feel the life pulsing beneath his skin. For once, I knew the meaning of the word *ecstasy*. I wanted to make a wild cry.

Our passion rose in a blaze, and I let his hands touch me everywhere. My knees went weak. I wanted to lie on the grass and let him hold me, to feel his weight on me.

"Jeer-remy!" Kate called plaintively. We could see her through the foliage of the garden on the back porch. Her eyes probed the dark.

"What a mindless old bat!" he said with savage irritation.

I stopped his lips with my fingers. "Stop. They only exist to test our love."

"I'll stay here. We'll wait her out."

"It won't work. She'll come looking or else round up everyone to help. You go on. Once she's inside, I'll slip over the garden wall."

"You could wait while I go in and slip back out again later."

"She'll probably lock you in your room tonight."

He smiled before giving me a last bonding hug and a kiss.

I sat alone in the dark rubbing the dog's ears. The poor thing even put his head on my lap. I told him all my fears, all the things I longed to tell Jeremy, but had not had the time.

About Aunt Thelma's madness. How she wanted to convince her deranged mother that Todd had murdered their little sister, and how my little sister was being made a pawn in the filthy scheme.

After a time, lightened of some of my burden, I decided to go home. The bank clock had finally broken down completely, so I couldn't know the time.

At the top of the wall I hesitated. Someone was moving around in the Broderick yard over by the shadow of the big house. Patiently, I waited and watched. A form moved out and went around the house. It was Bubba. He was probably out poisoning the poor songbirds.

Quickly, I slipped over the wall and scurried into the carriage house. In the morning I would show Ria the dog. He would belong to all three of us. He would be our true best friend.

40
Triumph

The next afternoon, when I came home from school, Black Dog was dead. He was swollen and bloated and covered with a mass of flies. Clotted foam hung from his lips. His eyes were blank and blind as night. He had been poisoned.

Taking the poor creature by a rear foot, I dragged him into our secret garden and sat in a lotus position on the bench amidst the heaped honeysuckle, brushing the flies away with a long, leafy twig.

I stared dumbly. I was inert, anesthetized by pain. After a while, Jeremy came up beside me.

"It had to happen," he said in a tone of acceptance. "Anything nice has to be destroyed by the Brodericks. It's like an iron law."

We buried the dog way back in the garden and stood there in silence staring at the humped-up black earth.

I was coming apart. Ria's eyes would not light with eager joy, because Black Dog was gone before I could show him off to her for even the first time. I was drowned by grief and fear.

"We'll fix him," Jeremy whispered. There was a vibrant tone in his voice. "It will be a purification ritual."

His face darkened with anger. Jeremy was beautiful to me. Jeremy with his outrageous stories. Jeremy with his knowledge of distant lands. I would seize his approval by drawing on his courage and being as strong as he was.

I put my fingertip against his nose, pressed in slightly, then laughed. I would be freed by action.

The sullen heat of afternoon descended. We were two teenagers with a purpose, trying our best to look casual as we strolled into the sweat-stained summer city. We traveled into a grimy world of which I had no knowledge: the area along the docks where the stevedores stayed when no ship was in the harbor.

A red neon beer sign hung on the propped-open door of a bar. In the cool, dark interior strangers' watchful eyes stared out at us. "Hey, bebby," someone called. "What's yore hurry?"

We scuttled on, suddenly aware of our youth and vaguely frightened.

"You need a bebby-sitter?" the voice hooted. "You can sit on my face, bebby!"

A flock of pigeons flapped away at our approach. We passed warehouses with sagging metal fire escapes, loose slabs of concrete with weeds growing thickly in the cracks, leaning light poles.

An old black beggar slouched away from us shuffling and smiling. "Yazzuh, yazzuh." His pencil-thin wrists stuck out of an old army overcoat he wore despite the heat. His chin jerked up toward his shoulder repeatedly.

Our slim figures slid among the broad shadows of the ruined old buildings. Our heeltaps could be heard on the broken pavement, then crunching among cinders. We crossed the railroad yard with its rank weeds, roofless roundhouse, and dusty windowpanes behind nailed-up boards.

We ventured on—along the narrow path into the kudzu-smothered trees, among marsh grass with its tracks of little wiggling creatures that love the mud, past old tires that piled up in the silt of the delta Congreve rested upon.

An eerie feeling overcame me when I spied Bubba's tiny shack. The shaggy masses of snaky green kudzu were slowly digesting the trees. Our shoes squished in wet patches where the marsh had leaked through the thin crust of topsoil and tangled in lines of old fishing line. On we went, seeking un-defined vengeance.

Jeremy made me wait in the bushes while he went to look. He passed through the ring of oil drums that stood forming a barricade around the shack. A red highway stop sign was nailed to the wall. Jeremy peered in the open door briefly, then gestured me forward.

Inside the oil drum ring was a litter of cans and plastic wrappers and bags. Empty grape drink bottles. The ashes of a campfire. A rubber truck-tire. A big X of polished river-stones in front of the door, like a warning or a curse. With his shoe, Jeremy kicked the stones contemptuously.

The air inside was humid and stifling, and the tiny room was cluttered with objects. There was a telephone-wire spool for a table, two stacked cinderblocks for a chair, an oil lamp and flashlight, a drink crate half filled with bottles of Pepsi. And—everywhere—weapons that gave evidence of paranoia and violence. A fireax. A cop's nightstick. A length of chain. Lead pipe inside a rubber hose. A boat gaff with the hook straightened out to form a spear.

Bubba had made a floor out of big chunks of linoleum and papered the walls with naked women foldouts from skin magazines. His bed had a tarp rigged over it like a tent. I figured the roof leaked.

An old bathtub was filled with auto engine parts that Bubba had obviously tinkered with using a variety of tools that lay on top. There was also a collection of small animal skulls and teeth, a car bumper, some oil rags stopping a low hole in the wall.

"What a rat's nest," I said.

Poking around, I found a cigar box with a switchblade inside. Also a set of brass knuckles and a knife you'd cut carpet with. A glass cutter. Playing cards with edges bent and dog-eared. A half-pint bottle of whiskey. Pack of cigarettes. Beside it was a box of rat poison. The cover had a rat with a big X through him.

"Let's do something profoundly original," Jeremy proposed.

"I'm yours to command," I said, truly meaning it.

He held up a can of gasoline. "Let's burn this dump to the ground."

Sweat was beaded on his upper lip. Filled with utter admiration, I raised myself on tiptoe and kissed him there, licked away the salty sweat.

We soaked the inside of the shack with gas, completely emptied the can. Then stepped outside. Before I even thought about it much, Jeremy had tossed in a match and ignited it with a whoosh and ball of flame.

We jumped back from the flaring heat. Grinned at each other and watched the flames mount.

Jeremy was actually dancing with excitement, making strange imprecations. I drew him away, both of us still glowing with triumph. The water made a sucking noise at the edges of the marsh as the tide shifted.

41

Intimate Conversation

From the narrow staircase of the carriage house, I saw my mother and Uncle Wheeler standing close together in intimate conversation. I hugged my knees and sat silently on a step. I held my breath. It was late at night, when Uncle Wheeler should have been at home with his wife and my mother should have been asleep. I watched them together in the living room. I should have been asleep myself.

As I watched, he bent his head forward and nuzzled her hair. She tilted her head and he browsed deeper in her neck. With a dreamy smile on her face, she offered him her parted lips. I was suddenly nauseated. The man who shared a bed with my vile aunt Thelma was kissing my perfect mother.

The kiss finished, they parted by silent consent. He left her slowly, gaping and stupid with lust, firmly caught in her subtle snares. His footsteps swished away on the lawn.

A stab of deepest pain pierced my heart.

I could remember being picked up at day-care, running and yelling, "There's my mommy!" and her grabbing me up and swinging me in a circle as I shrieked with joy. Did she remember holding my little hand in hers? Did she remember a child's eyes that stared with wide, trusting wonder at the world because she had been there to make me safe? Did she know how much I had relied on her for security and the orderly nature of the world?

Now she turned to see me sitting in darkness on the stairs.

"Alice?" she said. She was clearly flustered. My mother with her cat-green, seagreen eyes scuffled, scrambled, sought a nonchalant pose. Sitting in a chair and leafing through a magazine, her mind raced.

"Your uncle Wheeler came by to talk about Senior's Estate," she tried to explain. "I'm just amazed at how smart he is. Sure, plenty of people say he married for money, but he's done a lot with his life on his own. He's been acquiring businesses like crazy so he doesn't have to rely on Thelma's money. He's really wealthy in his own right. I'm just bowled over by what he's managed to achieve."

I rose up, standing like some solemn fate. She was not going to confide in me. She had no master plan to save us from evil. She was not acting out a charade—sacrificing her youth and beauty and honor to save my sister and me. In my heart I knew I had lost her for all time.

"Have you . . . been here long?" she questioned.

"Do you mean did I see what you were doing?"

Her face turned raw and ugly. "You little sneak!"

I had become Alice the street kid with all the smartmouth back-chat. "Are you lonely already without Todd?"

My mother didn't answer immediately. She let her silence join the nightmare mix of fate that had brought us to Congreve. I was so miserable that I longed to be swallowed up by this great rotting, lonely earth and swept out to sea with the silt of the Congreve delta to sink with fragments of dirt into the deep ocean's maw.

She spoke carefully, giving me an adult-to-child lecture on life. "Alice, we all have to grow up sooner or later. In your case, sooner than later." She smiled. "When I was a young girl, I was very pretty. Everyone fussed over me and said I was pretty as a picture. Anything I wanted, I could just smile and be cute and get it out of people. It was 'Daddy I want this' and 'Mommy I want that.' And I would get it. I learned to say 'oh thank you so very much it's what I've always wanted' and hug adults and it always got me lined up for what I wanted next.

"Most children can't seem to learn that lesson. They have a stubborn pride. They feel that all of life should be handed to them on a platter. And they get all belligerent when it isn't. If life isn't magical every moment, then it's tantrum time. Am I making any sense?"

"I'm not sure," I said slowly. I examined my hands, stared at the rough plaster of the walls, the stains of leaking plumbing.

"I was allowed to run wild, Alice. Oh, not in the streets exactly. It was Richmond, Virginia, after all, and I was a proper young lady. It's just that, whatever I didn't want to do, I didn't do. I can remember in first grade announcing that I hated arithmetic. And I was allowed to be a little saccharine belle and not know math at all. Math was for men who went to work in big offices and did important things."

She scowled and a deep cleft formed between her eyebrows. "I was supposed to be a beautiful blonde who sighed and baked cookies. I took ballet lessons, tap, ballroom, jazz, and all variety of modern dance. I had piano, too, but that was hard work and nobody admired you very much when you played the piano, so I quit it. I quit everything that didn't get me instant approval.

"I would dance and fling my body around extravagantly and undulate my shapely young limbs and the room would applaud. Boys would crowd round, falling all over themselves to anticipate what I wanted.

"I couldn't go to college. You had to be able to do math and science at least for two years before you could major in English literature. I couldn't stomach that even for two years. So I studied dance. It was all carefully arranged with family friends because for a Richmond girl to go to New York was something dreadful and frightening."

"And you met Todd?" I said, meaning things worked out perfectly.

"Yes, but first I was married to a Richmond boy from a

proper family who was sowing wild oats for a couple of years
before going back to the family real estate business."

"My father . . ."

"Yes. John McNamara. The father you've never
known."

I didn't want to hear about him. He had never been an
element in my life. It was always Todd. "But afterward you
met Todd."

"I was eager and ignorant. I was eager for the applause
never to stop. Todd was another boy with a background like
my own. He was rebelling against things he hated and fighting against strictures and social norms. We could giggle together about how brave and audacious we were in rejecting
our origins."

"But you got on. You were in love. You were happy."

"Over time, I became painfully aware that things were
not going to work out like love's young dream. Our marriage
—our lives—were going nowhere."

"Why?" I asked desperately. "How could that be? Everything was so perfect."

"Caught up in your little narrow world, you saw things
with the eyes of a child. I was like you once, too, but I had to
grow up. Unfortunately it was later rather than sooner."

"But . . ."

"You can't live on love, Alice. It takes money to pay the
rent and buy the groceries. Once in a while, you'll want to
take a vacation and go to some exotic land to see splendid
things. You may even want to stay in big hotels and dine in
fine restaurants."

I knew what she was saying. The message was only too
clear. But I couldn't accept it. Not my beautiful mother with
the seagreen eyes. She was a fairy princess. "But there's nothing fine or nice here," I burst out. "It's all gloom and rot and
dirty smells from the harbor and creeping, evil people who
live with death and madness."

"But we must stay here, Alice. We must stay here until
we get what we are owed."

"Owed?"

"The adult world misled me. Don't you see? I was never made to bear down and achieve anything, never made to acquire a professional skill. All my life I've been dependent upon weak men who betrayed me in the end and left me helpless and alone and without money. This time, I am owed money, and I intend to collect it."

"But Mother, we don't need it!" I cried. "There's you and me and Ria. We have each other."

"There is no love without security. If you're not secure, you can't love. That's why I never loved Todd. Oh, sure, we played at being in love, but he never provided for me. He never made me feel safe the way a woman has to feel safe before she can open up and give herself truly."

I had to lash back, to retaliate. "I loved Todd, even if you didn't."

"Because you were a child and felt secure. You don't know the pain and anxiety he put me through. Not just here, but in New York. The rent was always behind and there was the constant threat of eviction. We ate peanut butter and bean sprouts because we couldn't afford anything else. Don't you even remember that junky car we bought that we couldn't even afford so we had to turn right around and sell it at a loss?"

"You could love Wheeler Broderick? You could love that slime-bag just because he has money?"

"Don't be ugly, Alice. You're nosing into things you can't understand."

I screwed up my face. "You're as crazy as they are."

"I knew this day would come eventually, Alice." She sighed. "I knew you'd get so rebellious that I just wouldn't care what happened to you anymore. So, you've become quite expendable in my mind. I guess that's the biggest hurdle of adolescence, getting used to the idea of being expendable."

"Expendable?" I choked.

"Yes," my mother said, and her voice was cold as ice.

"Daria is one-fourth heiress to the bank and the Broderick fortune. Perhaps Wheeler will steal it all. But you see, he wants me very badly. Either way I win. And you . . . well, you just don't figure into the equation at all."

I climbed calmly up the stairs.

My mother had rejected me. But I still had myself—and Ria—and Jeremy. And I would be all right.

42

The Anodyne

"I love the dark," said Jeremy. "Everything is so cryptic. You can make it mean whatever you want."

"You do talk junk," I said. "That's a meaningless remark supposed to be all pregnant with hidden meaning."

I startled myself like I always do when I use a sexual word. And Jeremy was ringing my waist with his hands, as if I had given him an invitation to get me pregnant or something! Me, the little thirteen-year-old innocent. I pushed his hands off.

As had come to be our custom, we had met in our hidden garden after the lights were out in the houses. With our socks and shoes off, we stretched out on the old quilt Jeremy had brought, lay on our backs, and looked up at a clear sky spangled with stars.

A bat fluttered overhead and the air was soft and fresh-smelling with the faintest salty hint of a sea breeze. The secret garden with all the azaleas floating in the darkness seemed as innocent as we were. A nightbird called.

"What is it saying?" I asked.

"It's saying 'gerk gerk gerk,'" said Jeremy, and we both laughed quietly. Mute laughter. Whispering laughter.

"It is so nice here," I agreed. "You and I have become like hunted animals who find the dark friendly because it conceals us."

"We are hidden safe in the dark where the dreaded

Aunt Thelma can't find us to call down the curses of her angry God."

"She'd froth at the mouth if she saw us. Chew the rug. Eat broken glass."

"I don't think she'd be particularly broad-minded about the whole thing," Jeremy agreed.

I stirred uneasily, wondering about the passions that grew so easily within me. Jeremy pulled up a handful of grass, smelled of it, let it sift down. His eyes seemed in a trance as he stared at me in the dark. He leaned forward letting me smell his clean breath. With just the tip of his tongue, he traced the line of my lips.

I pushed him away again. Sobbing, I confessed the sordid secret of my mother and Uncle Wheeler, poured out my heart to my only friend in the world.

"I can understand her using him," Jeremy said. "They're so ruthless, your mother would have to be equally so."

"It's worse than that. I'm afraid she's caught their sickness. I'm afraid she's going to be very cruel . . ."

"To you?"

"Mostly to my little sister. Mother has come to see poor Ria as the key to the lockbox. You know what I mean. The heiress to the Broderick loot."

"Alice, we'll stick together. You know that."

"Promise?"

"I'm your anodyne."

"Will I know all these words when I'm in the tenth grade?"

"I relieve pain. I soothe."

He fished the witch's tooth out of my shirt and rubbed it against his chin. As he rubbed the smooth enamel, I felt as though he were rubbing my skin, my breasts. Then he did touch my breasts, pulling up my T-shirt, sucking with his lips.

I was too young for this. I knew that with great certainty. Still, I couldn't stop him.

The leaves rustled high in the treetops as a squirrel jumped from one branch to another.

Jeremy took my clothes off. He reached through the darkness to find the only snap and zipper on my jeans. I lifted my legs as he tugged them free and lay there expectant until he rubbed his cheek all over me.

"Your voluptuous body," he said.

"I'm a skinny teenager," I mocked, but I loved his love as much as his touch, as much as his tenderness. And I was impatient for his touch.

He pulled off his clothes, showing his skin pale in the moonlight, almost translucent.

I turned into him, locked my limbs onto his. I gasped as I felt the parts of him that made him a man and different from me.

"You hair is perfume," he said reverently.

"Mmmhm," I purred into his collarbone.

I subsided under his touch. His lips set me aflame.

"What we are doing is an old thing, but for us it's very new," he said, and I thought his words as beautiful as any poetry.

He did it with great caution. I lay stiff, receiving him, accepting each stage awkwardly, with surprise, wonder, and joy. The stars filled the sky above me and my fingers were rooted in his hair.

It was a soft and lovely experience. His hands stroked me. His vital part filled me.

A sudden emphasis like a miming of despair. A lurch. A shudder. And it was finished.

"Are you hurt or ashamed?" he asked anxiously once it was over. He lay beside me, his limbs drained.

So many girls claim to have felt incomplete after the first time. The boy does it so quickly. The arousal begins so late. But I felt warm and good and sensuous and complete.

I wanted Jeremy to like me as much as I did him.

"Of course I'm not hurt," I said. "I couldn't be hurt by someone as nice as you. And I couldn't be ashamed. But guys always wonder if it was worth it, don't they? I mean once they're drained of all that intense need, don't they feel sort of foolish?"

"Yes."

"I don't blame you. It's all right with me if you're ashamed."

He was very calm and wise. "Are you afraid I don't love you?"

I pressed my eyes against his bare shoulder and felt the radiance of his warmth. "Yes."

He fingered my witch's tooth on the long cord, laid it back between my teenage breasts. "This is my pledge to you. I will never ask for it back."

"Let's not go back to our rooms tonight," I urged. "Let's just stay here together."

We lay there surrounded by the seamless darkness. Tucked in and covered up. We slept in peace.

43
Authority

In blinding sunlight, we awoke. Blinking our eyes like animals, we sensed danger.

Aunt Thelma stood above us, holding our clothes. She was very angry. Her shadow moved over us. Her eyes bulged. Her mouth spit. Her knuckles were white and straining. She was holding the whip.

I clutched the quilt around my breasts. I could feel Jeremy's fear too. Except he was seething, longing to take the whip away from her. She sensed this and purred at him.

"Resist me," she sneered. "Jump at me and see what happens to you."

"We want to put our clothes on."

"Then you should have kept them on."

Jeremy rebelled, but only halfheartedly. I did not blame him. We were kids faced with adult authority.

The bright morning and the birds singing could not even cheer us. Everything was bleak and grim. I saw images of reform school with barbed-wire fences and dormitories locked up at night. Where every bit of humanity was packed together like wild animals for savage initiations at night after the lights went out.

My aunt herded us toward the big house. Norman and Kate were in the sunroom wearing bathrobes and fuzzy slippers. Kate was talking about how she really should start cooking breakfast.

Pushing us in front of her, Aunt Thelma displayed us

like hunting trophies. We stood facing the staring saucer eyes, the open mouths. A newspaper swished to the floor from fingers that could no longer grip it.

"Why . . . you're naked as Adam and Eve," Norman said stupidly. We are talking about absolute stupefaction. He had probably never seen a naked girl before.

"I found them this way in the garden," Aunt Thelma said proudly.

"In . . . in the altogether?" said Norman.

I could never believe how Norman talked.

"I don't think it's proper for me to be present," said Kate, retreating into her state of permanent abstraction. She patted her hair. "I don't think . . . it's . . . well, proper."

"You could well be right," said my aunt.

Kate waved at the air and slid out of the room. "We all need a good, hearty breakfast. It's the best meal of the day."

Aunt Thelma settled herself in a chair and laid the deadly whip on her lap. She was in no hurry. She wanted to relish this moment. "We must get to the bottom of this," she pronounced. "There is much to get to the bottom of."

Jeremy and I stood there naked. My shoulders were rounded. I put one arm across my breasts and the other over my crotch in the classic pose of the discovered libertine. Jeremy stood with his hands on his hips. He did not look fragile. He was slim as a sapling with lithe muscles.

Norman put on a show of good will, trying to give us the benefit of the doubt. "Jeremy, were you engaged in some enterprise?"

Aunt Thelma laughed sharply. "Sin flourishes amazingly."

Norman shoved on his glasses briefly, then took them off to wipe at the lenses with the sleeve of his robe. "Jeremy, I have always strived to be fair. You must put your side of the matter before us. We are willing to listen."

Always so glib, Jeremy was stumped. He could not come up with a plausible lie. "We spent the night in the garden," he said finally.

The glasses went back on. "I fail to understand."

I longed for Jeremy's poetic defiance. I wanted him to talk back to them. I wanted him to say that we had exulted in each other's limbs and in the warmth of human touch. We had found the love and joy and truth that lies buried in every human being. We had woven our love and longing into the fabric of the night.

Instead, he was a frightened teenager put on the spot, trapped by the deadliest of sins short of murder. "It was a hot night, and we slept out in the garden. It was nicer out there."

"They slept together," spit Aunt Thelma. "Naked."

Hands trembling, Norman took off his glasses carefully and rubbed his eyes. "Can this be true?"

"They did things to each other," my aunt added, with a supreme sense of satisfaction.

The trap was sprung. The Reverend Woolcott now saw it all laid upon the table.

"Alice?" he said, pronouncing my name as though he was not quite certain who I was. Perhaps I really was some demon in female disguise. "Alice, is this true?" His voice was actually kind.

And I, who had longed for Jeremy's eloquence, was as equally tongue-tied as he. "Yes," I admitted finally. "We slept in the garden."

"Your . . . clothes . . . ?"

"It was hot." The lie formed on my lips and came out in a rush. "We didn't do anything."

"Liar," spat my aunt. "I found them naked."

"But . . . but," spluttered Reverend Woolcott, aghast. "You didn't see them . . . do anything did you?"

Aunt Thelma opened her mouth and clapped it shut again. Her cunning eyes darted. She hadn't, of course, and she had said too much to make up a lie. "You know they did it. Why else would they be . . . *naked?*"

"But . . . but they wouldn't know how," Norman said

incredulously. "They couldn't possibly. Alice is barely thirteen."

"It's not Alice, I'm afraid. She's just a trusting innocent, a little child with a ripening body." My aunt rubbed her face to keep off a smile. "I'm afraid it's your son. He's fifteen. He knows."

In that second, it became instantly apparent to me that I was less important to Aunt Thelma than Jeremy. Jeremy was the other male heir to the Broderick millions. He was the competition for Bubba. Jeremy was the one who had to be destroyed. I was merely the tool for his destruction.

"He didn't, he didn't!" I protested. "He didn't do anything to me."

"Liar!" screamed my aunt. "Sins build one upon the other. One leads to the next."

"I asked him to take off his clothes. I wanted to see . . . I wanted to see what boys are like."

"I have given fair warning about such behavior," said Norman.

"I know. I did it anyway. It was all my fault."

"Do you expect us to believe that?" my aunt sneered. "I think the best way to get at the truth is the lie detector your uncle Wheeler keeps at the bank. It will smell out a liar sure as shooting."

"We can't have that," gulped Norman. "People would learn. The police would—"

"It is a police matter," interrupted Aunt Thelma. "You know that as well as I. A boy of his age and some little sprig of a girl. This is a serious jailable offense."

Norman squirmed uncomfortably. "But my position in the church would be hurt, and I'd never get another mission."

"Yes, I think we can safely say that your son has destroyed your career," my aunt acknowledged.

"No!" I screamed.

Aunt Thelma was obviously stunned by this rebellion against her authority. "You have no choice in the matter."

"I'll take the children's side," said Norman firmly. "I'll defend them against you."

I couldn't believe what I was hearing. Even if it was just a matter of salvaging his own career, he was actually standing up to her.

"You can lose that contest. Liars are often found out. I'll hook you up to the lie detector."

"You have no cause. I'm accused of nothing. I have some knowledge of the law."

"There's still a heavy risk for you. I'll spread this all over town. I'll go to your superiors. We'll lay the issue before them and ask their judgment.".

Norman swallowed hard. "If you feel you must."

My aunt was never without a fallback position. "Jeremy must be sent away to an all-boys military school. The rigid discipline will take his bad habits out of him."

It took a while for Norman to absorb this new information. "A military school? You mean where they dress the boys like soldiers?"

"Yes, you blithering fool. Where they dress them like soldiers. I want him out of here. I want him away from this girl. I won't have sinful behavior on Broderick ground. I won't have sin where Senior lived and raised his family."

"I'm industrious," Norman said wearily. "I work without cease." A nervous twitch began in his neck. It was a dissonant movement out of keeping with his placid face. It increased to a jerking and twisting of his entire head, as if his collar were strangling him.

It was then that Aunt Thelma realized she had won. It was suddenly clear that he would give up his son to maintain the shreds of his dignity. He did not want a violent contest over his position in the church. "Then it's decided," she stated, turning to Jeremy. "Military school. They know how to deal with liars there. Buck naked and they say they didn't do anything."

Jeremy lost it at that point. He began to cry, tears running down his face. Then just as suddenly he laughed. A shrill hysterical laugh. His carefully constructed world of dreams that had protected him against his parents' inanity and his aunt's wrath had come apart at the seams. He alternately laughed and cried, while Norman wrung his hands and jerked his head at funny angles.

Tears blinded my own eyes. He was my only link with some form of sanity. He was my protector. My hands came away from my sexual parts and covered my eyes.

Aunt Thelma grabbed my arm and jerked me out of the room. She dragged me into the kitchen and forced me to lay my torso over the table, buttocks up in the air.

"You are a sinful, evil child. You have tempted an innocent boy and ruined him. I shall show you the pain of sin."

The first sharp slap came down on me with intense, searing fire. I fought not to scream.

My aunt waited between blows. She waited for the pain to sink in deep so she could deliver the full shock of the next blow. As the blows were added one onto the next, her blood lust was roused. From my blurred haze, I felt the blows become multiplied, a whorling frenzy of lashings.

The pain became permanent, a part of my anatomy. Everything in my vision swam in a red haze. As the pain numbed me, I became almost caught up in the rhythm of the blows.

I must have fainted after a while. I had no more memory.

44

Hush of Loneliness

I remember Aunt Kate putting a bathrobe on me and helping me back to the carriage house, both of us moving unsteadily. She was talking about nothing in particular. How she couldn't get good bacon anymore. How there was too much fat in it. Things had been different in Congreve when she was a girl.

I lay in an agony in my bed all day. No one came to see about me. Not even my mother. I didn't even know where Ria was. I felt abandoned.

Night came and went. The next morning, noises from the Woolcott house woke me. I jumped from bed and threw open the window.

Jeremy was going away.

Through the upstairs window, I saw Norman loading the car and starting it up. Kate stood outside as if she didn't know whether she was going or not and waiting for Norman to tell her what to do.

Jeremy came out in a suit that was too small for him. Was he going to a cadet school somewhere off in the pine barrens of the midstate? He looked toward the carriage house. Was he searching for me? I waved frantically. He lifted his hand, then got into the car. Soon the car vanished and he was gone.

There was no thunder and lightning, no sound of trumpets or inspirational music—nothing that would set a mood of hoped-for return. He was gone.

I remember it was a Saturday with no school. Later that morning, I sat with Daria at the breakfast table, my heart buried in pain. My entire body hurt like fire. Every second was an agony. Aunt Thelma, Uncle Wheeler, and Gwen stared at me. My mother had disappeared somewhere and Ria was like a fragile plant.

My aunt ate with relish. As usual, she praised the bacon and eggs. Her enemies were falling one by one and my name had risen to the top of the list for execution.

Uncle Wheeler strutted off to the bank. It was Saturday, but the bank was open in the morning and he was an important man. He had to be there to keep everyone hard at work.

"Today is a very special day," Aunt Thelma said, beaming. "Today, Daria will be allowed to play in the attic."

Todd was gone. Jeremy was gone. My mother was lost somewhere in her own world. And I was too weak to resist.

Like a zombie, Daria went to Aunt Thelma's rough embrace. She was a small figure of a lost soul, a tiny husk of loneliness and fear.

"I don't want to play there," Ria whimpered. "I'm scared of the dark."

"Now don't be a problem," said Aunt Thelma. "You know it will be fun."

"Please. Please." Ria dragged back against the powerful hand.

The stairs were there, leading up and up to where Todd had hung suspended as if he had wished to launch his soul into flight. I was miserable, beaten, and powerless.

"Please," Ria said again.

With her normal servility, Gwen listened. Her body shook as though she had chills. Her fingers stretched and clutched. Her face contorted. Suddenly she mounted the third step—stood squarely in the middle barring her mother's path. "Why don't you leave her alone?" Gwen demanded. "Why can't you quit torturing people?"

I was stunned. Did Gwen know pity for someone other

than herself? Did she see herself in a small child and know the pain?

Aunt Thelma glowered at her.

"You hate us all," said Gwen. "You hate everyone. You hate Bubba because he's dumb. You hate me because I'm fat. You hate Daddy because he wasn't born a Broderick and no one will ever be as perfect as your daddy was."

"Don't you speak ill of Senior," Aunt Thelma warned.

"He didn't love you. He hated you. That's why you take it out on us."

Aunt Thelma lifted her hand to strike, but Gwen did not cower. She stood her ground.

"He knew the truth. He knew you killed Daria. He knew you set the tree on fire and put her into it."

Gwen had clearly struck a nerve. My aunt actually bellowed. "You don't know what you're talking about! That happened long before you were born. All you know is lies!"

Gwen kept on, spewing out her accusing words. "Senior knew you killed her. He told me one time. You destroyed Grandmother's brain the way you destroy everyone else. He knew the truth and he told me."

An icy calm descended over Aunt Thelma. "Gwen, you know what happens to bad girls, don't you?"

Gwen was shaken. Her resolve was gone just as suddenly as it had come. "No . . . no, please don't!"

"Bad girls go into the attic. They go into the attic where Grandmother waits."

Gwen's face crinkled as she squeezed her legs together. But it was in vain. Urine ran down them and puddled yellow on the floor.

"You are a disgusting child, Gwendolyn. You're wetting your panties just like you still wet the bed. You're a big baby. You'll never be an adult. I'll never be able to give you any responsibility. All I can do is show you the result of your sins."

"*No!* Please! I didn't mean it! I take it back! I swear I take it back!"

"You can't take back a thing once it's been said, Gwendolyn. You know that very well. You can't undo a sin."

Gwen was on her knees dabbing at the puddle of urine with the hem of her dress. "I'll clean it up. I always do. I'm a good girl, Momma. You know I'm a good girl. I never miss church. I sing in the choir. I don't do nasty things in bed at night."

"Go up the stairs, Gwendolyn," Aunt Thelma said as she took Ria from her. Ria squirmed in Aunt Thelma's arms and escaped her grasp. She came running up to me immediately.

Aunt Thelma's strong hands lifted Gwen up. Even so, Gwen's bulk was such that it would have been an impossible task without willing submission. Gwen's eyes were vacant with deathlike fears. "I don't mean to be bad. I swear I try to be good. I pray that God will make me good. I just slip up sometimes and do things I don't mean to do. Bad things just come out of me. I . . . can't help myself."

Aunt Thelma's smile widened. Her demon eyes were fascinated by her prey. "You're going to learn to help yourself, Gwendolyn. You're going to learn or you'll never be allowed out again."

My poor cousin's starched slip crinkled like footsteps in dry leaves. Her voice was puzzled. "I don't know why you have to punish me. I didn't do anything really bad. Not really."

As they mounted slowly, step by step, Gwen's meek voice became fainter.

"I didn't do anything."

At the top of the stairs I heard a door open, then close. A key turned in the lock.

I pulled Ria out of the big house. I gathered her to me. Gwen was sacrificed so that Ria could be saved.

45

Hidden Sins

As the day passed, I became stronger. My resolve was hardened. I was alone, but I was strong.

I went out into the night and dug up Black Dog's grave with a shovel. It was no trouble to see in the starlight. I felt as though I lived in the dark now. Darkness was my native element.

The dog wasn't buried deep. He stank horribly and looked worse, his gums and lips pulled back with his teeth in a snarl. White maggots swarmed in his burst-open belly. Ghostly little wiggling tools of the earth. White worms tidying up behind death. I thought I was going to be sick.

Overcoming my revulsion with fierce hatred, I dragged him by a rear leg across the yard and dropped him against the big house. Unafraid, I went down into the dark cellar. I hated my aunt and I was going to strike a blow. Feeling my way amid the rotting dampness, I found the crucifix Bubba had stuck full of nails and wooden screws. I brought it out.

Over creaking boards, I entered the evil house dragging the dog, scattering twisting, crawling maggots on the floor behind me. The back bedroom emitted a regular rasp of Uncle Wheeler snoring. I dumped the dog right at the door and lay the crucifix on it. Next I went to the kitchen and rummaged, found a candle in a pottery holder in the window. Returning, I lit it beside the dog.

I backed away from the flickering glare and stood admiring the effect fiendishly. I was reduced to their level. Inspired with yet another idea, I went back to the kitchen, got a carving knife, and stuck it in the dog. It went in between the ribs with a chunking noise.

I went outside and crawled under the bushes beneath their window, lay there looking at stars through gaps in the foliage like a castaway in an alien universe. As I watched, a shooting star let go and flickered through space in a sparking instant. Then it was gone—so fast, I wondered if I had really seen it.

I awoke as the sun was rising. I lay still, feeling stiff and wet with dew. But excited at what I had created. At what was about to happen.

Inside the bedroom of the big house, I could hear Aunt Thelma muttering. "A world of jukeboxes and women with painted eyes and dime store perfume."

"What are you going on about?" Uncle Wheeler yawned.

"You don't listen to a word I say."

He said nothing else. The bed creaked.

"I'm talking about how Beau Street has gone downhill with all those beer signs and girls in chiffon dresses. Their makeup is laid on with a trowel."

Uncle Wheeler mumbled something I couldn't distinguish.

"What are you going to do about it?" my aunt demanded.

"Hum?" said Uncle Wheeler as the bed creaked again.

Aunt Thelma crossed the room and opened the door. My heart was racing. She saw my present.

Her breath came in short, wheezing gasps and her voice changed. It was a lost voice from deep within her subconscious. The voice of a child.

"I didn't do it," she said. "It's not right to blame me. I was too far away. I was way across the room. I was just a small child. I couldn't have done something like that. Todd did it. Todd was the one. And Kate. They did it together. They were always jealous of her."

She was talking to someone. Not Uncle Wheeler. She was talking to someone who wasn't in the room. Someone who was dead or who had never lived at all.

"They're always sneaking around doing mean things to me because they hate me. I'm older and they're supposed to respect me and do what I say. I'm in charge and Todd thinks he's special just because he's a boy. He thinks one day he'll be like Senior and I won't count for anything."

By now, Uncle Wheeler had gotten out of the bed. "Thelma, what on earth are you going on about?"

He crossed the room, looked out to see the horrible dog carcass. "What the . . . ? God damn it, that sorry ass Bubba! I'll fix his lousy . . . !"

Still, my aunt continued her strange soliloquy. "I know you loved her best. Her and Todd. Him because he was the boy. Daria because she was so little and cute. I know you didn't love me. I know you hated me. But I didn't do it. I'm a good girl. I only do good things. I swear I didn't do it. I was too far across the room. Momma saw. She'd tell you if she'd just start talking again. She's going to start talking and she'll tell you I didn't do it. It was Todd who did it."

"Shut up, Thelma!" raged Wheeler. "I've had enough of your nonsense! Goddamn Bubba! That stupid-ass, sorry shit son of yours. You made him into the demented mess he is. You never let me take a strong hand with him."

"I was too far across the room!" my aunt screamed. "I was too far . . . !"

Uncle Wheeler shook her and even slapped her across the face.

Filled with a demoniac surge of triumph, I slipped away. I was winning. I was stronger than she was. I had discovered her weaknesses. I had no deep, hidden sins. I could win because I was cleaner.

46

The Chocolate Cake

Aunt Thelma spent Sunday behind the closed door of her bedroom. No doctors were called. Uncle Wheeler dragged the dog out in a plastic garbage bag and dumped it at the edge of the street. He called Alberta and told her to stay home, then he fumed in his study, making quiet phone calls to lawyers. He was readying some contingency. I was driving them apart. I could not let up. I watched from outside, lurking around the fringes of the house, fascinated.

Near nightfall, Aunt Thelma emerged from her bedroom seemingly under control. Since Alberta had not come to work, no one had made any meals. Aunt Thelma busied herself in the kitchen. I heard the whirr of a Mixmaster. Bubba appeared. Night fell and everyone slept.

When Monday morning came, Bubba left the house. Uncle Wheeler and Aunt Thelma went out together in his Cadillac. My aunt was staring and silent but hard again and back in full control of herself. I was not allowed to go to school until all of my whip marks were healed. The house was left to me.

Gwen had saved my sister from the attic. I was grateful to her and wanted to repay her deed with my personal loyalty, wanted to heal all wounds and do a valiant deed of my own. I was certain that she was locked in the attic. She had not been seen since she had stood up to her mother the morning after I had gotten beaten.

I entered the huge, ponderous old house that had once carried its message of wealth. Now it was only a dark monstrosity filled with demons. Obscure faded wallpaper. The dusty potted plant on the landing. The sickly colors of the stained-glass window with the head of the little girl in the corner. The wood, plaster, and masonry that had received all my cries of pain after I had seen Todd hanging there.

Listening with both ears, I crept up the broad staircase. I put my feet down carefully near the edges of each step so it would not creak. I was filled with the deep menace of the place.

Like a mute symbol of the secrets of the house, the attic door beckoned. My heart was in my throat.

But as I tried to get in, I realized that the door was strong as a bank vault. Aunt Thelma had the only key. There was no other way to get in. The lock held firm when I tried to jimmy it.

I crouched down and scratched at the door like some animal. Gwen had been in there for days. Was there a bathroom? Had someone brought her food? I wanted to at least talk to her.

I scratched again.

"Bubba? Is that you?" Gwen's voice asked faintly. There was eagerness in it. She was there. Just on the other side of the door.

"It's me—Alice McNamara," I whispered, though I knew the house was empty.

"Bubba?" she said more loudly. "Did you bring me some more? Please, did you?"

I glanced nervously over the edge of the stairwell. My body twitched. "It's Alice," I repeated, raising my voice a little more.

"Alice?"

"Yes. I want to help you."

"I'm sick," she whined. "I'm scared and I'm sick." Gwen began to cry. "It's dark here, horribly dark. Grandma's in here somewhere in the dark. There's all kinds of heaped-up furniture and stuff. She sits over there breathing in the dark. I'm sick. I keep throwing up. I've puked all over myself. I stink of it." She coughed and gagged as she spoke. It sounded disgusting. Like she was dying of lung cancer or something.

"What are you sick with?"

"Momma always said I ate too much even when I was little. She'd have me all dressed up at church and she'd say to the minister: 'Here's my little fat daughter.' Like I was deformed or something. It hurt me so much. I'd just go off all alone and cry. And then I'd eat stuff.

"It always tasted so good. I'd lie alone in bed at night and think about chocolate cake and candy bars with nuts in them. I'd sneak money and go down to the store and buy colas and peanuts and those nice pies and cakes that come all wrapped up.

"I'd lick the cream that stuck to the wrappers just real slow knowing that I had the cake to eat too. It was kind of like an appetizer and then I'd take that first bite. Chew it up real slow. Eat around the edge working my way into the center. It was all moist and chewy in there. That was the best part. Or sometimes I'd eat the cake and save the icing for last. It would get all gooey and smear all over my hands and I'd lick it off. Some of it would get under my fingernails. That was where Mumma would always look for chocolate—under my nails."

Gwen was sobbing. She bumped her head against the door and gave a gulp of pain. Her voice cracked. She coughed again.

"Grandma's over there—in the dark. If I see her face, I'm going to die. I'll just start screaming and die. She wants my cake. I know she wants it. She doesn't ask for it—she doesn't say a word ever—but she wants it. I don't want her to take it from me!"

"Cake? Are you eating cake?"

"It's mine. Bubba brought it to me. It's all rich and thick with big wedges of icing between the layers."

"Gwen, don't eat that cake," I said emphatically.

I knew what was happening. Why else would Bubba take her cake? Why else was he allowed to get in?

"You're just like them," she said sorrowfully. "Don't eat stuff. You're too fat. Well, I'm always going to be fat so who cares? I'll just go on and eat and get fatter and fatter. Nobody loves me anyway."

"Gwen, he's put rat poison in the cake," I whispered. "That's what's making you sick."

"I want my cake. It's all I've got. She wants it, and she's over there in the dark. She was always just an old hag watching us from the attic. I was always scared of her."

"Gwen, listen to me. You must not eat that cake. It's going to kill you. He's killed animals. Now he's going to kill you."

"I used to have a dolly. She would cry if she was hungry so I'd have little tea parties back in the garden with cups and napkins and things. Once I sneaked some cocoa in a tin. It was just the powder but I put it in the cups and I ate it with a little spoon. I just held it in my mouth and let my spit make it all chocolate and warm and runny and gooey. And I got to eat the dolly's cocoa, too. Little bits of it would fall off the spoon and I'd wet my finger and stick it on where it fell and lick it off my finger."

"Gwen, you did something nice for Daria. You did something nice and noble and good. You're a good person. You're not what they think you are. You're not one of them. You're not crazy like the Brodericks. They tried to make you crazy, but you're a good person. Please, please listen to me. Please don't eat that cake."

"I am a good person," Gwen said with new conviction. "I go to church. I sing in the choir. I don't pay any attention when the other girls poke fun at me. I don't touch myself in the bath where I'm not supposed to. I'm a good girl. I just sneak food sometimes. Can't anyone forgive me for that?"

I was shot through with a vast sense of pity and pain.

"Don't eat that cake." I sobbed. "Please, Gwen, please don't eat it."

"You go to hell," she refused stubbornly. Through the door, I could hear her gagging in dry heaves.

47
Boarding School Girl

Night came. Aunt Thelma and Uncle Wheeler returned. Bubba was in the car with them. They all went into the big house. Uncle Wheeler was talking about a new digital time-and-temperature clock he was having put up at the bank. Aunt Thelma was irate, calling the act an assault on Senior's memory. Uncle Wheeler told her to shut up. Since the dead-dog incident, my uncle had been exercising a lot more authority.

I was positive Gwen was being poisoned, yet I didn't know what to do. If I called the police, my aunt would twist it around somehow to get me blamed.

Bugs banged against the screens of the carriage house trying to get in toward the light. Mom came into the tiny living room.

"Alice, I want you to look over some of these catalogs. Take them to bed with you and read through them. You might be interested in going to one of these schools."

The catalogs were stamped with the Ashcroft library mark where Mom had checked them out. They were all from such ritzy boarding schools. Bewildered, I gaped at them.

"What is this?" I asked. "How can we afford boarding schools? Where would we get the money?"

Mom sat down and hugged her knees. She looked kind of excited. She stressed a lot of words to put enthusiasm in her voice. "Your uncle Wheeler has generously offered to pay. He's paying for Ashcroft as it is and this is really not that much more expensive. It would be such an opportunity for you, Alice. You would meet girls from all over the country. Girls who are interested in college and careers and achievement."

I flipped through a few of the catalogs. Teenage girls walked in autumn leaves holding books against their breasts with colonial buildings in the background. They seemed to be calling out cheerful greetings to each other.

"Aren't they lovely places with all the trees and old buildings?" Mother asked.

"Sure. I guess."

I didn't want to go to those places. I was the New York girl with an artist for a stepdad and a dancer for a mother. It was bad enough being stuck in Ashcroft, but boarding school? And Ria? What would happen to her?

What was going on?

"Don't you think it would be so nice, Alice? Just girls? No boys with all their demands. You could learn about boys later on in college when you were older and better able to cope."

"Yeah. I guess."

"We'd drive you to the school, Uncle Wheeler and I. He says he can get time away from the bank, which is a wonder to me, he's such a busy man. You wouldn't have to ride a bus or anything. And we'd come get you on holidays unless you have a friend who invites you home. I'm sure you'll make a lot of friends. You're so outgoing and friendly. I imagine a lot of the girls go skiing at Christmas."

I had never been skiing in my life. We had never had the money. I just didn't belong with such people. I was a sow's ear. And I was not going to be turned into a silk purse by being shipped off to a rich girls' school. "What if they won't let me in?" I asked.

"Don't be foolish, Alice. You're a very smart girl. Besides, the prestige of Ashcroft is such that none of these other schools would dare turn you away."

They seemed to have thought of everything. "You're

acting like this is starting tomorrow. I couldn't go until next year, could I?"

"Well, I know it would be the middle of the term, but if you're going to another school, why spend any more time at Ashcroft? We figure it's better to go on and get started with the new place. Get to know the girls and the teachers. You wouldn't be that far behind. In fact, your lessons would probably take right up where you are at Ashcroft."

My pulse throbbed. I couldn't believe we were having this conversation. "Mom, am I living in a nightmare? Am I going to wake up soon?"

"What are you talking about, dear?"

"Mom, Aunt Thelma has got Gwen locked in the attic with that old woman Gladys. She takes Ria up there to play with a burned Christmas tree and the toys of a dead girl. And . . . and we're sitting here talking about educational opportunities. What's going on?"

My mother stiffened. "I have told you to call your sister 'Daria.' And I don't like repeating myself." She paused only slightly. "It's never too early to start planning for your future. It's long been one of my regrets that no one ever tried to help me plan a career. I was just allowed to drift along without any discipline or structure."

"Mom, Aunt Thelma locks people in attics. She's not normal. She's sick."

My mother's lips trembled, then became a thin line. "I hate to be an adversary, Alice, and I know I haven't been the best parent in the world. I know Todd's death was a shock to you, but it was a shock to all of us. My pain is even greater than yours. Still, your behavior has not been the best in the world. Letting that strange young man Jeremy . . . well, do the things he did to you. You are working out your emotions —your adolescent confusions—in an utterly inappropriate way. This school . . . we feel it's necessary to help save you from your own emotions. It's necessary to get you away from boys and their temptations."

I stared at her soft curves. My beautiful mother of the

seagreen eyes. My heart had for so long been filled with the green of their sea—the warming ocean that bathed and protected me and kept me hidden and safe from evil.

"Mom, Gwen is being poisoned," I repeated, pleading with her to listen to what I was saying. "She's locked up there in the attic. Bubba is feeding her rat poison."

My mother continued with her harangue. A shade was drawn down over the seagreen eyes. The charm, the joy, the warmth, the laughter were all gone. "Your lies are quite intolerable, Alice. You may as well know that the schools we are considering are a great privilege, but they are also quite strict. They are accustomed to dealing with girls with emotional problems."

"Mom, don't you hear what I'm saying?" I nearly screamed. "Gwen's sick! She's lying up there in her own vomit. Bubba gives poison to her in chocolate cake. She can't stop herself from eating it. She is lying up there dying."

My mother shook her head angrily. "End of conversation. Finish. Terminus. I can see we are getting nowhere."

"What is wrong with you?" I shouted. "How can you let that man touch you?"

Her face held utter loathing for me.

"What is wrong with *you*, you filthy-minded, sick adolescent brat?"

Those were the final words before she stalked away. She left me in incredible inner pain. I was stripped of her love.

I pushed through the creaking screen door and ran smack up against my uncle Wheeler.

"Well, what do you think?" he boomed. "Some pretty fancy places, huh? No, don't thank me. Your happiness is reward enough for me. I'll be so pleased to see you growing up and realizing your potential." He took me playfully by the shoulders and kneaded the muscles of my neck. "After a few years in boarding school, you'll be so grown up we won't know you."

"Get your stinking hands off me!" I shouted. "You're not fit to touch my mother!"

"What?" He scowled. "What are you accusing me of?" His fingers sank into my shoulders.

I tore away from him and ran blindly into the dark. Tears were streaming down my face.

His vacuous, taunting laugh followed me. "Tantrums won't get you anywhere, Alice McNamara. They'll straighten you out good in boarding school if you have tantrums. All the more reason to send you. We've clearly made the right decision."

48

The Desperate Plan

A day passed. Bubba came home stinking and filthy and moved back into the house. Aunt Thelma threw his clothes out but otherwise welcomed him with open arms. He consented to bathe, put on army fatigue pants and a T-shirt he had decorated with a flaming skull before he bellied up to the table for the evening meal.

Okra soup. Roast beef and gravy. Mashed potatoes. Peas and corn. "This is a good supper," he said, chewing with his mouth open, "but I prefer breakfast." He looked toward his mother for approval.

"Good old bacon and eggs," she agreed.

Uncle Wheeler exchanged a significant glance with my mom. She excused herself when she was through eating and took Daria out of the house and to bed. My uncle got up from the table and made a lot of commotion in his study to let everyone know he was settling down to work on papers from the bank. When Daria was asleep, he would slip out of the house to rendezvous with Mom. Couldn't Aunt Thelma figure out what was going on? Or did she even care?

Poor old Alberta was doing dishes in the kitchen. Aunt Thelma ordered me to help and left the table. Bubba was on his fourth helping of roast beef.

I had something other than washing dishes in mind. I had a more desperate plan.

They hadn't confronted Bubba about the dead dog, the mutilated Jesus, and the candle. His calm told me he didn't even know about it. And he thought that no one knew he was poisoning Gwen. I laid my plans accordingly. I hung around in the dining room after Aunt Thelma disappeared.

"I know about the Jesus you stuck full of screws," I said to him in a low voice. "I'm going to tell her who did it."

He stared at me. His brain had to grind at the problem and figure out what I was talking about. He had performed that act of sacrilege so long ago.

"I'm going to tell," I crooned. Having laid the bait, I slipped through the kitchen and out the back door.

I went down the cement steps into the cellar, slammed the door real loud, and concealed myself among the boxes and rotting furniture. I crouched there, waiting patiently, amid the dark old worn-out things. Bubba was still packing his gut and trying to figure it all out.

Soon, I saw his leering face pressing up against one of the filthy windows. His nose squashed out and his mouth hung slightly open.

Back-lit, his hulk appeared at the door. He thrust his neck forward as he searched for me in the dark. "I know you're in there," he sang out. "I seed you through the winder."

I shuffled my feet to show where I was, but I didn't speak.

"I hear you. She ain't gonna believe you—not some whore like you. But you so dumb you done trapped yourself in here, and I'm gonna have me some fun with you."

"What kind of fun?" I asked.

"Mumma done told me about you and Jeremy. Mumma says you're a whore and I can do anything I want with you."

His voice held the sneer of debauchery. He was greedy with lust. He really meant to rape me, and my vicious aunt had virtually put him up to it. Oddly, I felt no fear. I knew I was in control.

"Yes, I'm in here, Wheeler Junior," I said in a mournful voice from back in the dark.

"Don't you call me that, you whore. My name's Bubba."

"Joo-nior. Wheeler Joo-nior, the banker's son. Do you think one day you'll wear a gray suit and carry a briefcase? Do you think you'll be able to add up a column of figures? You can't add two and two now."

"What are you talking about?" he said slowly.

"They're ashamed of you, Wheeler Joo-nior. They don't want you around because they're ashamed of their crazy psycho son."

He located me by the direction of my voice and came lurching at me. "Yeah, I'm a psycho. Ain't you scared?"

"I'm not scared of you, Wheeler Junior. You're coming down here in the dark where they've got hidden things. Things from the dead girl."

He stopped suddenly. "What kind of things?" The edge of his mouth jerked nervously.

"Come on and look," I lured invitingly.

He came on cautiously. I let him see me. He came swaggering at me, his belly thrust out. I threw a cardboard box over his head and dodged around him.

Bubba crashed into furniture, his legs churning, arms bashing against things. There was a cloud of dust. He choked and coughed.

"You damn bitch!" he yelled.

I dodged away and out the door. Slammed it and set the padlock. Bubba smacked up against it with his body, making it shake. It held.

"Hey!" he yelled.

In smeared flames, daylight was dying in the west. Night was coming on with its weary odors of sea and alluvial soil and rotting plants. The palmettos had turned to black silhouettes against the sky.

"It's getting dark out, Joo-nior," I said through the door. "You're all locked up in the dark."

He kicked at the door violently. "You lemme outta here!"

"I burned your shack, Wheeler Junior. I burned it to the ground. I'm not afraid of you."

"You was the one what did it! I knowed all along!"

"I poured gas all over it. All over your pictures of naked women. All over your knives and liquor and cigarettes and your rat poison. Then I set it on fire and watched it burn."

"I'll get you for that! I'll tell my Mumma! She'll fix you! She'll whip the hide right off your ass! She'll lock you in the attic with lard-butt Gwen!"

"No she won't, Wheeler Joo-nior," I crooned. "She doesn't really like you because you're dumb. You're so dumb they have to call you Bubba and let you hang around a gas station!"

"I ain't dumb! I'm smarter'n anybody! Don't you call me dumb!"

"You're so dumb you let me lock you in the cellar! You're so dumb you think no one knows you're poisoning Gwen!"

He went very quiet. "You don't know nothing about that."

"I know about the rat poison, Wheeler Junior. I know how you started out on little animals and moved up to a dog and now you're using it on Gwen. You're going to kill your own sister."

"I ain't doing nothing! Mumma is mad at Gwen because of what she said about her killing Daria. Mumma didn't kill Daria. Mumma is nice. Mumma makes me take Gwen that cake!"

"She's going to blame it on you, Wheeler Junior. You're so dumb that if she gets caught she'll blame it on you. She's set you up the whole way."

"No she won't! She loves me! I'm her first-borned son! I'm the son Senior wanted!"

"She's old and she's scared and she's crazy, Bubba. Just like you. You're scared and you're crazy. You've got the Broderick crazy streak. One day, they'll lock you off in the nuthouse in a straitjacket and you'll beat your crazy head against the wall until you die."

"She won't do that! Mumma won't put me in no nuthouse!"

"Bubba, don't you see? You'll just be thrown away when she doesn't need you anymore. You'll go to the boneyard. The glue factory."

"It ain't true! It ain't true!"

"They'll send you to jail, Bubba. The police will come and ask questions and you'll talk too much because you're dumb. They'll hook you up to your daddy's lie detector and make you tell the truth. And when they find you poisoned your sister, they'll send you off to the state prison where you'll be locked behind bars forever and the men will come and get you at night and no one will ever care about you ever again."

"Ain't true," he said in an unsteady voice.

"Yes it is. You've laid the trail. You killed all the animals. You had the rat poison. Your mother knows."

I waited in silence for a moment.

He gave out a thin sharp wail that rose like a cat yowling.

My plan was working!

49
Dead and Gone

"**Y**ou keep your fat stupid mouth shut!"
ordered Aunt Thelma.

"I ain't stupid!" yelled Bubba. "Don't you call me stupid!"

"Shut up, do you hear me! Shut up!"

"I ain't going to no jailhouse for you! I ain't going off to no prison where the men will hold me down and do stuff to me in the dark!"

"No one's going to jail! No one! Do you hear?"

Aunt Thelma had let Bubba out of the cellar and taken him into the house. He was near hysterical. I could hear the commotion from the kitchen where I hid in the darkness. He was railing at her, so intent on his own terrors that he forgot to mention my role in locking him up.

Bubba was dancing up and down with fear. His legs pumped, his arms flailed. "If Gwen dies they'll be cops all over this house. They'll find out. They'll hook me up to Daddy's lie detector and make me tell the truth."

Aunt Thelma took him by the shoulders and shook him. "Stop it, Bubba! You're my son. You're my Broderick son. I brought you into this world to please Senior. Nothing's going to happen to you. I won't allow it. Your father won't allow it."

"I ain't gone be faithful to you like some old dog and end up in the grave while you're out free!"

Frustrated and angry, she walloped Bubba across the

mouth. It failed to silence him. He turned his face, but kept yelling.

"Boneyard! Glue factory! Dead and gone in some dark hole! I ain't gonna die for you! I ain't gonna be lost in no sewage and black water where I can't breathe!"

She drew back to hit him again, but he slipped from her grasp and went pounding up the dark stairs. "I'm coming, Gwen!" he shouted. "I'll let you out! It ain't my fault you're in there! She don't like you 'cause you're fat and she wants you dead! Plus you know about Daria. You know she killed Daria."

It was clear that that was the last straw. Wheezing and gasping, Aunt Thelma lurched after Bubba. I couldn't see her face, but I could hear everything she was saying clearly. Her voice rang with a kind of panting, slavering desperation.

"I didn't kill her! Senior thought I did, but he was wrong. It was Todd and Kate. Not me. I could never do something so awful. Gwen's a liar. Liars burn in hell."

At the top of the steps, Bubba was tugging at the door-knob, calling out to Gwen. "I didn't mean it! I didn't mean to do nothing to you!"

I followed them up the steps. I wanted to see what I had created. I wanted to watch them fight it out.

Aunt Thelma caught Bubba at the top of the steps. She took him by the hair and shook him violently. Her mouth was twisted in a snarl. Her eyes were crazed with violence. She was screaming like a ghoul.

"You idiot! You shit! You sick-brained no-mind! I did not kill Daria, do you understand me!"

"Get away from me!" Bubba countered. "Get away from me you ugly old bitch!" With his big fists, Bubba pounded his mother in the face, and then took hold of the sides of her mouth as if he was going to tear her head apart.

Behind the locked door, Gwen was crying, "Killer killer!" Or maybe it was "Kill her! Kill her!"

Mother and son rocked and swayed. Then, with an outward fling of her arms, my aunt managed to throw Bubba from her. He arched out into space over the stairs.

He sailed past me. "WUHHHhhhhhh!" he shrieked as he went down.

On the landing, I pressed back into the wall.

I watched Bubba strike a step, bounce off, strike a lower step. Then he rolled—over and over—down, down. At the bottom, he lay strangely still.

My aunt came pounding down the stairs. Near the bottom, she halted and gripped the rail. Heaving for breath, she stared with saucer eyes at Bubba's motionless body. His head was twisted funny and one leg was under him. Thelma took the last steps tentatively. When she reached the bottom, she knelt beside him like a supplicant. She shook him.

"Get up from there, Wheeler Junior! Do you hear me? Get up from there! You're not hurt! You're just trying to scare me because I'm old and tired. All you and your sister ever want to do is scare me!"

A thin trickle of blood leaked out of the corner of Bubba's mouth and ran down his cheek. There was a curious smile on his face. He was dead.

From where I was standing, a bar of moonlight filtered through the stained-glass window with the Broderick coat of arms in blue, rose, and gold. The little girl's face looked solemn.

My aunt's shoulders shook with weeping and remorse. For the first time, I was witnessing an emotion from her other than anger. She knelt down beside Bubba. The smile on her face was ghastly.

"You're my boy. I brought you into the world for Senior. I made Wheeler take the Broderick name so you'd be a Broderick—so you could have the bank and be the heir. But you weren't good enough for Senior. He wanted girls. He wanted little girls in ribbons and bows. He said you were retarded and couldn't run the bank. Said he'd never leave it to you. The Broderick name would end in shame, he said!"

"You killed him," I said from up on the stairs. "You killed him."

Aunt Thelma looked up with stark, hunted fear in her eyes. "It was an accident!" she screamed. "It was an accident, I tell you!"

I did not contradict her. What was the point? My desperate plan had worked. My aunt was beaten.

50

Sweet Oblivion

Without resistance, Aunt Thelma gave me the key to the attic. I didn't hurry up the stairs. I was too frightened of what I would find.

Slowly, I trudged past the stained-glass window, its colors flowing now in the moonlight. Far below, I could hear my aunt talking to the corpse.

"I didn't mean it. You're not really hurt anyhow. You get up and quit trying to scare me. It was an accident I tell you! An accident! Nobody could have stopped it. I didn't push him. I couldn't have. I was too far away."

Reaching the top, I stood facing the dreaded door. I turned the key in the lock and pushed the door slowly open. Scanned the low dark room with its worn carpet, jumbled furniture, and shadows in blurred interplay. A dim light leaked through the salt-crusted windows.

It was a vision of the nightmare side of reality. There was a burned Christmas tree in a stand with toys underneath —scattered alphabet blocks—cloth-covered children's books scored by a long-ago flame—a cowboy hat—Daria's fuzzy yellow duck.

Over in the far corner, an old woman sat in a heavy rocking chair, her eyes clouded with impenetrable sorrow. All hunger, desire, love, longing, and hope had been extinguished in her. Her translucent skin hung slack on her bones. Her snow-white hair reached all the way to her shoulders. A meaningless smile twisted the corners of her thin mouth. Here she sat day after day while the sun baked outside or the sea fog crept in or the wind howled and the trees beat against the house.

She simply sat there, rocking gently in the chair, lost in the oblivion of madness.

I touched the string of broken ornaments on the tree. A bell tinkled. An angel fell to the floor.

Just inside the door, Gwen was lying curled up in a ball. Her clothes were stiff with vomit. Two plates were there. Plates that had held the deadly chocolate cake. She had licked them spotless.

"I'm sick," she moaned as she doubled up, constricted with agony and unceasing terror.

I tugged at her arms and tried to get her to sit up. "Gwen, you've been poisoned. We must get you to a doctor."

She cried piteously. "When I was little, I looked like Daria. Momma cut my hair the same as hers. She must have dyed it dark too. Twice a week she brought me up here and I was scared. I cried and wet my pants, but she made me come back. I was supposed to make Grandma well. That's what she would say."

"You've got to walk, Gwen," I urged. "I can't carry you."

Gwen got over on her hands and knees. Her head hung down almost to the floor. "She'd make me play like it was Christmas and I was Daria and the tree was on fire. I'd have to say 'Todd did it' and scream. She'd stick me with pins until I did what she wanted. It hurt. It hurt!"

"Please, Gwen, please get up!" I said desperately. "There's no one to help. There's only us!"

She looked up at me with blurred eyes. "Then one day I got fat and didn't look like Daria anymore so I didn't have to come up here. But Momma didn't love me anymore."

I dragged and pulled and pushed her. Gradually, she began to shift and she finally stood up with difficulty. Somehow I propelled her through the door. She reeled out and caught hold of the railing to support herself. I got around in front of her and coaxed her down step by step. Her eyes were feverish and she was sweating.

"I couldn't stop wetting the bed. I'd have nightmares of being locked up here. Momma used to threaten me with the attic when I was bad and sneaked food."

Looking back, I could see the old woman had shifted in her chair. She opened her mouth to attempt unaccustomed speech. "Daria?" she croaked.

Gwen made another step, then another and another. She whimpered sporadically, gripping the rail, fumbling at it as she shifted her handholds. I helped as best I could.

At last we reached the bottom. Gwen sat heavily on the final step—next to her mother. She looked down quizzically at her brother's dead body.

"Grandma won't get well," said Gwen. "Nothing I can do will make her well."

Aunt Thelma was still talking to Bubba's dead body. "You get up from there, Wheeler Junior. You get up this instant. I won't stand for this. You hear?"

I used the hall phone to call the hospital and explain what was going on. Twenty minutes later, the ambulance came with a siren wail that dimmed as it turned into the gate. I went outside and told them where Gwen was. Two earnest young men with crew cuts and big shoulders rushed in with a stretcher.

I sat on the porch and watched the dark world around me—the desolate Broderick mansion, a house of fiends and madness. The lawn was plumed with bits of rising mist. Sinewy coils of wisteria vine seemed to be choking the Woolcott house—that gabled house of Jeremy, my lost love. There was a damp odor of harbor water, a mix of salt and mud and oil sludge.

The arrival of the ambulance brought Mom to the door of the carriage house, peering into the darkness at the red blinking lights. Behind her stood Uncle Wheeler, who had been visiting with her for a purpose I knew full well.

The earnest young men carried Gwen out. She was humming a hymn and lightly moving her hands with the music. Aunt Thelma followed behind, staring with distant feral eyes. "You can't get good meat these days. It's an absolute disgrace. Senior never would have stood for it, I can tell you that."

The driver used the radio to call for another ambulance. "We got one dead and one poisoned," he whispered. "Better call the police."

As the ambulance drove off, Aunt Thelma lurched after it waving her arms. "Folks moved off the sidewalk for Senior Broderick!" she yelled. "We were somebody in this town when he was alive!"

And I am sure that all of Congreve heard her.

51

Best Intentions

The ugly brick hospital was sweltering in the hot sun. Window air-conditioning units dribbled puddles of water and moaned from the effort of cooling the building. I trudged up the steps between my mother and Uncle Wheeler.

"It's important that you pay your respects to your aunt Thelma," Mom said. Her tones were precise. My desperate plan had turned convenient for her and my uncle. It had gotten Aunt Thelma out of the way—neatly and cleanly.

"Social forms should always be observed," she continued. "That way, your intentions will not be misinterpreted. You can have the best intentions in the world and yet confuse people if you don't follow the forms."

In the waiting room, my mother sat down and declined to go farther. "I believe I'll stay here, Wheeler," she said. "I don't enjoy sickness."

My uncle and I rode the elevator to the top floor, where the mental patients were kept. Nurses with brooding eyes gave us directions.

We passed a woman trying to get a group of bedraggled patients to draw pictures of what was bothering them. Her voice had a brittle cheerfulness. "We can all work out our problems together through art," she chirped.

The group sat at long elementary school tables staring at their hands, fiddling with crayons. Their eyes were expres-

sionless. An old man with hair like silver Christmas tinsel
was tearing his paper methodically into long strips.

"That's very good, Chester," she said. "The uniformity
is ideal and the length of the strips might be telling us something. Would you like to talk about it to the group?"

"Get bent," muttered the old man.

"It's good to let out our emotions," she said approv-
ingly, talking as though she were one of the patients too.
"We have to remember that we're all at a crossroads in our
lives."

On we walked, through pea-green halls and rooms of
people in bathrobes watching black-and-white TV, another
group was working with modeling clay. We attracted only
languid interest. We were faint movement on the margins of
their world. A tired-looking old man slopped at the floor
with a mop and bucket of dirty water. Everywhere there was
the smell of urine and cleansing liquids.

From down the hall, I could see an attendant leading
Aunt Thelma toward us. She was wearing a straitjacket.

"Drugs aren't good for people," my uncle intoned sol-
emnly. "That's why I asked for the straitjacket instead."

As my aunt approached, Uncle Wheeler conversed in
hushed tones with Priscilla Davis, the staff psychologist who
had pronounced Todd a child molester. Their voices were so
low, I could only catch brief snatches.

Dr. Davis: "Some progress is being made . . . affect
apparently normal . . . some reality testing . . . memory
spotty . . ."

Uncle Wheeler: "Essential that she remain here if she is
to avoid prosecution . . . can't have a scandal that might
shake confidence in the bank . . ."

Uncle Wheeler straightened up and gave Dr. Davis a
significant look. She nodded, understanding. "Yes," she said.
"Of course Mrs. Broderick must cure herself. No drugs will
be administered. Her charts are clearly marked. The psychiatric staff is in total agreement."

We were shown into a small room with one chair and a wire-reinforced window that admitted a pale light.

The attendant, his white coat open to show suspenders and a belt, led my aunt in, drawing her along with the loose end of one of the leather straps that bound her up in the white jacket.

The solitary chair received her with a groan.

"Don't you push me," she yelped hysterically. "I am Thelma Broderick. Don't you dare push me!"

"Yes'm, Miz Brod'rick," said the attendant. "No pushin' here. None a'tall." He grinned at Uncle Wheeler and winked repeatedly, finally putting a finger beside his head to make a twirling motion.

"Yes, I know she's crazy," said Uncle Wheeler gruffly. "Now get out of here."

The attendant grinned hugely as he went out.

"Who's crazy?" Aunt Thelma snapped. "Who are you talking about?" She seemed to be trying to touch her shoulder with her chin.

For a moment I cringed and the old fears returned. It seemed to me this woman was a demon that could never be kept chained. She was the same as ever. She would demand to be released, and they would all fall down and do her bidding.

"No one," said Uncle Wheeler with his slick grin. "No one, dear. We've just come to check on you."

The momentary crimson drained from her cheeks. She settled herself in the chair.

Uncle Wheeler kept his lips drawn back over his teeth in a pretend smile. "Well, how are things, dear? Are they treating you well?"

"I don't like it here in the nuthouse," she said.

Uncle Wheeler made his *tsk*-ing noise. "Now, Thelma dear, this is definitely not a nuthouse. It's simply a place for you to rest and forget the terrible recent events."

"I don't forget anything," she argued. "My memory's perfect. They're always testing me and asking where I am and what time it is with a clock right there on the wall. I can remember everything that's happened." Her voice became complacent.

"I remember how every year Senior would get a brand-new Buick and drive it up to the house and honk the horn and all us kids would come running out all excited. We knew he was the most important man in Congreve because he could afford a new car every year, and the arrival of that car was like a reaffirmation of our place in society. We'd climb all over that car and want to play the radio and work the clock and—I could tell time even when I was five years old which they don't believe in here because they're always creeping around giving me sneaking looks and trying to make out I'm crazy. . . .

"Senior took insolence from no man. He exercised firm authority over the common people. We had to call him Senior because he didn't like any other name. It captured his importance. He was The Senior, the wisest elder of the tribe, the oldest of us all. 'The bank with a sound money policy and the church with a sound position on sin will salvage us all,' he'd say. And he meant it too. Senior was right about everything."

Suddenly, her voice turned oddly tender. "Daria was just as pretty as a picture. She was cute and smart and all dressed up fine as you please in black patent leather shoes. Why her eyes lit up as bright as the shine on those shoes. That's what Senior would say.

"He had big hands. Big, strong but affectionate hands. I can remember the feel of them as he'd stroke my cheek. I couldn't have killed Daria because if I had he wouldn't have loved me anymore. And that was the problem in the first place. He loved her the most because she was little and cute and not fat like me. I wanted to be loved more but I didn't kill her for that. It was the others. Momma killed her. And Todd. If they hadn't had that tree there in the first place, she never would have burned up. They killed her dead sure as anything!"

Smiling, Aunt Thelma seemed to be acknowledging to herself the importance of her strange, nightmarish memories.

"Daria could blush so pretty. She would turn all nice and pink. But she turned red in that fire. Then black. She got all black and stiff and the screams died in her throat. I was there, but it wasn't my fault. I was too far across the room to have set that tree on fire. It was Todd's fault. He always wanted a tree and Momma always gave him what he wanted. 'I want a big tree for Christmas,' he'd say, and she'd just tell the men to go out and get one and there it would be. Todd killed her."

My aunt coughed but it sounded more like she was strangling. A sudden look of pure joyous anticipation passed over Uncle Wheeler's face.

Her coughing turned to a choked gurgle. "Somebody help me! I can't use my arms. What's wrong with my arms?"

"Yes," mused Uncle Wheeler. "Your arms do appear to be useless. What do you suppose the problem is?"

"I . . . don't know," my aunt protested. "I can't understand it."

"Are you in a straitjacket?" Uncle Wheeler asked.

"No! I'm not in any such thing! I'm not crazy! There's nothing wrong with me! I won't die in the nuthouse!"

"If you can't accept reality, you can't be cured," Uncle Wheeler told her.

"I'm not crazy!" Aunt Thelma protested.

Uncle Wheeler stood up. "We must leave you now, Thelma."

"Who's this girl? Who's this girl you've brought? Is she one of them? Is she one of them sneaking, spying types out to prove I'm crazy?"

"You don't know her?" asked my uncle.

"Of course I know her," she countered. "Don't be ridiculous!"

"Who is she then?"

Aunt Thelma studied me carefully with her narrow eyes.

Put to the test, her mind wandered to more pleasant memories. "In summers, downtown, we used to go to the soda fountain and all us kids would sit up on the high stools. Senior would swagger up to the soda jerk and say we could have whatever we wanted. You could buy a lot for a quarter back then. It wasn't really so long ago when you think about it. Big balls of ice cream dropped with a splash into the fountain Coke. Daria would beat on the counter with a spoon because she was small and didn't know how to behave properly. But Senior would indulge her anyway and let her do whatever she wanted."

Suddenly, Aunt Thelma seemed to remember me. "I hate you," she said. "You're not one of us. You think you're going to get part of our money, but you're not. You don't have Broderick blood." She smiled in pride of possession. Thelma Broderick, imperial heiress to Congreve. Thelma Broderick, chief spider in the web.

I shifted toward the door.

"I hate you," she said stridently. "You and your ripe little body and full little mouth. You're going to die simply because you're inconvenient. Your sins will burn you in hell."

"We'll come back again soon, dear," said Uncle Wheeler.

"I need to powder my nose," my aunt whined. "I can't powder my nose all tied up like this."

In the hall, the attendant hovered. He gave my uncle a servile grin and Uncle Wheeler handed him a dollar bill. The attendant bobbed his head and smiled wider as though they shared a dreadful secret.

Slowly, we went out into the hall.

"My nose is all shiny!" Aunt Thelma yelled from behind us.

I couldn't resist looking back. She was leaning against the door frame with her head thrust forward. Ignoring her demands, the attendant was prodding her back toward the little room she lived in now.

"I don't like it here in the nuthouse! You take me home where I belong! I didn't kill Daria! I was way across the room when it happened!"

We got into the elevator. The doors closed behind us. My uncle put his hand to his mouth as though he was stifling an urge to burp. The elevator went down slowly, and opened up when we reached the ground floor.

Mom was waiting in the same chair, leafing through a magazine. As we approached she looked up with a remote smile.

Uncle Wheeler was quivering. It was then that I realized he was laughing.

"She's totally round the bend," he told my mother. "She'll never get out of here."

52
Careless Laughter

Uncle Wheeler quickly got rid of his mother-in-law. In the dead of night, a special car took Gladys to an expensive private nursing home. I didn't feel sad. She was locked in the protective security of her madness. She was no worse off than she had been in the attic.

With the death of Bubba, shipping me off to boarding school seemed to have been forgotten. I returned to the Ashcroft School, where life took on a hushed tone. Gwen survived the poisoning, but there were complications and she had to be sent away to a big hospital. The absence of Broderick women left an enormous vacuum that Headmistress Carson couldn't quite adapt to. All the girls seemed disoriented.

Daria made friends again, but I was a horse of a different color. I had been too close to the Broderick disasters. Almost superstitiously, the students steered clear of me, never speaking, avoiding eye contact. I even took to walking home for lunch to avoid having to sit by myself.

I would frequently find my mother lounging in the garden in a red bathing suit. Starting around noon, she'd begin sipping a gin and tonic. Uncle Wheeler would come home for lunch, driving up in his Cadillac, honking the horn even though he was only five feet away. My mother would jump up and act all startled.

"Oh, Wheeler," she'd say. "You're such a child."

First, she'd kneel there moving her abdomen and shoulders around. Then she'd sit back on the chair, pick up her drink, dabble a finger among the ice and look up at him through her eyelashes.

He'd peel out of his seersucker suit jacket, loosen his tie, and throw the jacket back into the car. Big sweat stains lurked under his armpits. He stank something awful, but Mom didn't seem to mind. She'd put her hand up against his chest and nuzzle all around him like he smelled of lilacs.

"I couldn't stay away," he'd say.

"Again?" she'd purr, acting so pleased that she was irresistible.

I was jealous. But not of my mom because she had a man I wanted. I wasn't infatuated with the gray-haired father figure of Uncle Wheeler. Despite what had happened in Congreve, Todd had been all the father I would ever want. He was the best father any girl could ever have. His memory was sacred to me.

Uncle Wheeler was different. With his pencil mustache and greasy hair, he was truly disgusting. Beyond that, he had heavy responsibility for Todd's death. He was a murderer the same as if he had hanged Todd himself.

It wasn't really jealousy. It was more a sense of moral outrage at seeing my mother—my very own flesh and blood —turn into a slave to this man. I simply could not understand her motivations.

She was my beautiful mother. My mother so beloved by Todd, Daria, and me. My mother who moved through life like a nymph from an enchanted wood. My mother of the seagreen eyes. Now under the baleful influence of Congreve and that horrible house, she had become as demented as the rest of them. Why? Why had it happened?

There was no doubt about her intentions. She wanted Wheeler because he had money. Big money. The money that ruled Congreve. She was willing to debase herself utterly for what? To live in the monstrous big house? To be forever haunted by the ghost of a little girl? To live in the house where her husband had been driven to suicide? It didn't make sense. Except that it was clear she had gone crazy. Life in Congreve had been too much for her, just as it had been too much for Todd.

Mom and Uncle Wheeler loved to go into the cavernous dining room and have lunch and more gin sitting together at the end of the long table. Some avocados and shrimp salad. Mom would stay in her bathing suit and sit with one foot tucked up under her like a girl. When I thought of the dark crises that bathing suits and booze had caused in that same house—how recently booze and bathing suits had been condemned as the devil's tools—well, I was sad and confused.

Each day near noon, when I was getting away from school at lunch, I'd creep in through the back screen door, holding it so it didn't slam. I'd stand there in the kitchen listening to the two of them chatter in the dining room. I even watched them through a crack in the door. Mom would lay her hand on his arm and give him meaningful glances. She'd tap his nose with her finger, rest her head against his shoulder, nuzzle his neck.

One lunch, I remember particularly noticing her rubbing her hand all up and down his leg. He smiled like a buzzard eating a dead animal in the middle of the highway.

"I really like your hair," he said, his eyes locked with hers. "I'd like to see it . . . well, really messed up and wild-looking."

"Your wish is my et cetera," she replied in a coy voice.

I thought I would choke as I watched them get up and rub against each other. Uncle Wheeler held her face in his hands and kissed her.

Their arms around each other, they went out of the room and up the stairs of the dark house. My mother's bare feet shuffled and his big, thick-soled shoes clomped on each step as they traversed the same identical stairs where Bubba and Todd had died.

I fled in tears and misery to the carriage house where I

had spent so many awful days. I longed to run away forever. I hate to admit that I never wanted to see them again.

The carriage house was horribly fetid and wretched. It was like a doll house with tiny rooms, ratty furniture, a groaning air conditioner, and a rusty refrigerator.

That day I couldn't bring myself to return to school after lunch. I hung around the St. Michael's graveyard, read the inscriptions on the gravestones, and wondered once again how miserable the people had been who had been born, lived, and died in this town. Born, lived, and died dominated and ruled by the Wheelers and Thelmas and Seniors. And in that instant I understood the desperation that Todd had felt when he tried to escape to New York.

When school let out, I met Daria and tried to put a brave face on things. Despite lingering heat, October had come with its promise of Halloween. Daria talked of trick-or-treating and how she intended to dress as either an angel or a unicorn. I could imagine a horn attached to her head, but couldn't figure out how to make the rest of her look like a horse. She said an angel would be fine.

"I'll have wings and a white dress and a halo," she said with great enthusiasm.

I shivered to think how close she had come to being an angel. I tried to tell myself that we had escaped evil and that now things would be better. We could actually think in terms of trick-or-treating, and even escape the confines of the Broderick mansion for bits of normal fun. Soon, Mom would wise up. She would come to her senses and be our lovely mother again and hug us and love us. The spell would break and Mom would have no memory of touching the awful Uncle Wheeler.

But there was no dinner that night. Alberta had been sent home, and Mom and Uncle Wheeler never came down from the bedroom. I fed Daria carrots and celery and cornflakes. When Daria asked about Mom, I lied that she was helping Uncle Wheeler redecorate the house.

I read Daria a story called "Small Pig," put her to bed,

and sat and talked with her until she was asleep. She lay peacefully, her tiny mouth breathing, her hands clutching the fuzzy duck. I left her there in her innocence and went to the front door, where I stood in the dark looking across to the telltale upstairs bedroom window in the big house. I felt sick to my stomach. Now my mother was taking Aunt Thelma's place.

There was a faint light on, like a bedside lamp way back in the room. The sound of careless female laughter wafted down.

53

Promise to a Child

In tearful misery I fled over the garden gate to my secret spot in the gazebo. I lay on the bench weeping. In my imagination, Jeremy appeared like a sympathetic ghost, sat down, rubbed my back, and stroked my hair. He let me know that in some way I belonged to him and so would always be under his care.

Never in my life had I felt so dependent on a male. I had never known and not even daydreamed much about my real father. Especially after Todd had come into my life. But Todd had never really seemed like a protective figure. Rather, he had been someone who was there who made my mother happy.

Now suddenly, at age thirteen, I thought of feeling warm and safe with Jeremy.

Like a magic visitation, I opened my eyes to see him standing there ghostly and shadowed before me. It was really him. He was actually there with his lean body and eyes of enchantment.

"Jeremy," I gasped.

"Alice!" he said.

And we hugged and held each other close, our two hearts pounding. He joked in his old way, making cracks about being home on leave from the junior army camp. Mater and Pater were busy reading a biblical passage.

"I hate them! I hate them!" I suddenly wept.

"My parents?" he asked, puzzled. "How could anyone

hate them? I find them odd perhaps. Even bizarre, but I can't hate them."

"No! I mean Uncle Wheeler and my mother!" I cried.

"Wheeler I can understand. We've long agreed that he's true slime. It's one of our most significant points of agreement. But your mom . . . she doesn't seem a bad sort."

"She's in his . . . in his bed."

"His bed? The man who married the dreaded Aunt Thelma? Now that's truly disgusting. Gosh, I'm sorry for you, I really am."

"Stop being so damn witty," I burst out. "Stop being someone out of a drawing room comedy. It's sick. It's horrible. I hate them."

He lifted me up and kissed my tear-streaked cheeks, my eyes, my lips. I melted into him, returning his kisses even though I was sobbing. His hands ranged my body, went under my shirt, stroked my back. I felt comforted. I had someone to talk to. Someone who would understand.

"Why has my mother fallen out of love with me?" I asked Jeremy. "What have I done to her?"

"Oh, Alice, she loves you still, in her own way."

"Give me a break," I said. "Her own way has nothing to do with me. It's like she has forgotten about her past life. Todd and Ria and me. She's gone crazy."

"It's her way of dealing with the reality, Alice. That's all. Don't blame yourself. You can't."

I lay up against his shoulders for a long time. He was right. It wasn't my fault.

"There is no more Thelma," he said, almost like a promise to a child that there was no bogeymen. "She's gone forever. There's only us in a world of sick adults. We can be in love. Our love can keep us pure. It can protect us against the whole world."

"Please stay with me," I begged. "Don't go back to that military school."

"I don't know about that. There's a chance—maybe—

of a reprieve now that Aunt Thelma's put away. And Mater and Pater are so vague they might forget to take me back."

I was determined to seize the moment. "Stay with me tonight," I pressed.

"The garden is ours," he agreed. "No Thelma to invade our sanctuary."

Then I remembered Ria and I shook my head. "My sister. I can't leave her alone. She might wake up and be afraid. My mom has abandoned her, but I won't. She'll have at least one person in the world she can rely on."

"Your mom's going to be with Wheeler," Jeremy said boldly. "We can have your charming little cottage."

I could find no fault with his plan—save Mater and Pater. "Your parents. Don't they ever check on you at night?"

"They can barely find the bathroom on their own. I'm not sure they even see me at the breakfast table. I'm like a poached egg or something."

The Reverend and Mrs. Woolcott's manner never seemed to bother him. In some inexplicable way, it was funny, yet comforting. He could be so strong and self-contained.

Once again comrades in intrigue, we scrambled over the gate with our old zest, went through the door and latched it. If Mom returned, she'd have to bang on it to wake me up. Jeremy could escape through the back window.

We crept upstairs in the darkness. Daria murmured in her sleep. I pushed Jeremy through the door into the bedroom where Todd had spent each night with my mother. Was there meaning there? Was I trying to exorcise a ghost? Was I trying to take their place and insert sanity and love where their madness had been?

I barely thought of it at the time. My mind was only on Jeremy, on his foot of height above me, the smell of his skin, and the taste of his mouth.

Shortly, we were naked together once more, stretched out on the dilapidated bed, our bodies touching on cool sheets, our souls entwined. We fondled and probed in all the secret places in a manner that was truly reverential. I was only thirteen. Did I dare make these forbidden delights into a habit when I was so young? By some kind fate, the decision was made for me. And, no doubt, it was for the best.

I remember feeling soft and cuddled in a sudden surge of weariness. I remember thinking of what was about to happen, thinking of his propulsion once more inside of me.

And then, somehow, his low, gentle voice simply put me to sleep.

54

Kind Fate

Morning came with the sound of birdsong. The marsh was a bright yellow. There was a hint of growing cool, a beginning fragrance of autumn in the air.

Daria was playing on her bed, sensing, as she always could, that it was Saturday.

"Jeremy!" she called out, running to hug him.

"We're playing house," I explained. "Mom went off for the evening so we decided to play house."

"You mean Mommy went away with Uncle Wheeler," Ria pouted. "She does it all the time now."

I ignored her insight and pushed her down the stairs playfully. "Jeremy will be the daddy and I'll be the mommy and we'll all have breakfast."

"What are my parents doing?" asked Jeremy. He was over at the window looking out.

I went to the window with him. The Woolcotts were on their knees in the Broderick yard praying. "I think it's pretty obvious," I said.

"Sure, smarty-pants, but what's the occasion? This is a bit dramatic even for them."

The three of us went out of the house and across the yard. Norman looked up. "Oh, Jeremy," he said. "And um . . . Alice." He always had trouble remembering my name. "We're having a small ceremony of thanksgiving."

"But it's barely October," Jeremy said.

Norman blinked at him. "Giving thanks is appropriate

at any time and especially when the Lord has seen fit to bless us so thoroughly."

"What's the big news?" Jeremy asked.

"Reverend Woolcott has received a posting," said Kate proudly. "His years of dedication and fine service have not been forgotten by the Board of Foreign Ministries."

"Oh," said Jeremy. His face fell.

"In Guiana," added Norman. "If you reference the atlas, you will find it an exotic tropical place in South America. The life will be hard, but we are used to hardship. It will be a good furtherance to your education."

"When are we leaving?" Jeremy asked. He looked crushed.

"Almost immediately," said Kate. "Or at least as soon as Reverend Woolcott can pack his library. I'm sure they'll have few books there. Your father's library will be essential if we are to provide spiritual uplift to these people who await our coming with such eagerness. That's what the letter said. We are awaited with 'such'—or was it 'much'?—eagerness. Do you remember, Reverend Woolcott? Was it 'such' or 'much'?"

"I'm not really sure, Mrs. Woolcott. It seems it was 'such.' But when you say 'much' that has a ring of truth as well. I don't know where I've put the letter." He searched his pockets. "I'm so forgetful about things. And yet the letter is such manna from heaven I don't know how I could have lost it."

"I don't want to go," Jeremy stated adamantly. "I think it's time I had a regular education instead of just reading books at random."

Norman and Kate exchanged confused looks. "They are expecting a family," said Kate. "They were quite explicit in the letter. 'We await the coming of you and your family with much eagerness.' It was 'much,' Reverend Woolcott. I'm certain now that it was 'much.' "

"We can't disappoint them" said Norman. "I'm sure it would be a disappointment if you failed to arrive along with us. They might begin to wonder if they had made the right choice. Small doubts could grow into substantive issues— even points of difference."

An upstairs window opened in the big Broderick house. My mother's voice called down. "Oh, Alice! Would you mind stepping up here, please?"

I looked up. Her hair was tousled. She was wearing only a slip.

"Hello, Kate," she said, leaning on the windowsill. "Norman, we're so happy to hear your good news."

"Oh . . . ?" said Norman. "How did you . . . ? Well, the Lord does work in wondrous ways. I've always said that, Mrs. Woolcott. Haven't I always said that?"

"Yes, Reverend Woolcott, you always have. And they're very true words."

Leaving Daria with them, I trudged into the house and up the dark stairs where Todd had hung twirling with the life gone from him.

Uncle Wheeler had arranged to send the Woolcotts away—that much was clear. He wanted them out of the way so he could have a free hand with the bank and the Estate.

With deep foreboding, I rapped on the door. My mother received me lying in bed with Uncle Wheeler. There was coffee on a tray beside them and stubbed-out cigarettes in a saucer.

"Come in, Alice McNamara," my mother said. Her smile was false. Her fingers slid inside the shoulder strap of her slip.

"You've heard the good news?" she asked.

"You mean about Guiana?"

"Isn't it simply marvelous?" she enthused. "Such a great adventure. A chance for Jeremy to live in a foreign place."

"He's lived in foreign places all his life," I said sullenly.

"And how lucky for him," Mom continued in her positive manner. "He's always in some place different and never stuck in a small town like Congreve. He's always meeting different people and seeing new and different things."

Uncle Wheeler lit a cigarette. I stood and stared at him. He puffed deeply and blew out a plume of smoke. He was wearing no shirt. Perhaps he was naked beneath the sheet.

Mother's voice probed carefully with her next question. "Alice, you've always been unhappy here, haven't you?"

"Yes," I agreed quietly.

"The Ashcroft School is really not your style. You're so much more of a free spirit than the girls there. They're being trained for rather tedious lives as housewives. You want to get out into the world and be an artist. See and do glamorous things."

I said nothing. I simply waited for the trap to be sprung. It was that business of boarding school again. I had to be gotten out of the way too.

"Wheeler and I have been thinking about your future. We want only the best for you." She lifted her cup and took a sip of the milky dregs. She smiled thinly. "In trying to think of your best interests, we've decided it would be a broadening experience for you to go to Guiana with your uncle Norman and aunt Kate."

I was utterly flabbergasted. In my wildest imagination I had never pictured this. "To Guiana? But have you asked them? What if they don't want me along?"

Uncle Wheeler smirked. "Norman will do as he's told. I arranged his posting, after all."

"I'll bet you did," I said sourly.

He laughed. "Do you imagine that Norman is capable of getting a job on his own? I give a bundle to that church. That's the only way he's remained employed all these years. Still, he periodically makes such a hash of things that they have to pack him up and send him home."

Mom laid a restraining hand on his chest. "Now, Wheeler, let's not make things seem dismal. Norman is a fine minister."

Suddenly I had a chilling thought. "Daria!" I blurted. "I can't go and leave her. It's out of the question."

"Of course, Alice," my mother said. "I can tell from the

set of your jaw that you're quite determined, my little hard-headed Alice. Well, I won't argue with you. Uncle Wheeler had already anticipated this." She ran her finger around the rim of her coffee cup. "I believe Guiana would be a good experience for Daria as well."

"But . . ." I began, "the will . . . I thought . . ."

Mother looked at Uncle Wheeler, who gave her a half nod. "Yes . . . you're thinking about the will and the fact that Daria and Jeremy are supposed to stay in Congreve."

I did not speak. I didn't want to stay in Congreve. But Todd had killed himself because we had been forced to stay here.

She took a long sip of coffee and smiled at me. "Uncle Wheeler has worked it all out with the lawyers. It was a strange stipulation in the will and had no real validity."

I left the room in a daze. It "had no real validity." Daria could leave Congreve. We really were going to escape this horrible place. I stepped carefully down the stairs. They were swaying beneath my feet.

The lawn was bright green in the sun. Kate and Norman were singing a hymn with their hands up in the air. Jeremy stood with them mouthing the words. As I approached, he rolled his eyes at me.

"Daria and I are going with you," I said, still in a state of shock.

Jeremy stopped singing and gaped at me. Then, a broad, warm smile creased his face. There was something purifying about his delight. He was happy. Ria and I would go. Jeremy, Ria, and I would be a family.

I hugged Daria to me as I looked up at the bedroom window. Mom and Uncle Wheeler were both there gazing down at us.

I did not want to think of the past. The past was over. I had loved Todd and my mother and I would always love them. They would always be there in my dreams and in my memories.

We were going to leave the spider's web of Congreve. We were going to go far away and be free.

My heart was no longer heavy. There would be no more prison walls, no more boundaries. I was traveling toward a world of enchantment bright with hope. And Ria was going with me. Together, Ria and I would be happy again.

We had a new family.